THE FATE OF THE FALLEN

BOOK ONE

AE WINSTEAD

First paperback edition September 2020

Cover design by MiblArt

ISBN 978-1-7352-709-0-6 (paperback)
ISBN 978-1-7352-709-1-3 (ebook)

www.aewinstead.com

TO MY FAMILY, *who were forced to consume far too many frozen dinners in order to make this book possible.*

ONE

Franklin, Kentucky
Present Day

I t hadn't been a typical Thursday night in the Reyes household, though not much is typical when your mother is an addict.

The evening started out ordinarily enough, with Ethan trying to force his mother to eat the microwave meal he'd heated for her.

"I can't," she said, waving him away. Her vacant eyes stared past him to the newscaster on the television screen as he gave an update on the latest earthquake to hit the globe.

"Unprecedented frequency," the man was saying, but Ethan didn't care. He tossed the mac and cheese onto the counter, stomped to his room, and slammed the door.

Collapsing onto his bed, he stuffed his earbuds in his ears and turned the volume up as far as it would go. But the music did little to drown out the cacophony inside his head.

The shadows were back.

The shadows.

The darkness his mother had battled his entire seventeen years of life, the negative energy that surrounded her, almost like a physical presence.

Everyone told him they weren't real, that he only imagined them. His grandmother had dragged him around to doctors for years before she died, but he knew something she didn't. No matter what meds they tried, or how many he took, the monsters never went away.

The dark clouds came and went, hovering over his mother like a silent stalker. Always absent during her dry spells, they'd appeared again a few days ago, leaving Ethan with an unsteady feeling in his chest.

The evening really took a turn, though, when Ethan walked back into the living room a short time later to find the couch empty and his mom's car gone from the driveway. If she'd been there asleep, as usual, he would've turned off the light, covered her with the dusty blanket from the back of the couch, and gone back to his bed to try to get some sleep. As it happened, though, he peered through the drizzling rain into the empty driveway and slammed his fist into the plywood that edged the window, cracking a concave dent that fit right in with the other fist-sized holes in the walls of their run-down trailer.

"Damn it!"

Ethan turned from the window, fists clenched. His heart thumped, and he worked his jaw until his teeth ached. A familiar burn boiled inside him as he pulled on a sweatshirt and ran out the door. He'd contemplated his course of action for only a moment, but there was really only one thing to do.

He had to find her.

Maybe this time I can actually talk some sense into her.

Ethan thought he knew where she would have headed. Even though his mother had a head start with her car while Ethan would be on his bike, he couldn't let that deter him. She was his mother. He had to try.

Thankfully, the heavy rain had subsided, but the fine mist that still hovered in the air caught in his black hair, plastering it to his face and down his neck as he sped through their neighborhood as fast as his rusty BMX would take him.

Riding through the dirty, overgrown streets of Franklin, the yards of the neglected houses filled with broken down cars and perpetually filthy children always reminded Ethan of the stories his grandmother had told him of the South Dakota reservation where she'd grown up—the same reservation his mother had run from while pregnant with him. Stories of poverty and addiction and waste.

From one hell hole to another.

Sloshing through the parking lot of the abandoned T-Mart shopping center, Ethan stopped his bike in the dark street in front of his destination. A streetlight flickered overhead, giving the street a haunted glow. The house loomed in front of him, the dilapidated wood porch rotten and splintering. Every window had been either boarded up or broken, and profanities decorated the chipped wood siding in colorful sprays. The house appeared to have been abandoned for years, but Ethan knew better. He knew the cockroaches that lived within.

He walked his bike up to the door, knowing if he left it on the lawn, it wouldn't be there when he returned.

On the other side of the busted-up door, a man slumped on the stairs like an inebriated sentry. He looked to be in his eighties but probably wasn't as old as the years of drugs and booze made him appear.

"Where's Elizabeth?" Ethan asked. "Is she here?" The man looked up at him through half-open eyes but didn't answer. A river of saliva ran down one of the deep grooves in his chin.

Ethan pulled back his foot and kicked the man—not too hard, but hard enough to rouse him from his stupor. "Where's my mother?" Ethan shouted but didn't wait for an answer. He stepped over the man and headed up the stairs.

Other bodies in varying states of consciousness lay scattered throughout the house: on the stairs, in the hallway, flung across

3

the rotting furniture. Pipes, needles, empty beer bottles, and soiled clothing littered the floor, a scattering of old, rotten debris. The stench of every imaginable bodily excrement mixed together and filled the air with a thick odor, but Ethan barely noticed. He could only think of one thing.

With no electricity in the house and the windows boarded, Ethan couldn't see a thing. Using his cell phone as a flashlight, he leaned down and examined each body he came to, relieved at each face that wasn't his mother's.

"Mom!" he called out to her but received only a few mumbled curses in response.

Ethan was beginning to think that maybe she wasn't here after all—maybe she'd gone to the market and would be back home by now—when his eyes landed on a familiar face. It didn't belong to his mother, but it punched him in the gut just the same.

The man sagged against the wall, a large duffel bag the only thing holding him up. "Hey, Ethan, you lil pansy. How you doin'?" His greeting slurred together as one long word.

It was Gary, his mother's on-again, off-again boyfriend. Gary had disappeared right before his mother's last clean-up attempt. If he'd slunk back into town, his mother wouldn't be far away.

Ethan glared down at the sorry excuse for a man lying in front of him. His clothes were rumpled, and he looked like he hadn't showered in days. Knowing that Gary had information he needed was the only thing that kept Ethan from pulverizing the man's face.

"Where's my mother, Gary?" Ethan asked through clenched teeth.

The man's eyes had drifted closed, so Ethan knelt and slapped him hard across the face.

Gary scowled at him. "Hey, man. Not cool."

"Where's my mom? I'm not going to ask you again."

Gary raised a shaky hand and thumbed toward the door next to him. "I don't know, dude. Probably in there with Jeffrey."

Jeffrey. The name made Ethan want to vomit. He realized that might seem like a pretty strong reaction for someone he barely knew, but how else should he feel about his mother's drug dealer? Especially the kind of dealer he knew to take more than one form of payment from females, no matter their age.

Ethan may have been angry before. Now he was livid. His pulse began to throb in his ears. *I should leave right now,* he tried to convince himself halfheartedly, but his brain was no longer in control of his body. The fire burning inside him was calling the shots now. He clenched his fists and burst through the door with no thought of what his next move would be.

TWO

The First War of Heaven

How you have fallen from heaven, morning star, son of the dawn!
You have been cast to the earth…you said in your heart, "I will
ascend to the heavens; I will raise my throne above the stars of
God…I will make myself like the Most High." But you are brought
down to the realm of the dead, to the depths of the pit.
Isaiah 14:12-15 NIV

The air exploded from Arael's lungs as her body slammed backward into the dry, orange dust of the battlefield. She tried to get up, *needed* to get up, but an immense pressure pinned her to the ground. She raised her head and stared down, disbelieving, at the angel's sword protruding from her chest. Surprisingly, the pain wasn't immediate. Numbness overtook her first, as disbelief morphed into shock and shock into confusion.

Then the fire erupted inside her. Heavenly Fire—the force that fueled the sun and the stars and gave the angels' weapons their power—flowed from the weapon in her heart and radiated throughout her body. The battle raged around her, but the agony chased all thoughts from her mind, turning them to a burst of red like blood exploding behind her eyes.

Above the noise of battle—growling, grunting, sword against sword—the screams and howls of a thousand shrieking voices pierced her mind. It took her a moment to realize the sounds were coming from her—her and the other angels who lay wounded and writhing on the ground as the Heavenly Fire worked its way through their bodies.

Lying helpless on the dirt of the battlefield, Arael became the pain. Nothing else existed in the expanse of time or space. Everything that had happened to her before that point—the ones she'd loved, the angel she'd been—fled from her. Staring wide-eyed at her assailant on the other end of the sword, another feeling crept in.

Betrayal.

Blazing emerald eyes, silver wisps of hair, and the outline of two menacing wings loomed against the backdrop of blue sky above her. He straightened, revealing more of the tawny face that belonged to her brother.

Michael.

This must be a mistake. She'd done everything as Michael had instructed. She'd infiltrated the rebel group and gained the leader's trust.

"He's planning an attempt to overthrow the Creator. He's gathering forces, building an army. We have to do something," she'd warned him.

All of Michael's intel on Lucifer and the rebels had come from her. And this was how he repaid his informant? By banishing her?

At that moment, the words she'd heard in the secrecy of Lucifer's meetings found their way to the front of her mind. *"Some of our brethren are not as honorable as they profess to be."*

Had Michael tricked her? Had this been his plan all along?

She closed her eyes. It didn't matter now…nothing mattered. She just wanted this torture to be over.

In the midst of the turmoil unfurling both inside her body and on the battlefield around her, someone called out to her. Her eyes jerked open as a voice intruded into her thoughts. A voice not her own, but just as familiar. It spoke two simple yet powerful words, louder than the battle raging around her.

I'm sorry, the voice repeated, ragged, even in her mind. She turned her head in the direction of the voice, and a flash of grief surged through her—grief so heavy, it would have pinned her to the ground had the sword not already immobilized her.

Another angel lay wounded beside her, another victim of the Heavenly Fire. She examined his face, his mouth set into a hard line. His eyes glowed the greenest shade of blue she'd ever seen. White hair curled around a delicate face, and his skin glowed the same greenish-blue hue of his eyes.

Uriah... Memories taken by the pain were beginning to come back to her now. She hadn't been alone in her undercover activities. Uriah was her confidant, her training partner, her protector, but most importantly, he was her *qanima,* her spirit partner in every sense of the word. They hadn't chosen one another, but perhaps more importantly, they'd been created *for* one another, their souls bonded at their creation by a power older than time.

How could I have forgotten him?

Only then did it occur to her that her brother had not only betrayed her, but he'd also included Uriah in his plan, which made her hate Michael all the more.

A moment ago, she'd been nothing but pain. No one. Just endless agony and torment. Now, looking at Uriah, she knew she needed to remember herself. And him.

I am Arael, a powerful Archangel in the ranks of Heaven. I am a Tempest in service to Elohim, the Creator. I am in Eden, the pass-through realm between the physical and spiritual worlds. I tried to help my brother, and he betrayed me...

She tried to respond with her mind, *I'm the one who's sorry,* but wasn't sure he'd heard.

When Michael and his army had executed their surprise attack, she and Uriah had been in their designated position near the Conclave Hall. They'd been told not to move, but things had quickly gotten out of hand, and they'd been pushed into the heat of the fighting. In the mayhem, Uriah had been struck first. She'd turned in an attempt to save him, her fierce protective instinct kicking in.

She had failed.

Her eyes scanned over his face again—his eyes, his hair, all spattered with blood. As her *qanima*, she could feel his spirit inside of her, an integral part of her true essence. Looking at him now, she could have been looking at a reflection of herself, except...his life remained more valuable to her than even her own.

Arael searched her mind, looking for more of him, wanting something pleasant to cling to in these last moments before her spirit was eternally cast out of Heaven. She didn't have much time, though, before another explosion of agony ripped through her body. Uriah's face contorted into a grimace, a mirror reflection of her own. He was feeling her pain. Or was she feeling his?

Moments before, everything had been moving in slow motion. Now, things were happening too fast. The innate connection that had always bonded them was being burned away, along with the rest of her. From her place in the blood-soaked dirt, she reached her hand out to Uriah and he to her until their fingers touched. They could usually draw strength from each other in this way, but neither had any left to give.

An eternity passed before Arael tilted her head up to look into her attacker's face—*Michael's* face. She struggled to breathe under the weight of his betrayal, which hurt almost as much as her physical torment. His face was taut and filled with something she didn't recognize.

Slowly the anguish began to subside. The fire of the physical pain turned to ice-cold emptiness and the emotional misery to white-hot hatred. Lucifer had been right all along. They were all liars. Michael, the Creator, all who still called themselves Righteous. Everything made sense now. The angels' weapons had always seemed a complete contradiction to their life of peace and harmony in the Heavens. They had no enemy, so why did they need weapons? All of a sudden, it was all so clear. The Creator had planned this all along. He had given them weapons to destroy each other, just as Lucifer had said.

This was Arael's last thought before the red faded to black.

THREE

Franklin, Kentucky
Present Day

Thursday night faded into Friday morning in a blur of flying fists and flashing lights. Ethan rarely got so angry that he blacked out, but a significant amount of time was missing from his memory of the previous night.

He remembered talking to Gary. He remembered entering the bedroom and seeing his mom splayed out, unconscious on the dirty mattress beside a sleeping Jeffrey.

The next thing he remembered, he was at the police station staring down at his bloody hands cuffed in his lap. He did a quick body check: flexed his fingers, moved his head from side to side. He wasn't hurt. So, whose blood was crusted on his hands? Jeffrey's? *His mother's?* Ethan jumped up.

"Hey!" He saw several officers standing at a desk down the short hallway. None of them moved. "Hey, assholes! Where's my mother? Elizabeth Reyes. Is she okay?"

One of them turned sharply, her ponytail snapping with the movement. She gave Ethan an *I-know-you're-not-talking-to-me-like-that* look but answered anyway.

"She's in lock-up. Little wisp of a thing jumped right on the officer's back who went in after you. Other than being strung out, she's fine. You just better be glad those officers were watching the place." The policewoman jutted out her chin. "Just sit tight," she added, turning back to her conversation. "Your representative is on her way."

Representative? Ethan didn't like the sound of that. "Representative" was just a fancy word for social worker—a stuffy old lady who'd want to "ask him questions" and "make sure he was okay." Ethan slammed his hands into the bars. "I'm almost eighteen, damn it! I don't need a babysitter!"

The state didn't see it that way, though, and a few hours later, Ethan found himself staring through rivulets of rain running down the back window of an aging blue Honda, vigorously chewing his thumbnail, and trying to control his rage. The day was still young, but the sky took on the dull grayness of dusk. Ethan thought it fitting, considering the circumstances.

The woman in the front seat had said her name was Carla. No last name. Just Carla. She was younger than Ethan would have expected: late twenties, early thirties, maybe. She gripped the steering wheel with both hands in a way that told Ethan she was either nervous or not a very good driver. Her short hair poked out from her head in random places, and her suit was wrinkled. She wore no makeup but seemed like the kind of woman who usually did. *It's almost like she was woken up in the middle of the night,* Ethan thought with a smirk.

They'd been driving for a while, and Ethan wondered how much longer he'd be stuck in the car with this lady, but there was no way in hell he'd open his mouth to ask.

Instead, he focused on the things he did know. One, his mother was a liar. Two, the cops were idiots. Three, this social worker was a tool, and four, he'd be in jail right now if it weren't for the simple matter of his age. Since he was still technically a minor, and his "victim," Jeffrey, had been in no position to press charges, he'd been released to the custody of the state. No one had said the word, but Ethan knew what that meant.

Foster care.

What a joke. He'd been taking care of himself since he was nine.

As she drove, Carla kept glancing back at Ethan in the rearview mirror. He had no idea what the lady must think of him, with his shaggy hair and baggy clothes, but he hoped she would break from social worker tradition and *not* try to make friends with him. He didn't think he could take another adult making fake promises just then.

He rolled his eyes when only a few moments later, she cleared her throat to speak. *So much for peaceful silence.*

"I hope they treated you okay back there," she said. "They should have called me much sooner than they did."

Ethan felt her eyes on him through the mirror again. "They told me what happened, but that's no reason…" Her voice trailed off before starting up again. "I know you don't believe me, but I do care about what happens to you. I had to bend over backward and call in every favor I had coming to me to keep you out of a juvenile detention facility."

Another glance.

"I read your file, and I know you're not a bad kid."

Ethan flung his hair out of his eyes and pressed his lips together, forcing the words he wanted to say back down his throat.

"I know this isn't ideal," she continued, undeterred by his silence, "but your mother is in a lot of trouble, and her court dates will likely drag out for several months. This was as close as I could get you to her under the circumstances."

Ethan rolled his eyes and finally spoke. "I don't care how close I am to her. I hope I never see her again."

"Your mother made a mistake, Ethan." Carla's voice was even, but her eyes were wide. "I spoke to her before I came to your cell, and she feels terrible about what happened."

"I bet."

"She told me she wants to get better for you." Carla glanced back at him again and rubbed her hand over her unruly hair. "You're her only son, Ethan, and she's your only mother. I know it's not your responsibility, but knowing that you're there for her will help her to do that."

Ethan's face twisted into a humorless smile. "Good try, lady, but she's been like this my whole life. She's never going to change."

Carla pulled her lips into a thin line. With any luck, she was now satisfied with her attempt to get through to him.

Another ten minutes passed before Carla spoke again. "I think you'll like the Morgans," she said. "They're pretty laid back. They didn't bat an eye when I told them about your…incident."

Ethan shot daggers at her with his eyes. If looks could talk, his would be saying, "Stop talking to me, lady. You don't know anything about my life."

As the view out his window morphed from city streets and office buildings into rolling hills and cornfields, Ethan's heart began to beat faster. Carla told him about the lame-ass town where he'd be staying, but Ethan didn't care. His fingers began to tingle, and the car began to shrink, closing in on him. Ethan focused on his hands in his lap and willed his pulse to slow. He knew what would happen if he didn't calm down.

Carla had taken him by his house to gather his things, but he'd put zero thought into what he'd thrown into his bag— except for his meds, of course. He didn't go anywhere without those. But in his anger and frustration, he'd stuffed his meds in his backpack then tossed the bag in the trunk…and there was no way in hell he would ask this lady to pull over so he could get them. *I'm okay. I can do this.* He traced the outline of the small object in his pocket, more out of habit than anything else. Not because he thought it could help him.

Beads of sweat popped up on Ethan's forehead, and he wiped his hands down his baggy camo shorts. He rolled down the window and leaned into the wind, but his lungs refused to expand. *Oh God, please not here,* he silently prayed. And somehow, thankfully, he managed to force his racing heart to slow.

"Okay, well," Carla said a few moments later, seeming not to have noticed his near-breakdown, "you'll be eighteen in a few months and free to do as you please, but until then, please take it easy on me, okay?" She pulled into the driveway of a white, two-story farmhouse that Ethan thought looked like something out of the Norman Rockwell painting his grandmother used to have. "I'm responsible for you until then. Well, the state is, actually, but I—" Ethan opened the door and slammed it on her words.

A middle-aged couple met Ethan and Carla on the porch. The woman wore a light pink dress that came down to her knees. Her hair was cut into a short bob, while the man was dressed in jeans and a white shirt.

At least he's not wearing overalls, Ethan thought as he stood stone-faced with his hands stuffed in the pockets of his shorts.

Carla greeted the couple with a smile. "Mr. and Mrs. Morgan, this is Ethan. He's gonna be a ton of fun for ya. I tell ya, he's just a little chatterbox. Could not get him to shut up on the drive over."

Ethan glared at her while the Morgans let out an easy laugh.

The couple took in his shaggy hair, lip ring, and 'Skate or Die' t-shirt and still managed to keep the smiles plastered on their faces. Ethan had to give them credit, he knew what they were thinking. Adults were always so manipulative, wanting you to think they loved you while betraying you behind your back. Ethan slung his bag over his shoulder and went through the front door without a word.

"This is Dale and Grace, by the way," Carla called after him, "in case you wanted to know."

"I'm sure he just needs a little time to adjust," Ethan heard the woman say as he wandered into the unfamiliar house. Footsteps came rushing behind him as the woman—*was her name Grace?* —followed him down the hall.

"Here you are, Ethan. Your room will be this way." Grace pointed down the hall to a doorway on the left. Ethan entered the room and dropped his backpack on the bed. The space was small and generic, containing only a twin bed, a dresser, and a nightstand. One small window looked out to the backyard and the trees beyond.

"The bathroom's across the hall if you need it." She wiped her hands on the front of her dress, looking like she wanted to say something more. Ethan hoped she wouldn't.

"I'm sure this is difficult for you," Mrs. Morgan said, her voice low. "I'll just give you some privacy."

Thank God. Ethan could feel the pressure building again, and he didn't know if he'd be able to stop it this time. He turned away from the door and clamped his eyes shut. No way was he staying here. He didn't need a social worker. He didn't need foster parents. He didn't need anyone.

He was already planning his escape, and once he was gone, he knew no one would waste their time looking for him. He walked over to the window and surveyed the distance to the ground. Maybe a ten-foot drop. He could make that easily.

"It's longer down than it looks," a voice said from the hall. Ethan turned to see Mr. Morgan standing in the doorway. Again, Ethan said nothing, just stared at the man as he walked back over to the bed. "Kid broke his ankle jumping out that window once. It was a shame, too. He coulda just used the front door."

Ethan lay back on the bed and closed his eyes.

"We hope you don't leave, but if you do, just know the door's always open if you want to come back."

Ethan raised his head and looked at the man. "Thanks," he said in a sarcastic tone and lowered his head back down onto the pillow.

"Dinner's at six. Grace's making some kind of casserole. And grilled cheese...just in case you don't like casserole." After another silent moment, the man's footsteps faded down the hallway.

Finally.

Ethan didn't want anything from these people. Not food, not this bedroom. Nothing. He only wanted to turn the clock back twenty-four hours and do this day over again. He would never have left his mother alone. If only he had been there when Gary had called, none of this would've happened. This time he'd have made her understand.

God! Why did he still let this bother him so much? He pushed his fists into his eyes to stop the tears from coming. He would not cry for her. Not anymore.

As he lay on the unfamiliar bed, thinking about all the other kids who must've slept there, his skin began to itch. He sat up and rubbed his hands down his legs as the room began closing in on him again. He poked his head out the bedroom door and looked down the hall. Voices drifted down from the foyer where they'd entered. He rummaged through his bag and pulled out a plastic baggie of pills, found the one he needed, and popped it in his mouth. He shouldered his backpack and sneaked down the hall in the opposite direction. He had to get out of there.

After a moment, he found a door in the laundry room and bolted out in a flash. Once outside, he took off at a trot through the drizzling rain across the soggy backyard.

Carla had talked a little about the town on the drive over, hadn't she? Ethan had tried his best to ignore her, but he was pretty sure she'd said the river encompassed this death trap of a town, and there was only one road in or out. He'd surely be spotted if he just took off down the road, though.

He knew the town wasn't big, so no matter which way he went, Ethan was sure that as long as he stayed hidden in the forest, he'd eventually find the river. He could follow it, and once he made it to the city limits, he'd be home free. With no other thought in his head and the prospect of freedom calling to him, he disappeared through the trees.

FOUR

Eden
After the Fall

The battle was long over before the deep aching pressure in Uriah's side wrenched him back into consciousness. This wasn't the same searing pain of the Heavenly Fire that had burned through him on the battlefield. No...this was much worse. A never-ending emptiness had been carved into his soul— a deep, hollow ache that spread all the way to his bones.

What happened? Uriah wondered as he brought his hand up to his face. His instincts were screaming at him to *Get up! Defend yourself!* But all he wanted was to wrap his arms around himself, curl into a ball, and disappear.

Instead, he drew a ragged breath and forced his eyes open.

Uriah found himself lying on the ground in a vast, dark expanse of blood-soaked dust in Eden. Nothing but orange dirt and bedraggled souls stretched out as far as his celestial sight could see. Weary and wounded angels were beginning to stir around him, each looking as lost and disoriented as he felt.

His right hand still gripped his sword and was covered in dark, red blood. His blood?

Or someone else's?

A small gasp escaped his lips as he looked down at himself for the first time. His chest heaved, and his side ached with every pulse of his racing heart. Uriah's robes were torn and stained red. He put his finger through the tear in the cloth and touched the wound on his side. A shudder brought the horror of the past few hours crashing back to him.

Lucifer's meeting. Michael's attack.

Arael!

He looked to the spot where she'd been, just a few feet from where he now sat. Her blood soaked the ground...*so much blood.* But she was nowhere to be found.

How could I have been so stupid? It had been Uriah's idea, after all, for the two of them to probe into Lucifer's group in the first place. He should have done it alone. He should have never involved her.

He jerked his head around in all directions, calling out to her with his mind as he'd done so many times before. But for the first time, Uriah received no response. He realized in horror that the emptiness he felt wasn't just the absence of Elohim's presence inside him, but the absence of *her.* He searched inside himself for something, anything...even a whisper of her, but found nothing. Her constant presence that he'd relied on since their creation was just...gone.

Unsteady, he rose from the ground and scanned the group again. Even through the dust of battle still hanging in the air, something strange nagged him. Through the orange haze, he saw angels from every order and rank, from Seraphim to Guardian, young recruits to experienced warriors, but he didn't see Arael.

The rare specks of color in the crowd indicated what was so amiss about the whole scene. Almost every angel in Eden had lost their distinctive colors that so vibrantly set them apart from each other; the red aura of the Seraphim, the pale-yellow glow of the Guardians, the deep lilac hue of the Archangels. Now, a few bursts of green, the distinct color of the Dominions, were scattered among them, but most of the angels were surrounded by a dreary gray haze.

Uriah's lips parted as he stared in horror. Angels wore their colors like a badge of honor. What would it mean for them to have their colors stripped from them, yet another thing taken by the Heavenly Fire? Was he still a Dominion? Was Arael still an Archangel? Uriah closed his eyes and hissed out a breath before opening them again. He would have to figure all that out later. At that moment, he had a more pressing concern.

Uriah moved with caution among the other angels as they sat devastated on the dusty ground outside the celestial bronze gate that led into the Garden. Inside lay a paradise of lush, green vegetation, bubbling streams of crystal-clear water, caves of emeralds and ruby, Elohim's most perfect creation. But outside the gate stretched a desolate landscape. Nothing but dry orange dirt spanned as far as the eye could see, the perfect place for Lucifer's clandestine meetings, or so he had thought.

Uriah looked into each despondent face he came to, searching for someone who might be able to help him, but each one reflected the same picture of emptiness and loss. He felt the despair wafting off them like morning fog. Some were beginning to stir, but most sat motionless, each lost in their own personal hell.

Warring emotions washed over Uriah in waves. As an Empath, he'd always viewed his power to feel others' emotions as a gift, but he'd never experienced such an overwhelming onslaught of negativity before. Nothing but sadness, hopelessness, and fear bombarded him from every direction, with a little anger and blood lust sprinkled in for good measure.

Their loss, added to his own, was almost too much for him to bear. It grew heavier and heavier on him until he could barely stand under the weight of it. He knew he needed to get away from there before it immobilized him, but he couldn't leave without Arael—if he could find her.

"Lieutenant?" A voice cut into his thoughts. A young angel with curly, black hair and a bright green aura came rushing up to him. Uriah recognized the fledgling as one of his Dominion recruits.

"Ronan?"

A look of disbelief and shock crossed the young angel's face, apparently registering the absence of color surrounding his former leader. Uriah felt Ronan's disappointment like a knife in his chest. Of course, Ronan wouldn't have known about Uriah and Arael's undercover activities within the rebel group. No one had. *Except Michael.*

Uriah felt compelled to say something like, "This isn't what it looks like," or "This is all a big mistake," but he didn't have the time or energy to try to explain. And what would he say if he did?

"We heard what happened," Ronan said, gesturing behind him at the other Dominions scouting the crowd. "Raphael sent us to contain the exiled. We were looking for you," he stammered. "We didn't know…"

Uriah felt Ronan's unasked questions ready to burst from his lips, but he had just as many of his own.

"I'm sorry, Ronan." Uriah held up a hand to him. "I wish I could explain this to you right now, but I can't. I don't know how much they told you, but I believe Lucifer will be the one you want to talk to—"

Ronan waved him off impatiently. "Well, the thing is, sir…Lucifer isn't here." Ronan consulted a small black tablet in his hand. "And neither are Marduk, Beliel, or Arael." He looked back at the exiled angels seemingly oblivious to the presence of the Righteous Dominions patrolling among them. "Any idea where they could have gone? They are the only ones missing among the Fallen."

The Fallen. That was the first time Uriah had heard the term. Fallen from what? He didn't feel like he'd fallen from anything. More like he'd been violently and suddenly purged from his home.

"What do you mean?" Uriah tried to make sense of Ronan's words, taking note that the young angel was still calling him "sir" despite Uriah's obvious change of status. "Arael is missing?"

Ronan shrugged. "Well, she's not here, sir. We came as fast as we could, but those three have already passed through to the physical realm, it seems."

The young angel continued talking, but Uriah wasn't listening. Arael was missing…and so were Lucifer and his top two advisers. Could they possibly know what she'd done? Word traveled fast in the celestial world, and Lucifer had made clear what would happen to anyone who talked of their activities outside of Eden. If she'd been discovered, would they follow through with their threats? Surely not. Lucifer was Elohim's second in command. Marduk and Beliel were leaders of the top two orders of angels.

Not anymore, they're not, Uriah thought as panic shot through him. Until the battle, Uriah had never fathomed one angel intentionally bringing harm to another, but now, all bets were off. Rules had been thrown by the wayside, and nothing was certain anymore. Arael *was* gone. Uriah knew she wouldn't have left him if she'd had a choice. Something had caused her to run. *Or she'd been taken.*

He knew it was useless, but he tried calling out to her again. And once again, his calls came back as an empty echo in his mind. He lowered his head. Without their connection, how would he ever find her? He growled in frustration.

Ronan finally grew quiet, freezing mid-sentence to stare at Uriah.

"I have to go," Uriah said.

"But sir…" Ronan shifted his weight. "I'm not supposed to let you leave."

Uriah put a hand on Ronan's shoulder and lowered his voice. "I understand that, but—" he paused, forcing the next words out. "I think Arael's in trouble."

Ronan's eyes widened.

"I know a lot has changed here today," Uriah continued. "But I still care about you, and I think you're one of the best Dominion recruits we have."

"Thank you, sir."

"So, you need to turn around and walk away." Uriah spun the angel by his shoulders. "I'm going with or without your permission, and I don't want this to look bad for you."

"But sir..."

Uriah stopped him with a hard squeeze. "I'm sure Gabriel will come with instructions. I'll be back before that happens. And I'll bring the others with me."

FIVE

C amryn Martin cursed the black clouds overhead as she pulled her Ford truck out of the parking lot of Hayden County High School. Even with the prospect of spring break in front of her, Camryn couldn't suppress the growing sense of dread swelling in her stomach. The rain had been steady for weeks with no sign of stopping. Coming from a family of farmers, Camryn understood the importance of rain, but she'd seen enough moldy cotton and waterlogged cornfields in her seventeen years to understand what would happen if these storms didn't let up. *It might be a bust already*, she thought as she drove past a pond that only two months ago had been a field of soybeans.

But it wasn't just the rain getting to her. Camryn never lacked for something to obsessively worry about: her fast-approaching graduation, the growing stack of college applications on her dresser, the thousands of different ways she might die on any given day.

Now something else nagged at her. She could barely discern it from the usual jumble of knots in her stomach, but it was there—a nervous panic, like the time she'd dreamt of coming to the end of the school year only to realize she'd forgotten to attend an entire class for the whole year!

Too many things in her life were changing. And she *hated* change. The transition from junior high to high school had been hard enough, but at least she'd still had the same classmates, terrible as they were, and she'd remained in the town she'd always known. School may have been torture for her for the past four years, but at least she'd known what to expect. College would be a whole new set of unknown horrors: unknown people, unknown professors, an unknown town, new, unknown ways to die.

As she turned into her employee parking space of Granny's General Store in town, Camryn tamped down the panic rising in her with a breathing technique she'd learned during her few months of therapy when she was a kid. She sucked in a deep breath, held it for a few seconds, then slowly exhaled, imagining all her fears, both old and new, being carried away in the hiss of air between her lips.

Her mother's words echoed in her ears, *"Life brings us enough worries without you conjuring up more of your own."* Camryn wished she could be more like her mother, always so calm and steady. Nothing seemed to ruffle Lindsey Martin, and no matter the situation, she always knew what to do. Camryn had always gone to her mother with her problems, and even though her mom didn't seem to mind, Camryn did. She would be an adult soon. She didn't want to keep running to her mother every time something scared her. *Time to start figuring things out on my own.*

The bell dinged behind her as she stepped out of the damp, gray day and into the time warp that was Granny's General Store. Rumor had it, Granny's hadn't changed a bit in the past sixty years, but then again, neither had the rest of the town. Kentucky Bend was located in an almost complete bend of the Mississippi River. Being surrounded on three sides by water and its proclivity to flooding didn't allow for much expansion, so there wasn't much of a draw for outsiders to migrate to their little town. The residents of Kentucky Bend were the descendants of the farmers who had settled there in the twenties and had been too dumb to leave.

Inside the General Store, most of the paint had chipped off the brick walls, and dust motes floated thick in the air. The racks of goods and display cases had to be the same ones used when the store opened in 1962, and Camryn often wondered if some of the goods were the same, too. She eyed the malted milk. *Does anyone even use that anymore?*

Granny Newman, the small, hunched woman behind the counter, had to be in her eighties, but still ran the General Store almost single-handedly. She only hired two or three part-timers like Camryn to make special deliveries to some of the elderly of the community—a group of which she did not consider herself to be a part. Granny had never had any children of her own, so she wasn't technically anyone's *actual* Granny, but no one knew her by any other name.

Camryn had arrived a few minutes before her shift, so she picked up a newspaper from the rack, scanned the front page, and instantly regretted it. The headlines only reminded her that while her little corner of the world was experiencing record rainfall, other places were enduring brush fires and volcanic eruptions. Severe drought had dried up water reservoirs in South America, and countries were threatening war over something as seemingly abundant as water. Another earthquake had hit in Mexico, leaving their capital city decimated and sending a renewed sense of dread into Camryn's gut. She sighed heavily as if these issues were somehow her own problems to solve, rubbed the back of her neck, and tossed the newspaper onto the rack. *Deliveries first, global warming later.*

The wood floor creaked under her wet boots as she grabbed her smock from the hook and looked at the delivery list for the afternoon. She released an audible groan at the last name on the list.

Kennedy.

As in Kyle Kennedy, the most insufferable brute at Hayden County High. His witty charm and killer cheekbones made all the girls at school swoon. The blue eyes and blond hair didn't hurt, either. Kyle was one of those disgusting people who was just good at everything. He'd made All-State in football the past two years but had injured his shoulder in the state championships a few months back. Hayden County had lost the game, and Kyle had lost his scholarship. It was a real tragedy.

Kyle had moved to Kentucky Bend to live with his grandparents in the fifth grade—about the same time Camryn's social life had taken a nosedive—and had joined in the extracurricular activity of ruining her life. His grandparents were nice enough, although they seemed completely oblivious to the fact that their grandson was a total perv.

She did her best to avoid him at school, which proved to be difficult since they had English Lit together, and he *always* asked to borrow her homework. She'd never let him, but that didn't stop him from asking...Every. Single. Day.

But it wasn't just his obnoxious homework habits that bothered her. It was the way he looked at her like he wanted to eat her, and that he went out of his way to touch her at every opportunity—it irked her to no end.

It might've been nice coming from another boy—one she thought might actually like her—but she knew Kyle wasn't really interested in her. She wasn't exactly his type.

Camryn considered herself pretty average in most ways, with thin, sandy-blonde hair and unassuming, amber eyes. The complete opposite of Kyle's girlfriend, Brooke Mason. With her model-thin frame, perfect skin, and perfectly straight, shining-black hair, Brooke stood out like a queen among her peasants. No way was Kyle really interested in Camryn. Not with a girlfriend like Brooke.

It was Brooke, Camryn assumed, who instigated Kyle's daily harassment. Brooke had hated Camryn since middle school. She'd gone from throwing gum in Camryn's hair and tripping her in the halls to stealing her homework and ripping it up right in front of Camryn's face. As they'd gotten older, Brooke's attacks had become more calculated. She used her popularity to blacklist Camryn from parties and spread vicious rumors about her, ensuring that everyone treated Camryn like a pariah. She couldn't help but wonder if Brooke was the mastermind behind whatever mind game Kyle was playing with her now.

He's just a stupid jock, Camryn told herself as she loaded down the back of her truck with the items from the orders. *Maybe he won't even be there.* Camryn smiled, proud of herself for "thinking positive thoughts." Another nugget of her mother's steady advice.

At Camryn's first stop of the afternoon, she had a nice chat with Mr. West, who never failed to have a new ailment to complain about. Camryn nodded along as he told her all about his gout and the incompetence of his new doctor.

At her next stop, Camryn found Mrs. Lewis fretting over her beloved cat, who appeared to Camryn to be struggling to hack up a hairball. But Mrs. Lewis was *certain* the animal was in labor. Camryn finally had to phone the vet in for an emergency house call before the lady would let her leave.

As Camryn pulled into the long gravel driveway of her last delivery of the evening, the heat blasting from the air vents did little to dispel the chill that raced over her body.

It was getting late. The grayness of the sky melted into a deep purple, and the rain pelted down on the roof of her truck. The knot in her stomach twisted again at the sight of the jacked-up Chevy truck, shining black in the glow of the barn light like a bad omen.

Camryn glanced around for Mr. or Mrs. Kennedy, but they were nowhere to be found. Kyle was there, though, standing in the wide-open door of the barn, grinning his stellar grin that drove the rest of the girls at school crazy.

Camryn's palms started to sweat. *Calm down, you idiot. This is how he wants you to feel.*

She hesitated a moment before pulling into the barn but decided unloading would go faster out from under this downpour. As she pulled through the open doors, the sudden absence of rain against glass was deafening. The wipers squeaked in protest, making Camryn flinch. She scrambled to turn them off.

Kyle leaned against a barn post, arms crossed, waiting for her. That alone made the massive barn feel ten sizes too small. He'd changed out of his school polo into a tight white t-shirt that clung to every muscle in his thick arms. Sucking in a breath, Camryn hopped out of the truck and slammed the door.

"Why don't you pick up these deliveries yourself, Kyle? It's pretty bad that a girl has to do your chores for you." She hoped she sounded annoyed, but she couldn't be sure.

"Bad shoulder, you know?" he replied, rubbing the injury. "Besides, if I did that, then you might not come visit me anymore."

A shiver ran up her spine, but she didn't blink. "Well, you're not wrong about that."

She tried not to think about him watching her as she moved around the truck and opened the tailgate. This was going to take a while, but she would keel over in a pile of cow manure before she'd ever ask him for help.

He walked over and placed his arms on the side of the truck bed and rested his chin on his hands, watching her unload the few bags of grain and gallons of pesticide. She didn't bother putting them away. Surely he could manage that himself.

By the time she finished, beads of sweat rolled down her face, despite the chill in the air. As she closed the tailgate and moved around the side of the truck, her eyes landed on Kyle, leaning on the driver's door, grinning again.

Camryn knew this game, but she wasn't playing. Not this time. She forced herself not to look away from him, though it made her sweat even more profusely than unloading the truck had.

After an agonizing moment of contemplating what her next move would be, Kyle finally stepped aside and opened the door for her. She willed herself to walk slowly and climb into the cab like a normal person instead of running and jumping in headfirst. She tried to pull the door shut behind her, but he still stood in the way.

"Wait," he said. "I'm having a party Sunday night to kick off the break. You should come." Then, as if realizing that might actually sound like a nice thing to say, he added, "It's not like you have anything better to do."

"Thanks," Camryn answered in a tone as dry as the Sahara, "but I wouldn't be caught dead at your party."

Kyle feigned a hurt expression. "Now that's not very nice. No wonder you don't have any friends."

"Goodbye, Kyle," she said, trying again to shut the door.

"Brooke won't be there," he added with a shrug, "just so you know."

Camryn wrinkled her forehead. Why would his girlfriend not be at his party?

Kyle continued to stare at her with his wide grin. "She has a cheer camp or something."

"During spring break?" Camryn wasn't buying that.

"Hey, it's competition season," he said in a perfect Brooke impression. "But whatever. Come. Don't come. I don't really care. I was just trying to be nice." He finally stepped away, allowing her to close the door between them.

Right. Camryn rolled her eyes. *Nice.*

SIX

Eden
After the Fall

Heading out of Eden after the battle, Uriah had never felt so alone. He was surrounded by hundreds of other angels facing banishment along with him, but he may as well have been floating in the darkest expanses of the universe with only the dust of burned-out stars surrounding him.

Uriah was surprised to realize that he'd felt this kind of emptiness once before—when he'd visited the Void. He didn't think of that day often, as it was quite possibly the worst day of his celestial life...until now.

Shadows filled the room despite the constant glow of light pouring in through the window.

"Where is that spear?" Uriah wondered aloud as the spark of panic inside him grew.

He and Arael would be making their training visit to the Void soon, and Uriah struggled to maintain his demeanor.

A visit to the Void was mandatory training for all angels before receiving their first assignment. They were required to explore all of Creation, but that was the one area everyone avoided, and for good reason.

The Void had been abandoned, left as a barren wasteland of nothingness that sucked the life and energy out of anyone who entered there. Why it even existed remained a mystery, but no angel dared question the divine wisdom of the Creator.

Most angels would put off this mission for as long as possible, but not Arael. She put their names in as soon as they became eligible for the trip.

"Better to just get it over with," she'd said.

Uriah tried to ignore his growing dread, not wanting Arael to know how terrified he was, but how could he when he knew what they were in for? They'd been briefed by their trainers as thoroughly as possible, but words could never express what feelings could convey. The harrowing hopelessness and gut-wrenching misery emanating from the other angels as they returned from the Void was something only he and the other Empaths could know.

Arael could know, through him—if he chose to share it with her—but he wanted to protect her from it for as long as possible.

As the time for their trip grew closer, the gnawing in his stomach became more troublesome. He hadn't said anything to Arael about his fears, but then again, he never had to when it came to her. She usually knew how he felt without him having to say a word. That's why it was so unexpected when she burst through the door to his quarters with a wide grin on her face and a bounce in her step.

"Will you please be quiet?" Arael exclaimed, hopping up on the table beside his growing pile of weapons, her raven black waves still managing to shine despite the shadows in the room.

Uriah looked up, annoyed, as he stuck a dagger into his belt. "I haven't said anything."

Arael pointed to her head. "I've been listening to you prattle on up here about this trip for ages. It can't be as bad as you're expecting." She picked up a stray arrow and twirled it in her fingers.

Uriah wrinkled his forehead. "You don't have to listen, you know," he said, taking the arrow from her and jamming it down into his quiver.

"I know. But I do have to keep an eye on you. Especially when you get so worked up." She poked him in the shoulder.

"I'm fine," Uriah said, strapping the quiver to his back.

"Yeah, okay," Arael teased. "What do you think you're going to need all those weapons for, anyway? It's not like we're going to run into any ravenous creatures out there."

Uriah tightened his sword belt around his waist. "I just like to be prepared."

Arael must've decided to give him a break then because she jumped down from her perch without another word and followed him toward the door.

"We got in with Michael and his recruits." She stopped and put a hand on Uriah's arm, her sapphire eyes burning into his. "We'll be fine. Nothing can hurt us there. This is a training mission, so there must be a reason it's required. Concentrate on that. We'll be in and out quickly, and Michael will be there the whole time."

Uriah nudged her with his elbow and managed a half-grin. He could never stay upset with her for long. "Let's just get this over with."

"Getting it over with" seemed to be everyone's top concern once they set foot into the Void.

"When can we leave?" Shia asked minutes after stepping into the darkness. Michael smiled knowingly as he escorted the rest of the group through the portal.

Even through the inky blackness surrounding them, Uriah could make out black clouds rolling overhead. Large, gray mountains loomed around them, and tiny, black pebbles crunched underfoot. The only illumination came from the large fire pits bubbling and spewing far in the distance.

Uriah cast long glances at Arael throughout the day. As the heaviness grew around them, she remained stoic, her steps only slowing once. She's trying to be strong for me. Or maybe she finally understood what he'd been so afraid of.

Uriah smiled as he set off from the battlefield to find her now. Arael had been right that day. His weapons had been useless, and his worry futile. The Void was just a place. Nothing scary or dangerous had happened, just as she'd predicted. Her ever-positive presence hovered over him in the memory of that moment.

He tried to draw upon some of her optimism and quickened his pace. If Arael had passed through Eden into the physical realm as Ronan suspected, he would need to find the doorway she would have created when doing so. He continued in the direction he thought she would've gone, hoping against hope the portal hadn't closed. He told himself she was fine—that even without their connection, he would know if she were in trouble.

But how could he be sure?

Before, he could've tapped into her consciousness and known exactly where to look or used her internal compass to draw himself to her. As it was, he didn't even know if he was going in the right direction.

Uriah growled and kicked the dirt. Orange dust flew up around him and hung in the air a moment before settling back in its original position. He let out a long sigh. *Maybe if I can retrace her steps, it might give me an idea of what happened.* He thought back to the last time he'd seen her and winced at the memory.

As she'd lain there in the dirt beside him, he'd never seen her so vulnerable, and the emotions he'd felt running through her had been new to them both. So much anger, hatred, confusion. If he were honest with himself, Uriah was confused as well.

What went wrong? He knew Arael believed Michael had betrayed them. And it had been Michael's sword that had sentenced Arael to this life of exile. But Uriah didn't believe it could be that simple.

The Archangels were a tight-knit group. Unlike the other angelic Orders, which could number in the hundreds or even thousands, there were only seven of them. They loved each other fiercely, and Michael was the big brother to them all.

Uriah had seen it with his own eyes. He'd watched Michael train with her, tend to her wounds. He'd felt Michael's love for her when they were together. Michael protected her. He adored her. There was no way for him to fake that, not with an Empath.

Michael had promised them immunity. As far as Uriah knew, there had been a clear plan to keep them both safe. Yet here they were, so the plan must have gone awry somewhere along the way. Or maybe there was more to it than he even knew.

Uriah blew out a breath. *This isn't helping.* He was now somehow even more confused and no closer to finding the portal.

Just when he was about to turn around, Uriah felt it—a slight disturbance in the layer of metaphysical particles that separated the realms. It was barely detectable now, almost completely closed, but it was definitely a door. Someone had been through here.

He stared at the spot for only a moment before steeling himself and stepping through.

SEVEN

Kentucky Bend, Kentucky
Present Day

On the drive home, Camryn replayed the whole encounter with Kyle in her head, waiting for her pulse to slow. Why did she always have to be such a coward? There were so many things she wanted to say to him, most only just now coming to her. Why would he think she would ever go to any party of his? And how gross was he to stand and watch her working like he had? Geez, he gave her the creeps.

Distracted by the fictional conversations playing out in her head, she didn't even notice the other truck in the garage as she pulled in.

One good thing about leaving this town, she thought as she walked through the back door, *I won't have to deal with Kyle or Brooke or any of them ever again.* That made her smile.

"What are you smiling about?" A voice sprang out of the darkness and snapped her out of her daydream.

Camryn jumped back in surprise. She dropped her backpack and pressed her palms flat against the door behind her, ready to make a run for it if needed. She was usually on the lookout for murderers and thieves, especially when her parents were out of town. She'd been stupid to come into the house distracted like this. *Stupid.*

All of this happened in the split second it took her brain to tell her that the voice she'd heard belonged to her mother. Lindsey Martin flipped on the hallway light and looked at her daughter with wide eyes.

"What are you doing here?" Camryn breathed in relief. "I thought you guys were on your way to Franklin."

Her parents spent most weekends in Franklin, a larger town about an hour south, selling whatever they could grow on their little farm at the Farmers Market there: squash, beans, watermelons, corn, even eggs.

Her mother gestured toward the sky and shrugged. "Can't sell much in this weather. Besides, I thought we'd take advantage of a few extra days with you before you go off to college in a few months and leave us here all alone."

Camryn knew her mother was only teasing, but she immediately tensed. Lindsey's gentle reminders of the decisions Camryn had yet to make only increased her paralysis to do so. She suspected her mother felt her pulling away from her, both physically and metaphorically, but was powerless to stop the rift from widening. Lindsey's frown deepened, and Camryn's hands grew clammy.

Her dad came in then, breaking the tension between them, as usual.

"Hey!" he said, his eyes brightening. "There's my girl." He kissed Camryn on the forehead on his way to the fridge. He still wore his work boots and a navy-blue t-shirt with the letters EMS printed on the back. His stocky build almost completely blocked the refrigerator as he opened it, pulled out a can of soda, and turned back to the two women.

Camryn returned his smile as best she could manage. These moments with her mom had been getting more frequent, and she didn't like it. *More changes.* The stomach knots started rolling again. Then came an uncomfortable twinge in her neck and the panicked thought intruding into her mind. *I need to check the floodwall.*

"I think I'm going to take the horses out for a ride," she said to her startled parents.

Her horses, Rebel and Romeo, helped calm her erratic nerves when she felt an episode coming on. Camryn understood why horses were often used as therapy animals. Grooming them, feeding them, sometimes just watching them eat was all it took to bring her back from the darkness.

Both her parents looked at her as if she'd just announced her plans to run off and join the circus.

"Honey, it's dark out," her mother stated matter-of-factly.

"And it's raining," her dad added. They blinked at her in confusion.

"Yeah, I know." She began rubbing her arms, which were suddenly crawling with invisible bugs. "I won't go far."

Her mom's eyes filled with tears. She stepped around the kitchen island and put her arms out to her daughter. "Honey, I'm sorry. I—"

Camryn instinctively stepped back from her. "It's okay, Mom. Really. I just have to get some fresh air. I'll be back for dinner." She didn't wait for permission. She turned and ran out the door.

Ten minutes later, Camryn had Romeo saddled, her flashlight in hand, and was headed out on one of the many trails she and the horses had forged through the woods over the years. Her parents hadn't come out to stop her, *thank God*, and she felt better already. The chilly night air bit Camryn's skin, and it felt good. It reminded her that she was still alive and not drowning as she'd felt standing in the kitchen a few minutes before.

She'd told her parents she'd stay close, but the lie had burned on her lips. She couldn't tell them the truth, though. They'd think she was crazy. *Crazier* than they already thought.

It *was* dark. And it *was* raining. So why did she find it so necessary to be out here in the woods, making her way to the river?

Maybe she was something worse than crazy. Maybe her brain was finally trying to kill her. It had been her brain, after all, that had convinced her she needed to check the floodwall at eight o'clock at night. "There are definitely cracks," it had told her. "People will die if you don't get to the wall and see for yourself," it'd said. And nowadays, when her brain told her to do something, she didn't even try to fight it. She wouldn't be able to eat, sleep, or eventually even breathe until action had been taken.

Her brain didn't tell her, however, what she should do if she did find a fracture in the wall. She was a teenage girl with her horse. What she was doing made no sense. Logical reasoning would tell her to turn around and go home, that she shouldn't be out in the middle of the woods so late. But her compulsions didn't listen to logic.

Things like this had been happening more and more over the past few months, these little ideas. Usually, they were small, easy to hide things, like incessantly checking the emergency supplies in the basement or her need to examine the headlines every day, as if she would find a hidden message in them. Camryn had read enough about OCD to know what symptoms to look for, but she wasn't ready to accept that diagnosis quite yet.

Probably because of the visions that had started about the same time: flashes of rushing water, the town in ruins, and bodies... The dead bodies of her mom and dad and Mrs. Sparks and Granny Newman. Real people, not the faceless blobs she usually saw in her dreams. Because they weren't dreams, coming to her in the night and fading from her mind as she went about her day. No, Camryn saw these things in Chemistry class and while driving down the road. She saw images so real, she thought they were actually happening. Until the images disappeared, that is, and she was left looking at Mrs. Meyers pointing to words on the blackboard as if a massive tidal wave hadn't just swept through her classroom.

Hallucinations were generally a bad sign in regards to one's mental health, but they weren't usually an indicator of OCD. Camryn wouldn't accept these symptoms as anything more than the effect of too much cortisol in her system. Surely they would go away after she'd made it through this transition in her life and settled into whatever dorm she would call home in a few months.

But she was nothing if not a realist. She promised herself that if the visions and the compulsions got worse, she would talk to her parents about them, or better yet, she would talk to her doctor. That's what an adult would do, right?

Yes, it is, she smiled. *I might just make it after all.*

EIGHT

Earth
After the Fall

As a Dominion, Uriah seldom found a reason to venture into the physical realm. His job consisted of upholding justice and order among his peers, and that usually took place in the spirit realm, in the higher courts of Heaven.

There had been a time, though, shortly after its creation, that he'd been dispatched to Earth to reprimand two young Tempests who were disrupting the delicate order of the physical world with unauthorized lightning storms.

In the end, he'd found the offending angels, diffused the situation, and had them both replaced and on restrictions with little incident.

Things like that didn't happen often, thank the Heavens, and Uriah hadn't had reason to return.

Looking around now, the landscape was much as he remembered, a much less vibrant version of Heaven: lots of green—trees, grass, all forms of vegetation—with a spattering of color from blooming flowers and plants. Birds chirped, and rodents chattered to each other. A few miles away, he heard the lapping of water, probably from a small pond. A light breeze blew, making the leaves shimmer in the sunlight. Animals of every kind roamed the fields, from giant beasts with antlers to tiny creatures who burrowed in the ground. He knew that if everything went according to Elohim's plan, the human population would grow exponentially in the following years. In its current state, though, the animals remained the true rulers of the Earth.

As Uriah stepped through the portal, he didn't know what to expect. The one thing he didn't expect, however, was another angel stepping through behind him. Uriah whirled around, his hand gliding automatically to his sword. Was this to be his existence now? Always on edge, expecting danger at every turn? He loosened his grip when he saw the face staring back at him.

Her auburn hair flowed around her pale face. She fiddled with a tear in her dusty robes as her colorless eyes darted around, taking in everything all at once. "Hello," she said in a small voice when she noticed Uriah staring at her.

"Akira?" Uriah asked in disbelief. Had he been so distracted that he hadn't heard her following him?

The angel before him looked pleased. "You know my name?"

"I heard you speak at one of our assemblies. I'm sorry," he rushed on, "but did you follow me?"

"Well, I—" She looked over his shoulder and rocked back on her heels. "Yes, I guess I did."

"Why?" Uriah thought back to the group of angels he'd just left. He didn't think any of them looked up for a trip like this, yet here she stood.

"I overheard you talking with Ronan. You're looking for your friend, right?"

Uriah nodded slowly, not sure where her comments would lead.

"I just thought I could help you."

"That's extremely kind of you, but I don't know how you could help me. And Gabriel is coming. You should probably wait for his instructions."

Akira's wings drooped a little. Uriah felt a small twinge of disappointment shoot off of her, but her face remained impassive. "Well, you don't remember everything, then, do you?" She smiled. "I know I'm a terrible gray mess now." Her smile wavered, and she ducked her head. "But, my aura used to be bright gold."

Uriah didn't know what to say. How could he have forgotten? She was a Tracker. He tried not to let himself get excited at the news. He couldn't possibly ask her to do what he was thinking of asking her to do. It was too dangerous. What if they found Arael with Lucifer? How would he explain that?

As he stood pondering a way to politely refuse her offer, Akira lowered her head and stalked past him.

"Gabriel will call for us when he arrives," she said. "We can look for your friend in the meantime."

Akira had already traipsed several yards in front of him and wasn't looking back. Uriah didn't know how he would explain this to her, but it appeared she was doing this with or without him. Knowing he would probably come to regret it, he hurried after her.

Uriah stayed quiet as Akira lifted her nose to the air then knelt to examine the forest floor. They'd been walking for a while now with little to go on. "I don't understand..." Akira's voice trailed off.

"What is it?"

"I don't know yet," she said, standing. "I'll let you know as soon as I figure it out."

Uriah didn't like the sound of that. "Um—"

"Shh." Akira shot a finger up to quiet him before speeding off deeper into the trees. Uriah frowned, wondering exactly when Akira had gained control of this mission. He shook his head and sped to catch up.

After twenty minutes of walking, weaving through dense trees and foliage of an immense cedar forest, they were no closer to finding Arael than when they'd first set out. Akira would occasionally say, "She's been here," or "Yes, she's definitely come this way," but Uriah grew more anxious with every passing minute.

"Any idea how close we are?" he asked for probably the hundredth time.

"You know," Akira said, impatience creeping into her voice, "continuing to ask me that question is not getting us to her any faster."

"Yes, I know. I'm just—"

"Listen," Akira interrupted. "I came here to help you, and that's what I intend to do. But I need you to trust me. I'm working as hard as I can, considering I *have* just been attacked, so I'm going to need you to cut me a little slack."

Uriah clasped his hands at his waist. "Akira, I am truly grateful for your help. I apologize if it seems otherwise. I'm just a little desperate, and I don't know—" He stopped, not knowing how to finish.

Akira tilted her head to one side. "Why are you so desperate to find her anyway? Everyone will have to return when Gabriel calls. Why don't you just wait and talk to her then?" The Tracker placed her hands on her hips. "What aren't you telling me?"

What could he say? He couldn't exactly tell her how he and Arael had been working undercover for Michael and essentially been the catalyst for the battle that ended in their exile and that Lucifer could be exacting his punishment on her as they spoke.

No, he couldn't tell her that.

"Arael is my *qanima*...was my *qanima*." He shook his head. "I don't know what we are now. But she would never have left me back there of her own free will. I'm afraid she's been taken."

Akira stared back at him with no expression on her face, but lucky for Uriah, he had other ways of knowing her feelings.

"I thought only Archangels had a *qanima*," she said.

45

He felt the confusion she tried to hide. And a hint of something bitter that he'd never felt before.

"That is partly true. Only Archangels are guaranteed one, but their *qanima* can be from another Order. Japhael's *qanima* is a Guardian. Gabriel's is a Cherub."

"And what? Your bond is broken now?"

Uriah winced. Just hearing the words spoken out loud caused the wound in his side to throb.

"Okay," Akira said before Uriah could make himself answer. "Okay, well…" she turned in a slow circle, examining their surroundings. "I don't know what you think could possibly have taken her. Nothing from the physical realm could've entered Eden, but if you're so certain, I could have been hiding our tracks."

"You can do that?"

"Of course I can do that." She lifted her chin. "I'm a Tracker."

Uriah smiled. So that's why he hadn't heard her following him.

Preparing to set off again, Akira swiped a dirty hand across her forehead. Uriah's face fell when he spotted a small bloody wound under her left arm. He rubbed the back of his neck. He could ignore the ache in his side because finding Arael was more important to him than his pain, but Akira had no real stake in this journey. She must be hurting but hadn't complained at all. He couldn't imagine why, but she *was* helping him, and he had to be thankful for that.

"I didn't see my attacker either." Uriah pulled back his robe to reveal a similar wound. "I don't even know who to be angry with."

A sympathetic smile pulled at Akira's lips. "Literally stabbed in the back."

They stood regarding each other for another moment. "Her scent is still faint," Akira said finally. "The moment it gets any stronger, I promise I will tell you."

Uriah nodded, and they set out again. Akira continued to lead the way, stepping gingerly through the thick brush, with Uriah close behind. The sun beamed down on them, intensifying the already stifling heat.

Another long while passed before Akira spoke again. "That's strange," she said, stopping in her tracks.

"What? What's strange?"

"She's doing it again. She's moving erratically, even backtracking in places. I don't understand what she's—" A cloud passed over Akira's face, realization dawning.

"What?" Uriah exclaimed. "You can't keep doing that. What are you thinking?"

"Well, it seems you were right. She is running from someone."

Uriah's head whipped around in all directions, his senses on high alert.

"Uriah, I think she's running from *us*."

Uriah let out a nervous laugh. "No, that's not possible."

"Why not?" Akira sat down on a fallen tree and placed her hands on her knees.

"I don't—I don't know. I just know I can't stop looking."

Akira straightened. "Will you listen to yourself? You need to face the facts, Uriah. I know it hurts, but she doesn't want to be found."

Uriah opened his mouth to argue, but something caught his eye. They had arrived at the edge of the forest, and a mountain range stretched out a few miles in the distance.

"I think I know where she is."

Akira turned to follow his gaze. "Yes, I believe you're right."

"I've been here before. Arael hasn't, but I told her about it. I'm going to take a look."

"Okay," Akira said, nodding thoughtfully. "I guess my services are no longer needed, then?"

"Oh." Uriah's excitement faltered. "No, you should come."

Akira shook her head. "No. She's your *qanima*. And she's avoiding you. I don't need to be there for that reunion. You have fun, though."

"She's not hiding from me," Uriah said, more for his own benefit than Akira's.

"Sure. Okay." Akira waved.

Uriah watched her walk away, the confidence of her words wafting back to him on the breeze. She believed Arael was running from him, but she was wrong.

No matter what Akira said, he knew Arael was in danger, and he couldn't stop looking for her now.

Nine

The North Woods of Kentucky Bend could be an ominous place at night for someone less familiar with the place than Camryn. The clouds parted enough to momentarily allow the moonlight to filter down through the canopy of bare trees. Spring would soon bring color and life back to the woods, but tonight the vacant limbs and brown leaves covered the forest floor like a wretched blanket of death. Only the occasional hoot of an owl or rustle in the bushes told Camryn that the forest was still, indeed, alive.

She should be scared. That would be the natural reaction for most people as they clomped into a dark, dead forest at night, but Camryn was more at home in these woods, day or night, than any other place in the world. For Camryn, these woods had been her second home, her classroom, and her sanctuary for her entire life. The memories of her childhood often came alive to her as she rode the trails.

Crossing Little Creek, she thought of her father expertly placing a worm on her hook and teaching her the art of casting a line. The deer that darted in front of her as she and Romeo ambled along took her back to the first time she'd held one in her sights, felt her father's steady hand on her back as she'd exhaled and released the arrow, just as he'd taught her.

Farther into the woods lay a clearing where she and the horses liked to spend Sunday afternoons when the sun was shining and the ground dry. It was also the place where she'd sprained an ankle while camping with her parents when she was eight and had learned how to make a splint out of two sticks and an old t-shirt.

She'd learned so much in these woods: how to catch and cook her own food, how to find and purify water, how to distinguish edible plants from poisonous ones. She'd been raised to take the art of survival very seriously. *"You never know when this world will go up in smoke,"* her father would say. With everything happening in the world, never had his words been more relevant.

Camryn checked the time and sighed. It would take hours to get to the levee and back, but her parents would be worried long before then. *I should probably call them.* That's what she was thinking when she heard it—a faint but recognizable sound. A sound that did not belong in the woods at night.

She stopped and listened.

There it was again.

Warning bells rang in her head, but something urged her closer. Shining her flashlight through the trees, she dismounted Romeo and followed the sound as stealthily as possible. As it turned out, it wouldn't have mattered how loud she'd been. The person in front of her wouldn't have heard her anyway.

The beam of her flashlight landed on a kid, probably about her own age, lying on the ground, soaking wet and shivering. A quick assessment of the situation told her that (A) he was not from around here and (B) he didn't have any visible outward injuries. She grabbed the blanket from Romeo's back and ran to him. "Are you okay?"

His chest was heaving as if he'd just run a marathon. His breaths came quick and shallow, and he had one arm flung over his eyes. His lips twitched, trying to form words, but his gasps for breath made them impossible to understand.

A more thorough check confirmed what Camryn suspected, she didn't see any blood or wounds of any kind. That was a good sign. But something was definitely wrong with him.

She placed her hand lightly over his wet t-shirt. He flinched at her touch and tried to scramble away from her, but it looked as if his limbs weren't obeying his brain.

"Go. Away," he managed to get out between gasps.

Camryn ignored him and wrapped the blanket around his shoulders. The wet earth gave way under her knees, and the water soaked through her jeans as she knelt beside him and pressed her hand onto his heaving chest.

She didn't consider that this person was a stranger or that he'd asked to be left alone. She didn't think about any of that. She didn't think at all. She began rubbing in slow, small circles on his chest, whispering soft words into his ear, just as her mother had done for her countless times before.

"It's okay. It's okay. Just take deep breaths. In and out," she repeated as she inhaled deeply and exhaled slow breaths, hoping he would follow her lead.

His eyes darted around wildly at her touch. She knew he was afraid but paralyzed by the anxiety pulsing through him. She gripped his face in her hands and forced him to look at her. In the darkness of night, his eyes were large black pools, both horrified for her to be witnessing this and pleading with her to help him.

For one frightening moment, she thought she would fall down into the darkness with him, but in a blink, she snapped back to herself and was able to focus again on the task at hand.

After a brief pause, she managed to continue her mantra. "It's okay. Just do what I do." She continued to breathe, in and out, and his eyes locked in on her face. As he began to mimic her, his breathing became more even, and his heartbeat slowed under her fingers. "It's okay," she continued until he was finally able to pull away from her.

He sat up and wrapped his arms around his knees, refusing to look at her. She grabbed a bottle of water from Romeo's satchel and handed it to him. He took it reluctantly and gulped down half the bottle while Camryn took the opportunity to get a better look at him. Even from his folded-up position, she could tell he was tall, with dark skin and dark hair. That was all she could make out without shining the flashlight right in his face, which she suspected he probably wouldn't appreciate.

After several more gulps of the water, he finally spoke. "How'd you do that?" he mumbled, still not looking at her.

Camryn shrugged. "That's what my mom does for me when I have them. It helps most of the time."

He pushed the strings of black hair out of his eyes. "When you have them?"

"Yeah. Sometimes." Camryn shrugged again. Her panic attacks were much less frequent than they'd once been, but the memory of the uncontrollable shaking and heart-pounding terror never left her. She glanced at the backpack lying nearby and wondered if he'd run away from somewhere. If so, why would he have come *here*?

"Do you have food and water?" she asked, gesturing to his bag.

The boy looked confused. "Huh?"

Only then did Camryn notice the ring of metal in his lip, glinting in the moonlight. *Yeah, he's definitely not from around here.* Camryn knew she should be moving on. It was getting late, and she still had to get to the river, but she couldn't bring herself to leave this stranger just yet.

"What are you doing out here anyway?"

"Are you always this nosy?" he snapped.

Camryn stared at him. She didn't need the flashlight to know he wore a scowl on his face. Here she was, covered in mud and soaking wet thanks to this kid, and he was going to be rude to her? But she couldn't find it in herself to be mad at him. Add this to her list of character flaws, but looking down at him with his own set of muddy, wet clothes and rain dripping from his hair, he looked more like a stray puppy than the vicious dog he was trying to portray.

"Well, where are you going then? I can take you somewhere." She jabbed a thumb toward her horse. The boy eyed the animal warily and shook his head.

Now she was just the tiniest bit annoyed. "Well, you can't stay out here all night. You'll freeze."

"Look, I don't need your help, okay. I'm fine," he said, pulling the blanket tighter around his shoulders.

"Yeah, okay," she replied, sarcasm heavy in her voice. "Well, good luck with that." She mounted her horse in one fluid motion. Right before she clicked the reigns, a panicked voice came from behind.

"Wait!"

When Camryn turned back to look at the boy standing alone in the dark forest, his face wore a mixture of fear, anger, and humiliation. She made him wait a moment longer before finally putting him out of his misery.

"Take that path to the big oak tree," she said, pointing to his left. "Then follow the trail to the fork and stay left. That'll take you to the south side of the park. The main road's about a mile east."

The boy stared at her, blinking.

Camryn rolled her eyes. "Just follow me," she said, thoughts of levee cracks and floods abruptly forgotten.

TEN

Earth
After the Fall

The mountain was just as Uriah remembered—a craggy, rock-covered mass of intersecting caves and tunnels. Inside, the darkness enveloped him, the only light coming from a few sporadic cracks in the rock overhead. The tomb of silence was broken only by the occasional echo of water dripping into a distant spring.

Uriah strained to exert his senses through the layers of rock around him, but he had no other ability to rely on in this strange new reality. He forced his concentration out, causing a vein to throb in his temple. He couldn't hear her. He couldn't smell her. He couldn't sense her at all. But she had to be there.

Uriah fought the urge to call out to her. Even though he didn't discern any danger, his instincts told him to tread slowly. He gripped his sword, ready for action, and found himself wishing Akira was there. She could have at least covered their tracks.

Uriah traveled what seemed like miles of tunnels before picking up something—not the spiritual presence he searched for, but something just as promising. It floated in the air like sulfuric gas, overwhelming him almost instantly; a mixture of grief, terror, and remorse, so strong it almost brought him to his knees. He strained to pinpoint from which direction it came.

After a few moments, when he'd determined only one source of the acrid air, he finally decided to call out to her.

"Arael," he whispered but received no response. "It's okay. I'm here. Just tell me where you are," he said a little louder.

The fear hung so thick that he could almost swat it away like a curtain in front of his face. She had to be close now.

Uriah rounded a curve in the passageway and stopped in his tracks. There she stood in a dead-end section of tunnel, sword outstretched, and a wretched look of terror on her face. Disheveled sprigs of black hair hung into her eyes, and her wings arched wide on either side of her.

He put his hand out to her. "It's okay, Arael. It's me." She stared directly at him but seemed to be looking through him. "You know me. I'm your friend." He took a step closer, and her eyes snapped into focus.

She jabbed her sword in his direction. "No!"

Uriah froze.

"You have to leave," she pleaded.

Uriah looked up and listened. "It's okay. There's no one else here. Come on. Come with me."

"I said, *no*!" She kept the sword trained on him and raised her other hand, palm outstretched, toward him.

Uriah took a cautious step back. "What are you doing?"

He'd seen her take this stance before, right before blowing a lightning bolt straight through a target. He knew the damage she could do, the power those hands wielded. Surely she wouldn't use that power on him.

As if reading his mind, she said, "I'll do it. Please don't make me. You have to go."

"I'm not leaving without you."

She shook her head but didn't say anything. He took another step closer. "I know what you're trying to do, but I'm not going to let you."

She looked at him, a mixture of hurt and anger on her face. "How, Uriah? How do you know what I'm trying to do?" She jabbed a finger at her head. "You're not in here anymore. You can't hear me. You might be able to feel some arbitrary emotions, but you have no idea what I'm thinking."

Uriah stood as still as a statue. "You're wrong. I may not be able to hear your thoughts, but I know you better than anyone. You think this is all your fault. You think you're responsible for an eternity of suffering for all those angels back there. You think you don't deserve to be happy, to even be alive, and you're going to isolate yourself from the only family you have left in order to punish yourself." He took a breath. "How's that? Am I close?"

Arael squeezed her eyes shut as a tear ran down her cheek. Uriah knew the tremendous anguish it took to bring an angel to tears, but he couldn't back down now.

"You give yourself a lot of credit, you know. Every one of those angels back there made a choice, just like you did. They made a choice to be where they were when this happened. This wasn't our fault, and if you want to stay here and feel sorry for yourself, that's fine—but I'm not leaving you."

Her sword began to tremble, and the bristled feathers of her wings settled back into place. He watched the tears fall silently down her face as the finality of their new life seemed to settle on her. The sword drooped and wavered until she gave up and collapsed to the stone floor, her black hair falling around her head like a tent covering her face.

Uriah went to her then. He knelt beside her and pushed her hair back off her shoulder. Arael turned her eyes up to meet his. "I'm sorry I left you back there," she said. "I can't believe I did that."

"Nonsense. You were scared. Anyone would have done the same thing."

"You wouldn't have. You never would have left me like that."

"Well, this is true," Uriah said, hoping to elicit at least a smile from her.

"I just couldn't bear to see you like that," she continued as if he hadn't spoken. "And I thought you would hate me."

"Hate you? For what?"

"For trusting Michael. For believing that he would protect us."

"I made a choice, too, you know. I trusted him, too. I could have talked you out of it if I'd wanted to." Uriah nudged her chin up, so her eyes met his again. "And nothing could ever make me hate you."

Arael shook her head and looked down at her hands. "What are we going to do?"

"Well, the one thing we're not going to do is act suspicious." Uriah stood, preparing to leave. "Right now, no one knows anything. You woke up. You got scared. You ran. Simple as that. Everyone is scared, so they will understand."

Arael shook her head. "I can't go back there. I can't face them."

"Arael," Uriah chided, "Gabriel will call us back soon. We can't stay here."

"I just can't, okay. Not yet."

"Okay." Uriah looked around. "Then I'll stay with you."

Arael started to protest, but Uriah remained firm in his response. "I'm not leaving you."

ELEVEN

Kentucky Bend, Kentucky
Present Day

"Someone slept well last night," Camryn's father said as she bounced into the kitchen the next morning.

"Yep. Not so much as a bad dream." She grabbed a cup from the cupboard and filled it from the coffee pot her mother handed her. Most nights, for as long as Camryn could remember, she'd been woken by horrific night terrors. Right in that moment between sleeping and wakefulness, she would be jolted awake by tortured screams. Sometimes the voice she heard was her own. Sometimes it belonged to…someone else.

"Maybe you're finally growing out of them like the doctor said you would," her mother offered.

"It's about time." Camryn could only hope.

"I was going to ask if you were okay after last night, but you seem to be feeling better."

"Yes, Mom, I'm fine." Camryn had come home the night before and gone straight to bed. Her parents had been waiting for her at the dinner table, but she couldn't even think of eating after her run-in with that mysterious boy. She'd told them she wasn't feeling well, but the truth was, she felt better than she had in a long time. "I'm much better today."

Her mom smiled and gestured to the window, bright with sunshine. "The rain's stopped. Since you're feeling better, perhaps we could make it to the Farmers Market after all." She raised a questioning eyebrow at her husband.

James nodded then looked to Camryn. "We may stay an extra night to make up for yesterday if business is good and the weather holds."

"That makes sense. I've got spring break next week anyway, so…" Camryn shrugged. "Be safe." She gave them both a peck on the cheek and headed out the door with her coffee. She stopped on the way to the stables and turned her face up to the sun. It had been too long since she'd felt its heat on her face. She couldn't help but smile.

Camryn had a feeling—today would be a good day.

"Good morning, guys," she said as she entered the stable a few minutes later. A loud whinny greeted her. "Oh, Romeo, don't be so dramatic." She smiled and rubbed his demanding snout. The brown and white Appaloosa had a heart-shaped spot right on his forehead, which was fitting, given his loving disposition.

Her other horse, a black Warlander named Rebel, possessed a regal air more appropriate for the noble steed of a Saudi prince than that of a rural Kentucky farmgirl. She rubbed his sturdy neck and dropped a scoop of feed into each bucket before clicking on the radio. A familiar, upbeat rhythm filled the barn, and she couldn't help but move her body along with the music as she shoveled the stalls.

Their little stable wasn't fancy; three stalls on one side and a couple of storage rooms on the other. She and her dad had built it when she was ten, right after they'd gotten Rebel, the first horse she'd ever called her own.

Her dad had rescued Rebel from a livestock auction after he'd been neglected and abused. He didn't trust people at all, especially men. When her dad had brought him home, Camryn had cried. She'd always thought of horses as the most beautiful, majestic creatures, but this one was a bony, frightened beast.

"If anyone can tame him, you can," her father had said to her. As a ten-year-old, that had been a huge weight on her shoulders, but she'd taken the responsibility with pride.

After several months and countless hours spent with him, though, Rebel had come about as far as he was willing to. Camryn could feed him, groom him, and pet him, but saddling him was out of the question.

Her father offered to take him to a trainer, but Camryn wasn't having it. "He doesn't want to be ridden, Dad. And that's okay. That's just who he is." And that's who he remained to this day. He was content to roam the fields and keep to himself, something Camryn could relate to.

She pulled Rebel out of his stall and gathered his brush, sponge, and hoof pick. Of all her chores, she most looked forward to this. She ran her hand down the length of the animal, feeling his coarse hair and the soft rise and fall of his belly as he breathed, so calm and trusting. She was just beginning to lose herself in the motion of the brush and the upbeat rhythm of the music when she got the uneasy feeling that she wasn't alone.

Whirling around, Camryn almost knocked over the stool beside her when she saw the figure standing in the doorway. It was the boy from the woods, a green backpack slung over one shoulder, leaning on the wood post with a smug grin on his face.

"I never would've taken you for a Taylor Swift fan." He looked out of place in his old Vans, cargo shorts, and faded black t-shirt. She could make out the word "CLASH" scrawled across the front in white letters dripping with crimson blood.

In the light of day and without the scowl, his face was surprisingly pleasant—all dark skin and angles and marble-gray eyes that pulled her into them from twenty feet across the dirt floor. He still had one corner of his mouth pulled into a grin as he twisted something absently between his fingers.

Camryn reached over and turned down the radio. "I don't—I mean—the horses like it," she stammered.

"Uh-huh." His head tilted to one side, allowing him to peer at her through the curtain of hair that hung unchecked like a veil between him and the rest of the world. His intense eyes examined her like she was a math problem he couldn't quite figure out.

Camryn's cheeks grew hot, the shock of his appearance blazing on her face. The boy straightened, dropping the object in his hand into his pocket, and flung the hair back out of his eyes. "What are you doing anyway?"

Camryn cleared her throat. Horses. Yes. Horses, she could talk about. "Just brushing them out. I have to do it about once a week."

The boy eyed the horses and the wiry brush she held in her hand. "And they like that?"

Camryn could barely process his words. A boy was standing in her barn. A boy who, the last time she'd seen him, looked more like a drowned rat than the tall, beautiful person standing in front of her now.

"Sure, they like it." She patted Rebel on the hindquarters and led him back into his stall. "It's kind of comforting for them...I guess." She had no idea what she was saying. Was she even speaking real words?

"Seems like a lot of work." He leaned away from the snout that reached out to sniff him.

"It is, but they depend on me." She shrugged. "It's just what I have to do."

Watching him try in vain to avoid the curious nose that sought him out, Camryn forgot about her nerves. "He just wants to say hi. Here, give him one of these." Camryn placed a few sugar cubes in the boy's hand.

"I don't know if that's a—" A giant tongue reached out and licked the cubes out of the boy's palm before he could draw it back. "Ahhh!" he shouted, wiping his wet hand on his t-shirt.

Camryn couldn't help but laugh. "Here," she said, handing him a towel.

"Okay. That was terrifying," he said, but he was smiling along with her.

"Well, he doesn't like everyone, so you should feel special."

"Really?" The boy looked pleased.

"I wasn't too sure about you until now, but if he likes you, you must be alright," Camryn teased.

The boy's face grew serious. "Well, I don't blame you for not trusting me." He stuffed his hands deep into his pockets, looking uncomfortable. "I guess I should apologize for the way I acted last night. I was pretty awful to you, and you were just trying to help, so..." He trailed off, looking down at his shoes.

"Oh, no." Camryn waved him off. "No big deal."

"Yes, it *was* a big deal, and I acted like a jerk."

"Yeah. You kinda did." They both smiled.

"So..." Camryn asked the obvious question. "How did you know where I lived?"

"Oh," the boy pulled the lip ring between his teeth, rolling it back and forth a few times with his tongue before he answered. "I'm at the Morgan's." He gestured up the road toward the house on the hill. "I came out this morning and recognized the horse. At least I hoped it was the same horse. I wasn't sure until I came down here and saw you...cleaning."

Camryn felt the heat rush to her cheeks again.

"Hope that's not too creepy," he added almost as an afterthought.

Camryn knew Grace and Dale Morgan were foster parents. Kids came and went from their house a lot—mostly younger ones, though. That did explain a few things.

"No. I guess not," she decided.

The boy blew out a long breath. "So, I never did get your name."

"Camryn. It's Camryn Martin."

"I'm Ethan." He leaned back against the wall, hands still in his pockets.

"So, what's your story, Ethan?" Despite his piercings and horrific-looking t-shirt, Camryn couldn't ignore her curiosity about him.

"Wow, you don't beat around the bush, do you?"

Camryn bit her lip. "Sorry," she said. "Is that too forward? I'm not very good at talking to actual people." She gestured to the horses. "I'm much better with animals."

"It's fine," Ethan said. "It's what you'd expect. My mom's a drug addict. She's in jail, and I'm here."

A stab of grief hit Camryn like a wave. *How terrible.* Romeo nuzzled her neck, sensing her unease. "What about your dad?"

"No dad. Just me and my mom. That's how it's been since my grandmother died."

"God, I'm sorry." Camryn decided she should probably stop asking questions.

"Don't be. It is what it is. Being sorry won't change anything."

"Wise words." She eyed the bag on his back. "So, what are your plans now?"

Ethan gave an ironic laugh. "Plans? I'm not very good at making plans. I'm too busy trying to dodge the shit life keeps throwing at me."

Camryn didn't know what to say to that. She looked up at the horse, examining Ethan with intense eyes. "This is Rebel," she said, patting the horse on the neck. "He's had a pretty rough life, too."

Camryn noticed Ethan's eyes lingering on her hand as it moved in a slow circular motion like it had on his chest the night before.

"Well, at least he has you now."

Camryn looked up into the horse's big, black eyes then back at Ethan's ashen ones. "Yes," she said. "I guess he does."

TWELVE

And it came to pass, when men began to multiply on the face of the earth, and daughters were born unto them, that the sons of God saw the daughters of men that they were fair; and they took them wives of all which they chose…there were giants in the earth in those days; when the sons of God came in unto the daughters of men, and they bore children to them, the same became mighty men which were of old, men of renown.
Genesis 6:1-4 NIV

A deep purple haze filled the morning sky as Arael made her way down the narrow mountain path toward the nearest stream. The dampness of the early morning air clung to her skin, and the earthy smell of the dew-covered ground filled her nostrils. Like a sonar, her ears picked up the faint rustling of dried grass and pebbles about twenty yards away as a small rodent scurried through the brush. Arael looked up and zeroed in on the eagle that nested on the ledge about a mile up the mountain just in time to witness the exact moment the bird spotted her morning meal.

You're about to be someone's breakfast, little mouse. Arael smiled as the whoosh of the eagle's wings reached her ears, the mother eagle diving toward her prey. She knew she needed to hurry, but couldn't resist watching—just for a moment—as the mother delivered the treat to the eaglets in her nest.

Arael and Uriah had made their home in the last and smallest peak of the Alborz mountain range that bordered the human villages of Tehran. They'd watched civilization from above as it grew and changed over the five hundred years since the Fall.

When the humans had first migrated there, they'd been cave dwellers who foraged for food. Now they lived in tents and herded cattle, using the animals for food and clothing. They'd begun to make their own weapons and jewelry, all strangely reminiscent of angelic artifacts. But Arael didn't concern herself with the business of the mortals—or the angels, for that matter. Not since the last Conclave.

For Arael—and all the other angels, she assumed—Conclaves had always been a joyous event. A social gathering of sorts. There was always a purpose, of course. Usually, just an efficient way for Gabriel to impart wisdom, hand out assignments, or give updates to all the Heavenly host at once. But more often than not, it turned into a celebration, a coming together of angels who otherwise would never cross paths with one another.

The Conclave after the Fall had been torturous. Almost as soon as Uriah and Akira had tracked Arael down after their exile, Gabriel had arrived at the battlefield with instructions, just as Uriah had expected. He'd blown his trumpet and delivered the set of laws the Fallen were now required to live by. If she'd had a choice, she wouldn't have gone. She would've stayed holed up in her cave and let Uriah report back to her whatever news Gabriel had delivered. But as a celestial being, Conclave attendance was not optional—her body was compelled to rise to the trumpet call like a flower drawn to the sun.

But as much as Arael dreaded seeing the faces of her fellow Fallen angels for all the reasons she'd explained to Uriah, she was most afraid of facing Lucifer.

Just act natural, she'd told herself. *Control your heartbeat, and don't talk too much*. It wasn't likely she'd run into him anyway, right?

Wrong. He'd been the first angel to approach her after Gabriel's meeting.

"Arael," he'd said, smiling. "I did hope I would run into you here."

Arael returned his smile. *Stay calm. You have nothing to be afraid of.*

Turned out, she'd been right. He'd sought her out to offer her a job, not to accuse her of treason. She'd been dumbfounded, but so relieved that she'd accepted.

The entirety of her existence now centered around patrolling the territory that encompassed their mountain range and reporting back to Lucifer any human activity—a mundane task if there ever was one, considering there *was* no human activity there, but how could she have refused? She was just thankful to have a job again and grateful to have escaped his wrath.

"Akira says Lucifer is trying to get every territory covered," Uriah had told her one day. "He's almost got it done, too."

It was smart of him, she had to admit. Elohim had Guardians assigned to every territory on Earth, so why shouldn't Lucifer? He was setting himself up as the leader of the Fallen angels, after all. She wouldn't have been surprised if he'd given her the job just to torment Clarion, her Guardian counterpart of the Alborz.

Uriah had accompanied Akira on the odd job here and there but hadn't committed to anything for himself just yet. "Just keeping my options open," he liked to say, but Arael thought it more likely that he was trying to keep an eye on her.

As far as Arael's assignment, though, she had done her job dutifully until now, not daring to tempt fate once again. But for some reason, at her last report, she'd failed to mention the two new human guests her mountain had recently acquired.

They'd be gone soon anyway. No need to involve Lucifer.

Arael traipsed down the mountain now, two empty water jugs swinging at her side. She kicked her way through the brush, taking no notice of the thorns and thistles scratching her ankles.

When she finally reached the stream, Arael plunged the first water jug into the cool water, tilted it against the current, and waited for it to fill. As the jug grew heavy with liquid, a familiar tingle bristled on the back of her neck. She sighed internally before pasting a smile on her face and turning to face her guest.

"What brings you down the mountain, Clarion?"

Beautiful was not a sufficient enough word to describe the angel before her. Clarion was radiant. Glorious. Glowing with a soft yellow light that was simultaneously comforting and powerful. Some of the Fallen had chosen to engage their Guardian counterparts in a battle for their territories, but she and Clarion had managed to live in harmony together for centuries, mostly because there wasn't much to fight over.

The Guardian of the mountain glanced toward the water jugs. "Interaction with humans is against the Law." Her voice, both soft and soothing, conveyed an authority Arael could not ignore.

"I'm not hurting them," Arael muttered. "I only bring them food and water, enough to survive." She thought of the two humans who'd shown up on her mountain a few months before, starving and weak. "They would be dead now if not for me."

"Is that not why they came to this mountainside? To die on their own terms?" Clarion retorted. "They are old and feeble. Why not let nature take its course, just as it does with the other animals?"

Arael lowered her eyes. "They're not animals." Her voice was almost a whisper. "Besides, it won't be long now anyway, no matter what I do."

Clarion's eyes regarded her, but before she could speak, another angel approached from the distance.

"I tried to tell her," Uriah said as he neared.

"Uriah," Clarion nodded in greeting.

67

Uriah turned to Arael and offered a playful wink. She wasn't sure where he had been (he hadn't been around much since the humans had shown up), but she wished he would've stayed there a little longer, at least until her groveling to Clarion was over. She turned away from Uriah, trying to pretend he wasn't there.

"I am a servant, Clarion. This is what I was created for. You know that as well as anyone. I cannot just erase that part of me." Words flowed from her mouth, almost against her will. "I am only trying to make my existence mean something again. Even if just for a little while."

She hadn't realized until that moment how much helping these humans actually meant to her.

Clarion relaxed her regal stance. "Don't worry. If I were going to turn you in, I would have done so a long time ago."

Arael sighed and raised her chin as Uriah tried to stifle a laugh. *Of course she knows.* The shame of her arrogance reddened her cheeks. Clarion knew everything that happened on her mountain.

"It must be hard living as you do."

Arael looked down at her scratched ankles and grimy hands. Prolonged existence in the physical form was not ideal for a celestial being, but much more practical when living with humans. "It's easier this way."

"I wouldn't know." Clarion's voice wasn't condemning, just matter-of-fact. Most angels only used their physical bodies to reveal themselves to the mortals, and even then, only briefly. Arael couldn't imagine Clarion ever finding occasion for such a thing.

"So, if you're not turning me in," Arael said, eager to change the subject, "why are you here?"

Clarion picked up a pebble and examined it with awe as if this were her first time seeing such a wondrous creation. "How long has it been since you've visited the villages?"

Arael glanced at Uriah, his white hair almost blinding in the light of the sun. He visited them often, but Arael preferred the seclusion of her cave.

"A long time. Why?"

"Things are not good," Clarion said, placing the pebble back in its spot. "I don't know how much Uriah has told you, but you are not the only one who has found living with mortals to be a fun way to pass the time."

"The Founders," Uriah said. "Those are the ones I told you about."

Ah, yes. Uriah *had* told her a little about the unfortunate decisions of some of the other Fallen, but not in great detail. Arael got the feeling it wasn't something he liked talking about.

Arael knew that the Founders were the angels who'd offered knowledge—everything the humans now knew about herding, weapon making, technology—as a dowry in exchange for mortal wives. By some unforeseen miracle, the mortals had been able to bear children from these unions—horrible half-human beasts called Nephilim.

Keeping to her mountain, Arael had never seen this with her own eyes, but Uriah told her of the carnage and destruction left in their wake. From his descriptions, the Nephilim were terrible creatures who bore their fathers' powers and had no regard for human life.

It was the Nephilim destruction that had brought Jacob and his wife, Salome, to their mountain for refuge. Arael had thought they'd been exaggerating. Perhaps she'd been wrong.

"He mentioned it," Arael said.

"And she told me it was none of our business." Uriah crossed his arms over his chest and rocked back on his heels. When had this become two against one?

Clarion nodded. "Well, it's your business now. Three of the creatures are heading this way. From what I can tell of their chatter, they have been sent by their father. And they are headed straight for this mountain." She glanced between them. "They should be here in half a day's time."

Arael thought again of the two helpless humans up in their cave. She wasn't worried, though. Not really. They had several hours to prepare for the Nephilim's arrival, and she was an Archangel. An exiled one, but an Archangel still. Surely she could defend a few humans against some half-human, half-angel hybrids, even without Uriah's help. "Thank you for the warning, Clarion. We will take precautions."

"I was thinking…" Clarion turned her eyes back to the horizon. "A thunderstorm might alter their course."

Arael wasn't sure she'd heard correctly. She glanced at Uriah, who seemed just as confused. "I thought I wasn't allowed to use my Tempest powers here."

Clarion turned back to Arael, her eyes burning as bright as the morning sun. "I don't want them here any more than you do."

As soon as Clarion had gone, Uriah turned to Arael. "I don't think this is a good idea."

"What?" Arael flinched away from him. "Why not?"

"There are too many unknowns. We don't even know if they're coming here. They could pass us right by, and you'll just be drawing unnecessary attention."

"You heard Clarion. Their father sent them here. To this mountain. She wouldn't lie to us."

"First of all, it isn't impossible for her to lie to us. Also…why would he send them here? There is nothing here they could want."

Arael thought for a moment. The realization sent ice down her back. "Unless someone knows about us." She looked up at Uriah. "What if someone found out what we did?"

Uriah's face contorted as it did when he was trying to decide if he would continue arguing or just give in and help her.

He finally deflated. "I'll see if I can find a way to distract them," he said, heading off on foot down the mountain.

Arael nodded but was already hurrying back up the path, water jugs in tow. Her mind raced with both fear and excitement. It had been so long since she'd utilized her Tempest power. Would she still be able to do it? Would it come back to her easily? Or maybe it had lain dormant for so long it would be useless to her now. One thing she knew for certain, though: she had work to do.

Later that night, her human charges asleep deep inside the cave, Arael stood on a ledge high above her mountain home. She scanned the mountainside and the valley below. The glimmer of the moon provided enough light for even a human to see by. Arael sat for a long time, hearing and seeing nothing except the chirping of crickets and the rustle of bat wings. She watched and listened until an unfamiliar sound reached her ears—a sound so faint, she would never have even noticed had she not been listening for it. She focused in on the base of the mountain where the muffled voices echoed. There they were, just as Clarion said.

Three enormous creatures walked the mountain path, each as big as two mortal men, their heads a strange, elongated shape. They wore animal skins, just as the other humans, and other than their size and oddly shaped heads, resembled the humans in almost every other way. That is, except for the dark aura surrounding them, even darker than that of the Fallen. Even though she sat hidden miles up the mountainside, Arael dialed in on their voices until she could make out their words.

"We have found it," the one on the right said. "Father will be pleased." Their eyes peered straight up her mountain. If their eyesight had been as sharp as Arael's, they would have been looking straight at her. She had no idea what they could want with her little mountain, but whatever their plan, it wasn't happening on her watch.

Arael stood, anticipation coursing through her. She hadn't tested her powers yet for fear of giving herself away. All her questions from earlier in the day still lingered, but she had to believe this could work.

With a shaking breath, she closed her eyes and flexed her hands. It only took a moment of concentration to put all her fears to rest. Her power hadn't left her. As she opened her mind to it, she felt it rising and stretching within her, like a cougar rising from slumber. She lifted a hand to the heavens, and giving a slight tug with the force inside her, pulled on the energies she knew hovered there, just above the clouds.

And nothing happened.

Arael opened her eyes and stretched her neck from side to side. *Okay. Maybe I'm a bit rusty.*

She planted her feet and tried again.

Raising both hands over her head this time, Arael concentrated on conjuring the electricity from within her. The veins in her neck throbbed. The energy consumed her as it rose up from her middle and inched its way up her arms, making them tremble with power. It had been so long since she'd felt the sensation, but it flowed from her core in a steady stream. The tingle of power climbed up her throat and escaped in a guttural scream so loud, a small shower of pebbles rained down on her from the rocky cliffs above.

Her chest vibrated with the boom of thunder that exploded in the sky. In the next instant, a burst of lightning shot down, lighting up the night as bright as midday.

She smiled as the brambly bush in front of the three enormous men burst into flames. Anyone looking would've thought it had been struck by the lightning, but Arael knew better. Uriah had figured a way to distract them.

Arael pulled again. More lightning flashed. More thunder boomed. As the power within her began to take control, she continued to pull from the sky with all her strength, and something else began to happen. The clouds opened up and began pouring out water on the earth. The rain fell on her and her visitors in sheets, plastering her hair to her face and her robes to her skin. That had never happened before, but she was glad it had. She watched the Nephilim as they turned sharply and headed for shelter in the nearby village.

It worked!

She stared down at her hands. The power she'd unleashed still stirred within her. For the first time in a long time, she felt *alive*. Her breath escaped in short bursts, and she couldn't wipe the smile from her face—not until she looked through her fingers down to the ground below.

Uh-oh. Arael felt the earth shifting—so infinitesimally that the mortals wouldn't detect it. Small cracks appeared in the ground, and water began spewing up from below as well.

She looked up the mountain. *Clarion is not going to like this.*

THIRTEEN

Kentucky Bend, Kentucky
Present Day

In the early hours of Saturday morning, Ethan had ironed out a fairly simple plan. He would wake early, gather his things— a chore that would probably take about thirty seconds—and walk out the front door of the Morgans' house and straight out of this town. He would stick to the main road and keep walking. No more trying to sneak away or hide. That had ended in disaster the night before. He wasn't quite sure what he'd do if someone tried to stop him, although he didn't think anyone would, but he'd cross that bridge when he came to it. Ethan figured that if it took an hour to drive to Franklin from Kentucky Bend, he should be able to walk it within a day. He had thirty dollars in his pocket for food, and he'd figure out the rest along the way.

What he hadn't planned on, however, was stepping onto the Morgans' front porch and seeing a familiar brown and white horse in a pasture down the hill. It was possible—likely even— that the horse did not belong to his mysterious savior from the night before, but somehow, Ethan was sure it was the same one.

He didn't remember deciding to venture down the hill toward the neighboring house, but here he was, twenty minutes later, standing in a barn, wasting precious daylight talking to a stranger about horses.

So much for plans.

Ethan leaned against the back doorway of the barn watching Camryn lead the horse she called Rebel out to the pasture to join the other one. She wore cutoff jean shorts, an old Kentucky Wildcats t-shirt, and muck boots. Her honey-blonde hair was pulled up in a wild mess on top of her head, and she had a smear of mud on her face—at least he hoped it was mud.

She definitely wasn't the kind of girl Ethan would ever have noticed if she'd ventured into his world of city lights and asphalt, but he hadn't been able to think of anything else since she'd stumbled upon him.

After sneaking back into the Morgans' the night before, he'd tossed and turned all night wondering where the strange girl had come from and where she might have gone after she'd guided him out of the woods.

What had she been doing out on a night like last night, anyway? Ethan had to admit, he'd been a little afraid that he'd imagined her entirely until he saw her again this morning dancing around in her barn.

Still…after learning that she was not only real, but completely ordinary, he couldn't fight his nagging curiosity about her.

Maybe because she seemed to really understand at least part of what he went through every day. He'd met plenty of girls who pretended to understand—who shopped at Hot Topic and dyed their hair black, only to shame their completely functional, middle-class parents. They had no idea what it was really like to wonder, every day, if today might be the day you give up trying to control the crazy and let it take over your life.

Ethan blinked away the thought and straightened as she walked back toward him. "I've got to get going," he said and was surprised to see a look of what might be disappointment on her face.

"Oh? Where to?"

He leaned in conspiratorially. "Don't tell anyone, but I'm busting out of this joint." He tapped an imaginary watch on his wrist. "I'm running behind already."

"Oh." She scrunched up her nose. "Like running away?"

"Exactly like that, yes."

Camryn either didn't catch his sarcasm or chose to ignore it. "Are you sure you really want to do that?" Her words came out in a rush, like they'd escaped her mouth by accident. She scratched her head. "I mean…"

"I know what you meant." Ethan chuckled. "But, come on, you know I don't belong here. I feel like I'm stuck in 1985. No offense, but I'm really not an eighties kind of guy."

"Oh, come on. I have a cell phone," Camryn said, taking her phone from her back pocket and waving it in his face. "*And* we have this fancy new thing called the internet. It can't be all bad."

"Again, no offense, but yes. Yes, it is all bad. There is literally nothing good about it." Ethan felt bad as soon as the words were out of his mouth, but he didn't know why. This girl meant nothing to him. He'd known her for a grand total of two hours. He shouldn't care about hurting her feelings a little.

Except he did.

Ethan reached into his bag and pulled out the blanket she'd given him the night before. "I wasn't expecting to see you again, but—" He held it out to her.

Camryn looked down at it but didn't take it right away.

"This might sound stupid," she said finally, "but since you do owe me for saving your life, hear me out, okay?"

Ethan dropped his hand and twitched his hair back out of his face.

"How about we make a deal? I'll show you around town today. You'll keep an open mind. And if you can't find one thing you like here, I'll take you home myself."

Ethan looked at her, uncertainty in his eyes. "To Franklin? That's like an hour away."

Camryn nodded to herself as if finally talking herself into a questionable idea. "Yes, I'll take you home—all the way to Franklin—if you promise to at least *try* to have fun today."

"Okay…" Ethan said slowly. "And your parents will be okay with this?" He hadn't met them yet, but most parents didn't let their daughters go on long trips with strange boys they didn't know.

"My parents are gone for the weekend," she blurted, then let the last word die on her lips like that was one bit of information she hadn't meant to divulge.

Ethan held up his hands. "Don't worry, I promise not to rob you in the night."

A look of slight embarrassment crossed her face before she held out her hand to shake. Ethan stared at her outstretched palm for a long moment, remembering the feel of it on his face as he'd laid helpless on the ground the night before. Adrenaline had been coursing through him then, but her touch had sent a numbing tide throughout his body, calming his spastic nerves until his heart had slowed and his shaking had stopped.

Would it feel the same to touch her now?

His heart thrummed in his chest when he finally took her hand in his but for a different reason this time.

Her small hand was warm but rough in places, making Ethan think she didn't spend a lot of time indoors. He let out an audible sigh of relief when he felt the same calming warmth pulsing from her hand into his, making his whole body feel like Jell-O. She grinned and shook his hand. If she was feeling the same thing, she was sure doing a good job of hiding it.

Oh well, that's probably for the best anyway. This girl was a dead end, just like this town. He'd be eighteen in a few months. She'd probably be heading off to college soon, and getting his feelings all tangled up over her was an all-around bad idea.

He could postpone his plan for one day, though. What damage could that do?

As they stood behind the barn, grinning stupidly at each other, Ethan's world shifted the tiniest degree. Things that'd seemed so important a few short hours ago were shoved to the back of his mind. He knew he was teetering on dangerous ground, but it was exhilarating, like being at the top of a roller coaster waiting for it to take a dive.

Don't be stupid, he warned himself. *Just stick to your plan.*

But Ethan already knew he was no good at making plans.

FOURTEEN

Alborz Mountains, 2348 BC

*So God said to Noah, "I am going to put an end to all people, for the
earth is filled with violence because of them…I am going to bring
floodwaters on the earth to destroy all life under the heavens.
Everything on earth will perish."*
Genesis 6:13-17 NIV

Back in the safety of the cave, Arael paced the floor of her
chamber. Uriah leaned against the stone wall, arms crossed
over his chest. The small space they now called home was dark
and sparse and contained their only possessions: two cots, a
lantern, a few water jugs, and their weapons.

Arael's smile stretched from ear to ear as she wrung her hands
and continued to pace, her whole body a complete contradiction
of emotions. "That felt *so good*," she exhaled. "And it came back
so quickly—like no time had passed at all." She closed her eyes
and reveled in the memory of it.

"Yes, well, are we not going to talk about the other thing that
happened out there? The thing that's still happening as we
speak?"

Arael peered up at a small crack in the rock above her cot, her
window to the outside world. Would Clarion know it had been
her? Would she forbid her from using her power again?

A rustling in the corridor caused them both to still. Uriah moved to the door while Arael inched toward her bow. She strained her ears for the slower heartbeats and loud breathing of her human guests but heard nothing.

Could the Nephilim have made it here after all? She realized in alarm that she had no idea what their powers might be. Maybe they had their father's speed. Maybe they were adept climbers. She'd been naive to think that she'd scared them away with a little rain and a bush fire. Without making a sound, she reached for her bow and made her way to the door of her chamber. Uriah already had his sword unsheathed and nodded for her to go first.

Arael steadied her breathing and pulled the arrow taut against the bowstring before stepping into the corridor.

"Oh!" she yelped, lowering her bow. "What are you doing in here? I could have killed you!"

"I doubt that," Clarion said. "And I think you know why I am here."

Arael opened her mouth, but it took a moment for her to find her words. "Yes, about that," she said finally, gesturing toward the mouth of the cave. "This isn't my fault."

Clarion looked out at the rain still pouring down and back at Arael without a word.

"I've never done anything like this before. I tried to stop it." Arael fiddled with her weapon. "I'm telling you. This isn't my fault."

Clarion turned back to Arael and spoke in her velvety voice, "No, this is my fault for assuming you could control yourself."

"What? I can!" Arael insisted. "I told you, this isn't me."

Clarion narrowed her eyes. "Even if you are correct. Even if you can't control it, you did start it."

Arael opened her mouth then slammed it shut. She couldn't argue with that.

"I will try to find out what's going on. You two—" Clarion said, jabbing a long, glorious finger at Arael and Uriah, "do not do anything until I return." As quick as she'd come, Clarion disappeared.

Arael met Uriah's stern eyes and smiled. It only took a moment before his stony face cracked, and they were both laughing. *What a night.*

They were still laughing when another noise pricked Arael's ears.

"Shh." Uriah placed a hand on her arm and held up a finger.

Arael followed close on his heels into the outer chamber occupied by the two feeble humans. The mouth of the cave was situated in such a way that they seldom had to worry about animal intruders, but knowing that three Nephilim giants were hiding out nearby had her a bit on edge.

As luck would have it, Arael still had her bow in hand, arrow in position, ready to release it on any intruder they might find. A quick inspection of the cave turned up nothing. She hurried out to the ledge and, looking up through the rain, saw Clarion's pale-yellow glow ascending up the mountain. She didn't appear to have heard anything. Arael looked back to Uriah, who shrugged.

Arael was beginning to think maybe she'd imagined it, making up noises in her edgy state, when the sound rang out again. She spun and ran back into the cave. She knelt down by one of the makeshift cots and placed her hand on the woman's forehead. "Salome, what is it?" She noticed out of the corner of her eye, Uriah backing his way out of the chamber.

"Water," the old woman croaked. Arael reached for the small, wooden bowl and raised it to the woman's lips. Salome raised a shaky hand to steady the bowl and patted Arael's hand. "Bless you, child," the woman said in a quavering voice reserved only for the old and dying.

Arael smiled down at her. "Try to rest now," she said, finally letting herself start to relax. The startling noise had only been the weak coughs of an old woman. Arael was berating herself for being so jumpy when, without warning, her insides seized. Her head jerked up and toward the door.

"What is it, child?" the old woman asked.

Arael shook her head. Of course, Salome couldn't hear it. This sound was meant only for angel ears. "It's nothing. I just thought I heard something. I'm going to go check it out. Go back to sleep." The woman smiled and lay her head back on the cot and closed her eyes, so calm and trusting.

Arael went back out onto the ledge where Uriah was already pacing. This time, Clarion stood at attention, looking down at them with unease. Arael looked back into the cave, unsure of what to do. She'd not left Salome and Jacob alone since the day they'd arrived on her hill. But now she would have no choice. The trumpet had sounded. A Conclave had been called.

Arael cursed under her breath. It'd been half a millennium since the last Conclave. What could possibly have happened to bring the Archangels back into the realm of the Fallen? She couldn't help but think it had something to do with the water that wouldn't stop falling from the sky.

Arael imagined her shame at being called out in front of the entire population of celestial beings. She couldn't even bring her eyes to meet Uriah's. She could just see the *I-told-you-so* look on his face. She worked on her explanation as she, Uriah, and every other Heavenly being were compelled toward the continuing trumpet call.

All thoughts of humiliation and punishment flew from her mind, though, when they arrived at the Conclave Hall and found, not Gabriel, the usual Conclave host, but Michael standing at the front of the group and two hundred angels in chains behind him.

FIFTEEN

Kentucky Bend, Kentucky
Present Day

The day with Camryn passed more quickly than expected. Apparently, there was much more to do in a place like Kentucky Bend than Ethan had thought. After he and Camryn had cleaned the stalls and fed the chickens, Ethan began to wonder if her offer had just been a ploy to score some free labor. But after watching her puff a loose strand of hair out of her face for about the fifth time, he decided he didn't care.

"Okay, let's go," Camryn announced when the chicken coop was clean, wiping her hands on her shirt. Ethan arched his back and swung his arms from side to side, stretching out his tight muscles. He said a silent prayer of thanks when Camryn headed for the garage instead of the horse stalls, as he'd been sure she'd try to persuade him to ride one of those monstrous animals again.

Relief turned to apprehension, though, when she directed the truck toward the trees behind her house instead of the paved road. "Is this what they call "off-roading?"" Ethan gripped the door handle as they bumped along.

Camryn only grinned.

She drove them through a clearing in the trees to a small muddy patch of land. "My dad made this into a dirt bike track for me when I was a kid," she said, straightening her spine and wrapping her arms around the steering wheel.

Ethan looked back and forth between Camryn and the parcel of land. "So…what are we doing here?"

Camryn seemed to be having an internal argument with herself. She gave him a tentative glance then looked back out at the water-saturated ground. "We're probably going to get stuck," she said to herself. "This is a bad idea."

When Ethan realized what she was thinking, a slow grin spread across his face. "I love bad ideas."

Camryn grinned right back at him and, without taking her eyes from his, reached under the dash and flipped a switch to activate the 4-wheel drive. Only a moment of hesitation flickered before she gunned the engine and spun the wheel, spraying mud high in the air. They both screamed with laughter as they listened to the mud rain back down on them through the open windows.

After a while, they did get stuck, but it didn't take Camryn long to pull her truck out of the mire using her dad's farm truck and tow cable. "My dad's going to be so mad," Camryn said, shaking her head at the mud drying on the seat of his truck, but she smiled around the words.

As Ethan had watched her clomping through the mud, attaching the cables and maneuvering the old farm truck perfectly on the dry patches of ground, he couldn't help but think Camryn would be a good person to have around in an emergency.

He'd tried his best to be helpful, but she seemed to know exactly what to do. His only job had been to steer her truck as she'd engaged the cable and pulled it from the pit they'd created.

Spatters of mud dotted Ethan's face and hung in Camryn's hair by the time they drove the two trucks back into the garage. He didn't know what else they could possibly do, looking the way they did. He expected Camryn to insist on a shower before they went anywhere else, but she surprised him again by dragging him back to the barn and telling him to wait outside.

The rumbling sound he heard a moment later sent a rush of blood through his limbs. He didn't even try to hide the smile on his face as he leaned back against the tree and stuffed his hands in his pockets.

"Well, what are you waiting for? Close your mouth and get on," Camryn prompted after pulling the green ATV out of the garage. Ethan unhitched himself from the tree and shook his head as he moved toward her. He ran his hand over the smooth leather seat before climbing on. "This is a Raptor 700."

"Uh, yeah. I know."

"This is amazing." His eyes greedily scanned the machine. "Can I drive?"

Camryn reluctantly turned over the keys after what seemed like a thirty-minute lecture on ATV safety and the added stipulation that they both wear a helmet. "There are hundreds of ATV deaths every year," she reminded him at least three times.

Miraculously, they both survived.

Steering the ATV in the wide-open space of the pasture behind Camryn's house had been the freest Ethan had ever felt. The speed and the wind and her laughter from behind him made him feel like if he willed it enough, he could rise into the sky and fly away.

Camryn directed him to a shallow spot where they washed away the mud in the waters of the swollen river. A thick strand of rope hung from a large oak near the bank, eliciting images of bathing-suit-clad kids swinging out into the water, screaming with delight as the rope carried them through the air before they splashed down under a scorching summer sun.

But summer was months away, and the spring rays had not yet warmed the water to a swimmable temperature. Too soon, they were shivering from the cold.

Camryn led them to a meadow where a large, flat boulder lay unshaded by the noonday sun.

"Come on," she said, reaching out her hand.

A jolt of electricity shot through Ethan as she helped him up onto the rock.

Camryn laid back and closed her eyes. "See, this isn't so bad, now is it?"

Ethan's stomach tightened with the almost imperceptible vibrations of her body as she spoke. He raised up on an elbow to look at her. A small smile played at her lips.

Ethan's eyes were drawn to the slight hints of red in her mostly sand-colored hair that spread out over the rock. He had the strange urge to lift a section of it just so he could release it— to feel the strands flowing through his fingers as they fell back into place beside her.

"I think I'll have to plead the fifth on that one," he said, lying back down. He closed his eyes, but not before he caught the grin widening on Camryn's face.

For lunch, Camryn provided him a proper southern meal of fried chicken and mashed potatoes from the diner in town.

"What if I'm allergic to chicken?" Ethan asked.

"No one's allergic to chicken," she said after she ordered for both of them. The rest of the afternoon they spent touring the town and scrolling through the music on each other's iPhones.

"I knew you were a Taylor Swift fan," Ethan joked, elbowing her playfully on the merry-go-round of the old Bailey Park.

"Oh my God, give me that." Camryn reached for the phone, but Ethan held it out of her grasp. "Those are so old. I need to delete them."

"Oh no, you're not deleting any of this. This is great," he said with a laugh.

Camryn's face reddened, but her lips turned up, pushing her cheeks into bright, shining eyes. Ethan felt something strange in his stomach, knowing that he was at least a little responsible for her smile.

As they meandered down Main Street in the late afternoon sun, munching on greasy fried pies from the diner, Camryn stopped and turned to him. "What's that thing you have in your pocket?" she asked through a mouthful of cherry filling.

"Hmm?"

"That thing you keep fidgeting with."

"This thing?" Ethan pulled a round piece of ivory-colored plastic out of the pocket of his shorts. Two arrows were carved into its face, surrounded by a thin, brown circle. "It's something my mom gave me when I was a kid. It's supposed to be good luck, but…" He looked at it uncertainly.

"Really?" Camryn asked through another bite of fried pie. "Does it work?"

"No, not really." Ethan rubbed his thumb gently over the face of the token as if it held a great secret.

Camryn tilted her head to get a better look.

"See these arrows?" Ethan explained. "By themselves, they represent protection because they were our ancestors' main form of defense. The circle around them represents family. It's basically supposed to mean that those who have gone before us will watch over us. It's just Lakota folklore, really."

"Lakota?" Camryn's eyebrows quirked up. "Like Native American?"

Ethan nodded as he stuffed the piece of plastic back in his pocket. "Yeah, my mom never talks about that part of her life, so I don't really know much about it." Actually, other than the meaning behind the charm, he knew nothing about it.

He avoided the quizzical look on Camryn's face. He didn't really want to get into a big conversation about his family, mainly because he wouldn't be able to answer any of her questions…or his own.

A few minutes later, fried pies devoured and good luck charms forgotten, they stood outside Granny's General Store. "Okay, you've got to try the Sugar Babies and the Firesticks," Camryn said. "I don't even think they make this stuff anymore. They may be the original candies from 1974, but they are *so* good."

Ethan leaned against the lamppost outside and crossed his arms. "If I didn't know any better, I'd think you were trying to ruin my dinner."

Camryn lowered her chin and looked up at him through long, dark eyelashes. "I'm sure Mrs. Morgan will forgive me."

Ethan tilted his head. "Well, that's very presumptuous of you. What makes you think I've decided to stay?"

"Haven't you? I know you had fun today. You have to admit, this life isn't all that bad."

She was right. Ethan couldn't think of a time he'd had more fun in all his life, which was kind of sad if he thought about it. Could he really stay here just because of a girl, though? He'd done a lot of dumb things in his life, but that would take the cake, for sure.

But he *had* promised her a day. And this day wasn't over yet.

"There are still a few things I'll have to try before can I make my final decision."

"Oh, is that right?" Camryn crossed her arms in front of her.

"Uh, huh. Let's see." He held up a hand and began ticking the items off on his fingers. "I've always wanted to go fishing. I mean, like since I was a little kid."

"You've never been fishing?" Camryn's eyes grew wide.

Ethan shook his head. "Nope." He raised another finger. "I've also never been hunting."

"I'm definitely not giving you a gun."

Ethan feigned a hurt expression. "Okay, then, what about taking me to a party?"

Camryn froze. "What do you mean?"

"They say you never really know a town till you've partied there." With that, he reached over her shoulder and pulled a flyer off the light post behind her. "What's this?" he asked with a fake tone of surprise. "A party!"

* * * * *

Camryn eyed the poster in Ethan's hand. It was a flyer for a party, all right. Kyle's party. "Yeah, if your idea of fun is a bunch of rednecks getting drunk out of their minds and making out in the backs of their trucks."

Ethan shrugged as if to say, "Sounds like fun to me."

Camryn rolled her eyes. "You're disgusting," she teased as she opened the door and headed straight for the candy barrels.

Ethan shrugged again. "I don't care. It was just an idea."

"Okay, grab a bag and a scoop. Put whatever you want in your bag, and we'll weigh it up front." Ethan's eyes followed Camryn's finger to the scales sitting on the counter in front of an ancient old woman who glared at him as if he'd just pissed on the floor.

"What's her problem?" Ethan glared right back at her.

"That's Granny Newman. She owns the place, and she doesn't like anyone. It's not just you." When they had chosen their candies, they placed their bags on the counter to pay. Granny and Ethan were still glaring at each other, and Camryn was scrambling to pull out her change to put an end to the awkwardness when a breaking news alert sounded from the small television on the counter, startling them all.

"This is Ann McClain with NBC news reporting on a breaking story of a massive earthquake that occurred in Los Angeles just over an hour ago. Justin Jenkins is on the scene to obtain some aerial footage, as we've been told that getting close to the scene on the ground is out of the question at this point. What can you tell us so far, Justin?"

The scene cut from the newsroom to a shaky shot out the side of an aircraft.

"Well, Ann, we are on the scene in Los Angeles, California this evening after a massive earthquake has devastated the entire west coast. As you can see, the area has just been destroyed. It looks like someone dropped a bomb, and it goes on for as far as the eye can see."

The camera panned out into the distance to an endless sea of crumbled concrete and bricks and dust-covered vehicles—no running, no screaming, no movement at all. Just complete destruction.

"The quake has registered at a magnitude ten," Justin continued to explain, *"making it the strongest earthquake in recorded history. As you can see from the footage, the damages and loss of life will be astronomical. The President has declared a state of emergency for the region and is sending the National Guard to aid in the search and rescue. This is all the information we have at this time, more to come on this story at nine."*

They all stood, mouths agape, staring at the television. "Good God." Granny's hand clutched at the fabric over her heart. "Search and rescue" was a joke. Anyone could tell from the footage, there would be no one to rescue. Camryn slammed her money on the counter and, not waiting for her change, fled the store. The cool air felt good in her lungs, but she couldn't seem to get enough of it in. An invisible hand clamped over her mouth as she struggled to suck in a breath.

Ethan came out behind her and placed a steadying hand on her back. "You okay?"

The heat of his fingers reached her skin, even through her clothes.

"Yeah. Good," Camryn said through slow, deliberate breaths. "Ready to go?" She tried to blink away the tears from her eyes. She so desperately did not want him to see her cry.

Ethan spun her toward him and brushed a tear away with his thumb. "It's okay to cry. That's a horrible thing that happened."

"Yeah, but it's not like I knew any of those people."

"It doesn't matter," Ethan reassured her. "They were still people. Someone knew them."

"It's not just that. Stuff like that always screws with my head." Camryn squeezed her arms around her middle and stared at the ground. "It doesn't matter what it is—a fire, a car wreck, earthquake. It doesn't matter. I'll think about it for weeks." She put her fists to the sides of her head and squeezed her eyes shut. "I won't be able to sleep for worrying about my parents and running through every possible scenario of what we should do if something like that happened here."

"There's no way to know every possible scenario." Ethan's voice was low as he leaned down to look into her eyes.

"*I know!*" Camryn wailed. "That's what makes it so bad." She wrapped her arms back around herself and stared over his shoulder, chewing her bottom lip.

Ethan stood in front of her awkwardly. He looked uncertain for a moment, then tentatively reached out and pulled her into his arms.

Without hesitation, Camryn melted into him, relief flooding through her. His arms felt strong around her like they could take some of the load she was trying so desperately to carry. She'd never had anyone comfort her like this before except her dad— *Oh God, don't think about him right now!*—but this was different. The feel of Ethan's arms around her and the faint sound of his heart beating so close to her just felt *right*. Heat radiated from his chest, and his warmth felt like it belonged to her, like it was hers to take from him. She stood there, soaking it up, thinking over the events of the past twenty-four hours and almost forgetting about the devastation they'd witnessed on the television.

Almost.

Camryn was surprised at her body's reaction to him. After a few moments, she was a little calmer, her thoughts a little less jumbled. *Maybe this is just what I need,* she thought, then immediately scolded herself. She was working so hard to be her own independent person. She should be able to handle her issues by herself. She shouldn't need anyone else for that.

Even though she didn't want to, Camryn forced herself to pull away from him, her exhaustion finally hitting her. "Come on," she patted his chest. "Let's go."

SIXTEEN

Conclave, 2348 BC

*F*ive *hundred years.* Five hundred years had passed since Arael had last laid eyes on Michael, but looking at him now felt as if no time had passed at all. He was just as intense and intimidating as he'd ever been, with broad, muscular shoulders, piercing eyes, and a fierceness most angels only ever hoped to possess. He wore the traditional warrior armor: breastplate across his chest, leather belt and tunic around his waist, and his—

Arael froze when her gaze landed on the sword. For a brief moment, she was transported back to the battle, lying in the dirt with Michael hovering over her with that same sword protruding from her chest. A tornado of emotion swirled inside her. The pain, betrayal, and confusion that she'd so diligently buried in the back of her mind were viciously unearthed and forced out like a violent sickness. It burned like acid in her throat. Tears sprang to her eyes, but she forced them away. She would suffer at Michael's hand no more.

Arael closed her eyes and willed herself back to the present.

They'd assembled in the Conclave Hall, a large circular colosseum in Eden, and made their way to their respective sections carved into the ancient stone—one for each order of celestial beings. Arael found Uriah right away among the Dominions. The apprehension on his face reached her from across the mammoth space. He had to know how hard this would be for her, seeing Michael again like this. He probably thought she would do something foolish. Arael forced a small smile to reassure him, then let her eyes travel on through the crowd until she found Clarion among the Guardians. When Arael's eyes met Clarion's, the angel nodded almost imperceptibly, confirming what Arael had feared. The angels in chains behind Michael were the Founders they had spoken of. Arael finally, reluctantly, gave her attention to Michael, who had already begun speaking.

He didn't seem to be speaking to the assembly, though. Instead, he faced the angels on the platform.

"You dared to think you could overthrow the Creator," Michael was saying. "Now you have the audacity to disregard the Law handed down to you through Gabriel. You are ungrateful for the life you have been given here. The Creator could have imprisoned you for your rebellion, locked you away in darkness for eternity, but He didn't. He allowed you free will and free reign of this Earth. You could have lived happily here, but you've disobeyed Him again."

Happily? Is he serious? The only ones who'd found any semblance of happiness were the ones chained on the stage behind him.

Fundamentally, Arael knew the Founders had been wrong, but seeing Michael's arrogance as he paced back and forth in front of them unleashed a fierce protectiveness in her for her fellow angels. She thought of her life of solitude and the humans she'd been looking after like pets. At least these Fallen had found some way to give their life meaning again. Maybe that's all it had been. Maybe their actions hadn't been as sinister as Clarion and Uriah wanted to believe.

"You have broken the Law and created these abominations that are destroying the Earth." Michael's voice grew louder. "And now they must be destroyed!"

With that, the angels behind him roared in protest. Some tried to stand but were quickly silenced with hard jabs to the ribs by Michael's guards who stood over them.

"And you—" Michael continued. "You will be punished. The Creator continues to be merciful. If it were up to me, you would be destroyed, your souls crushed into dust and scattered into the deepest recesses of the universe." Michael turned and paced back in front of the chained flock. "But your Creator is the only one who can destroy you. I can only imprison you."

Imprison? What does that mean? Arael glanced around for clues in the faces around her, but the other angels appeared to be just as confused as she.

Michael nodded to the guards who each pulled from their belt a long, thin rope of glowing orange light. Arael could tell, even from this distance, that these ropes were infused with Heavenly Fire, but they were new weapons, nothing she'd ever seen before. Whatever their power, it couldn't be good.

With glowing rope in hand, Michael hauled one of the kneeling angels to the front of the stage, putting him on display for everyone to see.

"This is what happens when you disobey the Law." In a flash, Michael flicked his wrist, and the rope in his hand twined around the hands of the bound angel.

The angel vanished from sight.

A gasp rippled through the crowd. The guards behind Michael followed his lead, flicking their ropes, entwining their captives' wrists. One by one, each chained angel on the platform began to disappear.

Arael couldn't believe what she was seeing. *Where are they going? What is happening to them? Why isn't someone doing something?*

When the bound angels realized what was happening, they began to struggle against their bindings. They cried out in pain and angry howls as the Heavenly Fire infused chains burned their skin.

95

While the spectators of this debacle murmured and fidgeted in the arena, Arael grew angrier by the moment. She clenched her fists so tight, her nails made deep grooves in her palms. In all her years as an Archangel, Arael had never seen Michael's men behave this way. True, her time with them had been peaceful. There'd been no enemy to fight, no giants destroying the Earth, but this was an atrocity! Arael looked at each soldier standing on the stage. She knew these men, knew every one of them, knew them as kind, loving creatures, not the violent tyrants she saw standing before her now. She agonized in her spot as the Founders continued to disappear.

"Stop!" She felt her voice rise from her throat before she'd even decided to speak.

Michael's head shot in her direction, and his icy gaze landed flat on her. She felt, rather than saw, the angels around her inch away until she was facing Michael alone surrounded by the gaping crowd.

Arael registered surprise on Michael's face when he saw who'd called out, but he remained firmly in control. "These men have disobeyed the Law. They must be punished."

Arael thought of the humans asleep in her cave. "We have all disobeyed the Law in some way." She gestured around at the crowd, who took another collective step away from her. "How are these men more guilty than any of the rest of us?"

Michael glanced around the room. "This is not my decision. I have orders. I follow them. And if we all did the same," he added, looking up to address the crowd again, "none of us would even be here now!"

"If we all did the same?" Arael repeated. "If we all followed orders, you mean?" She cocked her head at him, disbelieving he would dare to say such a thing to her. She *had* been following orders when he'd banished her.

"Arael," Michael said from his spot on the platform. "Maybe we shouldn't talk about this here."

Arael became immediately aware of the entire host of Heaven staring at her from the rafters. She glanced at Uriah, whose eyes were pleading. He was right. As furious as it made her, she couldn't say what she wanted to say here. No one else knew their secret, and she was dangerously close to raising a few questions from her comrades.

Arael knew she should be quiet, but her thirst for justice couldn't let this go. "Some of these angels were your warriors. They trained right alongside you. They were loyal to you."

"The moment they pledged their loyalty to Lucifer, they turned their back on me!" Michael spat.

"Or maybe it was you who turned your back on them!" Arael brought her hand to her lips. She forced her eyes away from Michael and found Uriah in the sea of faces as if he'd implored her to look at him. His face had drained of color, and he was moving now, undoubtedly coming to shut her up. Arael stepped back into the crowd. Some angels whispered and gave her strange looks. Some just shrugged and turned away. Michael looked stricken, but he thankfully didn't respond to her outburst. He turned away from her and back to the gawking crowd.

"You see the fate of those who disobey the Law. Do not let this happen to you."

"What will happen to the Nephilim?" someone called from the crowd.

"We need not worry about them or the sin they have spread any longer. They are being exterminated as we speak."

The angels looked at each other curiously. With every angel here at the Conclave—both Righteous and Fallen—how could anyone be hunting Nephilim in the physical realm?

"For forty days and forty nights," Michael said in the way of explanation, "the rain will not stop." He paused and looked from one side of the Colosseum to the other. "It will continue to fall from the sky and boil up from the earth. The Nephilim and all the evil they have spread will be destroyed."

Silence hovered over them like a thick blanket, and Michael's voice echoed off the stone walls. "By the water from the Heavens, the Earth will be cleansed! Judgment has commenced!" Michael turned then and nodded to the guards on stage who simultaneously lashed their captives with their golden whips until every Founder was gone.

Arael stood rooted to her spot. Could it be true? Clarion's words to her echoed in her ears. *"You may not be controlling it, but you did start it."* Had she really set in motion the events that would ultimately destroy every living thing on the Earth? She thought of Jacob and Salome. They would die without her. They would die *because* of her.

As other angels began drifting away, Arael couldn't make her feet move. The longer she stood, the harder her heart pounded until she thought it would explode from her chest.

She'd been used.

Someone out there knew where she'd been hiding, knew her power, and how eager she'd be to use it. Had Clarion done this? No. She'd been as angry and confused as Arael. They'd both been used. And she was fairly certain by whom.

By the time Uriah found her in the crowd, Arael was seething. She didn't hear him when he spoke and pulled away from him when he placed a hand on her arm. At that moment, her mind was consumed with one thought, and one thought alone— making Michael pay for what he'd done. To her, to the Founders, to the Nephilim…and to Jacob and Salome.

In her rage, a plan began to take shape. She looked up at Uriah, into his kind and innocent face. Uriah would never understand. He couldn't help her now. This was something she would have to do on her own.

SEVENTEEN

Kentucky Bend, Kentucky
Present Day

D riving home from Granny's and still reeling from the news of the earthquake, Camryn's insides vibrated with nervous energy. Thankfully, though, she could still form a few coherent thoughts and basically function like a human being, which was more than could usually be said of her in such situations. She looked over at Ethan in the seat next to her. Maybe because she'd never had such a distraction before.

Ethan stared out the passenger window, giving no indication of his mood. Was he freaking out as much as she was? His chest rose and fell evenly under the thin fabric of his t-shirt. A bruised and scabbed hand rested on the seat between them. The only sign of tension was the thumbnail he hadn't stopped chewing since they left the store.

They both jumped when Camryn's phone rang. "My mom," Camryn mouthed at Ethan when she looked at the screen. She put a finger to her lips before answering.

"Hey, Mom."

"Camryn," her mother's panicked voice filled the cab of the truck. "Honey, are you okay?"

"Mom, calm down. I'm fine."

Camryn's response was met with stunned silence on the other end of the line. Camryn couldn't help but smile.

"Did you—have you seen the news?" her mother asked with trepidation.

"Yeah, I saw it at Granny's. I'm on my way home now."

"You can come to Franklin, you know. I know you're always worried about the floodwalls—"

"I'm sure they're fine, Mom," Camryn cut her off. "There's an evacuation plan if anything happens."

There *was* an evacuation plan, thanks to Camryn's insistence to the town's fire chief. She'd championed that cause only after her demand for floodwall repairs had gone unanswered.

Her mother held her silence a beat more. "Well, you sound okay." But Camryn heard the uncertainty in her mother's voice. Clearly, she'd been expecting freaked-out-Camryn, not this semi-composed alien who'd taken possession of her daughter's body. Camryn understood her mother's confusion. Frankly, Camryn was a little confused herself. "So, how's business going?"

"Good," her mother replied. "Great, actually. But we can come home if you need us to."

"No, geez, please don't do that." Camryn knew her mother would think her concern would be the money they'd be losing, but more than that, she wanted a little more time alone with Ethan before she had to split her time with anyone else. "I promise I'm fine."

Camryn and her mother chatted a while longer, talking about nothing in particular, but Camryn conveniently forgot to mention the boy sitting beside her. When her mom had been sufficiently convinced Camryn really was okay, she finally said goodbye. Hanging up the phone, Camryn offered Ethan a guilty glance. He turned his head away without a word.

The blue sky had just begun its transformation into a giant canvas of bright orange and yellow when Camryn pulled into the drive. She had the sneaking suspicion that Ethan's serious demeanor had to do with something more than earthquakes.

When Camryn turned off the ignition, Ethan made no move to get out of the truck. He looked as if he had something to say, but couldn't find the right words.

"I've got one more thing to show you," Camryn announced. "If you have time." She'd hoped to elicit a laugh, but Ethan's jaw remained tight.

"I don't think I can take any more excitement today," he said, looking as weary as she felt.

"Nothing exciting," she promised. "Very dull, actually." She reached over and handed Ethan his sweatshirt from behind the seat.

Ethan got out of the truck and followed her up the steps to the swing that hung facing west. From where they sat, they had a perfect view of the sun approaching the trees in the distance. Ethan sat back on the swing and shoved his hands in the front of his hoodie.

Camryn wondered, not for the first time, why she was working so hard to keep this boy close to her. It was strange how quickly she'd decided to trust him. It didn't make any sense, much like most of the things her brain decided to do lately. And it didn't help that her brain wasn't allowing her to sort out her tumbling thoughts at the moment. They just bumped around in her head like clothes in a dryer.

She looked up at the sky and welcomed the distraction. "Look. We're about to miss it."

The sun had just touched the horizon and was creeping downward, disappearing behind the trees. The sky painted a mixture of bright yellows and flaming oranges. A fire in the sky. Camryn held her breath in childish excitement as the star of the show made its descent.

Camryn had always loved watching the sun set. She loved the dependability of it. No matter what else changed in the world, the sun would always rise, and it would always set. Every day.

She looked over at Ethan, whose face had opened in wonderment. For the first time since their meeting, he appeared completely unguarded, like a usually locked door had opened a crack, and she had been allowed a rare glimpse of the secrets hidden inside.

Too soon, though, the show was over. The sun disappeared, leaving a trail of pastel pinks and purples in its wake. A few quiet moments passed as the fireflies took to the air, and a chorus of crickets ushered in the night.

Camryn finally spoke, her voice no more than a whisper. "That's it. That's all I've got."

"Well, that was a grand finale if I've ever seen one." Ethan gave her an appreciative grin. "I've never really taken the time to watch a sun set before."

Camryn pulled her knees to her chest and looked up at the already starry sky. She couldn't remember the last time it'd been this clear and wondered how long it would last. Could they possibly be in the clear while the rest of the world was still suffering?

"Are you worried about the earthquake?"

Ethan shrugged. "I don't know. That was pretty far away."

Camryn stiffened. "You do realize we live on one of the biggest fault lines in the country, don't you? In the last two months, there's been a major earthquake on every fault line in the world. That's never happened before in our known history." Her voice drifted along with her eyes. "We're next. It's just a matter of when. And when it does," she emphasized, "we're pretty much dead with the floodwalls in the condition they're in."

"Well, I wasn't worried, but I am now." He bumped her with his shoulder. "Thanks a lot."

"Sorry." Camryn forced a smile. "But that's what it's like inside my head all the time, so welcome to my world."

"Well, since you think about it so much, what do you make of it all?"

"I don't really know." Camryn hesitated to say what she really thought. The words would probably sound crazier if she said them out loud than they did in her head. "It just seems odd. Everything has been escalating for a while now. The crazy weather, the natural disasters, and the wars. It all seems to be coming to a head at the same time. It's like a big cosmic riddle that no one's figured out yet."

"I thought that Harriet lady said it was supposed to be global warming or something like that."

"That lady that's on TV all the time? She's a kook. I know she's done a lot for the environment, but global warming doesn't explain everything. It definitely doesn't explain the earthquakes or why everyone is so suddenly ready to go to war over the slightest little thing."

Ethan mulled it over for a minute. "I never really thought about it, I guess."

"Are you kidding? It's literally *all* I think about." She gave an exasperated shake of her head.

The air turned cooler around them with the sun gone from the sky. Ethan leaned forward and put his elbows on his knees. "Thank you...for everything. No one's ever done anything for me like what you did for me today."

Camryn smiled a sad smile. This was the moment she'd been trying to postpone. "But you're still leaving, aren't you?"

Ethan let out a long sigh. "Cam."

The familiar way he said her name squeezed her heart. "It's okay. You don't have to explain. It was selfish of me to ask you to stay."

"No. It's not even about me anymore."

"I get it. I told you, you don't have to explain." Camryn stood abruptly and dusted off her shorts.

"I know I don't have to." Ethan jumped up. "God, will you just—" Ethan pulled his fingers into a fist in front of him.

Camryn crossed her arms over her chest, not wanting to hear whatever he had to say but not knowing how to shut him up.

"You were right," he continued. "You have a great life here. And if I stayed…it just wouldn't be good."

Camryn opened her mouth to say something, but Ethan cut her off. "I'm trying to do the right thing here, okay? For once in my life."

"How is running away ever the right thing to do?"

Ethan's eyes darted around the porch, searching for the right words. "I know you don't understand it now, but you don't need a person like me in your life."

"Well, I'm glad you're such an expert on what I need."

"Why didn't you tell your mom about me?"

Camryn shrugged defiantly. "Why should I? You'll be gone by the time she gets home, right?"

"It's because I'm not like you, that's why." Ethan didn't appear phased by her obstinance. "You know your mom is going to tell you to stay away from me, and she would be right."

Ethan's face softened. "I like you, Camryn. Probably a little too much. You deserve to be with someone…not like me." He reached out and tucked a piece of hair behind her ear. "I would hurt you eventually. It's just what I do."

Camryn closed her eyes. "I don't believe that."

"I could tell you some stories that would probably change your mind."

She took a few steps back, putting some distance between them, and bumped into one of the ceramic planters her mom kept on each side of the front door. She placed her hands on the edge to steady herself. "I seriously doubt that."

Ethan gave an ironic laugh and stuck his hands back in the front of his shirt. "Really? Let's see." He glanced up at the roof of the porch as if he'd somehow find the words he needed there. "I could tell you about the time when I was in eighth grade that I smashed my math teacher's windshield with a baseball bat."

Camryn shook her head at him. "Ethan—"

"Oh, I can do even better than that." He stepped closer. "I could tell you about the kid I almost killed last year. You'd probably like that one." His eyes held hers with a fierceness she couldn't fight. "The little punk stole my bike." Ethan shrugged as if that were reason enough. "When I found him, can you believe he actually wanted to fight me for it?" Ethan laughed at the memory. "*He* wanted to fight *me*. It only took one hit for me to know…I wasn't going to stop." Ethan looked at her with such intensity, Camryn got the feeling he was trying to scare her.

"It felt so good to just let it out…" His voice trailed off, and for a moment, the sharp inhales and exhales of their breaths were the only sounds that could be heard. "Eventually, someone pulled me off of him, but I have no idea what would have happened if they hadn't."

"Stop," Camryn pleaded. She didn't want to hear this—not because she didn't believe it, but because it didn't matter. Whoever did those things wasn't the boy she'd spent the day with. *It couldn't be.*

"And have you not noticed these?" He held up his fists, covered in greenish bruises, the knuckles spotted with scabs. "This is why I'm here, and I don't even remember how it happened. I was *so angry* that I completely blacked out." His voice rose, and a small vein pulsed in his neck. "That's the kind of shit you don't need in your life."

What Camryn did next, she blamed on a lack of experience with confrontation. She knew even before she did it, it wasn't the best way to end the conversation, just the quickest.

She'd felt the pine cones in the planter when she'd placed her hands on it a second before. She remembered helping her mother place them there for some kind of nature-themed decor. Without thinking, she wrapped her fingers around one and hurled it in Ethan's direction.

He flinched and raised an arm in front of his face, but it was too late. "Jesus Christ, Camryn!" he cried as he touched his fingers to his face. "What the hell?" He drew his hand away, and a small spot of blood dotted the palm of his hand. He looked back at her with wide eyes.

"Just stop, okay. I told you I understand, and I'll take you home like I promised. You don't have to do this."

She turned and fumbled with her keys to let herself in the house. Dropping them from her shaking hands, Camryn knelt to pick them up. When she stood, Ethan was leaning beside the door, his hands in his pockets and eyes closed. You would never have guessed that moments before he'd been yelling at her.

When Camryn had finally gained control of her hands, she tried again with the lock, but Ethan placed his hand over hers before she could get the key in.

"I'm sorry," he said. "I didn't mean to upset you more than you already are." He inched closer to her, never moving his hand from hers. "Listen, are you going to be okay after—" he waved his hand in the air, "you know."

He didn't have to say the words for Camryn to know what he meant. "I could sleep on your couch if you want."

Camryn thought back to last summer when she'd tried to diet for a few weeks. She hadn't realized the abundance of sugar in the world around her until she couldn't have it anymore. She'd eventually learned to walk away from the temptation rather than salivating over something she knew she couldn't have.

"Don't worry about me." She shook her head. "I'm used to being alone."

EIGHTEEN

Babylon, 2060BC

And Noah and his son and his wife and his sons' wives entered the
ark to escape the waters of the flood...Every living thing on the face
of the earth was wiped out; people and animals and the creatures
that move along the ground and the birds were wiped from the earth.
Only Noah was left, and those with him in the ark.
Genesis 7:7, 23 NIV

Shades of green, blue, red, and yellow illuminated the land as
Arael peered down at the mortals from atop the city wall of
Babylon. She could tell a lot about a person by the color of their
aura. More than just splashes of joy, excitement, or sorrow, it
displayed their strengths, fears, and sinful tendencies, all in a
swirling halo of color the mortals didn't even know they
possessed.

Most of the angels she saw these days had no significant aura
left, just a gray cloud surrounding them. But the mortals, they
wore their weaknesses like a banner, like a beacon for the Fallen,
screaming, "Come get me. Here I am."

Arael was appalled that their celestial existence had been
reduced to this. They'd once been mighty Warriors and
Guardians, tasked with the order and protection of the Universe.
Now, their immense collection of power and intelligence was

being spent on the pursuit of the demise of the human race—a race that had miraculously survived the Great Flood through a mere handful of survivors. Arael saw it as a testament to their resilience, but Lucifer had seen it as another opportunity to destroy Elohim's creation.

Arael didn't have to wonder why this had become the main objective of their existence. She knew their so-called leader had harbored a jealous hatred of the mortals since their creation and now had an army of malevolent angels at his disposal with nothing better to do with their time.

Arael couldn't blame him. She might not like it, but she understood it. She knew, all too well, that hate was a seed that, when nurtured, could grow into something much darker.

Something uncontrollable.

Besides, Lucifer...or *Apollyon*, as he'd demanded to be called since returning to Earth after the flood, wasn't at fault for her pathetic existence. She had Michael to blame for that.

Arael watched the mortals a few moments more, even though she wasn't supposed to be there. The City of Babylon lay within Marduk's territory, and he didn't like sharing the spotlight with anyone. But Marduk was a fool, so she could safely assume that she wouldn't be noticed.

Today was to be a special day for Babylon. It was the first day of the Babylonian New Year, a week-long celebration in honor of—to Arael's great horror—Marduk. Arael was outraged at the mortals' worship of him as their most beloved deity when he actually happened to be the dumbest being of higher intelligence Arael had ever encountered.

The day would be clear, she could feel it in the air. Arael wanted nothing more than to open up the sky and pour out all the rain in the clouds, just as she'd done the year before.

The year before that, there had been a lightning fire in the wheat field. Arael smiled as she remembered the shrieks and screams of the Babylonians as they'd retreated into their homes or to the fields to save their crops. As much as she wanted to ruin Marduk's celebration, she knew the number one rule of using her Tempest powers: no suspicious weather patterns. Arael crossed her arms in front of her to keep her hands from twitching. *Ridiculous rules.*

Just then, as the Babylonians congregated in the center of town, preparing to follow the king and his court in an elaborate procession through the city gates to continue their worship at the temple, Marduk sprang right into the midst of them, jumping and dancing around like a buffoon. The mortals couldn't see him, but Arael felt embarrassed for him just the same.

How had Elohim not turned his back on this world already, burned these mortals to ashes like they deserved? True, some of them still worshiped Him and followed His Law, but their numbers grew smaller and smaller with every passing year.

It won't be long now, Arael thought as she canvassed the city with her celestial sight for the unmistakable light of the Clean Ones. Their bright white auras stood out like glowing lamps in the night among the other tarnished souls. There were so few of them now, it would only be a matter of time before Elohim's followers would be eradicated, and with them any knowledge of the God who had created them.

She had to commend the Fallen for their efforts. They had corrupted whole cities with their spiritual attacks. And Arael couldn't take credit for any of it. She hadn't worked for Lucifer since the flood. She'd reserved her energy for someone else—someone who'd consumed her thoughts every second of every day since the last Conclave.

Her brother, Michael.

While the others schemed ways to destroy the mortals, Arael planned her revenge on the one who'd lied to her, betrayed her, then used her to kill thousands of innocent people. There was only one problem: thus far, Michael had been virtually inaccessible to her. She was but one Fallen angel with a score to settle while he remained a heavily guarded Archangel never without several layers of protection. Disappointingly, not even Lucifer—er—*Apollyon* had been able to help her get to him. But that hadn't stopped Arael from planning. And waiting. She knew one day, her time would come, and she was nothing if not patient.

Arael tensed as someone joined her on her perch. She turned to see Akira, one of Apollyon's messengers, glaring at her through narrow eyes. "Master would like to meet with you," she said in a harsh tone.

"I bet he would." Arael turned back to the scene below.

"Your absence has been noted from the last two assemblies." Akira tapped her finger on the dagger in her belt.

"I've been busy."

"I'm sure you have. Listen, Apollyon knows what you've been up to. Between you and me, I don't think you deserve this, but he has an assignment for you."

Arael groaned.

"He says this is an assignment you will want. Not that you deserve it," Akira added.

"You sure are improvising a lot for a messenger," Arael said without turning around. "If I didn't know any better, I'd think you don't like me much."

"You're right. I don't like you." Akira raised her chin to look down her nose at Arael. "I don't like how you disregard our master and the kingdom he's established here. It's disrespectful."

Arael clamped her lips together to keep from saying something she'd regret. She hated how the angels had mindlessly fallen in line under Lucifer's rule, calling him Apollyon and Master and worshiping him like some kind of deity. Of course…they didn't know what she knew.

They didn't know how he'd used them all as disposable pawns in his plan to overthrow Elohim.

"He's lying to them," she remembered telling Michael after she and Uriah had worked their way into Lucifer's group. *"He's telling them there is no chance of resistance, that your army is foolish and weak. He's luring them into a false sense of security, and they don't even know what they're risking! All for his futile attempt to take the throne!"* Arael had known, even then, that Lucifer wanted to be a god, and he didn't care what he had to do or whom he had to hurt to get there.

Things had not changed. If anything, they'd gotten worse.

"He says he can give you the thing you want," Akira smirked.

Arael turned to peer at Akira over her shoulder. Arael wanted only one thing, and Lucifer knew exactly what it was.

Akira crossed her arms over her chest. "When should I tell him to expect you?"

Arael stood, silly mortal festivities forgotten. "I'm right behind you."

NINETEEN

Kentucky Bend, Kentucky
Present Day

E than jerked awake from a fitful sleep. He scrambled for his phone to look at the time. 8:04 AM. Relieved that he hadn't overslept, he lay back onto the stiff pillow that smelled mostly of detergent and only slightly of dust and the children who'd slept on it before him.

Sleep had never come easily for Ethan. Having an addict for a mother and frequent late-night visitors were not conducive to very good sleep habits. But last night's tossing had been for a different reason.

Camryn had done something special for him. She'd allowed him to feel like a normal kid for the first time in his life, even if just for a day. And she'd allowed him to feel...something else, too. He hated that the day had ended the way it had. His brain told him he was doing the right thing by getting the hell out of her life, but his gut said something different.

Ethan got out of bed and grabbed the only other pair of shorts he had with him, the ones he'd been wearing when Camryn had found him two nights ago. Grace had been so kind as to wash them, even though he'd done nothing but give her the silent treatment since he'd arrived. He'd have to remember to thank her before he left.

Thank her? Ethan grimaced at the thought.

Ethan walked across the hall to the bathroom and stared at the shower curtain for a long moment before pulling it back and getting in. He hated showering in strange places. His bathroom at home was tiny and dark and smelled faintly of mildew, but it was familiar. He knew exactly how long the hot water would last, and he knew how to adjust the knobs.

He did his best thinking in the shower, though, and right now, he needed to think.

Under the hot spray, he closed his eyes and let the water run over him. Immediately a small, delicate face appeared in his mind, but it wasn't the face he'd expected. Camryn had pretty much dominated his thoughts for the past thirty-six hours, but now someone else was trying to push her way in. The only other female who could rival Camryn in his brain—this face belonged to his mother.

Elizabeth Reyes had tried to shimmy her way into Ethan's thoughts several times over the past couple of days, but he'd succeeded in pushing her out every time. The easy calm of the past few days here with Camryn was such a stark contrast to the turmoil of his life in Franklin that he couldn't allow them to occupy the same space in his head.

But this isn't real, he thought. *That is.* That *is your life.* "Yeah, okay," he said to himself, and standing in the heat of the water, he finally let her in.

One day, when Ethan had been five, during one of his mother's dry spells, she'd taken him to the zoo. They'd walked for hours and raced to eat ice cream cones before they melted. Nothing spectacular had happened that day, but the memory had stuck with Ethan because it was the first time that he remembered seeing his mother genuinely happy. They'd watched the monkeys play, and she'd laughed—a loud and infectious sound. He'd rarely heard it, and five-year-old Ethan had decided it was one of his favorite sounds.

Ethan hadn't thought of that day in such a long time. He kept his happy memories safely tucked away in his mental filing cabinet labeled "Do Not Open." Somehow recollections of baseball games and birthday parties made the memories of overdoses and foster homes even harder to bear. But the memories were there.

A strange resolve washed over him in the warm flow of the water. He opened the drawer a little wider and peeked inside.

The images came to him, fuzzy at first, then crystal clear.

He saw his mother's smiling face chasing him around their backyard with a water hose while a soaking-wet Ethan squealed with delight. He saw his mother leaning over him as he lay in bed with a fever. The little boy in his memory closed his eyes as she rubbed his hair and sang a soft hymn from her childhood. Ethan didn't understand the words, but he did understand the tranquil feeling that drifted with the melodies through the air.

He saw now what his anger had never allowed him to see before. She had wanted to be a good mother. She'd done the best she knew to do.

For the second time since waking, Ethan wondered what the hell was going on in his head. Where was the anger? Where was the angst? Where was the fireball of raw emotions that had fueled him for most of his life?

Finished with his shower now and standing in front of the mirror, he wondered who he would be without those feelings. His life had always been dictated by emotion and impulse. Whatever he felt like doing, he did, and what anyone else thought about that, he didn't care because life was shit, and nothing meant shit, and nobody mattered, including himself.

But now things were different. Someone mattered. And that someone made him feel like maybe he did, too. His head drooped between his shoulders, leaning against the bathroom sink. He watched the drops of water fall from his hair and land in tiny droplets on the porcelain.

He wasn't sure he liked this new Ethan. Was this even real? Or a passing phase that would be gone tomorrow and his old friend, Anger, would be back with a vengeance?

I need to see my mom, he decided. That would be the only way he could know for sure. If he could see his mother and still keep his anger at bay, maybe he would be able to trust this new version of himself.

The smell of fried bacon broke into Ethan's thoughts. He couldn't remember the last time he'd had a home-cooked meal, and the aroma made his mouth water. He couldn't imagine sitting down and eating with his too-gracious hosts, though. He didn't know if he could withstand the awkwardness, even for bacon.

Camryn had sent him one brief text after he'd left her the night before, letting him know she'd pick him up at nine o'clock for the drive back to Franklin. So he was surprised to find her standing in his room when he entered a few minutes later, his hair still dripping from the shower. She startled and turned when he came through the door, stuffing her hands in the pocket of her pink hoodie.

"Hey," he said, acutely aware that he wasn't wearing a shirt.

"Oh," she said in response, her cheeks darkening again as she averted her eyes to the floor.

Ethan smirked a little as he reached for the shirt on the foot of the bed and pulled it over his head. "You're early."

Camryn cleared her throat. "Um, yeah. I should've just called." He couldn't help noticing her eyes darting around the room, looking everywhere but at him. "I just wanted to tell you that we may have to postpone our trip just a little."

"Oh?" Ethan's eyes narrowed. "Why?"

Camryn took a deep breath and held up the crumbled-up piece of paper he'd left on the nightstand—the flyer he'd stuffed in his pocket outside of Granny's last night.

"Because we have a party to go to."

"Cam, what are you doing?"

"Believe me, my motives are completely self-serving. I need to go to this party, and I don't want to go alone."

"You *need* to go to this party?" Ethan still wasn't convinced.

"Yes. For personal reasons. I'll explain later. So, will you go with me?"

Ethan flicked his tongue over the ring in his lip. His trip to see his mother could wait another day, right? He threw up his hands, realizing he couldn't say no to this girl. "Sure. Why the hell not?"

At Camryn's insistence, they did eat a quick breakfast. She'd apparently known the Morgans all her life and was quite chatty with them over toast and bacon. Ethan watched them all with caution, like a spectator in an extremely odd tennis match. They didn't offer to include him in the conversation but didn't completely ignore him either. They all kept glancing at him, giving him silent permission to join in if he wanted. Each time, he just stuffed another piece of bacon in his mouth.

"Ready to go?" Camryn asked finally, rising from her chair.

"I thought you'd never ask."

"What are you two up to today?" Mrs. Morgan asked.

"Uh…" Ethan realized he had no idea what they were doing. The day was still young, and the party didn't start for another twelve hours. The thought filled him with both excitement and dread.

"Fishing," Camryn said and gave Ethan a wink.

On the porch, Camryn stopped and turned to him. In her face, he saw a lightness that hadn't been there before. He wondered what had changed since he'd seen her last. When he'd left her on her front porch, she'd been pretty pissed. Then she pulled her lips up into a shy grin, and Ethan was overcome with the urge to pull her close, to hold her like he'd held her outside the General Store the night before.

Twelve hours of this? He didn't know how long he could keep being such a nice guy. Camryn reached up and brushed her fingertips over the small scrape on his cheek. "Sorry about this," she said. "I can't believe I threw a pine cone at you."

"Yeah, you could have taken my eye out."

"Especially since I was aiming for your chest."

"What? We've finally found something you're not good at?"

"Shut up," Camryn laughed. "I could still shoot you in the leg from a hundred yards."

"Noted." Ethan gave his head a light shake, bouncing down the steps after her.

TWENTY

Babylon, 2060BC

When Abram was ninety-nine years old, the Lord appeared to him and said, "I am God Almighty; walk before me faithfully and be blameless. Then I will make my covenant with you and will greatly increase your numbers…you will be the father of many nations…kings will come from you. I will establish an everlasting covenant between you and me and your descendants after you, to be your God and the God of your descendants."
Genesis 17:1-8 NIV

Arael followed Akira down a series of elaborate tunnels that snaked beneath the Zagros Mountains to the west of Mesopotamia. The air grew thick around them. Past the mouth of the cave, all semblance of the physical world disappeared. No vegetation grew, no creature wandered. Not even the scurry of insects could be detected in these caves. Arael didn't know if it'd been enchanted to keep intruders out or if the evil hung so thick that no living organism dared pass into Lucifer's domain.

"Not that I really care," Akira said as they walked, "but I wouldn't speak Apollyon's former name in his presence if I were you. It makes him quite angry."

Oh, right. Arael rolled her eyes.

"That name was given by Elohim and is detestable to his ears."

"Yeah, I got it." As ridiculous as she thought it was, Arael knew she would comply. She would have to respect his wishes if she expected to get this assignment. And she had a feeling this was an assignment she wanted.

"So, do you know anything about this new job Apollyon has for me? I mean, have you heard…anything?" Arael didn't want to talk to Akira at all, but her curiosity wouldn't let her keep quiet. Had he discovered some new Archangel outpost or caught wind of an upcoming Conclave? Or had he finally found a loophole allowing them access to the Archangels where there hadn't been before?

"No clue. I do know there have been a lot of hushed whispers around here the past few days, though. Lots of Watchers in and out." Akira paused to look at her. "It feels like something big."

Questions swirled in Arael's head, but Akira's words overshadowed them all. *It feels like something big.* Anticipation hummed through her body as they walked on. The farther down they went, the hotter and heavier the air became. A stench worse than the mortal world assaulted her senses—the smell of rotting flesh and festering waters.

The caves were dark—the kind of dark that would make a mortal man positive he'd gone blind, but Arael could see well enough. Her celestial eyes cut through the darkness and down the length of the narrowing tunnel they traveled. Condensation ran down stone walls that appeared slimy and smooth with age, and she heard faint dripping coming from somewhere above. She looked up and saw that, not only did the tunnels lead down into the earth, they connected to other tunnels above them, reminding Arael of an elaborate beehive. She drew her eyes back in front of her. She didn't even want to think about what could be lurking up there.

When they finally reached their destination, Akira ushered her through the arched entryway and bowed out silently.

The room before Arael loomed large and open compared to the narrow tunnels they'd just traversed. Small flickers of flames danced from the sconces on the walls, providing the only light in the space. In the middle of the room sat a throne made of smooth black stone. Several higher-ranking angels stood guard around the throne, staffs in hand.

Even though Arael thought it strange to see these Seraphim who'd once loyally guarded the throne room of Elohim now guarding this place, she could only be grateful for their presence. Even after so long, she appreciated having witnesses to their encounters.

Apollyon didn't rise when Arael entered but remained motionless as she stood in the doorway, twisting her hands. *Does he expect me to bow?* The thought horrified her. She'd never been invited to the throne room before, and Akira had failed to bring her up to speed on expected etiquette.

Unsure of what to do next, her eyes fixed on Apollyon's snow-white hair that stood in stark contrast to the cool black throne in which he sat. His smooth, pale skin and open, inviting eyes lent an innocence to his face, hiding the evil she knew lurked inside. An image of a wide-eyed loris came to her mind. The small, adorable animal seemed harmless enough. But Arael had seen the creature attack, killing its victim with its fatal venom.

"Arael," he began, "you have been one tough angel to find."

Arael cursed herself for the unease she felt in his presence. "I—I didn't know you were looking for me."

"You don't come to my assemblies. You ignore my messages..." He spread his hands in front of him. "If I didn't know any better, I'd think you were avoiding me."

"Ha," Arael barked out a nervous laugh. "I haven't been avoiding you."

Of course she'd been avoiding him.

"I've been...busy."

"Busy?" He cocked his head. "You aren't working for me anymore. What could you possibly be doing that's kept you so busy?"

Arael pressed her teeth together. "You know what I've been doing."

Apollyon steepled his hands and blew air out his nostrils. "I don't feel I ask too much of you, Arael, I really don't. I do not force you into service. I do not require sacrifices, as *some* tyrants do. All I ask is that you report to me periodically and respond to my summons when I call."

Arael bowed her head, sufficiently ashamed of her insolence, her usual contempt for him quickly replaced by admiration for the great leader sitting in front of her. *Apollyon has worked so hard to make a home for us here. I should really be more grateful.* She strode toward the throne and bowed before him. He placed a hand on her shoulder as she raised her eyes to look at him. Anger and surprise shot through her as she jumped up, looking around. *How did I get over here?* Hadn't she been standing at the door?

A wicked grin spread across Apollyon's face. "That's right," he said. "I've acquired some new abilities." His smile disappeared. "Nice, right?"

"How did you—" Arael didn't even know what to ask because she still wasn't sure what had happened.

"Oh, it's much easier than you would imagine." Apollyon's eyes brightened. "I won't bore you with the details, but it seems that if you are able to suspend an angel in between life and death for enough time, you can suck the power right out of him. It's quite a brutal process, but it's amazing, isn't it?"

Arael didn't even try to hide the horror on her face, but Apollyon didn't seem to notice.

"Oh, and I do hope I can count on your discretion about this. Could you imagine what would happen if everyone knew?" Apollyon clucked his tongue and shook his head. "The bloodshed…"

Arael nodded, but her attention roamed elsewhere. Her mind wandered to the poor angel who'd been tortured and killed just so Apollyon could take his powers. He had to have been some sort of Empath, able to manipulate emotions instead of just reading them, as Uriah could. The thought of Uriah sent a jolt through her. She hadn't thought of him in a long time.

Apollyon's face opened in surprise. "Oh, dear," he tsked. "You miss him, don't you?"

Arael stared back at Apollyon. How did he know she'd been thinking of Uriah?

A slow grin spread across Apollyon's face, but his eyes remained hard. "That's right, Arael. My power has grown tremendously since our last chat. There are no secrets anymore."

Arael's heart raced, and she didn't even try to control it.

He knew.

He knew about her treason. He knew about Uriah. He knew everything. Had this all been a trick to get her here and pilfer through her mind?

"I—" Arael started, but Apollyon interrupted her.

"Shhh." Apollyon snaked out of his throne, causing Arael to take two steps back. "That's not why we're here today. And no, I didn't ask you here to get information from you. Uriah has been more than useful for that." He stalked toward her, one step forward for every one of her steps back. "Now that everything is out in the open, I am willing to let your little transgression slide…temporarily. If you do something for me."

Arael swallowed hard. "What do you want me to do?"

Apollyon ignored her question, pausing in the middle of the room. "You aren't even going to ask about him?"

An ache hit Arael in the chest, making it impossible for her lungs to expand. Of course, she *wanted* to ask. She wanted to know everything: where he was, what he was doing, if he was safe. But she couldn't say any of this to Apollyon. She couldn't even say it to herself. She had to tell herself she didn't care. He had not been a part of her life in a very long time.

"What do you want me to do?" Arael asked more firmly this time.

If Apollyon noticed her unease, he didn't show it. He circled around to face her. Arael looked up into his intense face, reminding herself why so many adored him.

He clasped his hands in front of him and pursed his lips. "It has recently come to my attention that a covenant has been established between Elohim and one of the Clean Ones, a man by the name of Abram." He turned and strode back toward his throne. "A covenant to establish a nation, a chosen people among them. This nation has been decreed to rise up among the mortals and overcome us."

Arael tried and failed to stifle a laugh. She couldn't imagine anything more ridiculous. "The Clean Ones are virtually nonexistent, sir. How would they ever form an army?"

"I know." Apollyon continued his pacing. "I didn't believe it at first, either. But it has been spoken. By Gabriel, nonetheless, and guess who has been declared protector over them?" He gave Arael a knowing look.

Without hesitation, she knew the answer. "Michael."

"Precisely." He smiled. "Here's the chance you've been asking for. What you've wanted for so long." He raised his hands and shrugged. "The opportunities are endless."

Arael's mind raced with excitement.

"I will give you whatever you need." Apollyon sat back down and studied his nails with great interest. "If it is angels, you shall have them. If it is powers, they can be yours. I know you want this as badly as I do, and now that I know why, I feel we can be an effective team." He held her gaze as she shuddered. "I am putting your former transgression out of my mind...for the time being. I am trusting this will be incentive enough to get the job done."

When his eyes rose to meet hers, Arael caught a glimpse of the manipulative, power-hungry, dictator he'd become. She knew he'd disclosed his knowledge of her treason only to remind her who still held the control here, not to entice her to accept this mission. She would have done that anyway.

A cold chill washed over her. Arael offered a small bow before exiting the room. "I won't let you down."

TWENTY-ONE

Kentucky Bend, Kentucky
Present Day

By late Sunday morning, Ethan found himself sitting in a grassy patch of dirt, holding a fishing pole and wondering how the hell this could possibly be his life. He should've been home already, playing his Xbox, riding his skateboard, sleeping till noon. Instead, he was working through an existential crisis while fishing on a creek bank with a girl he barely knew. He glanced over at Camryn, who sat beside him on the bank, a Styrofoam cup of squirming worms between them.

Camryn had been quiet since leaving the Morgans', and she kept scrunching up her face like she did when she was thinking hard about something. "You still worrying about the earthquake?" he asked.

"Uh…no. Yes. I mean, I am, but not any more than usual."

Ethan laughed. "Well, what's the matter then? I can tell something's bothering you." Ethan realized it didn't even seem odd to say that he could read her emotions so well. It should. They'd really only known each other a few days, but somehow it seemed much longer than that.

"Um…" Camryn looked like she might throw up, and there was that nervous laugh again. "It's just that, I did something I wish I hadn't done, and now I don't know how to undo it without you knowing." She finally looked up at him, pulling her shoulders up to her ears.

"What is it?" Ethan laughed. "Whatever it is, I'm sure it's not that bad."

Camryn sat for another minute before stuffing her hand into the pocket of her hoodie and pulling out a small baggie of pills. "I found these in your room this morning, under your pillow."

The anger that had been mysteriously absent all weekend poked its eager head around the corner of his subconscious. "Why were you going through my things?"

"I wasn't!" she exclaimed. "I swear. I just sat down, and your pillow fell..." She trailed off, biting her lip. "And there they were. I swear I wasn't looking through your stuff."

Ethan studied her face. It held such a look of mortification and dread that he decided he believed her. He waved the anger away for now. "I'm not a drug addict, Camryn. I'm not my mother."

"I know that." The words came out in a rush.

"So, what's your question?"

"What do you mean?"

"You found some pills in my room. I'm sure you have at least a few questions, and they could go one of two ways. I'm just curious to hear which way it's going to go."

Camryn looked down at the bag in her hand. "I know what they are," she said in a voice so low, Ethan barely heard her. "And I know why you have them. I just—" She paused before going on. "I just wanted you to know that I know, that's all. And we can talk about it if you want." She handed the bag back to him.

Ethan took it without saying a word. Once again, she had surprised him. They sat for a long moment, both staring down at the bag of pills.

"You don't have to," Camryn said.

"Yeah, it's fine," Ethan's voice was gruff. He cleared his throat, unsure what to say or where to begin. He'd never talked to anyone about this before. He'd always been so good at hiding, good at keeping secrets. But at that moment, he decided he didn't want to keep any more secrets from her. He also knew that if he did this, if he opened up to her, it would be over for him. He'd be in it with her, with no going back.

Ethan sat his pole down on the bank beside him and stared out at the water. Camryn did the same but didn't press him.

"I went to my first psychiatrist when I was six." Ethan pushed his hair back out of his eyes. "My grandmother took me. I was seeing things that weren't there." He shook his head and tugged at the clumps of grass at his side. "I was doing things."

"Doing things?" Camryn jerked her head toward him.

Ethan shrugged. "I don't know. Just things that aren't normal for a kid. It scared her, I guess. My mom was so messed up, she didn't notice or care, so my grandmother took me." He held up the bag of pills. "And that's where this got started."

"At six?" Camryn sounded surprised. "It's unusual to start kids on meds so young."

"No. Not right away. They tested me for everything under the sun." Ethan shrugged. "I tried psychotherapy for a while. Nothing really worked. So, I got my first prescription when I was eight. Risperdal. It helped some, I guess." He didn't want to tell her that nothing helped completely, but some things made him forget to care. "Then came the Xanax. She died not long after that—my grandmother. My mom couldn't be bothered to get me to the doctor, so when the prescriptions ran out, I had to find them on my own."

He paused for a moment and tossed a few pebbles into the water.

What he wanted to say— "My mom hooked me up with her drug dealer"—was a little too real, and he couldn't force the words out of his mouth. "I know a guy," he said instead. "It makes me sick every time I have to call him, but I don't know what else to do. It gets really bad when I try to quit taking them, you know?"

Camryn nodded. "Yeah."

"Anyway, street drugs aren't always the best. I never know what I'm really getting from him, but most of the time, they do the job."

Camryn twisted her ponytail between her fingers. "That's terrible."

"It is what it is." He raised one shoulder.

"Is that your motto or something?"

Ethan offered a sad smile.

"I had Xanax for a while," Camryn said after a pause. "I quit taking it. I didn't like how it made me feel."

Ethan nodded. He could understand that. He wasn't a huge fan of the grogginess and mood swings, either. "It's not much of a choice for me."

"The Haldol." She pointed to a round, orange pill. "That's an anti-psychotic."

A jerky nod was the best answer Ethan could give. He wanted to come clean with her, for her to know everything, but this was turning out to be harder than he'd expected.

"For your hallucinations?"

His lips tightened. "Yep."

Camryn nodded, then said in a voice that seemed a million miles away, "How did you know what you were seeing wasn't real?"

"I didn't know at first. The shadows had always been around, so they were completely real to me. But my grandmother—I mentioned the shadow people to her one day. She asked me a lot of questions about them and then took me to the doctor. That was the first time I ever thought something might be wrong with me."

He glanced at Camryn. She hadn't said anything in a while. He thought maybe she didn't believe him, but when he looked, he saw that wasn't the case. She hadn't even heard him.

With the color washed from her face, she stared across the creek at something in the distance.

"Shadow people?"

So, she had heard him after all. Following her gaze, Ethan's world ground to a halt around him. The birds stopped chirping. The breeze died down. Every sound vanished except the heartbeat pounding in his ears. In the distance, a dark cloud had descended out of the sky, taken on a slightly vertical shape, and rested in the crook of a branch in the tree. It was one of his shadow people, all right, and it was looking right at them.

Ethan was almost afraid to ask the question. "Do you see that?"

Camryn gave a slight twitch of her head that might be interpreted as a nod. He gave her shoulder a shake. "What, Camryn, what do you see? What is it?" Could she possibly be seeing it, too?

When he looked back to the tree, it was gone. Camryn sat blinking rapidly.

"You saw it, didn't you?" He tried to keep his excitement at bay, but she didn't answer. Before Ethan could think of what to do next, Camryn stood and started walking robotically toward her truck.

Heading back to Camryn's house, Ethan had given up trying to get any answers from her. He'd resigned himself to just getting her home safely when she'd started muttering under her breath. He was still worried but relieved that she'd started talking again, even if he couldn't understand a word of it.

Standing in her bedroom, Camryn continued mumbling to herself and frantically flipping the pages of some professional-looking books that had overtaken every flat surface of the room.

Ethan picked up a less ominous looking one, *How to Stop Worrying and Start Living,* and absently flipped a few pages. "What exactly are you looking for?"

"I know I've read something about this. I know it's here somewhere."

"You do know it's kind of weird that you have psychiatry books in your bedroom, right?"

Camryn shot him a look. "I like to know what's going on inside my brain, okay?"

Ethan held up his hands in surrender. "Okay, yeah." He thought it best to keep quiet while she did...whatever she was doing, and took the opportunity to look around the room.

He'd never been in a girl's bedroom before and felt as if he were in one of those living exhibits in a museum: *Here, ladies and gentlemen, we have the bulletin board where the girl likes to keep mementos and small photographs, usually of friends, but in this case, of her parents and many various animals. Here you see the dresser where the girl has on display all of her hair care and cosmetic products, which the purpose of most still remains a mystery. And on this wall, we see her collection of riding awards.*

Ethan inspected each trophy and ribbon, each adorned with images of horses in various states of motion and wondered what kind of rodeo hell he was getting involved in. *That's strange.* There had been several ribbons for each year up until about three years ago. She still had her horses, so why wasn't she still competing?

Continuing his exploration, Ethan examined a few photographs propped on a shelf. Most were of Camryn and her parents. She seemed to be pretty close with them. That could be a problem for him, he thought, glancing over his shoulder at her. He never made a very good impression on adults. What if they wouldn't let him see her after they returned? A spark flared in his belly, but he tamped it down. He didn't have to worry about that yet.

A few other pictures were there as well, two of just her horses and one of her standing between the two of them. He picked up the last one and ran his finger over the smiling face looking back at him. That smile—it was a genuine smile, not forced or fake like in the other photos. She was happy when this picture had been taken, he could almost feel it. She hadn't been worrying about natural disasters or the uncertainty of the future.

Under different circumstances, Ethan thought Camryn would probably have been self-conscious about him being in her room, but in that moment, she was too focused on throwing books around to worry about him seeing her stuffed animal collection.

Several books and lots of mumbled curses later, she found what she was looking for. "Yes! Here it is!" She sat down on the bed, and Ethan lowered himself onto the mattress beside her. "Shared hallucinations. It's called *folie à deux*. It's very rare and happens mostly with twins or people who live in social isolation, but it *is* documented: two or more people sharing the same psychosis or hallucinations." She pointed at the words on the page.

"Wow, that's—" Ethan waggled his eyebrows, "—weird. But what does it mean?"

"I have no idea," Camryn said with the enthusiasm of someone who'd just found the cure for cancer. "But it means something. It has to."

Ethan had to agree. Even though he wasn't entirely convinced that his shadows were hallucinations, Camryn *was* the only other person who'd ever been able to see them. "Has anything like this ever happened to you before?"

The excitement drained from Camryn's face. "Well, yes, actually. Nothing like what we saw back there, but other…stuff."

"What kind of stuff?"

Camryn explained about the visions she'd been having for the past several weeks. Add that to the earthquake yesterday and the shadow man showing up today, and Ethan was growing more and more uneasy. "Maybe this party tonight is a bad idea. Too much is happening right now, and we don't know what any of it means."

"So, what are we supposed to do?" Camryn threw up her hands. "Just sit here and wait for something terrible to happen? That's what I've been doing my whole life, and I don't want to do it anymore." She got up and walked over to her closet. "I'd much rather be stressed about what I'm going to wear tonight than freaking out over some hypothetical thing that might or might not happen."

Ethan smiled. "Fair point. I just feel responsible somehow, like I brought all this bad stuff into your life. And if anything happens to you…"

"Whatever's going to happen will happen no matter where we are. And at least we'll be together, right?"

Together. The word sounded new to his ears, like it held a meaning it never had before.

"Right?" she asked again, poking him in the shoulder.

Ethan wondered what had brought about this sudden change in her, but he wasn't about to argue. Maybe they'd have a chance to talk about it at this party.

"Yeah, yeah." He swatted her hand away. "Whatever you say."

TWENTY-TWO

Mesopotamia, 2060BC

Arael stood at the front of the dark mountain gorge and scanned the crowd before her. The moon illuminated the flat, rocky ground, leaving the walls and crevices in shadow. Apollyon had been true to his word. He had given her space to prepare, angels, weapons, and the freedom to do whatever she saw fit to complete her mission.

Arael swept a scrutinizing eye over the angels now at her service. Many she recognized: Norah, Shia, Raglan, Anzel. Some weren't as familiar to her, but that was okay. Now that she knew she and Apollyon shared the same goal, she trusted his judgment—with this mission, at least.

Arael had just opened her mouth to speak when her eyes landed on the one face she hadn't expected to see there. She coughed on the breath that lodged in her throat.

He stood alone, arms crossed, leaning against the back wall of the chasm. Arael turned to Akira, who had been so thoughtfully gifted to her as an assistant. "What is he doing here?" Arael hissed, gesturing with her eyes to the angel sulking at the back of the crowd.

"Uriah? You asked for the best, and he *is* the best."

"At combat and battle strategy?" Arael asked incredulously. That was not the Uriah she knew.

"Uh, yeah. Where have you been?" Akira's lips spread into a sly grin. "Oh wait...that's right."

Arael held up a hand to her. "Not now. I need to take care of this." She hammered her sword against the ground twice, quieting the murmuring crowd. Immediately, all eyes flew to her, eager and expectant.

"Thank you all for coming. Before we get started, Uriah, I need to have a word with you in private." Uriah detached himself from the wall and began to make his way slowly through the crowd. "The rest of you, I'll thank you for your patience." With that, she turned and exited through a crevice in the rock behind her.

Uriah followed as she knew he would. Not because he was ever so obedient to her, but because, thanks to Apollyon, she was now his superior. Arael waited until they were out of earshot of the others before she turned and spoke. No light filtered into the narrow passageway, and Uriah's face remained hidden in shadows. "So, Akira tells me you are an expert in combat now."

"That's what you wanted to talk to me about?" Uriah rested his hand on his sword.

"I haven't been completely oblivious to what goes on around here. I know the only way you could have those powers."

Uriah raised his chin. "I've done what I've had to do to survive. You should understand that as well as anyone. I'm sure that's not going to be a problem, is it?"

"Not at all. I'm just surprised, is all. After...what happened."

Uriah shifted his weight. "This is different."

"You left me because I wanted to destroy Michael. Now our entire mission revolves around trying to destroy Michael. How is this different?"

"This isn't your personal vendetta, Arael. This is a real mission."

Arael wouldn't have been more shocked if he'd slapped her. "You don't think I had a *real* reason to want him dead?"

"I didn't mean it like that. I—"

"It doesn't matter," Arael said, cutting him off. "Listen—"

"No, you listen." Uriah took one large step toward her until his face hovered inches above hers. Arael had to look up to see into his murky gray eyes. "I've gone over in my head a million times what I would say to you if I ever had the chance, so please let me talk."

Arael stared, too shocked to respond.

"I tried to be supportive of you for so long. All I ever wanted was for you to be happy. And if getting revenge on Michael was the way to do that, then I was going to make that happen for you." His voice was almost a whisper now. "And we tried, didn't we?"

Arael nodded. He had tried—in the beginning.

"But after so many years and so many tries, you couldn't see that it was never going to happen. With every failed attempt, you grew more and more obsessed. I couldn't stand seeing you like that. It was like nothing else mattered. Not me, not us…not anything." He paused then as if the words were thorns in his throat. "And as much as that hurt, it was worse that you didn't see it. You didn't even notice what it was doing to me."

"Uriah—"

"I'm not finished." He took a deep breath. "I've beat myself up every day since I left you, and wondered if maybe I could've done more. I've busied myself with mindless assignments for a cause that I don't even believe in because I just… I missed you. And yes, I've done some things I'm not proud of, but I'm still me. I'm still the same angel who's given you everything in me, even at a cost to myself. And that hasn't changed." Uriah relaxed a little then and stepped back. "And that's all. That's all I wanted to say."

"Well…" Arael cleared her throat. "That was a lot." She looked into Uriah's face, engraved with years of pain. "I'm so sorry about what I put you through. I guess I never took the time to think about how things were affecting you. And I'm sorry about that, too." Arael's gaze fell along with her voice. "For what it's worth, there's no one else I'd rather have by my side on this mission, new powers or not."

Uriah's mouth twitched into a reluctant smile. "Well, what are we waiting for then?"

TWENTY-THREE

"Maybe this is a bad idea," Camryn said before they got in the truck to head to the party on Sunday night. She'd started having second thoughts as she'd picked at her noodles during dinner. The kids who would be at this party had made her life miserable for the past seven years. And this being the first party where she'd ever dared to show her face, she was sure to be the center of attention. She tried explaining this to Ethan, but she couldn't make him understand the seriousness of the situation.

"What do you want to do then, just sit around here and wait for something terrible to happen?"

Camryn glared at him. "Using my own words against me? A lousy and ineffective tactic."

Ethan laughed, taking the keys from her. "Get in the truck. I'm driving. That's the only way I can be sure we'll make it there."

Camryn stuck out her bottom lip but climbed in on the passenger side.

"What are you so worried about?" Ethan asked. "I'm with you. Me and you, remember?"

A small smile played at the corners of Camryn's mouth.

"It'll be fine," Ethan assured her. "I know things have been weird today, but really, what could possibly happen?"

"Have you ever seen the movie, *Carrie*? That's what I'm imagining right now."

Ethan grimaced. "Nothing like that will happen, I promise. I won't let it." He reached over and wrapped his fingers around hers. She savored the unnatural warmth she had now come to associate with his touch and smiled when he didn't pull his hand away.

Ethan squeezed her fingers. "Better?"

Camryn strained to keep the smile on her face and nodded.

"I feel stupid," Camryn said as they hopped out of the truck in the middle of the Kennedys' back pasture. There seemed to be a hundred other vehicles back there, and she felt the thump of the music as soon as she opened the door.

Camryn wore jeans, a loose-fitting gray t-shirt, and a pair of black boots. Her hair, usually pulled into a sloppy mess on the top of her head, now fell over her shoulders in loose waves. Ethan had on one of the two outfits he'd brought with him, camouflage cargo shorts and a black t-shirt.

"You're good." Ethan grabbed her hand again and squeezed. "You look great, and you said he personally invited you, right?"

They followed the herd of people migrating through the field toward the music. It seemed that everyone had come out tonight. Some she recognized from school, but some she'd never seen before. *There must be more than just our school here*. That might actually work in her favor, Camryn thought.

As they approached the throng, they found a scrawny boy in a cowboy hat who couldn't have been a day over sixteen priming a keg. Camryn wondered at first if Kyle's grandparents knew he had alcohol in their bean field but decided that was the least of her worries just then.

Thankfully, the kid didn't offer them any as they passed. Camryn didn't know how she would turn it down without looking like a prude. Ethan must have misunderstood her long glance at the keg because he asked, "Do you want something to drink?"

"Oh, no, I'm good."

"Because they're not going to just hand it to you. You have to pay for it. Kegs are expensive, you know?"

"No, I didn't know. And how exactly do you?" Camryn teased.

"Well, I'll let you in on a little secret. This isn't actually my first party."

"No? I never would have guessed."

Camryn looked around to see too many faces staring at her, making her feel like an animal in a zoo. "You know what," she said, pulling some bills from her pocket. "I might just have one glass." She told herself she would just hold it, to give her something to do with her hands, but she also hoped it might keep her from standing out like a sore thumb.

"Are you sure?" Ethan asked.

She nodded and handed the bills to the kid who gave her a red plastic cup full of amber liquid.

Ethan waved her off when she offered to buy him one, too. "Got to get you home tonight."

A few kids stood close to the big fire, but Camryn and Ethan hung back a little with the larger group. Despite her best efforts to look casual, Camryn still got a few curious stares. Were they looking at her? Or the dark-skinned boy with the facial piercing beside her? Probably a mixture of both, she decided. But no one screamed or threw anything at her, so maybe this might not be as bad as she'd thought.

"So, this is how country folk party, huh?"

"Well, I wouldn't know, but I'm assuming so." Camryn shrugged, bringing the cup to her mouth. The liquid slid down her throat, foamy and cold. She grimaced at the bitter taste.

"Honestly, it's not much different from parties in the city. Except for the big fire, terrible music, and the faint smell of cow manure." Ethan poked her with his elbow.

Camryn laughed. "Well, I can't argue with the rest of that, but this music is good, unlike the screaming crap that's on your phone. That music cannot be good for your anxiety."

"Hey, my music is good. It has meaning and emotion. Every country song I've ever heard is about driving a truck, a girl in a bikini, or drinking beer. Where is the meaning in that?" He raised his fist for dramatic emphasis. "Where is the emotion?"

Camryn rolled her eyes and took another drink from her cup, barely tasting it this time. "It doesn't have to mean anything. It's fun, and it's easy to dance to." She closed her eyes and began to sway along with the music. When she opened them a moment later, her body went rigid. Over Ethan's shoulder, Camryn's eyes fell on someone else, someone looking back at her with a ravenous grin.

Ethan must have registered the surprised look on her face because he spun around, his body tense. Kyle strolled over to Camryn, not even giving Ethan a glance.

"Camryn! You came."

Camryn inched closer to Ethan, who took a protective step in front of her. Kyle finally acknowledged him with a dismissive look. "Who is this guy?"

Camryn didn't feel the need to explain anything to Kyle. Except this *was* his party, and he *had* invited her.

"This is my friend, Ethan. He's visiting from out of town."

Kyle pursed his lips. "Well, you two have fun," he said finally, giving Camryn a wink as he sauntered past. He leaned closer when he reached her and wrapped a cold hand around her arm. "Maybe I'll catch you around later." His breath on her ear sent a shudder through her.

"Who the hell was that?" Ethan stared after Kyle as he disappeared into the crowd.

"That," she said with a shaking voice, "was Kyle," as if that was explanation enough.

"What a douche."

A nervous laugh escaped Camryn's lips. "Come on," she said, holding up her cup. "I need another one of these."

Twenty minutes and two glasses later, the encounter with Kyle had been forgotten. Ethan leaned back against a fence post and crossed his arms, looking amused as Camryn threw her head back and swayed along with the music.

"Oh no," he said when Camryn reached out a hand to him. He shook his head. "I don't dance."

"Come on," she said, forgetting why she'd been so afraid to be there. "You know you want to." She reached out and took his hand. But instead of pulling him away from his post, he pulled her closer to him. The electricity in his touch and their sudden closeness made her forget to breathe for one beat of her heart.

Ethan took the cup from her hand and set it on the post behind him. It was almost empty. He chuckled. "Maybe no more of these tonight, huh?"

Ignoring him, Camryn exhaled her next words in one breath, like she'd been holding them in for a long time. "Can I tell you something, and you promise not to freak out?"

"There isn't much you could say that would freak me out at this point." Ethan grinned.

As they stood there, chest to chest, her hand still entwined with his, the rest of the world fell away until just the two of them stood alone in the field with only their unspoken words between them.

"I know you think that you and I are too different to be together. I know you've been trying to push me away, and I understand why. I understand that our lives couldn't be any more different," she continued, "but I can't remember a time when my life has made more sense." She ran a hand through her hair. *I'm not saying this right.*

Suddenly desperate for him to understand her, Camryn rushed on, doubting she would gather the courage to talk like this to him again. "It's like…when I'm with you, whatever is broken inside me…doesn't feel quite so broken anymore." *Oh God, did I really just say that?* Camryn squeezed her eyes shut, struggling to regain some of the dignity that was slipping from her grasp. "But not like that. Just like, I mean…I was fine by myself. But since you got here, things are just…different. I don't know." She looked down at their feet, only inches apart. The alcohol and this sudden rush of bravery were making her head swim. "Maybe that doesn't make any sense," she said in a low voice.

Ethan reached out and brushed the hair off her shoulder. "It makes perfect sense. Why do you think it's been so easy for you to convince me to stay in this god-forsaken town?"

Camryn looked up at him, her eyes full of hope and apprehension.

Ethan's free hand moved down to her waist, and she leaned forward, resting a hand on his chest. His other hand came up to brush the side of her face as his eyes bore into hers, asking a silent question.

She closed her eyes and tilted her face to his. In her mind, she was screaming, *Yes! Yes! Please, yes!* so loudly she feared Ethan would hear it. Camryn could already feel his hot breath on her lips and the electric hum of anticipation thrumming through her body when a voice broke through their bubble, like nails on a chalkboard.

"Oh. My. God!"

It was Brooke Mason and her entourage. Camryn stumbled, and Ethan put a hand on her back to keep her from falling.

"Look who it is, guys. It's the little freak—" Brooke continued as they stopped beside Camryn and crossed their arms in unison,

"—and her little freak friend. Where did she find you?" Brooke asked Ethan. "At the annual witches convention?"

Ethan narrowed his eyes to slits.

"Shut up, Brooke," Camryn said through clenched teeth. What was she even doing here? Kyle said she would be at cheer camp. *Kyle said...* Well, that explained that.

Brooke pretended not to hear her. "I thought we had a deal," Brooke said, referring to their longstanding, unspoken agreement that if Camryn pretended to be invisible, Brooke would leave her alone. Which for Camryn, meant not going to parties such as this.

Camryn had bowed down to Brooke for years, finding it easier than dealing with her constant harassment. But now, with three glasses of alcohol in her and Ethan by her side, she wasn't about to let Brooke's three-hundred-dollar extensions and manicured nails intimidate her.

Camryn shook her head. "I'm not going anywhere, Brooke. I was invited here. If you have a problem with that, you need to talk to your boyfriend."

Brooke glared at her with fists clenched at her side. Camryn prepared herself for a full-on Brooke attack. But Brooke whirled on Ethan instead. "Did she tell you about her superpowers?" Brooke asked, fury exuding from her every word.

To his credit, Ethan didn't blanch, just continued to glare at her. But Brooke didn't seem to be phased by the venom in his eyes. She opened her mouth to say more, but never got the chance.

Camryn had never considered herself to be a violent or impulsive person, but at that moment, the only thing she could think about was how to stop the words coming out of Brooke's stupid mouth. So she did the only thing she could think to do. She raced toward Brooke, letting out a guttural scream, fully prepared to tackle her to the ground. She'd almost reached her

143

when a massive arm came out of nowhere, swept her up mid-stride, and set her down a few feet away.

Kyle.

"Is there a problem, ladies?" Kyle drawled while Camryn squirmed in the grip of his two giant hands.

Brooke opened her mouth to speak, but Ethan's quiet voice cut through the night like a blade. "Take your hands off her."

All eyes turned to him. Kyle cocked his head. "What did you say to me?"

Camryn knew Ethan would want to fight him, but Kyle was six inches taller than Ethan and twice as wide. "Nothing, Kyle. Just let me go, and we'll leave."

"I said, take your hands off her," Ethan said, a little louder.

"Ethan, don't. Please." Camryn pleaded with her eyes, but no one seemed to be paying any attention to her.

"And how are you gonna make me?" Kyle asked, tightening his grip on her arms. Camryn winced.

Ethan had seemed pretty calm until that moment. Almost too calm, Camryn thought, considering what he'd told her on her porch the night before. At Camryn's evident pain, though, his whole demeanor changed. His fists clenched, his jaw tightened, and he seemed to grow two inches taller. His eyes met Camryn's and communicated a million things in that one look.

Then several things happened at once. Camryn leaned forward and stomped down hard on Kyle's huge foot. Thrown off balance by her sudden movement, he released her with an *umph* of pain. At the same time, Ethan came in with a quick jab to Kyle's nose, creating a horrid stream of dark, spurting blood. Brooke screamed and ran to Kyle's side.

All eyes on Kyle now, Camryn and Ethan took the opportunity to slip through the crowd before everyone figured out what had happened and burned them at the stake. They were lost in the sea of cars before Brooke's screams faded from their ears.

Camryn was almost in tears by the time they reached her truck. Why had she thought this would be a good idea? Had she learned nothing in the past seven years? She'd almost gotten Ethan killed. If anything would've happened to him, she would never have forgiven herself. And drinking? What had she been thinking? At least her parents weren't home to witness it. They would be so disappointed.

She couldn't imagine how this night could get any worse until Ethan turned on her with angry eyes and said, "Okay, we need to talk."

TWENTY-FOUR

Jerusalem, 587 BC

…Nebuchadnezzar king of Babylon marched against Jerusalem with his whole army… By the ninth day of the fourth month, the famine in the city had become so severe there was no food for the people to eat…Nebuzaraden, commander of the imperial guard, an official of the king of Babylon, came to Jerusalem. He set fire to the temple, the royal palace and all the houses of Jerusalem…The whole Babylonian army broke down the walls of Jerusalem…and carried into exile the people who remained in the city.
2 Kings 25:1-11 NIV

Arael tapped her sword and paced back and forth along the rampart of the wall surrounding Jerusalem, the capital city of Israel. It was ironic, she thought, that her journey over the past thousand years had started atop a city wall just like the one under her feet. The scene unfolding before her, though, was strikingly different from the festive celebration of Babylon so many years before. Below her now, Arael watched the Israelites starve and die.

For months the Babylonian army had surrounded the city, holding its citizens captive within their own walls, waiting for the Israeli army to weaken. But now things were starting to happen.

"The battering rams are mobilizing," Uriah said, adjusting the bow strap across his chest. A thousand years, and he still wasn't used to the heavy warrior armor.

If Arael hadn't been so apprehensive, she would've smiled. Her own armor fit like an extra skin. She'd hoped the same would happen for Uriah over time, but it seemed he would always be a Dominion at heart.

"I can see that." Arael reached over and straightened his breastplate without taking her eyes off the Babylonians below them. She stared out over the massive army. Countless hours of planning and plotting and manipulating mortals, hundreds of smaller attacks against Michael's beloved Israel, all leading up to this, their last strike.

The first part of their two-phase mission had been successfully executed years before. The northern kingdom of Israel was firmly under Assyrian rule, its people exiled from their land as the Fallen had been exiled from Heaven. It may have taken a thousand years, but that was of no consequence. Time did not exist in the spirit realm as it did in the physical. To the angels, years passed like days, days like minutes. A few hundred years was nothing but a spark in the infinite fire of eternity.

"I've waited a millennium for this moment," Arael said under her breath.

The key player in this second phase, King Nebuchadnezzar, had been a more-than-willing participant in her schemes. Arael found most kings fairly easy to sway. Offer them power and riches, and they'd do most anything. She'd only needed to whisper the idea into his mind, and a few short years later, here they were.

"What if he doesn't show?" Akira's white messenger robes fluttered in the wind as she sat, twisting a dagger between her fingers, perpetually uninterested in Arael's plans.

Arael sighed. After so many centuries, she'd come to the conclusion that Akira had only stuck around this long to annoy her. "He'll be here."

"After everything we've done to them, what makes you so sure this time will be any different?"

"Because," Arael growled, "this isn't a feeble attempt at turning his people against his God. If we are successful in this mission, it will mean complete annihilation of them. He won't leave such a significant outcome up to his army." She turned and glared into Akira's smug face. "He'll be here."

Arael wasn't surprised they hadn't seen Michael in their previous battles with Heaven. He trained soldiers, and he trained them well. He couldn't be everywhere at once. He wouldn't need to be bothered with every little skirmish and attack. But every step to this point had been meticulously planned. This was much bigger than a simple famine or a few plagues. Arael had bet all her cards that he would not risk something this significant on anyone's skills but his own.

As the Babylonian army advanced their battering rams, though, and the Israelites stood watching from the tower, gaunt and feeble, Arael stopped pacing and glued her eyes on the horizon.

"Where is he?" came Akira's voice, syrupy sweet.

Arael spun toward her. "He'll be here!" she snapped. Akira turned her face away, but not before Arael caught the smirk she tried to hide.

Arael continued her pacing, not ready to admit that Akira might be right. It wasn't likely, for all the reasons Arael had just explained, but what if…?

The Babylonian army had surrounded the city for months. Cut off from their fields, the people inside the walls were starving. Unable to transport their dead to the cemetery outside the walls, the bodies piled up in the courtyard. The streets flowed with putrid waters, and the city ran rampant with disease. Arael and her army were on the precipice of the complete destruction of his people, and Michael still hadn't appeared.

"He'll come," she said more to herself this time. "And when he does, you two remember I want him for myself."

"I still don't understand why we can't help you. Three against one are much better odds."

Arael gripped her sword and clenched her teeth. "We're all going to pretend you didn't just say that."

She knew Akira was trying to rile her, and Arael wasn't falling for it. Not today. "Now is not the time for your infantile behavior. Stick to the plan and stay out of the way." Arael turned to face Akira, her coal-black hair billowing around her face. "If you get yourself killed trying to be some kind of vigilante, don't expect either of us to come to your aid."

Uriah glanced between them, blinking rapidly.

Akira shrugged as if it didn't matter to her one way or another.

Just then, Nebuzaraden, the commander of the Babylonian army, let loose a battle cry, and his archers released their arrows, providing cover for the infantry to advance.

Arael's heart thrummed with anticipation. She thrust her sword into the air, signaling her own army to action. "Ready your arms!" she called to the hundreds of Fallen angels standing with her in the spirit realm and interspersed with the Babylonians outside the gate. The angels pulled their weapons at her command. She and her army had, thus far, not been permitted entrance into Jerusalem, but that would soon change.

Arael widened her stance to steady herself as the battering ram pounded into the gate. The wall shuddered, and the earth trembled under her feet with the force of the blow.

The humans were scarce in the square today. Those still able-bodied enough to make it to market had been warned to stay indoors. Still, a few stubborn souls lingered in doorways and whispered over neighboring fences. But with each consecutive strike, people emerged from the buildings to investigate the noise.

But Arael saw with her celestial eyes what the humans could not. As the huge, wooden weapon crashed into the city gate for the fifth time, a vision appeared in the sky above the city that only the angels were privileged to witness: The Army of Heaven descending from the clouds, and there in front—was Michael.

Arael's eyes grew wide at the sight of him. She could hardly believe this was happening. She hadn't so much as gotten a glimpse of him since he'd walked away from her at the Conclave. And now here he stood, right in front of her.

Michael and his army moved slowly, methodically, even as the wood splintered and cracked, and the cries of the invading army grew louder.

The tension bled from her soldiers behind her itching to strike. Arael signaled to them, and they stilled. She had waited so long for this moment, she wanted to savor it.

Arael held her place on the wall as Michael's army came to light on the carnage of his city.

"Michael, the great warrior," Arael sneered. "I have waited a long time for this moment."

"I don't want to fight you, Arael."

Arael let out a small laugh. "And why is that?"

"I don't want to hurt you."

Arael clenched her jaw tight. "Well, it's a bit late for that." Below them, the gate finally gave way from the blows, and the Babylonians came pouring into Jerusalem. With that, Michael's protections were breached like the popping of a bubble and Arael was able to make the flight from the top of the wall, down into the city. Her army followed. Soon the two angels stood face-to-face in the courtyard with their armies behind them, surrounded by the decaying corpses of the dead. Screams rang out as the soldiers' spears flew through the air, finding their marks in the backs of the fleeing Israelites.

"Arael," Michael spoke slowly, as if speaking to a child. "Your issue is with me, not them," he said, gesturing to the oblivious mortals scurrying and screaming around them. "And I can explain everything if you would let me."

Arael narrowed her eyes at him. "Do you think I'm a fool?" she spat. "You know you're going to lose this fight, and this is your last-ditch, sorry attempt to save your people." Her fingers twitched on her sword. *It would be so easy to take him out right now.* "And I'm not falling for it."

She knew he'd seen her practically imperceptible movement. His eyes had never left hers, but he'd seen it and chosen not to act. *He underestimates me. That's good.*

"I don't want to hear your words now. They change nothing." In a flash, Arael had her sword unsheathed and a hair's width from puncturing Michael's throat. His army tensed behind him, but Michael didn't move.

A flash of orange flame shot past as the building beside them ignited into an instant inferno. The soldiers who weren't dragging women into the streets were launching fiery arrows into the buildings, the homes, the temple.

Michael's head rose with the pressure of Arael's sword, even as he put up his hand to halt his men. For a brief moment, everyone stood tense, unsure what to do. Michael glared down at her through slitted eyes.

"There's that righteous anger," Arael spat. "Now, maybe we can get down to business."

After a tense moment, Michael took a step back. "Stand down," he ordered his men.

"No!" Arael yelled. "You can't retreat. Look at what is happening. Your people will be destroyed, don't you understand that? The covenant made by Elohim and Abram will be extinguished. You must fight for them."

Michael looked around as the Israelite soldiers fell in bloody heaps and the city burned. Screams echoed as children were wrenched from their mothers' hands.

Michael turned with resignation and lifted his sword, giving his men the signal they'd been waiting for. Both armies let out a growling battle cry as they collided with each other in a frenzied rush of wings and weapons.

Arael and Michael were the only two who advanced with purpose. They circled, weapons drawn, each waiting for the other to strike first. Arael didn't mind being the one. She jabbed her sword toward Michael, which he deflected with his own.

"What is it you want, Sister?"

"Do you even have to ask?" She lunged forward again, her sword just missing its target as Michael stepped out of the way. "I want you locked away in the deepest, darkest prison in the abyss to rot in solitude for eternity." Arael lunged at him again. "And I'm not your sister."

Michael faded back, allowing her to advance on him. "Having me imprisoned, what would that accomplish? Just to make you feel better? Will it change your fate?"

"Perhaps," she said as they parried their swords. "With you out of the way, Apollyon could take his place on the throne in Heaven. And we would all be able to return home."

Michael locked his sword with Arael's and pulled her in close to his chest. "You think it would be that easy? That you'd be able to just waltz into Heaven like nothing ever happened?" Michael shook his head in disgust as Arael struggled to free herself from his grasp. "Heaven exists where Elohim is. He is Almighty. All Powerful! Only the Righteous will ever be permitted to enter there. Apollyon is delusional if he thinks he could *ever* defeat Him." Michael strained at the pressure of her sword.

"We'll see about that," Arael said through gritted teeth as she pushed Michael away with surprising force. He stumbled back but righted himself quickly. He raised his head, never taking his eyes off her.

Then he laughed.

Michael stood with his sword at his side, all pretense of fighting gone. "Can't you see? Everything that's happened…everything you've done. None of it has been a surprise. It's all been foretold, even our defeats." He raised the point of his sword to her. "But let me commend you. You are playing your part well." He looked around at the burning city and the warring angels around them.

"Your fight is not with these people. I know it, Apollyon knows it. Everyone seems to know it but you. This fight has nothing to do with you or me or the people of this nation. He is using you, Arael. He's using you to get rid of me before the real fight can happen, and you don't even know you're his pawn."

Arael narrowed her eyes to slits. Was he making fun of her? Belittling her accomplishments? She lunged at him, screaming in fury. Michael sidestepped her again, throwing her off balance. He grabbed her from behind as she fell forward and squeezed her arms to her sides, his lips at her ear. "Don't believe me? Why don't you ask your beloved leader what he knows?" Arael tried to jerk away from Michael, but his hold was too tight. "This covenant will not be broken. You can kill every last one of these countrymen, and it would not stop what is coming. God's chosen people will soon encompass more than just the Israelites. No matter what you do. No matter how hard Apollyon tries. He cannot stop it."

Even though she couldn't see Michael's face, Arael heard the smile in his words. Her struggle to free herself from his grasp lessened slightly as she sought to comprehend their meaning.

"Apollyon knows what is coming. And he won't let it happen without a fight. You know as well as I do, he will bring every force he has to stop it because he's stupid enough to think it will make a difference. But let me assure you, it will not."

He shoved Arael away from him then, and with one beat of his mighty wings, flew backward onto the stone wall dividing the upper and lower parts of the city.

"He will lose, and it would behoove you to stay as far away from that fight as you can."

In a flash, Arael sailed to the wall beside him, advancing on him again. "What makes you think I would heed any warning from you?"

"I am no fool. I know you will not do this for me or even for yourself. But please, listen to me. For him." Arael followed Michael's glance down to Uriah, holding his own against three of Michael's warriors. Arael didn't even have time to be annoyed that Akira was right there with him, nothing but two daggers in her hands.

"It will not end well for Apollyon and anyone associated with the storm that is coming. If there is any chance for Uriah to avoid this, you will back down." Michael sidestepped her again, barely avoiding the point of her sword this time. "Stop fighting, Arael. Look around. This battle is over."

And with that, Michael slammed his sword into the ground, knocking Arael back with an unseen, concussive force. She flew off the wall and landed hard on the dusty ground, dazed. Her eyes burned with the afterglow of a blinding light. A buzzing filled her ears as she sat up and looked around. All her army, along with Akira and Uriah, sat on the ground with her, dizzy and disoriented.

Every sword in Michael's army had given out the same electromagnetic pulse, scrambling their senses, ending the fighting in an instant. A shadow came between her and the sun as she looked up to see Michael staring down at her.

"You may have defeated my people in this battle here today. But you will never defeat me." Arael expected to see malice in his eyes, but all she saw was sadness.

With that, he turned to walk away, leaving her and her army still stunned and sitting in the dirt.

"What should we do?" Uriah asked. "This is it. We won't get another chance."

Arael had believed that, too. But something Michael said had given her pause. "Don't worry," she said to the confused faces looking back at her. "This isn't over yet."

TWENTY-FIVE

Kentucky Bend, Kentucky
Present Day

Camryn couldn't think of any good conversation that ever started with the words "we need to talk." She also couldn't imagine what Ethan could need to talk about so badly that it couldn't wait until they'd driven away from this party and out of danger.

"What we need to do is get out of here. We can talk about whatever you want anywhere else but here." Camryn rubbed her eyes, the effects of the alcohol wearing off. The weightlessness she'd felt moments before was quickly being replaced by a familiar nervous energy. Ethan backed out of the throng of cars, side-eying her as he did so.

No sooner had they turned out of the long drive onto the narrow country road than Ethan started in. But he didn't sound angry anymore, something more like concern seeped from his voice. "What did she mean back there, about you having…powers?" He said the word like he didn't know what it meant.

"Oh my God, are you serious? *That* is what you took away from that whole situation?"

"Well, what was I supposed to take away from it? That everyone in this town is a prick?"

"I tried to warn you."

"Cam, I'm serious. Do you really—? Is that something—?"

"No! Of course not! You actually think I believe I have some kind of powers? I might be crazy, but I'm not that crazy."

"Stop saying that. You're not crazy. And just so you know, I'm not one to judge. You know that, right? If you did…think that…it would be okay."

Camryn's mouth fell open. "Well, thank you, Ethan," she said, her voice dripping with sarcasm. "That is so kind of you, but I don't think I have superpowers, okay? That's a rumor Brooke started when we were kids, and she has the whole town believing that it's true."

"The whole town thinks you have powers?"

"No!" Camryn wailed. "They think that I *think* I do."

"Huh?" Ethan's face scrunched in confusion.

"Just…never mind."

Neither of them spoke for a while. Ethan tapped his thumb on the steering wheel as he drove in silence. He seemed to be navigating the truck back to Camryn's house, which was fine with her. It had been an exhausting day. Scratch that, it had been an exhausting weekend, and Camryn was coming down off a serious adrenaline rush. She rubbed her hands over her face.

"Did she tell you about her superpowers?" How could she have *not* seen that coming? And Kyle? She looked over at Ethan. She couldn't put her finger on it, exactly, but something extraordinary had happened between them in the middle of Brooke's little tantrum back there.

"Hey," Camryn said, the word full of caution. "That was pretty cool what we did to Kyle, huh?"

A reluctant grin spread across Ethan's face. "Yeah, it was, wasn't it?"

"Yeah—it was like I knew what you were going to do before you did it."

"Well, he was hurting you. It wouldn't take a genius to know what I was going to do."

They'd arrived back at Camryn's house by then. As soon as Ethan shifted the truck into park, she jumped out and ran around to the driver's side before he'd even shut his door. "Yes, but I knew. I didn't just think you might. I knew you were going to hit him. And I knew where and how hard, just like—"

Ethan grabbed her arms then as if he feared she might run away from him. She looked up into his tormented face. His eyes searched hers with an intensity that chased all thoughts from her mind. Excitement and anticipation froze the blood in her veins. He wasn't asking for permission this time. He was issuing a warning.

In the next second, his lips were on hers, and her back was pressed against the cool steel of the truck bed. The tension of the past few days seemed to melt away as Camryn pulled him closer to her.

This.

This was sweet relief. The knots in her stomach and all the tension she held in her body vanished the moment their lips touched.

Camryn had often wondered what her first kiss would be like, but she could never have imagined anything like this. This kiss wasn't gentle or sweet or innocent. It was a kiss of desperation, all hands and lips and skin and hair. And she returned it with just as much yearning, like this was all she'd ever needed or would ever need again. His hands burned against her skin as he brought them under the hem of her shirt and squeezed her hips above her jeans. Camryn slid her hands under Ethan's shirt and ran her fingers up the curve of his back, over his shoulder blades, feeling his muscles move as he buried his hands in her hair. For the first time in her life, Camryn's brain was silent. Her body was in charge now, and it knew exactly what to do.

Ethan picked her up and set her on the seat of the truck, never taking his lips from hers. She wrapped her legs around his waist, pulling him closer.

A tiny voice in a deep, dark well in her brain yelled at her to stop, that this was happening too fast. But her body was screaming so loudly she couldn't hear it. She couldn't hear anything or feel anything or think about anything but the firestorm happening inside her...until Ethan pulled away from her, breathing hard. "Did you feel that?"

"Uh...yeah." Camryn's hands rested on Ethan's chest. His heart raced under her fingers.

"Not that." He flashed a shy grin that made Camryn's stomach clench. "I thought I felt—" Just then, the ground rumbled like a warning to them both.

Camryn stilled, jolted back to her senses. She knew what it was before Ethan could say the word.

"Earthquake."

Strangely, Camryn wasn't scared. Something more like excitement shot through her veins. At least some of her incessant planning was going to pay off. Camryn gave a nod and jumped down from the truck, survival mode activated.

She didn't take time to deliver any instructions, just trusted that Ethan would follow her lead as she ran headlong for the stables. A clap of thunder boomed overhead. She heard Ethan right on her heels.

She tried to tell herself they had time. *It could be days before a larger earthquake hits if one comes at all.* But the hammering in her chest and her persistent visions of the town in ruins shoved her forward. She knew they needed to be in the truck heading far away from here. But there was something she had to take care of first.

"Open the gates!" she yelled to Ethan over a sudden gust of wind.

"What?"

"The gates!" she yelled again, pointing to the stalls that held her two beloved horses.

She ran into the stable and unlatched Romeo's stall. Both horses bucked and whinnied, spooked by the earth's vibrations. Beside her, Ethan unlatched Rebel's door and swung it wide. As soon as the door opened, Rebel shot past them and into the night.

Romeo was not as cooperative. Camryn patted the air in front of her. "Whoa, boy. Whoa." A rearing hoof came dangerously close to striking her head. She crossed her arms over herself defensively and felt two hands pulling her back out of the doorway.

As soon as she was out of the stall, Romeo darted out and disappeared.

She stood stunned for a moment. The horse hadn't been spooked. He'd been trying to tell her to get out of his way. In her vain efforts to help him, she'd only been delaying his escape.

Had she done the same thing to Ethan? If it weren't for her, he'd be long gone by now, in relative safety.

"Why did we just waste five minutes doing that?" Ethan demanded. "We need to get as far away from here as we can."

Camryn couldn't look at him. "If we get a quake like California got yesterday, the levee won't hold. They were trapped in here. At least now they have a chance," she said. *Which is more than we can say for ourselves.*

"All right, well, now that that's done, can we get the hell out of here, please?"

"Still no luck?" Camryn asked when Ethan slammed his phone against the seat of her truck as they drove through town.

"No. I think the towers must be out." He'd been trying to get through to the jail to check on his mother since they left Camryn's with what few supplies they could grab in the bed of the truck. Thunder still boomed all around them, and continuous flashes of lightning illuminated the sky.

"You've got to be kidding me," Camryn said, inching forward on the road. Everyone else in town had apparently had the same idea—to get the heck out of Dodge—but there was no reason traffic should be moving this slow.

Something else must be wrong.

It didn't take long to see what that something else was. Once they'd reached the main road, Camryn saw blue flashing lights, and orange police barricades were blocking a section of asphalt that had crumbled during the tremors. Two cops were doing their best to direct traffic on one very narrow strip of asphalt that led out of town.

"Yeah, I'm not getting through to my parents either." Camryn tried to distract herself with conversation. "The last I heard they were on their way home, but I have no idea how far they made it before the tremors. Hopefully, they heard about the evacuation and are trying to get to safety."

Ethan gave her a daft look. "You're their daughter. They're coming to get you," he said. "I have a crappy mother, and even I know that."

Camryn chewed her lip. She hoped her parents wouldn't be heading back here into the eye of the storm, but she knew he was probably right. She could see the silhouette of the two officers in the headlights up ahead now, but they may as well have been on the moon, as long as it was taking to reach them.

"What is it now?" Camryn craned her neck to see what was causing the commotion up ahead. A car had pulled up to the police barricade. Someone was trying to get into town. "Who is this crazy person?" she wondered aloud as two people came out of their car and stepped into the headlights, creating two black shadow puppets flailing their arms and yelling. Camryn drew in a breath as she realized who those silhouettes belonged to. Without thinking, she jumped out of the truck and ran toward them.

As she drew closer, she heard her mother's screams. "My daughter! My daughter is in there!" The officers tried to hold her mother back while Camryn's dad stood in the middle of them, being the mediator, as usual.

"Mom!" Camryn screamed over the howling wind. "Mom, I'm right here." Somehow her mother heard her through the thunder and wind. Lindsey's face emerged from the shadow into the headlights of the cruiser. Camryn recognized the relief on her mother's face and saw her father's posture relax.

Only four cars separated Camryn from her parents when a violent and unrelenting shaking knocked her to her knees. She pitched forward to steady herself. On her hands and knees now, Camryn looked to where her parents stood. They clung to the hood of the police car to keep from falling to the ground, their faces twin masks of horror and helplessness. She thought of Ethan in the truck behind her, trapped here because of her.

Her parents.

Ethan.

Forward.

Back.

It was a surprisingly easy decision to make. Camryn put her hand on the car beside her on the road, pulled herself to her feet, and took a shaky step toward her parents. *Ethan will be fine. He'll know what to do.* Her hair stung her face as the wind whipped it around her head. She heard the crunch of metal and breaking glass as a tree toppled across the road, crushing the minivan in front of her.

This is a big one.

Screams of the passengers in nearby cars rang out through the wind. Camryn tried to keep moving but had that stomach-churning feeling she remembered from childhood after she'd been riding the merry-go-round a few spins too long. She was somehow managing to put one foot in front of the other until, mid-stride, the earth opened up in front of her.

TWENTY-SIX

Israel, June 11, 1967

This cannot be happening. Not again. Arael's eyes soaked in the action dying down around her. Orange and yellow flames lazily flicked from the Syrian tanks and combat vehicles that sat deserted on the dusty road leading into Israel near the northern bank of the Sea of Galilee. Gray wisps of ashes danced in the air like meandering snowflakes.

The Israeli planes that had laid waste to their attackers could still be heard overhead, returning to their airfields. The Syrian vehicles that hadn't been destroyed were retreating.

Arael wanted to chase after them. She wanted to scream at them, "Come back! Finish this!" But she couldn't blame them. In the past six days, she'd watched Israel launch air strike after air strike against Egypt and Jordan, and now Syria, wiping out their air forces and sowing confusion among their troops.

The Arab coalition, as the media had begun calling the trio of allied nations, had the Israelis outnumbered three to one, but that hadn't stopped the Israelis from cleaning house with them.

This was just the latest in a string of devastating defeats for not only Arael and her army, but every one of Apollyon's teams: Marduk in Masada, Beliel in Germany, and the most epic defeat of them all, the one attack Apollyon had headed up himself at Golgotha against the one who called himself the Messiah.

Michael hadn't been wrong when he'd warned her away from that one. Everyone involved had been captured, never to be heard from again. Everyone except their leader, of course.

And Michael had been right about something else, too. In the years following the crucifixion of the Messiah, the number of Clean Ones had multiplied many times over.

In Israel now, in the aftermath of her own massive loss, Arael and her army had been decimated. In the distance, Uriah staggered and wiped long streaks of celestial blood from his sword. He clutched at his side and crumpled to the ground, along with the rest of her army, who sat tending their wounds. He'd come so close today—as close as he'd ever come—to being killed by one of Michael's soldiers. And it had been Akira, not Arael, who'd gone to his aid.

Not far from Uriah now, Akira knelt down on the rocky beach, sucking in heavy, defeated breaths. Smears of dirt and streaks of blood adorned the faces of the army around her. No one had escaped injury. Arael didn't know how many soldiers she'd lost here today, but the number was sure to be substantial. Apart from celestial casualties, hundreds of human bodies, mostly Arab, littered the ground around them. The familiar smoke and smog of battle filled the air—if you could even call it a battle. Arael would more accurately call it a massacre.

When Michael had told her during their first battle in Jerusalem that Israel's story was far from over, Arael had been overjoyed. To her, that meant she would have another chance to defeat Michael. Looking back on it now, she could never have imagined the cost. For the first time, she found herself wondering if it had all been worth it.

Seeing them all come so close to death today, she finally realized what Apollyon was too arrogant to see: Michael's army was more powerful than hers. She would never defeat him. Apollyon would never defeat him.

Arael collapsed in the dirt, both from exhaustion and from the gravity of the realization. What did that mean for her? Apollyon had made himself clear. He'd grown impatient with her, and he had every right to be angry. He'd given her ample time to take care of Michael, and Heaven knew she'd tried. Thoughts of destroying him were all she could ever remember, and she'd given it every ounce of her time, energy, and concentration over the past three thousand years. She had every weapon, every power, and the sheer hatred to complete the task, and yet she failed at every attempt.

Six days ago, she'd stood in this very spot, prepping her army for battle. "Defeat is not an option here. The Arab countries have Israel surrounded, and Israel's army is far inferior." She'd looked to Uriah, who'd given her a reassuring smile. "They will never even know what hit them."

Six days later, and she was the one wondering what had happened.

As Arael sat in the dirt going over in her mind what she might have done differently, Akira hauled herself up from the ground and trudged over to Uriah. Sitting there on the beach, watching Akira console Uriah when it hadn't even occurred to Arael to do so, an idea niggled in her brain, threatening to make its way to the forefront of her mind. It was more of a plan of sorts. A plan she hadn't even known she'd been making until that very moment. A plan so absurd, she immediately dismissed it. There was no way. It wasn't even possible.

Just then, a blue shimmer appeared in the distance, visible even through the dusty air. Every angel left on the bloody banks of the sea turned to watch as, through the shimmering portal, stepped their leader and ruler of the powers of the air, Apollyon.

The air thickened around Arael as she stood motionless in the sand.

This can't be good.

Apollyon would never show his face in a battle like this. His presence could only mean one thing. Her time was up.

What would he do to her? The most merciful thing would be to take her powers and send her to the dungeons, but Apollyon was far from merciful. More likely, she would be doomed to spend her days in a lake of burning sulfur, feeling her skin burn and melt away from her bones over and over again for eternity.

Apollyon floated past the destruction surrounding him as if it weren't there. He scanned the defeated faces of the Fallen army. Arael's eyes darted to Uriah and Akira—Akira, who stood protectively over Uriah as Apollyon passed by. Apollyon nodded to her in greeting. *She is still in his good graces.* Any other time that would have angered Arael, but now...now that meant Uriah could be safe. Akira would protect him.

That was all the push Arael needed to do what she did next. The plan that was barely even a plan had already been set in motion. And in the instant before Apollyon's eyes found her in the crowd, Arael disappeared.

TWENTY-SEVEN

Kentucky Bend, Kentucky
Present Day

Camryn stared down into the bottomless chasm of darkness in front of her. She'd watched the car beside her descend into its depths when the road had split and crumbled beneath it. Now it was as if it had never existed at all.

Camryn teetered on the edge of the fissure, the black hole welcoming her. Her arms pinwheeled wildly as she caught nothing but empty air. Her heart seized with the realization that she was going to fall into this abyss. All her life's worries about random illnesses, floods, spiders, and snakes, and what would finally do her in was a giant hole in the ground, something she'd never taken the time to worry about. She would've laughed at the irony if she'd had time.

The half-second she balanced on the edge of the earth seemed to drag on forever, the moment frozen in time. She stared down into the blackness and wondered if she would fall forever. She heard her mother scream, but it was far away now, her mind already lost in the nothingness of the hole in front of her.

Her feet slipped over the edge, and for the briefest of moments, she was floating, touching nothing. She had been certain the moments before death would be filled with terror, but she was surprisingly calm, almost peaceful. *This is it.* She closed her eyes and waited for whatever would come next.

What came next was a whiplash-inducing jerk from behind. She was no longer floating but flying backward through the air. The ominous darkness of the crevice was replaced in her vision by the inky blackness of the sky, covered again by fast-moving clouds. *Is this death? Am I dead?* If so, this wasn't so bad. This was home.

Then a frantic face appeared over hers, screaming at her to move. "Get up!" Ethan grabbed her hand and pulled her to her feet.

Nope. Not dead.

She looked down to see Ethan tying something around her waist. She was still drifting in the endorphin-induced serenity of her near-death experience and could only stare down at his moving hands. "That's a very efficient knot," she said. "How'd you learn how to do that?"

Ethan tied the other end around himself. "Boy scouts," he said, but somehow Camryn didn't believe that. Then his arms were around her. She felt him lock his hands behind her back and bring his lips down to her ear. "I may not be able to keep hold of you. If we get separated, I need you to hang on to this rope and try to keep your head above water.

What? What water?

In answer to her internal question, the chilly water hit her feet only a second later. In a breath, it was at her knees, hips, waist. The deep gorge in the earth caused by the earthquake must have cut straight across the river on both sides of them, giving the swollen river an easy escape. The gorge had now filled with water and was quickly overtaking them.

When the water reached her chest, it lifted them like a buoy. Ethan had to let go of Camryn with one hand to keep his head above the freezing water, moving fast around them, bringing a ton of trash and debris with it.

The water pushed them, pulled them, swirled around them like a menacing weapon of nature.

"Tree!" Ethan yelled as the spindly branches came into view up ahead. If they could grab onto it, maybe they could use it to keep themselves afloat. She felt the rope tugging at her waist and saw Ethan not far in front of her. If she'd had time, she would've wondered where he'd gotten it and how he'd known what was coming, but at the moment, she could only be grateful. If not for his forethought and impressive knot-tying skills, he might be lost to her forever.

The tree rushed at them too quickly. Camryn knew they'd only have a split second to grab on, and only a slim chance the limb wouldn't break with the weight of them, sending them right back out into the swirling water.

"Now!" she yelled to Ethan, but he was already stretching out, grabbing the only limb he could reach and using it to pull himself closer to the stronger, thicker trunk of the tree.

The water rushed around them, threatening to rip them from their refuge with every movement. She saw Ethan in her periphery and was relieved that he was, at the moment, latched securely to the thick limb.

Using her whole body and all the strength she had left, she wrapped herself around the trunk and began to pray. She hadn't prayed many times in her life and wasn't sure there was even anyone out there to hear it, but this seemed like an appropriate time if there ever was one. *Dear Lord,* she prayed, *Please help me. Please help us—*

That was as far as she got before something—a very heavy something—crashed into her leg, crushing her knee against the tree. Camryn screamed out in pain.

"Are you okay?" Ethan yelled from his position a few feet from her.

"Something hit my leg," was all she could manage to say as pain shot from her knee down her shin in a hot fury. There was no way to assess the damage now. She just hoped the adrenaline pumping through her veins could keep her hanging onto this tree until help arrived. "We need to get to the other side!"

Ethan shook his head. "No, don't let go!"

"We have to move!" Camryn insisted as what looked like a propane tank rushed past them in the water. "We're right in the path of anything coming this way." Ethan's eyes widened at the sight of the tank. He looked back at Camryn and nodded. "Okay, we just have to move slow. Don't let go of the tree, just inch around. Let the water push you."

When they'd moved their position a few inches, Ethan called out, "I can't go any farther. There are too many branches."

"Can you go under?" she asked. He reached under the water, feeling around the lower branches then shook his head. "There's too many. I'm stuck." Camryn's mind raced through all the things her dad had ever taught her about survival. She heard his voice in her head, clear as if he were treading water beside her. *"There is always a way out. You just have to find it."*

Then Ethan's words from the night they stood together outside of Granny's came to her. *"There's no way you can be prepared for every scenario."*

True, this was one scenario they'd never prepared for. So, which one of them was right? Was there a way out of this?

Camryn looked all around, searching for a way out, an escape. She turned her head back to Ethan just in time to see a huge tree, roots and all, racing toward them in the water. "Ethan! We have to let go."

Ethan turned his head and apparently came to the same conclusion. There would be no escaping that. They pushed off from the tree in unison just as the uprooted tree crashed into theirs, right where they'd been.

And once again, they were at the mercy of the river.

The water swept them away, assaulting them with everything in the town that hadn't been bolted down.

The rope still tethered them to each other, but neither could stay above water long enough to speak. There was so much Camryn wanted to say to him. But every time she was pulled under, the words faded further and further away. *Thank you, Ethan, for staying with me, for showing me what it's like to really have a friend.*

Every surge of water over her head, the pain in her knee, and all the debris pelting her under the water were quickly draining her strength. She felt the rope around her waist tighten and a hand tugging on her shirt, trying to keep her above the surface. She wanted to tell him to save his strength, to leave her and save himself, but she couldn't make her mouth form the words.

They'd been swept far past the city and the road leading into town now. How far had they traveled? She tried to tell herself they were almost to dry land. *You just have to hang on a few minutes longer.* But the quick glances she could get when she was above the surface showed no end in sight. The river had been loosed from the cage of its banks and was filling the world.

I can't. I can't do this. Ethan... I'm so sorry.

Something crashed into her then, pulling her under one last time. Something big and heavy and rough. It might have been another tree limb or a dog house or a car. She didn't know. She couldn't even find the strength to care. She felt the rope tethering her to Ethan snap, and finally, she was free.

TWENTY-EIGHT

New York City, 2002

U riah had never liked using his physical body. Even when Arael had chosen to dwell in hers for years, Uriah could never commit. It was just so confining. He hated putting limitations on his senses, and that's what it felt like as he walked down this crowded New York City street, like he had a glass bowl over his head. He could only hear a few hundred yards in either direction, and the sun shone too bright in his eyes. Even the people rushing by on their way to work or school or wherever mortals went at noon on a regular weekday, made him uncomfortable. They were just...dirty, and even with his diminished sense of smell, they stunk. As a matter of fact, the whole city stunk. It was just the smell of the world these days, a rancid mixture of chemicals and sewage. He wouldn't even be here like this if it weren't crucial to his mission today.

It had taken Uriah decades to convince Apollyon that he didn't know where Arael had disappeared to after their loss in Syria. He'd spent the last thirty years "looking for her" at Apollyon's command, only to come up empty on every lead.

It had been smart, on the one hand, for Apollyon to come to Uriah for help; no one in creation knew her better. On the other hand, though, did he really think Uriah would just find Arael and hand her over to him?

Apollyon had begun to lose patience with Uriah about ten years ago. He'd sent out Trackers and offered a position in his hierarchy as a reward for her capture. As time passed, he'd begun to depend less and less on Uriah and more and more on his other resources.

But it had taken years more for Uriah to grow certain that Apollyon was no longer tracking his every move. It had been torture, going through the motions year after year, decade after decade, doing nothing while he knew Arael was out there somewhere in danger of being found.

And while he truly didn't know where to find her, he did have an idea.

The only trace of Arael he'd picked up in his whole time searching for her had been in New York City about ten years ago. It hadn't been a scent or a sighting. Just a feeling. A tingle in the air that had turned up nothing at the time, but the memory stuck with him. And right now, that feeling was all he had to go on.

He wasn't technically supposed to be in New York, though. He was supposed to be in Miami. Apparently, the spirits of the Nephilim there, now referred to by most humans as demons, were getting a little out of hand, and as eager as Apollyon was to sway the mortals, he was nothing if not strategic. He didn't want another Sodom and Gomorrah on his hands. Uriah grimaced at the memory of *that* debacle.

The stories of Sodom and Gomorrah were the stuff of legends among the underworld. Any kind of evil you could think of had been present, even accepted there. The Nephilim of those cities still bragged of the debauchery they'd spread. The ones who were left, anyway.

Two Archangels had arrived one day, burned the neighboring cities to the ground, and imprisoned a whole legion of demons in one night. Beliel's battalion had been virtually wiped out in one fell swoop.

Apollyon wasn't risking another episode like that in Miami. Uriah had been dispatched to employ his Dominion authority and get the rowdy demons under control. He just had to make a quick stop first.

Marching through the streets now, Uriah began to sweat, yet another thing he hated about this physical body. Even though it wasn't a human body, it resembled one in every outward way. He could eat, drink, and yes, even sweat. Inwardly though, was a different story. He was still an angel in every way. If he were still a Righteous angel of Heaven, his distinctive celestial aura would still be visible, even in his physical form. And the Fallen's lack of an aura would be even more noticeable.

So how, he wondered, had Arael kept herself hidden all this time? And how would he find her when no one else had been able to?

The rock that had settled in Uriah's gut grew heavier. He'd searched the city, above and below ground, every building, under every bridge and down every sewer grate. So far, the only thing he'd gained was a hole in his shoe.

Frustrated, Uriah meandered into Central Park and sat down on an iron bench. Maybe if he could clear his mind of her for a while, he would be able to make sense of things. He closed his eyes, sucked in a few deep breaths, and coughed from the smell. These mortals really did stink.

He looked around for the first time, not looking for clues, just seeing the world around him—the mothers pushing strollers and joggers running by. Even the vendors selling popsicles and hot dogs provided a needed distraction from his failure.

Humans had always fascinated him. Though the world changed and civilization grew, people stayed the same. They loved each other, killed each other, stole from each other, and comforted each other much in the same ways today as they'd done throughout history. Uriah had always marveled at how each human could be so different from the next. There were big ones, small ones, and every size in between. How could there be so many variations of the same thing?

He stared now at the backside of a very short, very wide woman selling flowers from a cart. She had a loud, boisterous voice, but that wasn't what had first drawn his attention to her. His eyes had been drawn to the flowers in her baskets. White carnations, simple and small. Arael's favorite. She always said they looked like little explosions of color.

Uriah let out a heavy sigh. And now he'd come back to Arael again. He'd just started to look away when he did a double-take, his eye catching something...unusual.

A woman had approached the flower vendor. A plain, normal-looking woman with short, curly, brown hair that framed a small, round face. Her baggy clothes hung from a too-thin frame, and a small white scar adorned her right cheek. He never would have given her a second look if he hadn't seen her eyes—tiny black pupils surrounded by a swirling gray cloud. The color in her eyes was moving, shifting like the foam atop rippling waves. Uriah sat mesmerized, but the flower lady didn't seem to notice.

As Uriah watched the women talking, he must have risen from his seat because the next thing he knew, he was standing. The woman with the swirling eyes glanced in his direction. Uriah didn't know what he'd expected when their eyes met, but when she looked back to the flower vendor, continuing their conversation as if she hadn't even seen him, Uriah was surprised by the disappointment that dropped in his chest. He'd expected something. Some recognition, some acknowledgment. After all, she couldn't be human—not completely.

Her aura was weak, but nothing that would have alarmed him had it not been for what he'd seen in her eyes. Could she be Nephilim? If Apollyon had sanctioned *that* again...

When the curly-haired woman turned and started walking toward the street, Uriah couldn't help but follow her. He didn't want to frighten her, but he couldn't just let her walk away. He didn't think she'd seen him fall in step behind her, but when his feet hit the pavement a few beats behind hers, her step quickened. Uriah did the same until a few moments later, she was running.

"Wait!" he called out to her. "Hey!" *Is she running from me?* Uriah smiled at the challenge. Even though she had a full block's lead on him, Uriah caught up to her in three long strides—careful not to move too fast so as not to draw attention to himself.

Catching her by the elbow, he spun her around. "Hey," he said, breathing hard. "I just—"

She jerked her elbow away from him. "Let me go, you creep." People slowed as they passed, casting wary glances their way. Uriah dropped his hand to his side and backed away from her. The woman turned and started running again, this time disappearing into a storefront a few buildings down.

Uriah rushed through the doors after the woman to find himself standing in a very large, multilevel bookstore with what seemed like hundreds of rows of shelves and its very own escalator. Uriah twisted his head from side to side. *It's like a maze in here.*

Lucky for him, though, he'd gotten close enough outside to catch her scent, a mixture of cinnamon and clove. He sniffed the air and followed the smell to a secluded alcove on the first floor with a circle of oversized, fluffy chairs in the middle of several rows of books. Uriah chuckled to himself when he looked up and saw the sign that read *Spirituality and Religion*.

Of course.

Uriah spotted the woman in the second row among the shelves of personal devotionals. She stood in the aisle, thumbing through the pages of a book like she hadn't just been chased through the streets by a stranger. She glanced up when Uriah started down the aisle toward her, pulled a piece of paper from her pocket, and very deliberately placed it inside the book. Next, she slid the book back onto the shelf. She gave Uriah a long, steady look as she did this, then hurried past him and out of the store.

Uriah walked over and pulled the book off the shelf. He flipped the pages until the note fluttered out. Uriah grabbed it from the air and read:

1468 Madison Ave. Room 402
Make sure they don't see you.
There is something there you need.
You won't see me again until you have it.
I'll be watching.

And then, as if that wasn't cryptic enough, scrawled across the bottom in thick ink, two more words made his mouth go dry.

Destroy this.

Uriah crumpled the note in his hand and looked around. Spotting the security camera in the corner, he made his way to the restrooms. Inside the stall, he opened his palm, and the wad of paper burst into flames. When it had properly disintegrated, he dropped it into the toilet and flushed.

Overkill? Maybe. But if she wasn't taking any chances, neither was he.

Fifteen minutes later, Uriah stood puzzling outside the address the woman had given him. He'd shed his physical body, per instructions, so as not to be seen. Still, his chest tingled. The building before him was a hospital. He'd never had reason to enter one. As a matter of fact, he avoided them intentionally.

Hospitals reeked of mourning and despair, and he would feel it all as if it were his own.

Uriah couldn't imagine what he could ever need that would be inside, but the woman's eyes implored him.

Room 402 was a patient room in the Intensive Care Unit. He stood in the hall, trying to block out the misery and loneliness that assaulted him from the surrounding rooms. He thought it strange, but he felt nothing coming from the door in front of him. He stepped inside, thankful that she'd warned him not to come here in his physical form. No way could he explain his presence here if anyone asked. He cast his eyes around the room but saw nothing out of the ordinary. Just a television, a bed, a nightstand, a man lying in the bed, and several machines that were keeping him alive.

That was it.

What in this room could Uriah possibly need in order to see this mystery woman again? Did she want him to steal the television for her? Surely he could have gotten a better one at the Radio Shack on the corner. Was it medicine she needed? If so, why this room specifically?

Uriah looked around again, this time his eyes landing on the man in the bed. He was tall and unnaturally thin, with dark hair cut close to his head. Uriah thought again how fragile the mortal body was. It took next to nothing to kill them. What had happened to this one? He walked to the foot of the bed, where a chart swung from a metal rope. He couldn't open it, being in the spirit realm, but he could use his other senses to get the information he needed. He narrowed his eyes and, with his celestial sight, bore into the file.

Name: John Doe
Address: unknown
Age 25-30yrs

According to the doctor's notes, the man had been pulled from the bay two weeks ago after an apparent double suicide attempt. He and an unidentified woman had been seen jumping from the Brooklyn bridge. They'd been in the water for almost an hour before being rescued. He was now on seventy percent oxygen with no brain activity since arrival. Chance of survival: slim. No other mention of his companion anywhere.

A mound of grief swallowed Uriah whole. Not from someone else this time, this pain belonged to him.

Death was the way of the mortals, but not like this. Suicide was a terrible way to end things. So many times, lives were ended with the best parts right around the corner.

He grieved for the man but still wasn't any closer to figuring out his purpose for being there. By that time, Uriah was almost sure it had something to do with the person in front of him, as he was the only variable factor between this room and any of the others.

Maybe the man's suicide partner could provide some clue. Lucky for him (not so much them), he was almost certain how she would be identified in the computer. He went to stand behind the nurse's desk, barely noticing the two young women who sat there discussing the color of another patient's feces as he looked into the computer's hard drive and scanned its files for the name he wanted. After a few minutes of scouring, he could only find three Jane Does registered at this hospital. One, an elderly, homeless woman brought in with an apparent heart attack, one a middle-aged woman being held on the psych ward after attacking a clerk at the liquor store on Fourth Street, and a third who was in the morgue.

Oh no.

Morgue-Jane-Doe was the only one who fit all the criteria: young white female dead from an apparent suicide. It had to be her. He looked to the room across the hall and felt a renewed sadness for the man. His friend was dead. Even though that had been their intention all along, Uriah's heart ached for the comatose man.

Still unsure of his mission, Uriah headed to the morgue. It took only a minute to find the room and the silver metal drawer that held the body of his Jane Doe. He stood a moment, wondering what he thought he would find or how it could help him. With no answer but nothing else to go on, he looked into the chart attached to the drawer. His whole body began to vibrate as if he'd been connected to a low electrical current. A small square picture stared back at him from the corner of her chart, obviously taken postmortem. The person was covered by a sheet, leaving only her head visible. Her eyes were closed, but Uriah didn't have to see her eyes to know they would be a swirling gray.

It was his lady from the park.

But she's not dead.

Is she?

She'd been talking with the flower vendor, and people had heard her yelling at him, so...no. She was definitely alive.

But according to this chart, she wasn't. A quick peek into the drawer told him it was empty. The body that should have been in there was gone. Uriah placed his hands on top of his head and stared at the picture. *What is going on?*

In a blink, Uriah was back in room 402, staring down at the frail body in the bed. This man's friend had sent him here to get something. Did this man have something that belonged to her? A quick search of his room told Uriah he had no personal belongings. Not even a change of clothes. Nothing.

Maybe she'd been mistaken. But she'd seen Uriah and somehow knew he could come here unseen and get what she needed.

What, Jane Doe? What do you want?

Just then, a long, blaring sound rang out from one of the machines attached to the man's body. His heart had stopped beating. In a matter of seconds, people came rushing into the room and right through Uriah as if he wasn't even there, which he wasn't—not really. The nurses shouted to each other, and a doctor climbed onto the bed to begin chest compressions. To most humans, this would look like chaos, but not Uriah—what he saw was beautiful.

Everyone had a job to do and did it well. One nurse taped pads to the man's chest and another called "Clear!" before placing the paddles onto the pads. Another pressed a button, sending a pulse of electricity from the machine directly into the man's heart. His body rose off the bed for half a beat before slamming back down again. Uriah watched in fascination as the doctors and nurses moved in perfect order, trying to save this man's life.

Then, as understanding blossomed, Uriah's fascination turned to horror. Horror, not at the terrible desecration happening to the body in front of him, but horror at the idea forming in his mind. He thought he knew what the woman wanted.

But no. There was no way. It couldn't be done.

But it had been done, at least once before. And if his hunch was right, he was much closer to Arael than he'd thought.

By the time Uriah worked through it in his head, the activity in the room was dying down. The doctors and nurses took off their gloves.

"Time of death 9:05 PM," one of the doctors announced.

If he was going to do this, Uriah had to act fast. Thinking of Arael and hoping to God he hadn't misunderstood, he closed his eyes and jumped.

TWENTY-NINE

Kentucky
Present Day

E than knew the moment the rope was cut. He felt the absence of Camryn's weight that had been tethered to his, like an extension of himself. He dove under the water, his hands searching the murky depths but coming up empty. He scanned the surface for her, but in the darkness, he couldn't see much. Large, bobbing objects floated by, and the tops of barns and silos could be seen standing immobile in the rushing waters—but no Camryn.

Lightning flashed all around. One bolt anywhere near here and they'd all be fried anyway, Ethan thought. Maybe he should give up. He'd tried, right? When the rope had been severed, she'd barely been holding on. She was probably dead by now. He should stop fighting and join her.

Ethan's lungs burned, and his muscles ached. It would be so easy to stop.

Just stop fighting.

Just close his eyes and succumb to the water.

But the spark of hope burning in his belly wouldn't let him do that. Not yet. He had to believe that as long as he kept fighting, she would do the same—that every breath of air he took into his lungs would somehow provide her the oxygen she so desperately needed. As easy as it would be, Ethan knew he wouldn't give up, that as long as he had an ounce of strength in him, he would fight for her. He would never stop. But as much as his brain was on board with that idea, his body wouldn't cooperate.

Ethan's brain screamed at his legs to kick, at his arms to move, but they weren't listening. A surge of water came over his head, and his muscles, wrought with fatigue, didn't protest.

Don't stop! You can't stop! he screamed at himself, even as darkness enveloped him.

Ethan floated in oblivion for only a moment before something soft and feather-light brushed against his fingers, chasing away the unconsciousness closing in.

It could've been a number of things: river weed or a fishing net or the soggy leaves of a tree. Still, he swiped his hand through the water, searching for what he could only believe were soft wisps of Camryn's hair. When he felt it again, he latched on, intending to pull the object toward him but found himself being pushed upward through the water instead. Ethan didn't have time to be surprised before he broke through the surface, gasping for breath, with a massive, hairy body underneath him. In front of him, something red caught his attention. He wiped his eyes and looked again.

A bridle! And that bridle was attached to a black Warlander who carried Ethan through the churning waters. Ethan sputtered water from his mouth and whooped with a sudden rush of energy. The appearance of the horse filled him with new hope.

"Rebel, we have to find Camryn," Ethan yelled at the animal. He'd never be able to live with himself if he survived this and she didn't. Ethan placed his hands on Rebel's back and pushed off, preparing to jump back into the water to search for her again when a brown and white Appaloosa appeared by his side. Camryn's dark blond hair floated in the water, a rippling web of hope that seemed to be reaching for him as she lay sprawled across the horse's back. Ethan couldn't tell if she was breathing, but just by seeing her, he had to believe she was okay.

The two horses trudged through the water as if they knew exactly where to go. Ethan and Camryn were at their mercy, having no other choice but to trust the animals' instincts.

Mercifully, it didn't take long for the horses to find solid ground, and as soon as he could safely dismount, Ethan ran to Romeo and pulled Camryn from the horse's back. Her lips were blue, and her skin, cold as ice.

It's just from the water. She's fine, he told himself even though her chest was eerily still.

He laid her on the ground and placed a finger on the vein in her neck. A faint pulse fluttered under her skin, but he didn't let himself celebrate. She still wasn't breathing. His shaking hands hesitated over her rib cage. He'd never done CPR before. *What do I do?* He'd only seen it done on TV, but that was nothing compared to having a real person lying on the ground in front of him.

"Think!" he berated himself. "Air. She needs air." Yes, that was it. He needed to get air into her lungs. He placed his hand on her forehead and tilted her head back. He pinched her nose closed, leaned forward and blew a quick, hard breath into her mouth.

"Shit!" he screamed into the air when nothing happened. He swiped the back of his hand across his mouth and leaned forward to try again.

Come on, Camryn, you can't give up now.

Right before his lips landed on hers for the second time, she sputtered and spit a lung full of water right in his face.

Ethan let out a relieved cry and slumped back on his hands, chest heaving as if he were the one who'd almost drowned. *Shit...* Camryn rolled to her side and coughed several times, clearing her lungs.

He leaned toward her and pushed her wet hair back off her forehead, needing to touch her, to feel her, to know she was really there.

"Are you hurt?"

Camryn brought a shaky hand to her forehead. "I don't think so. Just my knee."

Ethan looked down and noted the swelling even through her wet jeans. "We need to get you some help."

He stood and offered her his hand. She took it and pulled herself up, wincing with the movement. Camryn clung to him to steady herself. He put his arm around her and pulled her close, glad to have a reason to hold her.

She looked up at him with worry in her eyes, the lines on her face a window into her mind. She had to be thinking about her parents. They had been right on the other side of the road when the earth had opened up. They must have been there when the water overtook the town.

"We'll find them," he promised, though he had no idea if that was true.

Camryn didn't say anything, only looked out into the vast expanse of water from which they had just emerged.

Ethan glanced around as the sound of an approaching motor hit his ears. He didn't see anything at first, but a few moments later, a small boat came out of the darkness and slowed about twenty yards from them.

A man in a red life vest steered the vessel and four other people who looked to be in the same shape as Ethan and Camryn huddled together under a blanket in the small space of the boat.

"You kids okay?" the driver asked.

"Her knee. I don't think she can walk on it."

The man nodded. "There's a first aid site about two miles that way." He pointed up the road. "That's where we're going. I'd take you, but we're about full here." He gestured to the occupied seats. "I can come back for you, though."

"That's okay. We've got a ride." Ethan glanced back at the horses, grazing on a tall patch of grass nearby.

"Alrighty then. Take this blanket. It'll help with the cold."

Ethan waded out into the water and took the silver "blanket" from the man. It looked more like a deflated balloon to Ethan, but he would take any help he could get.

"You kids be careful now." The man nodded and sped off.

Ethan unfolded the blanket and wrapped it around Camryn's shoulders. He took one last moment to look at her, dripping wet and shivering. This moment was quite possibly the last normal one they would have. What would they find up the road?

Ethan had no idea how their life would change depending on the answer to that question. They didn't know how bad the earthquake had been, how much damage had been done, or who had died.

He could only be sure of two things. They were alive, and for the moment, they were together.

THIRTY

New York City, 2002

How do the Nephilim do this? Uriah looked down at his new body. *How did I do it?* The demons could easily possess a human body.

Well, "easily" was a loose term, but they made it look easy. Perhaps because their souls had once been confined to a human body and were used to its constraints. Uriah was not. He looked down at the hands that, two hours ago, had been lifeless in a hospital bed, swollen from non-use. Hands that now belonged to him.

If walking around in his own physical form had been hard, this would be next to impossible. Not only was this a physical body, but it wasn't even his own. This body was all wrong. Too tall, too thin, too hot. He could barely hear or see a thing. It seemed all his superhuman abilities were gone.

Is this what it's like for humans all the time?

Uriah had never known sickness before, so the weakness he felt staggering out the back door of Mount Sanai Hospital was disorienting.

Leaning against the wall, he planted his palms on his knees and closed his eyes. His head throbbed, and his veins ached where needles had just been ripped from his arms. Uriah had felt pain before, in both the spirit and physical realm, but this was a different kind of pain. This pain was going to last.

Fear mingled with his misery as he thought of all the muggings and murders that happened in dark alleys, just like the one in which he stood. *I need to get out of here*, he thought, and at the same moment, he heard footsteps rushing at him from his left. Was it one person or two? He couldn't tell the difference with these useless ears! He raised his arm over his head, knowing he couldn't defend himself in his weakened state, even against a mortal. He tensed his body and braced for the blow he knew was coming.

"Took you long enough," a breathless voice said. Uriah looked up into the anxious face of his Jane Doe.

Well, she did say she'd be watching.

The woman looked different now through these human eyes. She still *looked* the same, with her brown, curly hair and the small scar on her right cheekbone. But he noticed different things now. He noticed the soft curve of her nose. The delicate skin just under her ear that disappeared under the collar of her jacket. But the most striking difference was her eyes. Now, in this body, with his own mortal vision, her eyes were a milk chocolate brown. Where had the churning gray clouds gone? He uncurled his body from the wall and stood as straight as he could manage. In John Doe's body, he stood an easy foot taller than her petite frame.

Darkness had fallen on the city, but the moon shone down on her face, highlighting every dark freckle. Even without the swirling clouds in her eyes, Uriah knew his suspicion was correct. Somewhere inside this strange, beautiful human body…was his *qanima*.

"Good job," she said. "I didn't think you could do it."

"Couldn't? Or wouldn't?"

She shrugged. "Both, I guess."

As angry and confused as he was at what she'd asked him to do, all Uriah wanted was to go to her, to protect her from everything, but he felt that, if he moved, he might vomit.

He leaned back against the wall and closed his eyes. "I feel...I feel..."

"I think the word you're looking for is nauseous. Don't worry, take some deep breaths. It'll pass."

"I have so many questions," Uriah said.

"I would imagine you do, but we can't talk here. It's not safe." She handed him a pair of dark jeans and a long-sleeved cotton t-shirt. "Here, put these on." Uriah took them and grimaced in pain as he removed his hospital gown before stiffly pulling on the clothes.

They were both quiet as Uriah followed Arael out of the alley and onto a much brighter side street. From there, they walked several more blocks to a corner store where Arael sat him down on a bench outside.

Uriah rubbed his hands down his pant legs. The clothes she'd given him were just another layer of confinement and felt like sandpaper against his skin. He wanted the hospital gown back.

"This is awful," he said.

"Yeah, it's pretty disorienting at first, but you'll get used to it."

"Really?" Uriah couldn't imagine ever getting used to this.

"No. Not really." Arael smiled. "I'll be right back. Don't go anywhere." A few minutes later, she returned with a bottle of orange liquid and handed it to him. "It's orange juice. Drink up."

Uriah wrinkled his nose. He'd eaten human food before, but tried to avoid all liquids except water.

"It'll make you feel better."

Without hesitation, Uriah unscrewed the top and took three big gulps. The liquid was cold going down and tasted sweet on his tongue even after he'd swallowed it all. A few more drinks and the container was empty. He handed it back to her. "Thanks," he said as she threw the empty bottle in the trash. "I do feel a little better. Still hurts like hell, but I think I can walk now." He rose shakily to his feet. "Where are we going anyway?"

"Someplace safe," was all she said until they stopped about ten minutes later outside a towering brick building. When Arael started up the steps, Uriah grabbed her arm. "This is a church. I don't think—"

"It's okay." Arael gestured to their borrowed bodies. "These things offer more than one kind of protection." She reached down and grabbed his hand. "Come on."

Even through the aching and discomfort of this strange, new body, Uriah registered the softness and warmth of her hand in his, something he'd never noticed before.

Once inside, the door had no sooner shut behind them than her arms were around his waist. This is what the mortals would refer to as a hug. Their very nature caused the mortals to thrive off physical touch. Angels did not need such things, but this felt good…and strange…but mostly good. He wrapped his arms around her small body and hugged her back.

"I knew you'd come," she said into his chest then jerked her head up at him. "How did you find me?"

"Oh no, no, no," Uriah chided. "I'm the one asking the questions here."

"Yes, of course." Arael led him out of the foyer and further into the church.

As ecstatic as he was to have found her, Uriah couldn't stop his eyes from darting around the large space. Their fall from grace having come before the formation of any religion, the inside of a church was one of the few things he'd never seen before. About twenty rows of dark wood pews lead to a choir stand flanked by a pulpit on the left, a lectern on the right, and a beautiful, full wall of stained glass behind the altar. Stairs off the foyer led up to a balcony that overlooked a row of glass chandeliers that led to the front.

They settled into a hard, wooden pew right inside the back of the church. "I'll answer all your questions," Arael said, "but please. I need to know how you found me. Because if you were able to—"

"Apollyon may be able to as well?" Uriah said, finishing her thought. "Well, I think you're safe because I didn't even know it was you—not for sure. Not until I came out of the hospital."

Arael pursed her lips and tilted her head, confused.

"In the park, when I first saw you, there was something different about you." He paused. "This is going to sound strange, but it was your eyes."

"My eyes?"

"Yes, they were moving like clouds." He shrugged. "And I was curious."

Arael sank back against the pew. "So, you did this—" she touched his arm, "—without even knowing it was me."

"I—I hoped it would lead me to you, but yes, I didn't know for sure."

Arael stared at him, her mouth slightly agape. "You are…" She trailed off, shaking her head. Then she launched herself at him, knocking him back against the pew as she hugged him again, tighter this time. He didn't hesitate to return her embrace and felt her shoulders begin to shake in the circle of his arms.

She raised her head and pointed to the tears streaming down her face. "This happens a lot." She laughed as Uriah reached out to swipe at a tear. "It's ridiculous."

"No, it's not," Uriah smiled. "It's endearing." A small grin threatened against the corners of her mouth, and Uriah felt a strange warmth start in his chest and spread all the way down to his toes. Physical touch was so different in these bodies. While all his other senses were dulled tremendously, the nerve endings that existed under the skin of this body were hyperaware. From the clothes on his back to her skin against his, every touch was electric.

From the longing in the eyes looking back at him, Uriah thought she must be experiencing the same thing. Uriah pulled his hand back from her, and she straightened, clearing her throat. So much was happening inside him that he didn't know how to process it all.

He took a lock of Arael's strange, brown curls and twisted it between his fingers. "This is bad, Ari," Uriah said after a pause. "This is really bad."

"Shh!" Arael shushed him. "You can't call me that. My name is Skylar. Your name is Gavin. Also, I think it's fine. These bodies were dying anyway. It's not like we've hijacked a valuable human life."

"You *think* it's fine? The rules are pretty clear…" Uriah raised a shoulder then squinted at her. "Wait a minute. Two weeks ago, these two were living human beings. You've been gone for thirty years. How many times have you done this?"

Arael shrugged and looked away. "A few." The tone in her voice let Uriah know this was not something she wished to discuss. He let out a long breath and drummed his fingers on the pew behind her. "Are those really their names? Skylar and Gavin?"

"What, you think I made them up?" Arael looked insulted. "I found their ID's in their apartment. Oh, and to make matters worse, it seems these two had a pretty serious drug problem."

"What?" Uriah blinked twice.

"Yeah. And…due to some strange, recent events, I've found out they owe a lot of money to some very bad people."

"Wow, you really know how to pick 'em." Uriah laughed. "And how did you find their apartment? There was no address listed in their files."

"I just did, Gavin." She made a point of emphasizing the name. "Those are not the important questions here. What's important is that some bad people are looking for these two. I think they attempted to end their lives because they saw it as their only escape. But apparently, they didn't take their IDs with them, so the people looking for them have no way of knowing what's happened."

Uriah thought he knew what she meant. "And if we're seen by the wrong people in these bodies, Skylar and Gavin will be dead...again."

He pinched the bridge of his nose. "I think I understand why you had to do this." Uriah turned his gaze to the front of the church, unable to look Arael in the eye. "Back in the park...I didn't even recognize you for what you were, let alone who you were, in that body."

"And neither will anyone Apollyon sends to find me."

Uriah nodded. It was a solid plan. It had been a solid plan for thirty years. No one would suspect that a Fallen angel even could occupy a live human body, let alone purposefully do so. He knew firsthand what an extreme sacrifice it was. "So, you've had this body for a week, and you're still here? If you knew these people were after you, why haven't you left town?"

Arael looked up at him, her eyes glossy with unshed tears. "I've been waiting for you."

Uriah's breath hung in his throat. He thought back to that feeling he'd had on his trip to New York ten years ago. Had she been here all this time?

"I know things haven't been the same for us since the first Conclave," she said. "I'd been so consumed with revenge... I was worthless to you. I gave everything I had to Michael and nothing to you. I just—" her voice cracked, threatening tears again. "I thought I owed it to you to stick around."

Uriah took her face in his hands and brought their foreheads together. He wanted to say so much, but nothing would be enough. This was the first glimpse he'd gotten of his *qanima* since Syria, and he didn't want this moment to end.

"I understand if you can't stay with me," Arael continued. "This life is not easy for beings like us. But I'm so glad you're here." Her voice wavered, and she wiped the back of her hand across her cheek. "Even if it's just for me to tell you this one thing."

She pulled away slightly to look him in the eye. "I want you to know I didn't leave *you*. Back in Syria… If I could have taken you with me, I would have. I even tried to go back for you, but it was too risky and I—"

Uriah shushed her then by pressing his lips to hers. He couldn't bear to hear the anguish in her voice any longer, and with her face so close to his, he thought he knew the perfect distraction.

For a moment, Arael remained frozen, but then she relaxed into him and was kissing him back. She brought her arms up and wrapped them around his neck, brushing her fingers through his hair.

"I'm not going anywhere," Uriah said when he finally pulled away from her. "My place is with you, no matter what." Arael scratched under her ear. Uriah knew she wanted to protest. He also knew she wouldn't. He stood and reached a hand down to her. "Let's find this apartment of ours, get what we need, and get as far away from this town as we can."

"Don't turn on the light," Arael warned as they entered the dark apartment twenty minutes later. She crossed the room to peek out the window that opened onto the back alley. "Give it a minute. Your eyes will adjust."

Uriah had never had a need to turn on a light before, but now, for the first time, he couldn't see a thing. *This is going to be harder than I thought.*

Even in the dark, Arael moved with ease around the apartment, checking all the locks on the doors and windows. Of course, she would have the layout memorized. By the time she finished, Uriah could see well enough to move away from his spot by the door and closer to her. After so long apart from her,

194

he never wanted to leave her side. She stood in the center of the room, twisting her hands and looking uncertain. He strode over to her and pulled her into his arms, longing to feel the hum of his body that he only felt when they were this close. He was not disappointed as her body relaxed into him. She put her arms around his waist and buried her face in his shirt. This he could get used to.

There were so many things they needed to talk about, so many things he needed to know. But he couldn't think through the fog in his brain, the effects of the day finally hitting him all at once.

Unable to stand another minute, Uriah tugged Arael over to the couch. "These human bodies are pretty inadequate, aren't they?" He sat down, and Arael found her place beside him. He lifted his arm, and she snuggled in close to his side.

"When we leave tomorrow, we may have to split up," she said. "Maybe even stay in different cities for a while. Just to be safe. I can get us passports, but that will take some time. We'll have to lay low until we can get to Cyprus."

"Whoa. Cyprus?"

"It's the only place we can truly be safe. I have it on good authority that the Righteous will allow us asylum there. We can start a new life."

"You've been planning this for a while, haven't you?"

Arael laughed. "I just don't want to take any chances."

Uriah smiled. "If we need to split up, we split up." He turned and stared into her strange, chocolate brown eyes. "I've found you twice already. No matter where you go, I'm sure I can find you again."

"I'm glad you're here," she said through a yawn. He reclined his head on the back of the couch and gave her shoulder a squeeze. He meant to say he was glad, too, but before he could get the words out, he was asleep.

A sliver of light woke Uriah as it shone in through the slit in the curtain over the window. He squinted and raised a hand to his face. Arael stirred beside him. "We must have fallen asleep," he said.

"Mmm..." was all the response he got before she leaned over and curled up on the other side of the couch, wrapping herself into a small blanket. Uriah put his elbows on his knees and turned his head to stare at her, taking a moment to really look at her in the daylight. The sunlight illuminated her brown curls, giving them a golden hue he hadn't noticed before. He wanted to reach out and touch her but didn't want to wake her again.

His head swung around to take in the rest of the apartment. This was the first time he'd had a chance to really get a look at the place. It wasn't much to speak of, just a studio apartment with dirty carpets, a couch and television in the main living area, and a microwave and refrigerator in the kitchenette. A mattress on the floor must have served as their bed, but Uriah wasn't sure he would've slept on it. The place was tidy, though, which was more than he would have expected from two junkies. He imagined Arael with a broom in her hand, those springy curls falling down into her face as she tried to clean the place like an average mortal. That made him smile.

Uriah's stomach rumbled then as if he needed another reminder of his humanity. He walked over and pulled open the fridge. He'd never quite understood hunger before. Angels could eat but didn't need it for survival. Still, the gnawing pit in his stomach made him wince. There really wasn't much to like about these bodies.

"There's no food here," Arael mumbled from the couch.

He spun around. "I'm sorry. I didn't mean to wake you."

Arael didn't appear to have heard him. She still hadn't even opened her eyes. Uriah realized then she probably hadn't had many opportunities to sleep like this in the past thirty years. What had this life been like for her? What had she been through?

Had she met people? Had friends? Uriah was sure he'd have time to hear all about it. After breakfast.

"I've been getting food from the bakery downstairs," Arael mumbled. "They have good bagels."

Uriah smiled, remembering the scent he'd picked up from her outside the bookstore yesterday—cinnamon and clove. "Bagels, huh? Well, how about I go down and get us some?"

"Why don't I go?" Arael said, curling herself deeper into the blanket. "They know me."

"No. Go back to sleep. They know me too, remember? Skylar isn't the only one who lived here." Arael mumbled something in response and closed her eyes again.

Uriah stopped at the door and looked back at her, wondering if they could really pull this off.

Yes, he decided, they definitely could. Eventually, these bodies would wear out, but they would find more. And more and more. They could do this as long as they needed to. And they would finally get to be together, just as they'd been created to be.

Uriah looked around and found a few crumpled bills in the purse she'd been carrying, then quietly shut the door behind him. Even without his celestial powers, he felt oddly carefree. Knowing that he, as Arael's *qanima*, hadn't even recognized her in her new body gave him a peculiar sense of security. As long as they were careful, no one would ever find them.

Blame it on his newfound optimism or maybe just blind stupidity, but what happened next…Uriah never saw it coming.

THIRTY-ONE

Kentucky
Present Day

Camryn stood with Ethan at the edge of the water, petrified with fear. She wanted nothing more than to stay right there, safely wrapped in his arms where she could pretend that the life she'd known for seventeen years, her school, her town, maybe even her family weren't gone forever.

She didn't want to think about what might lie ahead. Her mind couldn't process it. She'd almost died twice tonight, wasn't that enough? The fog in her brain was almost as heavy as her limbs, but something the man in the boat said urged her into motion.

Help was near. And if there was a first aid site, maybe her parents would be there, too.

"Well, you heard the man," Ethan said. "We've come this far, what's two more miles, right?"

As it turned out, two miles was a lot longer than it should have been with one person hurt and the other having zero experience with horses. Once they'd managed to wrangle themselves onto the back of Romeo and settle into a steady pace on the country road leading into town, Camryn let her mind work through the last few disastrous hours of her life.

What the hell happened? She remembered getting separated from Ethan and losing her fight with the water. She understood that the horses had shown up and saved them. But so much didn't make sense.

"How did you know what was going to happen?" she asked Ethan, who held her a little tighter than necessary from his spot behind her on the horse's back.

"What do you mean?"

"Back in town. You had that rope. How did you know we would need it?"

He didn't answer right away. "Because you told me," he said after a moment.

"No, I didn't. I didn't even know—"

"When you told me about your visions of the town flooding," Ethan continued as if she hadn't spoken. "I remembered what you said about the fault line, and I thought it sounded more like a premonition than a hallucination." He took a deep breath. "Then, when I felt the earthquake, I thought that had to be it. And if what you'd seen was really going to happen, I didn't want to take any chances. I saw the rope when we were in the stable, and I just grabbed it." He shrugged. "Just an impulse, really."

Camryn couldn't believe her ears. How could he make her insanity seem so completely rational? She pulled the horses to a stop and twisted in her seat to look into his tired and dirty face.

His lips pressed together, trying to suppress a grin. "What?"

The words trying to escape her mouth were, "I love you," but what came out was a small, "Nothing." She couldn't make herself say it, no matter how true it was. She did love him. She'd realized it right after the rope had been cut and right before she'd given in to the water. She hadn't wanted to die, but if drowning in the river would've saved Ethan, she would have gladly done it. Wasn't that love?

But they *had* only known each other for a few days. It sounded ridiculous, even in her own mind.

Ethan leaned forward and touched his lips to her forehead. He grinned down at her with eyes that made her feel a little dizzy. In that small moment, Camryn let herself feel a tiny bit of happiness despite the circumstances. She didn't know why, but she knew she'd get another chance to tell him. It didn't have to be tonight.

As they made their way into the city, Camryn surveyed their surroundings, trying to determine their location, but nothing looked familiar. How could it? Nothing was as it had been just hours before. With smoke wafting from the rubble surrounding them, they were riding through a war zone.

A few minutes later, they came to a more populated area dotted with more buildings and houses—what was left of them, anyway. People screamed, sirens blared, fires blazed. The sound of helicopters overhead drowned out people's cries for help.

They'd seen the helicopters almost immediately after the man in the boat left them and assumed they were searching for more survivors in the water, but as they topped the hill and saw the activity in the distance, they realized the first aid site was also serving as an evacuation point.

People in all types of uniforms—National Guard, fire and rescue, first responders, even police, ran back and forth between incoming boats, stretchers, and helicopters. People, injured and uninjured alike, were being loaded into choppers and whisked off into the night.

Camryn and Ethan wandered into the middle of the activity, but no one paid them any attention. People were literally dying all around, so two kids who seemed to be unharmed didn't warrant much alarm. How would she ever find her parents in this mayhem?

Camryn hopped down off the horse with a yelp of pain. Ethan managed to slide off Romeo much faster than he'd gotten on and was by her side in a flash. "Slow down. Let me help you," he said, but Camryn didn't have time to slow down. She looked around as if she were just going to see her parents sitting on a bench, waiting for her arrival. Not surprisingly, they were nowhere in sight.

Out of nowhere, a young man with close-cropped, blond hair and striking blue eyes stepped in front of them, looking way more excited than the current situation called for. He wore the uniform of the National Guard, but his wide grin didn't quite fit with his military persona.

"Hey." He glanced between them. "You look like you need some help."

"No, I'm fine." Camryn tried to move around him, but her leg wouldn't cooperate. She lost her balance and would have fallen on her face if both men hadn't reached out to steady her.

"Yes, she does," Ethan retorted.

"No. I don't. I need to find my parents. James and Lindsey Martin, can you tell me if they're here?"

A look of confusion flickered on the soldier's face, but just as quickly, the grin returned. He produced a small, digital pad from an inside pocket and scrolled down a few pages.

"Martin...Martin..." The soldier continued to scroll. "Oh, Martin—wait, sorry. That says, Marlin. No Martins yet, but don't worry. People are still coming in, and there are other sites set up along the perimeter. I'm sure they'll turn up."

Camryn's face twisted into angry confusion. "How?" she demanded. "How can you be sure of that?"

The soldier stammered, looking thoroughly reprimanded, "Uh, I...um."

The next thing Camryn knew, Ethan's hand was on her back, and her anger had been obliterated and replaced by blissful nothingness. Everything around her slowed, and she was suddenly floating on a cloud.

Of course! This is just a dream. This had to be one of her night terrors. *Wake up,* she prodded herself, *please wake up.*

Voices surrounded her, but the words didn't register at all.

"...sorry..." "...look at her leg now?" "...think she's in shock."
None of it meant anything.

* * * * *

"My name's Jay, by the way," the soldier said as he began poking at Camryn's knee. "And your names are?"

When Camryn didn't respond, Ethan gave him both their names, and the soldier entered them in the strange little pad he held in his hand. Ethan had never seen anything like it, kind of a mix between and tablet and a smartphone.

"Is she going to be okay?"

"Yeah, I think her kneecap is just bruised. She'll need an X-ray when you get to Langley, but it'll probably just be swollen for a few days."

"Langley?"

"Oh, yes. Sorry." Jay pointed to a helicopter landing about a hundred yards away. "The life-threatening injuries are being taken to the nearest operational hospitals, mostly north of here. The others are being transported to Langley Air Force base in Virginia. They're taking the displaced for now. And they have a small clinic on base where she can get an X-ray. The powers-that-be will figure out something more permanent from there."

"Virginia? Why so far?"

"This area is too dangerous right now. There are still tremors being detected. The worst may still be ahead of us. Virginia is the closest, safest place."

Ethan thought of his mom, locked up in a cell in a building made of metal and bricks.

"How far are we from Franklin? Was it hit like this?" Ethan asked.

"We're about forty miles from there, but I don't have any specifics about damage there. I've been here since the beginning of the rescue efforts, and our information is mainly need-to-know."

Finished wrapping up Camryn's knee, the soldier pulled out a penlight and shone it into her eyes. Concern crossed the man's face.

"What? What's wrong?" Ethan asked.

The soldier straightened. "Nothing at all. Everything looks good."

He did a quick evaluation of Ethan, giving him a thumbs up. "You guys should head over there," he said, pointing to the make-shift landing zone in the middle of a football field. "You'll be out of here in no time."

"There's no chance we can stay here? Try to find our parents?"

"Afraid not. Everyone out. Those are our orders. We'll have all names and locations in here." He pointed to his digital pad. "We'll work at reuniting you with your family when everyone is safe."

Well, there was no arguing with that, and Camryn was in no state, mentally or physically, to make a run for it. Ethan put his hand on her arm, helped her up, and started in the direction of the helicopter.

"Wait." Camryn's sudden alertness startled them. They both turned to look at her. "What about my horses?"

Rebel and Romeo were tied to a nearby fence post, drinking from a bucket of water someone had placed there for them.

Jay looked back and forth between her and the animals. "Um, I don't think we can get them on a helicopter. They're going to have to stay here, I'm afraid."

A pained expression crossed Camryn's face. She looked as if she would protest when Jay said, "We could probably use their help. Horses are great work animals, especially in situations like these. We'll take good care of them, I promise."

"They saved our lives," Camryn said. "They're not going to understand." Tears welled in her eyes.

"Well, maybe you could just talk to them," Jay suggested. "They understand more than you think."

"You have horses?"

Jay smiled and nodded and shooed her toward the animals.

Camryn limped over to them and rubbed their heads. Ethan hung back with Jay, giving her some privacy.

"So how long have you two known each other?" Jay placed his hands in his pockets and rocked back on his heels.

"Just a few days, I guess. It seems like longer than that, though."

"Ahh." Jay nodded. "And what were you doing when the quake hit?"

"We were uh…" Ethan scratched his head, remembering what they had been doing when he'd felt the first tremor. "Why do you need to know that?"

"No reason. Just making conversation. I was home. Watching TV. I live pretty close to here."

"That right?" Ethan rubbed his chin, wondering what the hell this guy was talking about. Thankfully, Camryn returned just then, rescuing him from any further awkward conversation with Jay.

"All good?" Ethan asked her.

"Can I get them back? When this is all over and we're settled somewhere?"

"Of course." Jay took a card from his pocket. "This is my name and armory number. You call, they'll be waiting for you."

"The white one is Romeo. He's very affectionate and kind of lazy. The black one is Rebel. Do *not* try to ride him if you know what's good for you."

Jay gave a salute of understanding, and Camryn surprised them both by wrapping him in a quick but meaningful hug.

Inside the helicopter, two shell-shocked people sat across from them, and a few stretchers were loaded into the back. Three crew members with red crosses on the arms of their uniforms seemed to be too busy with the injured to even notice the people in the seats in front of them.

No one spoke a word, just made lots of hand gestures over the loud noise of the propellers. Jay handed them two headsets and gestured for them to put them on. He pointed to his ears and yelled, "You'll be able to talk to each other with these."

He gestured to the pilot in the cockpit. "They're all connected, so everyone can hear everything." He gave them a wink. Camryn and Ethan waved at him in thanks.

He waved back, flashed them both a goofy grin, and disappeared back into the crowd.

Ethan reached out and found Camryn's hand. Her face reflected his own feelings exactly: fear, uncertainty, grief.

For now, and maybe forever, they had nothing in this world except each other.

THIRTY-TWO

New York City, 2002

The blow came from behind. If Uriah had been paying the least bit of attention, maybe he would've ducked. Maybe he would've run the other way. Maybe he could've avoided it altogether.

Or maybe not.

It was more likely he wouldn't have seen them, no matter how cautious he'd been. He still wasn't used to this peculiar, new body with its strange human perceptions. He was used to his celestial instincts—used to sensing an opponent, the anticipation of an attack, the instinctive way his body would react. None of that happened this time.

This time, the only thing he felt was a blinding hot pain on the back of his head.

Uriah's vision went white. Fire wrapped around his wrists as the awkward heaviness of Gavin's human body fell away from him. Free from the almost unbearable confinement of it, he felt his powers return to him, but little good they would be to him now, not with these chains of Heavenly Fire around his wrists.

Uriah looked up to see Michael glaring down at him with fierce eyes. He barely registered the two winged figures flanking him before noticing that, over Michael's shoulder, everything around them—the buildings, the people, even the sun in the sky—was just a shade dimmer, as if he were looking at his surroundings through a thin veil. And he was, really, the veil of space and time. If someone looked down the alley right now, they would see only Gavin's body, lying alone on the dirty pavement at the bottom of the stairs.

Where Uriah, Michael, and the other angels stood now, time and space did not exist. He and everything else that existed here would never age, never die—not in the way humans thought of death. They would never change in any way unless purposefully so.

The same could not be said about the things that existed in the mortal realm. In time, the buildings would decay. The people would grow old and pass away. The streets would crack and become so overgrown by weeds and vegetation they would no longer be recognizable as what they were. Even the sun would burn out eventually, a star collapsing in on itself. Nothing there would last forever. Gavin could attest to that.

"They told me it was you," Michael said with a mixture of disbelief, horror, and rage. "But I didn't believe them. Didn't believe you had it in you."

Uriah shook his head. "I don't know what you mean. I haven't done anything."

"But haven't you?" Michael directed his eyes to the roof of the building on the opposite side of the street. With his celestial sight restored to him, Uriah saw Nephilim spilling out of a portal onto its rooftop—just black, shapeless shadows swirling out in a demon tornado.

"The protections we have around this building will be useless in a few more minutes. They'll search every building within a twenty-mile radius. We have to get her out of there."

Michael's words bounced off Uriah as he stared at the portal, still spewing demons like an erupting volcano. There had to be a thousand of them. *Why so many?*

The demons themselves were not discernible from one another, just shapeless, black forms. But their leader, standing like a statue at the edge of the rooftop, staff in hand, Uriah recognized immediately. His name was Dagon, but he was more widely known as the Punisher.

Uriah swallowed hard. Dagon was Apollyon's hammer of justice. He'd earned his nickname over centuries of increasingly creative yet cruel punishments for anyone in his charge. The staff at his side glowed a familiar orange light. How he'd come to possess a Heavenly Fire infused weapon was not known, but what he did with that weapon had become lore among the Fallen.

Uriah paled. He could never allow that to happen to Arael.

He didn't have time to think about how exactly he would prevent it, though, before Michael shoved him into the hands of one of the robed men. "Raphael, you take care of this one. Samael," Michael said to the other angel, then gestured down at the body lying at their feet, "get that body back to the hospital before someone notices it's missing." He shot daggers at Uriah with his eyes while still talking to the other men. "I've got to clean up this mess."

If Uriah thought Raphael would be any gentler than Michael had been, he would've been wrong. Raphael shoved him back into the darkened alley where an angel stood guard at their own portal.

"Raphael. I didn't bring them here! I swear to you!" Uriah pleaded, but Raphael stared straight ahead as he pushed Uriah through the shimmering blue doorway.

With his hands bound, Uriah lost his balance as he stumbled through the portal onto a bed of hard, jagged rocks.

Immediately, a pressing weight landed hard on his chest, an invisible boulder crushing him farther down onto the rocks. The collective grief of a thousand mourning souls hit him all at once. If there had been anything good or right or pleasant in his life, it was lost in that instant.

Unnatural darkness welcomed him. Uriah sensed that he was inside, even though he couldn't see any sign of a ceiling or walls. Just the feeling of some kind of enormous enclosed space. In front of him, a stone tunnel led off into...more darkness. *I've been here before,* Uriah realized in horror. *I know where I am.* But this time, he'd had no time to prepare. Michael wasn't here to protect him, and Arael wasn't here for support. He was all alone.

Just then, Raphael stepped through the portal behind him and stared down in disdain, seemingly unfazed by the atmospheric shift of the Void.

"You have to believe me." Uriah clutched at Raphael's leg in desperation. *They won't leave me here, will they?* "I would never do anything to put Arael in danger. I—"

"Silence," Raphael said in a voice so low the air seemed to tremble. "Your intentions are irrelevant. You knew Apollyon was looking for her. He specifically asked you for help. Whether you agreed or not, you led him to her. And for your carelessness alone, you will be punished."

"What? You can't punish me for that! I was going to warn her. I was trying to help her. She had a plan. She already..." Uriah's voice trailed off as he realized what he'd done, how stupid he'd been. Apollyon must have known what he would do eventually. Uriah had been ignorant to believe he would ever stop monitoring his movements. Apollyon would have waited a thousand years if it had taken that long.

Arael's plan had been airtight. If Uriah hadn't shown up and led Dagon right to her, she never would've been found. She'd still be safe right now, just as she had been for the past thirty years. *If I hadn't been so selfish.* Uriah's stomach roiled. He was surprised he could still feel this very human impulse without a human body, but the memory of the nausea he'd felt coming out of the hospital in Gavin's body still lingered inside him like muscle memory.

Raphael looked around impatiently while Uriah worked through all this in his mind. The Archangel didn't give him long, though, before he reached down, hauled Uriah to his feet, and marched him down the corridor. Uriah knew there was no point in resisting. The only way out of the Void was through a portal, and he was sure Raphael's had closed immediately. He wouldn't leave that gateway open for just anyone to meander through.

Even though he couldn't see anyone, Uriah could sense the presence of others around him. It didn't take him long to realize the corridor was not solid. Cells were carved into the walls of the tunnel with some sort of celestial reinforced bars holding the cells' inhabitants captive. This had to be Apollyon's infamous dungeon, an extension of the Void, because, what better place for a dungeon, really?

He'd heard of this place but had never been here himself. He avoided it for the same reason he avoided hospitals.

"These are Apollyon's prisoners." Uriah's voice sounded unfamiliar to his own ears as he struggled to brush off the misery that oppressed him from every direction.

"They are prisoners, yes," was all Raphael said in response, and Uriah understood. Some of these prisoners were Apollyon's. Some were Michael's. He'd never thought about it before, but of course, Michael had to keep his prisoners somewhere. Uriah guessed he should count himself lucky that Michael was only planning to lock him up and hadn't killed him on the spot as he'd seen done to others. As bad as this was, the death pits that lay below were far worse.

The slower they walked, the faster Uriah's mind raced. But now his thoughts had turned from his own fate to Arael's.

"Do you think they got her out in time?" he asked a silent Raphael.

He hadn't expected a response, but the energy pulsing through him pushed the words from his mouth. "Where is he taking her?" he asked, trying again, but Raphael acted as if he hadn't heard. "Why is he helping her?"

Still nothing.

Uriah decided to try another approach. "If you think I'm in league with Apollyon, what's to stop him from coming down here and releasing me once you're gone?"

That got a reaction from his captor. Raphael whirled, towering over Uriah in the corridor. "You think Apollyon holds any authority down here? He does nothing without the permission of Elohim!" Then, looking surprised by his own reaction, Raphael backed up, straightened his robe, and drew back his shoulders.

Uriah winced at his words. He hadn't expected an answer from Raphael at all, let alone that. Raphael spun and resumed his silent march once again, leaving Uriah with his mouth hanging open. He wanted to say something more but couldn't think of a single thing. *He does nothing without the permission of Elohim?* What did that mean?

If he had been Marduk or Beliel or one of Apollyon's thousands of loyal followers, this most certainly would have infuriated him, caused him to jump to his leader's defense. But Uriah was not loyal to Apollyon. Uriah had lived more of his existence as a Fallen angel than a Righteous one, but he could never forget that he didn't choose this life. He had known before the Fall that Apollyon was a liar, and nothing Uriah had experienced on this side of Heaven had proven otherwise. That was why he and Arael had been spying for Michael in the first place. But even with his disloyalty to Apollyon, he'd never imagined such a scenario.

Uriah might not have believed it, had it not been for what they ran into at the bottom of a particularly steep drop in the stone floor. Raphael and Uriah practically slid down the sloping embankment into another larger section of the Void. He looked up to see row after row of cells containing angels he recognized. Angels he hadn't seen since the second Conclave after the Fall. These were the Founders that had disappeared off the stage at the hand of Michael's soldiers.

Darkness still surrounded them, but small torches burned from the walls around the cavernous space, giving off just enough light to see the grotesque disfigurement of the once beautiful creatures. Hair had been ripped out, long bloody grooves ran down their cheeks as if they'd clawed their own faces. They were naked and filthy. While Apollyon's prisoners on the top level had slunk back and cowered in their cells, these angels pressed their bodies to the bars, burning themselves in the process. They looked as if they'd gone mad.

"Just so you know, they did that to themselves," Raphael said before he shoved Uriah into his own cell. Their moans and cries filled Uriah with a terrible dread. Was this what was to become of him? How could he protect Arael from here?

Raphael stood outside the cell and stared at Uriah with a strange look on his face. He opened his mouth to say something then closed it again. He turned his head, clenching and unclenching his jaw.

Uriah felt a small twinge of emotion seeping off of him. He'd felt those twinges before—the distinct pang of someone trying to hide their emotions from him.

"Please spare me your guilt," Uriah managed to say. "I don't think I can take it in addition to everything else I'm feeling right now."

Raphael turned back to stare at him with intense, blue eyes. "I'm not much for conflict, you know. I'm more of a lover than a fighter." He held up his palms, waggling his fingers in the air. "But you intrigue me, Uriah. You are a curious angel, indeed."

Uriah was already struggling to draw in breaths. "I'm sorry, I don't know what you mean," he heaved.

"I've been watching you for a while. Did you know that?"

Uriah managed a slow shake of his head.

"I have." He narrowed his eyes at him. "And you know, I can't help but wonder exactly whose side you are on."

THIRTY-THREE

Kentucky
Present Day

Strapped into his seat behind the pilot, every minute carrying them farther and farther from danger, Ethan still couldn't let himself relax. If life had taught him anything, it was to never get comfortable. Things could seem okay, then *Bam*! Circumstances could change on a dime.

Camryn's fingers were still laced with his and rested in his lap. She leaned her head on his shoulder and closed her eyes. Ethan could only imagine how exhausted she must be. He hoped she could fall asleep and escape the hell that was their life, at least for a little while.

Ethan, too, was numb from fatigue, but he wouldn't be sleeping anytime soon. Even though his body was bone-weary, his mind wouldn't rest. He traced his thumb over the top of the fragile hand in his and shuddered at the thought of any harm coming to it—or the person it belonged to. He knew she was strong—stronger than she gave herself credit for. She knew a lot about survival and had good instincts, but she was also naive. There was a big world out there that she knew nothing about.

Ethan, on the other hand, knew a few things about the world. He knew the true nature of the human spirit and how depraved it could be. He looked over at her sleeping face and thought about everything they'd lost in the flood—their phones, all their supplies, his meds, any semblance of a normal life.

The thought of not having his pills made his stomach flutter. Images of night sweats and nausea made him cringe, so he pushed them from his mind. He had a responsibility now, greater than any physical need.

He had to keep her safe.

I won't let anything happen to you, he silently promised her. He just hoped he could hold his demons away long enough to keep that promise.

They weren't long in the air before the sun made its appearance over the horizon, giving Ethan his first hint of visibility since they'd lifted off. The other passengers seemed to be sleeping, but Ethan craned his neck to take in the devastation below. He could hardly believe he was seeing his own country and not some war-torn, third-world nation.

A dusty fog filled the air, the floating residue of buildings that had once been people's homes and businesses, now nothing more than piles of concrete and ash. Even the trees had toppled to the ground, crushing anything that dared to stand in their path. The whole scene reminded Ethan of footage he'd seen after Hurricane Katrina. *But we're too far inland for a hurricane.*

Ethan squinted to read a large piece of a green metal road sign that had lodged in the top of a downed tree. The blood in his veins turned to ice as he read the words printed in big white letters, "Franklin County Jail." The sign had been uprooted and could have traveled a long way, Ethan tried to tell himself. *It doesn't mean anything.* But a quick look around told Ethan they were, indeed, flying over his hometown.

Ethan stared through the fog as they passed over a large pile of white bricks surrounded by an open yard and a double-layered, gated fence. People who appeared as small as ants scurried in and out of the rubble, pulling out limp and lifeless bodies. A fire burned on one side, pushing back the rescuers with its licking flames. Ethan turned in his seat to peer out the window as they passed over. White specks dotted a section of grass. It took Ethan only a moment to realize the specks were white sheets covering what could only be dead bodies. Numbness crept down his limbs as the truth slammed into him like an unexpected punch to the gut.

My mother is dead.

She'd been in that building when the earthquake hit, trapped like a caged animal. And there was no way anyone had survived.

Ethan thought of his mother stuck in her cell, knowing what was happening and being powerless to save herself. Or maybe it'd happened quickly and she hadn't felt any pain. He hoped it had been the latter. No matter what his feelings ever were for her, she was still his mother, and he hoped she hadn't suffered.

Ethan squeezed his eyes shut as his mother's voice came to him as clear as if she were sitting in front of him. "I'm going away for a while," a much younger Elizabeth Reyes had said to a much younger Ethan. "But I'll see you again soon."

He'd been six at the time. No one told him much back then, but he heard things. Words like "addict" and "rehab" didn't mean anything to him, but the fear that clawed its way into him as he stood before his mother inside the cold and sterile-smelling clinic, he understood.

"Be brave for Grandma," she'd said with a wink. "She's not as tough as we are."

She'd stood then, suitcase in hand. "The next time you see me, I'll be better. I promise." There had been so much hope in her eyes that some of it had spilled over into Ethan's six-year-old heart.

"I'm going away for a while."

Ethan conjured a more recent image, her face older and lined with consequences. He imagined her saying those words to him now.

"The next time you see me, I'll be better. I promise."

Ethan gripped the seat beneath him and bit down on his lip until he tasted the metallic tinge of blood. He remembered their day at the zoo and the sound of her laughter as she'd wiped ice cream off his nose. He hoped he'd never forget that sound.

I love you, Mom, he said silently to her. *I'm sorry...*

And he was sorry—for so many things. Mostly he was sorry he'd failed her, that he hadn't been able to save her. She'd died a junky just as she'd always feared, scared and alone in a jail cell. The image punched him right in the chest, and Ethan felt something break inside him. The pressure that had been building over the past few days finally erupted, and Ethan doubled over in his seat. It hurt as badly as a bone cracking, but this was no bone. The chasm splintering through him ripped his heart in two.

Ethan turned away from the others as he knew he couldn't hold back the flood that was building. He didn't even want to. He knew if he tried to hold this in, it would gut him—rip apart his insides, leaving no part of him intact.

He'd hoped to do this quietly, with some semblance of dignity, but trying to reign in this heartache would be like trying to pour the river back into its shores with a bucket.

He was swept up by the current of his tears, tossed around and drowning. Just like the waters of the muddy Mississippi, the pain filled his lungs and pressed out all the air until he was fighting for breath.

Almost immediately, Camryn's hand tightened in his. He tried to pull away from her, but where could he go? In the next instant, she was out of her seat and sitting across his lap as her small arms snaked around his neck like a life preserver.

The pilot's words blasted through their headsets. "Ma'am, you must remain in your seat!"

Camryn yanked her headset from her head and tossed it to the floor. She gripped Ethan's shirt and clung to him until Ethan didn't know which of them needed saving.

Ethan returned her embrace, wrapping his arms around her waist. He buried his face in her neck and let himself be swept away.

Ethan stayed there with her even when no more tears would come. Camryn's shirt was soaked, and his throat was dry, but even then, he didn't move. After everything that'd happened, he couldn't find the strength to lift his head from her shoulder. The pilot had long since given up trying to prompt Camryn back to her seat. She sat rubbing circles on Ethan's back with one hand while the other remained tangled in his hair.

He didn't know how much time had passed before he felt a tap on his shoulder. Ethan looked up and was greeted by a pair of ghostly pale eyes outlined by a band of thick, black eyeliner. A delicate band of metal adorned her arched eyebrow.

He hadn't taken the time to look very closely at the two other passengers the night before, but their faces appeared much younger in the light of day.

Right now, the girl was gesturing to her headset and pointing down to the ground. "We're landing," she mouthed, then pointed to the seat next to him.

When he looked up at Camryn, her eyes were red and puffy. She'd been crying, too—for him or for her own loss, he wasn't sure. Even their pain seemed to be connected now. The second their eyes met, a new fear overwhelmed him, and he knew.

He couldn't lose her. He wouldn't survive it.

He lifted her gently from his lap and helped pull the straps back around her shoulders. Her eyes set in a glassy stare as the helicopter met the ground.

When the propellers had powered down, and the doors swung open, Camryn, Ethan, and the other passengers emerged from the helicopter. One look around told Ethan they weren't on an Air Force base. They weren't on land at all. They'd stepped out onto the flight deck of an aircraft carrier, surrounded as far as the eye could see by deep, blue water.

Ethan heard Camryn's sharp intake of breath as she stepped out behind him, and he put a protective arm around her. She was already trembling. What must she be thinking? If Ethan had to guess, she was imagining all the possible ways one might die in the middle of the ocean.

He wanted to tell her it would be all right, that they'd be back on dry land soon, but even if he'd been able to make himself say the words, he wouldn't have had time. A man in a green flight suit came rushing up to them. Ethan didn't know whether to be afraid or angry, but the man's friendly eyes and welcoming smile didn't seem menacing. He almost seemed happy to see them. Above the left breast pocket were the words "U.S. Navy," above the other, the name Ray. He passed a gaze over the four of them.

Ethan glanced again at the two other passengers. Almost identical in height and build, both were slender and tall for their age, which Ethan guessed to be about fifteen. Their faces held the same shape, long and angular, reminding Ethan of two Russian athletes. They could have passed for siblings, except for the stark contrast of their appearance. The girl wore black jeans, black combat boots, and a tight black crop top with the words "I regret nothing" smeared across the front. Her silver eyes seemed to glow against the rust-colored curls that blew loosely in the sea breeze.

The boy could've stepped out the front door of prep school, with a red polo, khaki pants, black, curly hair that was somehow flawlessly styled despite what they'd just been through, and eyes the brightest blue that Ethan had ever seen.

Their faces were drawn into the same distressed expression, but they showed no sign of comforting one another that you'd expect from siblings or even strangers who'd gone through something traumatic together. In fact, they seemed to be making a concerted effort to not look at each other at all.

Maybe they don't know each other. Maybe they're all alone.

Ethan was overcome by a desire to protect them all—the only adult among a group of helpless kids. Taking in the scene around him, his good friend, Anger, showed his ugly head again.

Who would bring four kids onto a warship in the middle of the ocean without their parents? How could anyone think that would be okay? These people had to be breaking at least a handful of laws, not to mention what they were doing to these poor kids.

Ethan's grip tightened around Camryn, who was trying to bury herself into his side as he stepped between the officer and the other two passengers.

"What's going on?" Ethan demanded of the officer as he drew closer. "Where are we?"

"Welcome aboard," the man said in response, not noticing Ethan's irritation. "All I'm authorized to tell you is that we're somewhere in the Atlantic Ocean. The captain will explain everything else you need to know."

Ethan felt Camryn take a step behind him and grab onto the back of his shirt sleeve. He looked around to see "U.S. Navy" written on the side of the other aircraft on the deck. They were just a group of kids, and they hadn't done anything wrong, so they shouldn't have anything to worry about, right?

But why would the captain of a warship want to meet with a bunch of kids? And why go through all the trouble to bring them here now when so much was happening on land?

Not seeing any other option and hoping to get some answers, Ethan took Camryn's hand and followed the man down a flight of steps onto a narrow catwalk then through a watertight hatch to the interior of the ship.

"First things first," Officer Ray began, nodding to the limping Camryn, "we need to get you to medical."

The man led them down a maze of narrow corridors lined with wires, pipes, mechanical boxes, and hoses. The place felt cold, all hard surfaces, fluorescent lighting, and metal. At the end of one corridor, he stopped and opened a door to a small room. "We can get you an X-ray in here. Hop up there on that exam table, and the doctor will be right with you."

Camryn and Ethan both peered inside the tiny room. A blood pressure cuff and some other random medical equipment that Ethan couldn't identify hung from the drab-colored walls. Neither of them made a move to step inside.

"How did you know she needed an X-ray?" Ethan asked, only then noticing the two other passengers weren't with them. "And what happened to the kids that came here with us?"

"Well, the medical information from the pick-up point was relayed to us through this handy gadget right here." The officer pulled out a small digital pad identical to the one Jay had used back in Kentucky. "And the other two passengers were not injured. They were taken to a stateroom where they'll be staying until we're ready to move you again."

Ethan narrowed his eyes. "What do you mean, move us again?" He glanced at Camryn, whose eyes were somewhere far away. He clenched his jaw and glared at the man. "We're not just some cargo you can move around wherever you want. She's in no condition to be bouncing around from place to place."

He gestured back to Camryn, who stared past the man with the same glassy expression she'd worn most of the night. "And somebody better tell me where we are. Why are we here? The last we were told, we were supposed to be landing in Virginia. She's lost her parents, for God's sake. How are we ever going to find them out here?" Ethan's voice had escalated as he spoke until he was almost yelling now.

The man's face grew ashen. "Oh dear," he said before forcing a smile back on his face, infuriating Ethan even further. "I will inform the captain of your concerns." He drew the curtain and disappeared down the long corridor.

Camryn and Ethan stood in stunned silence. *What is happening?* Ethan pushed his hair back out of his eyes. Not knowing what else to do, he turned and helped Camryn up onto the exam table. She followed his instructions without protesting. At least they could get this one thing taken care of.

Ethan put his hand on her arm. "Does it hurt?"

Camryn shook her head, but the pinched look on her face told him otherwise. Ethan's chest tightened with the realization that she hadn't said a word since they'd gotten into the helicopter the night before. Maybe she was still in shock. Maybe she was grieving. Maybe she was just processing it all.

He put his hand on her cheek and turned her face to his. He touched his forehead to hers and closed his eyes. "I wish I could help you," he opened his eyes and pulled back to look into hers. "The way you've helped me."

Her eyes focused briefly on his, but she didn't speak. Ethan wasn't even sure she'd heard him. He let out a long sigh, leaned back against the wall, and crammed his hands deep into his pockets. His lips twitched into a sad smile as his fingers wrapped around something small and familiar inside. He pulled out the ivory token and held it up for Camryn to see. It was his little plastic good luck charm, his only possession left in the world.

Ethan sat down on the only other seat in the room, put his elbows on his knees, and twisted it between his fingers.

"Yeah, that thing definitely doesn't work," Camryn said.

So relieved to hear her voice, the chair almost toppled to the floor as he stood and pulled her to him, squeezing a little harder than necessary.

Camryn laughed. "Okay, okay, I can't breathe."

He pulled away to look at her. "I don't know. I'm feeling pretty lucky right now."

"I'm sorry," Camryn said. "I'm trying—"

"God, don't apologize. We just got our asses handed to us."

Camryn laid her finger on the little token Ethan gripped in his hand. "You want to talk about it now?"

No. He most definitely didn't want to talk about it. But he knew Camryn did. And right now, that was all he had to give her.

When Ethan spoke, his voice was raspy with hesitation. "My mom gave this to me on my first day of kindergarten," he began. "I was nervous about starting a new school. She was doing good at the time, and she knew how scared I was." He stopped and cleared his throat. "She tucked this into my pocket and told me about the spirits of my ancestors and that they would watch out for me. She told me that as long as I had it with me, I would never be alone." He looked down at Camryn, whose eyes glistened with unshed tears.

"And it worked. For the longest time, I really did believe it was magic or something." Ethan coughed away his growing emotions. "So, before her first stint in rehab, I hid it in her suitcase...because I didn't want her to be alone."

He paused again. "I didn't see it for a while after that, and I was pretty sure she'd lost it. But it showed up again right before Grandma's funeral." He swiped a hand across his eyes. He wanted to stop talking, but the words were spilling out now, almost beyond his control. "We passed it back and forth a few more times. The last time she gave it to me was right before my last court date."

Ethan looked up at the ceiling. "God, that seems like such a long time ago, but it was just before all this happened." Ethan glanced up at Camryn. He hadn't told her any of this yet. "Vandalism. But it wasn't my first offense. I ended up getting like, a million hours of community service, but I should've gotten a lot worse."

Camryn finally spoke, her voice a hoarse whisper. "Well, maybe it is good luck, after all."

Ethan shrugged. "I haven't really believed that since I was a kid. You know, I've never admitted this, not even to myself, but I always just knew that whenever I held it, I felt a little bit closer to her. Even when I hated her so much." His voice faltered, and he turned away from Camryn, pushing his fists into his eyes.

At that exact moment, the curtain swung back, revealing a petite woman with a bright smile and hair so black it almost looked purple pulled into a tight bun on the back of her head. "Hello," she crooned, pretending not to see Ethan wiping his eyes. The woman wore the same green uniform and the same conspicuous smile as the officer before.

She walked over to Camryn and placed a light hand on her leg, just below her knee. "My name is Lailah. I'm the doctor here, and I'm going to take a look at your leg, okay?" She raised her eyebrows, waiting for Camryn's response.

Camryn gave a slow, silent nod, and the doctor began massaging the area on Camryn's leg, above and below the knee. The doctor closed her eyes, wrapping her hands around to the back of Camryn's leg. Camryn glanced back and forth between Ethan and the doctor and jumped when, a moment later, the doctor's eyes snapped open, the smile widening across her face. "There you go. Looks like you're going to be just fine."

"How can you tell? Wasn't she supposed to get an X-ray?" Ethan asked.

"No need." The doctor patted Camryn's knee before she turned to walk back toward the door.

Camryn tensed as if bracing for the pain at the woman's touch, but relaxed slowly and gave Ethan a bewildered look.

He crossed the room in one stride. "It doesn't hurt?"

"No, it's fine," Camryn said, swinging her leg off the side of the table. Camryn opened her mouth to say something to the doctor, but the woman was gone.

"Things are getting very weird around here," Camryn said.

Ethan stared out the door where the woman had just exited. *I couldn't agree more.*

THIRTY-FOUR

New York City, 2002

As soon as the door clicked shut behind Uriah, Arael sat bolt upright on the couch. In her in-between state of sleeping and wakefulness, his leaving the apartment hadn't quite registered to her. Now, with him on one side of the door and her on the other, she was filled with an unexplainable dread. Well, maybe not quite so unexplainable. There were some very bad people out to get them.

Arael shot up off the couch and grabbed her shoes. *You're overreacting,* she told herself. *Uriah is smart and capable, and you'll look like a crazy person running down the stairs after him.* But she couldn't stop herself. What if those thugs showed up again looking for their money? Uriah wouldn't even know who to look out for.

She had one hand on the doorknob, one shoe on, and was struggling with the other when she froze in her tracks.

Someone was in her apartment.

She hadn't seen anything—not a reflection in a window or a movement out of her periphery. She hadn't heard anything. No, she just felt it. An eerie, goose-pimply feeling that she wasn't alone. Arael forgot about her shoe and straightened. Before she even had a chance to turn, a giant hand came around her head and clamped over her open mouth.

"Quiet," a husky male voice said in her ear, "if you don't want to get hurt."

Arael's pulse quickened, and for a moment, she heard nothing but the sharp intake of her own breath between the man's clamped fingers. A dozen questions rushed through her mind: *Who is this? How did he get in? What does he want?* But none of them were pertinent to her immediate survival. She only needed to know how she was going to get out of this.

In Skylar's body, she was small and weak, and her celestial powers were virtually nonexistent. Never in the millennia of her existence had she ever been so vulnerable. She cursed herself and her decision to give up her powers in exchange for the "safety" of this body. What was she safe from, exactly? Being found by Apollyon? She'd learned quickly in her pretense of mortality that people in this realm were capable of just as much evil.

Think! Arael willed herself to calm down. *How are you going to get out of this?* Because there was no doubt, no matter how much bigger or stronger the intruder was, she would get away from him or die trying. The lone act of making that decision gave her strength. Not supernatural strength, but the innate, primal instinct to survive. Her body grew rigid, and her fingers clenched into fists. Determination bloomed within her, drawing her up, making her stronger.

Arael bit down hard on the hand covering her mouth. She'd seen a screwdriver around here somewhere, she just had to get to it and—

The man behind her stifled a yelp and spun her around. "Arael, it's me!" Michael gave her a frustrated shake then put a finger to his lips to silence her.

Arael blinked in stunned confusion. She didn't know which was worse, Apollyon finding her here or Michael.

The confidence that bolstered her a few moments ago disappeared. Seeing Michael standing in front of her now, she realized there was nothing she, as a mortal, could do against a fully armed and powerful Archangel, no matter how determined she'd been. She was trapped. She wasn't fast enough or strong enough, or even smart enough, she admitted to herself, to get away from him. And if she dared to leave the cover of Skylar's body, Apollyon's Trackers would be on her like lions on an injured wildebeest.

Besides, she couldn't leave Uriah.

Arael let out an audible groan. Uriah, who'd gone down to get bagels from the bakery, was about to unwittingly walk straight into danger.

She crumpled to the floor like a marionette whose strings had been cut, her failure a solid mass holding her in place. "I'll go with you," she said, squeezing her eyes shut. "I won't fight you. You can do what you want with me, just leave Uriah out of it. Anything he's ever done against you has only been under my orders. He is innocent."

By this time, Michael was at the window, using one finger to draw back the curtain ever so slightly. "Uriah is far from innocent," Michael said, "but he is not my concern right now. Now get up."

He pulled her back to her feet and dragged her toward the door. "Dagon has found you, and if you want to survive, you have to come with me." He put a hand on the knob, but even Arael, in her mostly human body, felt the dark energy of the underworld wafting up the steps, making the hairs prickle on her arms. Michael's words only then clicked into place. *Dagon has found you.*

Dagon. The Punisher.

Apollyon had sent Dagon after her? *Well, that's just great.* Would he and Michael fight over which of them would get to torture her first?

Michael pushed Arael back into the apartment. "You're going to have to lose that body." His eyes raked over her strange new form. "I can portal us out, but not with you in that state."

"There's no time," Arael said in a harsh whisper. "They're right outside the door." She almost laughed. Demons prowled at her door, and her immortal enemy stood right in front of her. Uriah was in danger, and she was powerless to help either of them.

"Right." Michael rubbed his chin. Arael jumped when a loud scratching sound rattled the door. The wood splintered but held. Michael must have some kind of protection around the apartment, she realized, or the demons would have been in already.

"On second thought, keep it," Michael said. "I have an idea."

"Michael!" Arael cried in quiet desperation, "Uriah is out there! We can't leave him here."

"Uriah is with Raphael," Michael said with no more care than if he were reporting the weather.

Arael's face froze in confusion. Michael's words wouldn't compute in her brain. "Why is Uriah with Raphael?"

Michael ran back to the window and looked down. His wrinkled brow and frustrated growl told her there must be more demons coming up the side of the building now.

Time seemed to stand still as Arael's fate came crashing down around her. Her eyes darted around the apartment. There was nowhere to run. Nothing else she could do. It was over. All her planning and preparation and precautions had all been for nothing in the end. Before the end of this day, she would be at the mercy of one of the two most powerful beings in all of creation—Michael or Apollyon.

Her fate with Apollyon would be horrendous. She'd seen him rip the heart out of a prisoner for much less. But apparently not before Dagon had his way with her first.

Her fate with Michael was less certain. The Righteous Ones weren't much for torture. But with the fate of the Founders still unknown, she couldn't get too excited at the prospects. Maybe Michael would just send her wherever he'd sent them. It was a big risk, but sure to be less agony involved than if Dagon got hold of her. And also…Uriah was with Raphael, whatever that meant, and sticking as close as she could to Michael was her only hope of ever seeing Uriah again. As much as she hated it, she was rooting for Michael to win this one.

"What are we going to do?" Arael asked. Again, Michael didn't answer. He just reached back, wrapped his massive arm around her waist, ran toward the window, and jumped.

Arael tensed, bracing for the screams of the people on the street below. Wouldn't they be able to see them? She was in a human body, for Christ's sake. And Michael was in his corporeal form. But Michael would never allow that, she realized as she noticed the warm pressure tightening around her—Michael's shield of protection wrapping around her like a comforting hug.

For a moment, they plummeted toward the ground, her hair blurring her vision as it whipped around her face. But then…they were soaring. Up, up, up into the morning sky above. Arael looked down at the scene below, surprised she could now see into the spirit realm with her very human eyes.

The black, lizard-like creatures that snaked the building like a hundred living vines whipped their heads around in unison when Michael and Arael shot out the window. Now they scurried back down again. Some took to the air, their shrill screeches filling the sky.

While the demons weren't restricted by the confines of gravity, they wouldn't be able to follow them. Such was the beauty of transporting. Unlike floating through the air in direct defiance of physics, Michael was manipulating interdimensional particles in a way that made it *seem* as if he was flying. In reality, he was folding space, like you would fold a piece of paper, accordion-style, to make two dots on the paper meet up. It was the best way to travel short distances within a dimension, like walking straight down a hallway instead of going out one door and back in another. Arael wasn't sure where the other dot on Michael's piece of paper was, but neither did the demons. To them, Michael and Arael had simply disappeared in the air over the street. That would buy them some time, but not much.

"Here we are," Michael said after a minute, then landed in a crouch on the ground, graceful as a cat, in front of a familiar building.

Arael blinked twice then collapsed to the ground.

Michael was over her in an instant, waving his fingers in front of her face. "What's wrong? Can you hear me?"

His faces faded in and out. *Wait, he should only have one face.* Arael shook her head and struggled to focus her eyes.

"What just happened?"

"It must have been the transporting," Michael answered. "It was foolish of me to do with you in that body. I had no idea how it would affect you."

Michael pulled Arael to her feet and spun her around, inspecting her from every angle. "Are you hurt?"

"What? No." Arael jerked her arm from his grasp, coming back to her senses. "Don't touch me."

"Arael, I know this must be hard for you to believe, but I'm trying to help you. I don't want to hurt you. I've never wanted to hurt you. And I don't want anyone else to hurt you, either."

Arael jerked her head toward the building in front of them. "So why did you bring me here?"

"This is the only place you will be safe for now. Until we figure out our next step. But we need to get inside." He placed a hand on her back to urge her toward the door. "This is going to be the first place they look."

Even with everything that just happened, Arael was still taken aback by the stark contrast of the centuries-old architecture backlit by the modern New York skyline. They were back at the church she and Uriah had visited the night before.

"Why bother?" Arael threw up her hands. "Why don't you just pull out your magic handcuffs and send me to…wherever it is you like to send us and be done with it?"

"I'm not sending you anywhere," Michael growled. "Can we continue this conversation inside?"

"And what about Uriah? Where is he?"

"Inside. Inside!" Michael said, more insistent this time, and Arael finally conceded. She'd be no help to Uriah if Dagon found her out here on the sidewalk.

Once inside, Michael seemed to relax. His shoulders dropped the tiniest bit, and the flow of words wasn't as hurried from his mouth. "Arael, I have tried to explain this to you so many times, but you could never—would never—hear me."

He looked down and shook his head. "I never thought you could hate me this much. I thought eventually you'd be able to hear me and really listen. Unfortunately, that has never happened. And now we've run out of time."

Before Arael could ask what he was talking about, Michael snapped his head to the front of the church.

"What? What is it?" Arael was afraid she already knew.

"A Tracker demon. He's outside."

"How do you know that? Isn't that the whole point of a Tracker demon?"

Michael opened his mouth to answer, then shut it quickly, as if just realizing who he was talking to. "It's not important, but they're everywhere now," he said, looking around as if he could see through the building to the outside. "They've signaled the others. They know you're in here."

"Oh, God." Arael tipped her head to the ceiling.

"I have an idea, but you're not going to like it."

"I wasn't expecting to like anything you had planned anyway. What is it?"

"We're going to have to portal out of here. But you can't do it with that body."

Oh...*oh.* Arael drug her head back and forth on her shoulders. "I–I can't do that."

"Yes, you can." Michael took her face in his hands. "It won't be pleasant, but I swear," he said with his bright blue eyes boring into hers, "I won't let anything happen to you."

Yeah right. I've certainly heard that before.

Arael drew in a breath and held it, keenly aware of every quickening beat of her heart, each one marking time, drawing her closer to whatever hell would come next. She knew what happened to the Nephilim who found themselves exposed in hallowed places such as this, and it was never pretty. Outside the protection of this very ordinary human body, she would just be Arael, a Fallen angel, standing undeniably on forbidden, holy ground.

"I'll open the portal first," Michael explained, "so we can get you out of here as quickly as possible once it's done."

Arael nodded her head a little too vigorously. "Okay. Just do it." She had no choice, really. Better to just get it over with.

As Michael turned from her, her thoughts flew to Uriah. Michael's words kept repeating in her mind. *Uriah is with Raphael.* With Raphael where? And why? How had Michael and Dagon come to find her at the same time? Could they be working together? Arael had so many questions, and so far, she hadn't gotten any answers. She just hoped that, if she was patient and stuck with Michael long enough, she would eventually discover the truth.

THIRTY-FIVE

Somewhere in the Atlantic Ocean
Present Day

T HANATOPHOBIA. The Diagnostic and Statistical Manual of Mental Disorders defined thanatophobia as the extreme or irrational fear of death. Other symptoms included increased anxiety, dizziness, sweating, heart palpitations, nausea, and stomach pains. Even though there were no guaranteed treatments, there were several effective options.

Camryn could tell anyone anything they wanted to know about the subject. She'd had this particular part of the DSM memorized since she was twelve.

Ever since she could remember, she'd been wary of the world around her, from the rushing waters that surrounded her town to the tiniest insects that crawled on the ground. But even though she saw danger in places where none existed, she couldn't say she feared being dead exactly. The thought of her body not existing in this world anymore didn't frighten her.

Camryn feared the things that could cause death. More specifically, a slow and painful death, like drowning, being crushed to death, venomous snake bites, or being eaten by a shark in the middle of the Atlantic after the aircraft carrier you just landed on sank to the ocean floor.

And while there still existed a possibility of each of those things happening, especially the latter, she'd looked death in the face twice in the past twenty-four hours and had beaten it both times. Now, even the one injury she'd sustained had been miraculously healed.

She was still swinging her leg back and forth, hopping around in different directions, waiting for the pain to return, but it didn't. She looked up at Ethan feeling triumphant.

"I don't care how weird it is," he was saying. "If you can walk, that's one less thing we have to worry about if we have to make a run for it."

"And where exactly are we going to run to?" Camryn asked, still testing out her knee. "I know this is going to sound strange, but I think we should hear them out." She stood and faced him. "So far, these people have done nothing but help us. We are in the middle of the ocean, and unless you know how to fly one of those helicopters up there, we really have no choice but to do what they say."

Ethan looked uncertain, but before he could argue, another uniformed man popped into the room. Like the doctor before him, he seemed to appear out of thin air.

"Camryn! Ethan! So glad you're here!" he said with a smile. "Now that you're all fixed up, let's get you settled in, shall we?"

Camryn took note of the annoyance on Ethan's face, but he just gave her a long glance that said, "Are you sure about this?"

Camryn nodded and gestured for the new officer to lead the way.

Ethan fell in step behind him, positioning himself between Camryn and the officer. Ethan looked back at her and gave her hand a reassuring squeeze, but for once, she didn't need reassuring.

It was strange, this new power she felt. She'd given death the middle finger and was now free from the crippling fear of it.

As they marched behind the man, Camryn prayed her newfound strength wouldn't leave her. Within the calmness, like a set of Russian nesting dolls, one egg-shaped doll nestled snuggly inside a slightly larger one, she found confidence, clarity, and a sense of control she'd never felt before. Was she naive to hope this could last?

Doing her best to prove that it could, she wouldn't allow herself to think of her parents or the impossible circumstances they'd found themselves in. That was sure to bring back the panic.

Instead, she forced herself to concentrate on the span of Ethan's shoulders in front of her and the grace with which he walked. His gait was already so familiar to her, like she could pick him out from a mile away just by the stride of his step. It'd freaked her out at first, this familiarity they shared, but she was getting used to it now.

He wasn't very big or muscular, but Camryn had seen him move. His wiry frame allowed him the agility of a fox, and even though he didn't have the bulky muscles of guys like Kyle, he was strong. His t-shirt clung to his skin, accentuating the definition of each muscle.

Heat rose in her cheeks as she remembered the way those muscles had moved under her fingers when he'd kissed her the night before. Camryn shook her head. This was not the time or place to be thinking about that.

She moved her gaze from Ethan's shoulders down to their hands, clasped in front of her. She smiled at the contrast of their skin, hers pale white and his, a golden bronze. Staring at their hands, she thought she could discern a slight rise in Ethan's heart rate, an uptick in his breathing.

He's upset.

But that was silly. How could she know that just from the touch of his hand? Camryn took a deep breath and blinked several times. Lack of food and sleep were muddling her thoughts.

"Okay, here we are," the officer said finally, sweeping his hand into what had to be the tiniest sleeping quarters Camryn had ever seen. The room was all metal—not unlike everything else on this ship—except for the mattresses on the two bunks that only held enough room between them for someone to crawl in and lie down. About eight square feet of floor space separated the door and the bunks, barely enough room for the two of them to stand.

Camryn had to appreciate the fact that she wasn't claustrophobic, but taking note of the tight look on Ethan's face, she had to consider that maybe he was. Maybe she'd been right about him being upset after all. The officer didn't seem to notice, though, as he told them to make themselves at home...or something. Honestly, Camryn wasn't listening. She just wanted him to leave.

He rambled on a few more minutes before he said, "I'll let the captain know you're here," then disappeared as fast as he'd come.

Camryn turned to Ethan, whose breathing was coming in short gasps. "What is it?"

"Nothing," he said in a pinched voice as he sat down on the side of the bed.

"Hey." Camryn lowered herself to sit beside him. She wanted to reach out to him, put a hand on his back...something...but decided against it. She didn't know what she would do if he pulled away from her. "There are doctors here," she said in a gentle voice. "I'm sure if there's something you need, they can get it for you."

"I said I'm fine," Ethan snapped, giving her a glimpse of the scared boy she'd first seen, wet and cold, in the woods a few days ago. Ethan gripped the knees of his shorts and rocked almost imperceptibly back and forth on the side of the bed. Camryn thought she now knew how her parents must have felt all those times she'd had an "episode," and they'd been powerless to help her.

"I know what you're doing," Camryn said. "I've been in your shoes lots of times, trying to play it cool when you're actually losing your shit inside." She watched beads of sweat spring up on his forehead. "And I know how well that doesn't work, so please don't push me away." She reached out and placed a tentative hand on his arm. "Let me help you."

When her hand touched his skin, he drew in a sharp breath and closed his eyes, but he didn't pull away.

"I hate this," he said, his voice wrought with agony. "I thought I could control it. I gave my mom such a hard time, but I'm just like her."

"Hey!" Camryn scolded. "Needing meds for a disorder and needing drugs for an addiction are two completely different things." She realized then that his hands were shaking, too.

"Speaking of meds, when's the last time you had them?"

"Day before yesterday, I think. What does that have to do with anything?"

"Because I don't think you're having a panic attack. I think it's just withdrawals."

Ethan choked out a breath. "I don't see how that's any better."

"Sure, it is. What you're experiencing now is probably as bad as it's going to get. You just need to distract yourself. Think about something else." She thought about how he'd helped her back in the medical bay. "We could talk about your mom."

"I don't want to talk about my mom."

"Okay, bad idea. You could tell me about your grandmother. What was she like?"

"My grandmother?" Ethan stood abruptly and started to pace. "She was a lot like you, actually. Stubborn and impulsive." He almost smiled. His nostrils flared, and he chewed his lower lip, but Camryn thought she was getting through to him.

"She loved you a lot."

"She practically raised me. She used to tell me stories about the reservation where she grew up." Ethan threw a glance up to the ceiling. "I wish I would've actually listened."

"Maybe we could go there someday, find your family. You're sure to have more family there, right?"

A look of surprise crossed his face as if the thought had never occurred to him. "Yeah, I guess I probably do."

She wanted to go to him, to put her arms around him and press her cheek against his chest...so she did. This new Camryn wasn't holding anything back. All her fears of rejection and humiliation that had kept her paralyzed her whole life were gone. She no longer cared how it would look or what he might think of her. She just wanted to be close to him.

She squeezed him and smiled when his arms wrapped around her and his heart began to slow against her cheek. Even with everything that was happening, she felt a little lighter as she thought of everything she had to be thankful for.

For one, she was alive.

More importantly, Ethan was alive.

And most important of all, there was no immediate threat to their lives. That had to count for something, right? Surely the force that guided the universe wouldn't allow them to come this far just to let them fail now.

As they stood there holding each other, a loud rap at the door made them both jump.

Before either of them could answer, the door swung open to reveal a giant of a man in a green flight suit standing on the other side, so tall and broad that his chest was almost the only thing visible through the open doorway. Camryn wondered how he maneuvered through the tight corridors of the ship.

He ducked into the room, his gaze sweeping from Camryn to Ethan, changing from warm and welcoming to harsh and cold.

"Hello, you two," he said without taking his narrowed eyes off Ethan. He held out a large hand to each of them. "I'm the

239

captain here. I heard you had some questions, as would be expected. I will do my best to answer them, but first—" his gaze still pinning Ethan to the wall, "—I have some questions for you."

For one small moment, Camryn let her fear creep back in like an icy claw in her chest. This man was trying to appear friendly, just as everyone else on the ship had since their arrival. But he was clearly holding back some feelings, specifically toward Ethan. Was he angry at him? For what?

Before Camryn could formulate any especially terrifying scenarios, Ethan drew up beside her. In a matter of seconds, she witnessed a transformation that she'd seen only once before— when he'd faced off against Kyle at his party the night before. Instead of being frightened or intimidated, as would any rational human being on the planet, the man's ire seemed to embolden Ethan. Ethan sidled up to the man, who was easily twice his size and offered the same icy glare right back to him.

"I don't think that's how this is going to work," Ethan said. "I know we don't have to answer any of your questions without a representative present. You brought four minors onto a military warship in the middle of the ocean against our will and without anyone's consent. I'm sure so many things about this whole situation are illegal. And unless you want every news crew investigating the Navy for human trafficking, you're going to be the one answering questions. Then you're going to find her parents. That's what's going to happen."

"Ah, yes." The captain turned and gave a knowing look to a man they somehow hadn't yet noticed standing in the doorway. The man nodded back as if to say, "I told you so."

Camryn and Ethan's mouths dropped open.

"You!" Camryn said.

It was Jay, the National Guardsman who'd helped them into the helicopter.

Ethan pointed a finger at the two men. "Someone needs to tell us what is going on here right now."

"What?" the captain said as if this were a perfectly normal occurrence. "Him?"

"Yes, him! We just left him back in Kentucky with the National Guard! Now he's here? On a Navy ship?"

"Well, yes," the captain said. "He's a floater of sorts. He helps out wherever he is needed."

The two teenagers shared dumbfounded expressions. "I don't know much about the military, but I'm pretty sure that's not actually a thing," Camryn shot back.

"Ah, well." The captain shrugged as if he were bored with this particular conversation and stepped toward Camryn with outstretched hands.

Ethan stepped between them. "You're not touching her."

"I'm sorry," the captain said, backing up. "I didn't mean to frighten you." He lowered his hands and pulled out a penlight similar to the one Jay had used on them back in Kentucky. He leaned forward and flashed the light first into Camryn's, then Ethan's eyes. They both drew back from him, but he'd apparently seen enough. He put the penlight back in his pocket and looked back at Jay.

"It seems you were correct." His gaze swung back toward Ethan. "That does explain a few things."

Jay's proud smile evaporated when he saw the scowl on the captain's face.

"How could this have happened?" the captain asked with forced calm in his voice.

"I–I don't know, sir," Jay stammered. "The human brain is—"

"Do not lecture me on the human brain!" the captain shouted. "I know more about the human brain than you ever will. I want to know why I wasn't notified."

Ethan's hand snaked around Camryn's waist while she backtracked in her mind, trying to remember the layout of the ship, thinking they might have to make a run for it after all.

"I assure you, sir, you knew as soon as we did."

"So, you didn't know?" The captain stalked toward Jay. "All this time, and you had no idea?"

Jay looked down at the ground. "Well, sir, some had their suspicions, but orders were—well—we didn't think it would be a problem."

Veins popped from the captain's neck as he roared, "You didn't think it would be a problem?" He gestured back toward the two kids cowering in the corner. "What are we supposed to do with them? There is no way these two children can complete this mission!" By this point, he was towering over Jay, screaming. "Do you understand what this means for humanity?"

"There's always a restoration, sir," Jay offered in a trembling voice.

"That could take weeks," the captain said through his teeth. "Or even months. And we don't have that much time."

"I'm sorry," Camryn heard herself say, "but I think you have us mistaken for someone else. We're just kids. Just simple, ordinary teenagers who go to high school and vandalize private property—"

"Hey!" Ethan interrupted.

Camryn shot him an apologetic glance. "We got separated from my parents during the earthquake, and we really need to get back to them. Whoever you think we are, or whatever you think we can do for you...or humanity," she added with a gulp, "I assure you, we're not those people."

Jay gave her a pleading head shake, as if the more she talked, the more trouble he would be in, and from the look on the captain's face, that was probably the case.

"Just ordinary teenagers, you say?" The captain glanced back and forth between them. "Let me ask you, have you ever done

242

anything you couldn't explain? Or seen things other people couldn't see?"

Camryn thought of her visions of the town flooding and Ethan's shadow monsters.

"No," they both said in unison.

The captain pinched the bridge of his nose then began shoving Jay toward the door.

"Give us a moment, please." He pushed Jay out into the hallway and closed the door.

"What the hell was that all about?" Ethan asked when he and Camryn were alone.

Camryn took two steps and put her ear to the door. "I don't know," she said. "But something weird is definitely going on."

"Weird?" Ethan asked, pacing again and running a hand through his hair. "More like insane."

Camryn heard only muffled voices at first. Then silence. She put a finger to her lips, but still heard nothing. Just as she put a hand on the knob, preparing to peer out down the hallway, the door swung open, knocking her back against the wall. The captain stalked back into the room alone.

"Okay, this is what we're going to do," he said, pointing a finger at Camryn, who hadn't moved. "We're going to find your parents."

Then, turning to Ethan, he asked, "What about you? Any parents you need us to find?"

Ethan appeared taken aback by the question, so Camryn answered for him. "No, but there is something you can do for him," she said. "He needs Xanax."

When the captain cocked a questioning eyebrow at her, she added hastily, "He has a prescription. He lost them in the river. We can wean him off of them, but he needs enough to get him through the week." The captain opened his mouth to speak, but Camryn cut in, "And make sure it's the good stuff, not any of that generic crap."

"He doesn't need—" the captain started, but clamped his lips together. "Fine," he said, jaw clenched. "Two parents, ten Xanax. Anything else?"

They both stared at the man, afraid he would tell them this was all a big joke and he couldn't help them after all.

"No? Good! Great! Let me just get right on that," he huffed, then turned and stomped out of the room.

As soon as the captain was gone, Jay entered, carrying an overflowing tray of assorted foods. Mostly meats, fruits, and vegetables, but Camryn would've eaten bugs at that point if that's what he'd brought. She hadn't expected to have much of an appetite, but knowing the entire Navy would be looking for her parents, her body's systems came fiercely back to life. She clutched her stomach as it gave a loud rumble.

"Sorry about him," Jay said, seeming not to hear her growling tummy. "He's a little cranky today."

"What is his deal?" Ethan asked.

Jay shrugged. "He's been a little overworked lately." He set the tray down on the bed.

Camryn grabbed an apple and tore into a chicken leg. "Where are my horses?" she asked.

Jay looked up at her, startled. "What?"

"If you're here, where are my horses? I left them with you."

"Oh, yes, they're fine," Jay said, smiling. "I promise you, they are in the finest of care." He raised his right hand as if taking an oath. "I swear."

His confident smile put Camryn's mind at ease. She was glad Jay had shown up, actually. It was nice to get an update on the animals who'd saved their lives, but as much as she hated to admit it, her horses weren't her biggest concern at the moment. He had been the first person to show any interest in helping to find her parents, and whatever he'd said to the captain in the hall must've worked. Whatever reason for him being here, she was glad.

Ethan came around the bunk and slapped Jay on the shoulder. "Jay," he said. "You seem like a good guy." Jay smiled as if the opinion of this teenage stranger meant a lot to him. "I need you to tell us where we are and why we're here."

"Oh, no." Jay shook his head. "Are you trying to get me killed?"

"Killed?" Camryn's head shot up from the tray of food.

"No, not literally killed, but you know…in big trouble. I can't tell you anything. But look." He pulled out two cookies from underneath some broccoli on the tray. "I snuck these in for you."

Ethan snatched a cookie from Jay's fingers. "Gee, thanks, Jay," he said with an exaggerated roll of his eyes.

"Look, I'm sorry. I really can't. Not just because of him." Jay looked back at the door. "But because I know you wouldn't be able to understand it all right now."

"What does that mean?" Camryn asked.

"Nothing. Forget I said that," Jay replied, backing toward the door. "I have to go, but if I can offer some advice, just try to get some rest. Really." He nodded from the hall. "Go to sleep. I promise things will make more sense when you wake up."

"Wait…Jay," Camryn called after him, but the man was already gone.

THIRTY-SIX

New York City, 2002

Michael drew his sword ceremoniously and pointed it at the spot between the pews in front of him. *"Aperta sunt in nomine Domini,"* he said in a low, reverent voice.

Arael bristled at hearing the old language again. She'd once thought it an elegant and beautiful tongue, but now, she couldn't understand a word of it. None of the Fallen could—yet another thing lost to them after the Fall.

Whatever he'd said must have worked, though, because the view in front of her began to change. She still saw the pulpit and the sun shining through the stained-glass windows, but now they shimmered as if they came to her through a sheer mist. A soft circle of iridescent light appeared, first as small as a fist, then growing to the size of the angel beside her, a perfectly-sized passageway.

It all happened so fast, but the whole procession of it sent a pang of something Arael didn't quite recognize right through her. Was it wistfulness? Nostalgia? She hadn't had time to quite put her finger on it before the portal opened, and an unfamiliar angel stepped through.

"This is Nathanael," Michael explained. "He's going to take Skylar's body back to the hospital once it's done."

Arael nodded in greeting and offered a tight smile.

"Okay," Michael said. "Now comes the fun part." He pulled what looked like a set of metal bracelets from inside his robes, each about three inches wide and bound together in the middle like iron, glowing gold with Heavenly Fire. "I'm going to need you to put these on."

Arael grimaced. "Is that really necessary?"

Michael shot her an incredulous look. Arael huffed but reluctantly held out her hands.

"As you know, this situation is unprecedented," Michael began. "I'm not sure what's going to happen—"

"Stop talking." Arael closed her eyes. "Just do it."

Michael cleared his throat and shook his head as if to say, "Okay, you asked for it," then snapped the cuffs around her wrists.

Immediately, Skylar's body began to seize around Arael like a cocoon ridding itself of its pupa. Michael grabbed her—or Skylar rather—and gently laid her now lifeless body on the floor.

That part Arael had been prepared for. She'd separated from a few human hosts in the past thirty years and knew the unnatural ritual of it. What she wasn't prepared for, standing inside this holy place—inside the house of Elohim—was what would happen next.

For a moment, nothing happened. Arael, in her celestial form, stared in alarm at Skylar's body as if she were a puppy Arael had witnessed being hit by a car. She had never met the real Skylar, the girl who'd been so strung out on heroin that the only solution she'd seen to her problems was throwing herself off a bridge.

No, she hadn't known that girl.

So why did she feel, at that moment, like she'd lost a friend? Arael was reminded of the pain she'd felt on the battlefield during the First War when Uriah's soul had separated from hers. She and Skylar hadn't shared a soul, but they'd shared a body, and somehow that was just as intimate.

She might have knelt down and brushed the curls from the girl's face. She might have whispered words of farewell to her before she was whisked away by Nathanael. She might have done any number of things if she'd been able. As it was, though, she was frozen—paralyzed by an unseen power that had begun swirling around her like a hurricane.

She'd heard the Nephilim tell of being cast out of human hosts in holy places such as this. All their accounts were the same. They told of being sucked into a vortex, swirled around in a dark tunnel, then dispensed from the grounds like a cannonball from a cannon.

Arael could feel it now, swirling, tugging—something from the outside trying to pluck her up. But she was being held at the bottom of the tornado, presumably by the cuffs around her wrists, the power in them holding her in place.

For a moment, she felt no pain, just the uncomfortable sensation of being pulled in two. Then a tingling started in her feet. Arael wanted to shake them, but she couldn't move. As the tingling crawled up her legs, it grew hotter and hotter, turning from a numb warmth to intense heat to scorching fire, licking at her legs, her thighs, her stomach.

Oh God.

She wanted to cry out, but even her vocal cords were paralyzed. In seconds, her whole body screamed through the invisible flames.

Michael and the other angel had their backs to her, walking toward the front of the church. Michael appeared to be giving instructions to Nathanael, who carried Skylar's body in his arms.

Please, Michael, please turn around.

What is he doing? She screamed inside her own head and felt like a fool for trusting him again. She cursed him a hundred times before she became lost inside the pain. Just like being back on the battlefield, the Heavenly Fire burned through her body.

But this time, the Heavenly Fire wasn't just doing a job. It was angry.

Arael screamed, but no sound came out. The heat billowed around her, lifting her up, swirling around her in a crazed frenzy. Her hair, even though she smelled it singe, floated around her face as if she were submerged in water, not engulfed in a blazing inferno.

Not a single inch of her body was spared. The heat pressed in on her face and squeezed the breath from her lungs. She saw the skin of her hands turning black and flaking away, smelled the putrid aroma of burning flesh so pungent she didn't think the memory of it would ever leave her nostrils.

In her mind, she was moving, flailing, jumping, running, screaming, but in reality, standing behind Michael in the church, she was as still and quiet as the tomb the Heavenly Fire had become.

Arael didn't know how long she stayed like that—it couldn't have been long—but just when she thought she couldn't bear it any longer, that she would surely lose her mind from the excruciating torment, she felt a hand on her arm, then under her legs and lifting her up. Not just in her mind this time, she was actually being lifted off the ground, carried by some unseen force.

She couldn't even wonder what was happening. Her brain couldn't think of anything other than the pain.

Just fire and pain and more pain.

And then it was gone. So swiftly that it might never have been there at all. Her paralysis left her, and out of her mouth came a blood-curdling scream, finally able to escape the confines of her throat. As soon as her limbs were back in her control, she frantically ran her hands over her body, her hair, her face, gasping for clean, cool breaths. There were no burns, no soot, no evidence of the hell she'd just endured. Outwardly, it was as if nothing had happened.

She then became aware of Michael standing in front of her. He stood back from her, his eyes darting over her body, looking just as frantic as she felt. His arms fanned at his sides, and his brows squeezed so close together they could have been one. He was saying something, she realized, but she couldn't make out any words.

She held up a finger to him and sucked in a few more breaths of blessedly clean air. Michael extended a tentative hand and laid it on her shoulder. A simple gesture, but so much power flowed from that hand. Warmth spread down her body. *Calm* was the only word she could think, as if he were pushing it into her mind over and over, peace oozing down her body with each pulse of the word. *Calm. Calm. Calm.*

"Well...now we know what happens," she said in a shaking voice when she could speak.

"Are you okay?" he asked, his voice dripping with relief. "Are you hurt?"

"No, no. I'm fine." She waved him off stoically but realized...she *was* fine. Completely fine. She would never forget the pain she'd just endured, but free from that place, there would be no lasting effects.

Arael looked around then and realized where they were. The valley was blanketed with the purple darkness of night, but the moon still shone overhead. Olive and cypress trees dotted the grassy meadow around them. To her left loomed the granite face of a mountain. Her mountain, the small peak of the Alborz, her first home after losing her place in Heaven.

"No one is here," Michael said. "No one else has been assigned since you left, and I've sent Clarion away for a while. It's just the two of us for now."

Arael leaned away from him, unsure of his intentions.

"This territory was a pity assignment from the beginning," she said, trying to sound casual. "I doubt Apollyon has given it a second thought since I left."

"You're probably right."

"What do you want, Michael?" Arael asked wearily. "You say you don't want to hurt me, yet you're dragging me around in handcuffs. What's going on?"

Michael gestured to her hands. "This is just a precaution. I will remove them once you've made your decision."

"My decision about what?"

For the first time Arael could ever remember, Michael looked uncertain. He spoke with caution as if she were a wild animal who might attack.

"Arael, I want you to come home with me."

THIRTY-SEVEN

Somewhere in the Atlantic Ocean
Present Day

"I ate way too much." Camryn leaned her head back against the bed. She and Ethan sat on the floor of their bunk room, the tray of food between them.

"Oh my God…" Ethan groaned. "I don't think I've ever tasted food so good."

"Yeah," Camryn agreed. "It was almost too good. Now all I want to do is crawl in that bed and sleep for about two days."

"Mmm," Ethan grunted from beside her. She looked over and saw that his head was resting back on the side of the bed, and his eyes were closed. She scooted closer and put her head on his shoulder. Maybe she would just sleep right here.

Ethan leaned his head onto hers and rubbed his nose in her hair.

Camryn smiled and glanced up at him. She'd been ready to swat his arm, but all airs of playfulness vanished when she turned her face to his. The smile fell from Ethan's lips, and he sucked in a sharp breath. Camryn wasn't entirely sure what was happening, but the effect was instantaneous. Her heart hammered in her throat.

Ethan skimmed his fingers down her arm, leaving a sizzling trail in their wake. Camryn's stomach did a flip. He'd only touched her like this once before, and she still wasn't used to the explosion of sensation that happened where his skin met hers.

"Ethan…"

"Yeah?"

"Uh, nothing, I just—" She looked down as her cheeks burst into flames. "I don't know."

Ethan lifted her chin and searched her face. Agony seeped from every facet of his features as if he had an itch he was trying desperately not to scratch.

"Can I kiss you?" he whispered as his fingers grazed her cheek. She leaned into his palm and closed her eyes. "It's okay if you say no. I know you're upset, and we don't really know what's going on, but…" He brought his forehead down to meet hers. "Even with everything that's happened, I can't stop thinking about last night."

His lip pulled into that bashful grin that never failed to melt her insides. "I mean, it could have been a fluke, but that was the best damn kiss I've ever had."

A nervous laugh escaped Camryn's throat. He was right. She should be upset…about everything. But being this close to him, alone in this tiny room, it was easy to let herself believe they were the only two people in the world.

She drew upon her newfound confidence and leaned forward, pressing her lips to his. She let him take the lead at first, fearing she'd do something wrong. But as he kissed her, his lips gliding easily over hers, she came alive again, just as she had the night before, some primal force inside her taking over.

She brought her hand up and clutched Ethan's shirt, pulling him closer, kissing him harder. He seemed to lose control the same moment she did, biting her lip and twisting his hands in her hair.

She raised herself up and in one swift motion, was sitting over him. He looked up at her in surprise, but she brought her mouth down hard on his again, losing herself in the taste of him.

His hands hesitated under the hem of her shirt, burning her again with his touch. She knew he was holding back, and she knew why, but she didn't want to be treated like a porcelain doll. She pulled her face away from his just long enough to offer him a quick nod.

"It's okay," she said before lowering her lips back to his. She wanted him to know how strong she was, that whatever he wanted to do, she could take it. He squeezed her hips with so much force, Camryn was sure she'd have bruises, but she didn't care. It somehow egged her on, knowing he was feeling the same frenzied power.

"Ahh!" It was Camryn who broke away this time, grabbing at her head, overcome by dizziness.

"What is it? What's wrong?" Ethan panted, but Camryn couldn't answer. She pulled herself up and sat down hard on the floor beside him.

"Camryn, what is it? Are you okay?" He managed to ask again before he fell back against the bed. "Whoa," he groaned.

"Yeah," Camryn agreed. "Whoa."

"What's happening?" Ethan asked, but Camryn had no time to answer before his eyes closed and his head landed in her lap.

The food. We've been drugged. She looked down at an unconscious Ethan, panic just beginning to creep back in when her eyelids fluttered shut.

THIRTY-EIGHT

Alborz Mountains, 2002

Arael replayed Michael's words in her head. *"I want you to come home with me."*

Surely she'd misunderstood. "What do you mean, home?"

"You heard me. No questions asked. I can take those cuffs off you, and you can come back home with me, back to Elohim. You will take your rightful place beside me as an Archangel in the Septitude. It will be like you never left."

Arael would have laughed in his face if he hadn't looked so serious. "I don't understand. I've spent the last three thousand years trying to kill you."

"I haven't forgotten," he smiled.

"Yet you are willing to give me a pass for that? Why me and no one else?"

"Arael." Michael looked at her as if she should already know the answer. "Because you aren't supposed to be here."

Arael stiffened. She could remember a time, in the beginning, when those words were all she'd wanted to hear. For Michael to admit his mistake. To go home. To go back to the way things used to be. But so much had happened. Did she even want that anymore? Could it ever be the same?

She couldn't even consider it, but, nevertheless, found herself asking, "What about Uriah?"

Michael pinched his lips together and shook his head. "Uriah is a different situation."

"How?" Indignation ignited inside her. "We were both working for you. We were both supposed to be protected. How is it different?" Arael was almost shouting now, but she didn't care.

"It's...complicated."

"Let me tell you what isn't complicated," Arael said, bringing her voice back under control. "I go nowhere without him."

Michael, who'd been doing a good job of giving her space, lurched toward her, grabbing her by the shoulders. Arael clenched her teeth as his fingers dug into her skin.

"Don't be hasty in this decision, Arael. You have no idea how hard I've worked to make this happen. This is my fault, I understand that. And I have pled your case to Elohim from the beginning, even when you were actively trying to kill me. It wasn't until you walked away from Apollyon that He began to consider my request. Do you have any idea how rare this opportunity is?"

Michael gave her a gentle shake. "This is a one-time offer, Arael. Don't let your loyalty to Uriah keep you from happiness. Especially when his loyalties lie elsewhere."

Arael forced the air in and out of her lungs before she spoke again. "You do not get to question Uriah's loyalty to me. You don't know anything about him."

Michael loosened his grip but didn't let her go. "I know more than you think."

Michael's earlier words crept back into her mind. "Uriah is with Raphael," and she finally put her finger on what had been bothering her. Raphael was a Healer. He wasn't normally involved in Michael's processes of justice. Arael could only think of one reason Raphael would be involved in this.

"Is Uriah hurt?" Arael accused. "What have you done to him?"

"We're not getting past this, are we?" Michael huffed. "No, Uriah is not hurt. But he is in prison. I didn't want to have to tell you this, but it was Uriah who led Dagon to you. If you want to know who is responsible for blowing your cover, it was him."

Arael shook her head. She understood now why Michael hadn't wanted to remove the cuffs. If she'd been free, she would have killed him with her bare hands.

"How dare you," she growled. "Even if he wanted to do such a thing, it would be impossible. We were *qanima*. He could never betray me like that."

"Anything is possible with the right motivation." Michael's face lost its harsh edges and turned back to pleading again. "Think about it, Arael. You've managed to hide for thirty years. You've stayed in the same place and changed bodies only a few times, all undetected. But as soon as Uriah shows up, so does Dagon. That can't be a coincidence."

"You know who else showed up the same time as Dagon?" Arael glared at him. "You." She thrust her cuffed hands toward Michael again. He grabbed them and jerked her toward him, so close she could see the orange flecks in his blue eyes.

"Don't be a fool! How could you think—" he began but seemed to reconsider the question. "Just think about this. If you stay here, you will die. You will be running and hiding all alone. Until Dagon finds you. And I assure you, Dagon *will* find you. And Uriah will still be in prison. There is nothing you can do about that. With him out of the way, you can be safe—have the entire host of Heaven behind you. Live the life you were created for."

Michael waited another beat before finally removing the cuffs from her hands. Arael rubbed her wrists while she glowered at him, all the pent-up anger and hatred for her captor exuding from every pore on her body.

She needed to get away from him. She needed time to think, and she couldn't do it with him staring at her like he was. But she wasn't stupid. She knew Michael had to have some kind of protection around them. Otherwise, Dagon's army would have found her by now.

"I need time," she said.

"I'm afraid we don't have much of that. As you know, my shield only keeps them from picking up your scent and my aura from the air. It doesn't keep them from showing up here. They will find us by process of elimination eventually."

"I know," she said. "I just need a minute."

Michael finally nodded. "Stay on this side of the mountain," he said, but Arael was already running.

Arael hadn't felt her own physical body in decades. It felt good now, like a familiar winter coat—confining but comfortable. In her physical form, sprinting through the grass, arms pumping at her sides, Arael fought to clear her mind.

Michael's words about purpose and new opportunities volleyed against images of eons-worth of battles, injuries, floods, and most vividly of him hovering over her with his sword stabbed into her chest. Feelings of hope and betrayal wrestled for a place in her heart.

Arael didn't know what else to do. So she ran on, chest rising and falling. She wanted to feel the burn in her lungs and the sting of her feet. More than anything, pain brought her into focus. Right now, she wanted to break things. She wanted to scream. So she pushed herself harder.

When she reached the base of the mountain, she kept running. Up the path, around trees, hurdling boulders until the terrain became too steep for her to propel herself with her feet, and she began pulling herself up with her arms.

Yet the clarity she so desperately chased still evaded her. The higher she climbed, the angrier she became. How could Michael fathom in the farthest reaches of his imagination that she would ever go back with him? And leave Uriah? How deranged did he have to be?

But what else could she do? Her cover was blown. The only foolproof plan had been ruined. She had nowhere to go. On the other hand, she would rather live her life as Michael's prisoner than to ever work with him again. He had accused Uriah of unthinkable things and put him in prison. And she was just supposed to go along with that?

She climbed with the stealth and grace of a panther, remembering every cliff and crag from her time living there. Blood oozed from her feet and hands as she approached the summit, but she hardly noticed. She pulled herself up onto the rock, a dizzying height for any mortal, and stood with her hands on her hips, chest heaving. Every muscle in her body screamed, and tears threatened to spill from her eyes.

This was an impossible decision. She couldn't go with Michael, and she couldn't stay here.

But the heaviest of all the weights pulling her down—she couldn't save Uriah. If he was in prison, she had no authority to release him, and she couldn't break him out. She could plead his case, but that would require a lot of groveling, and she didn't think Michael would be in any mood to grant her any favors after she refused his offer. Maybe accepting it was the only way.

Arael collapsed to the ground, letting her head sag between her shoulders. She was calculating her odds of just sulking there until one of them found her—just let fate decide—when an unexpected sound reached her ears.

She stood, her own problems momentarily forgotten, and looked around. She hadn't laid eyes on this terrain since before the flood, but nothing had changed much. The mountain was still a huge, rocky mass dotted here and there with sparse vegetation.

To one side, she now saw roads and tiny villages, to the other lay the Caspian Sea. That side of the mountain held nothing but steep slopes and jagged cliffs, some rising thousands of feet in the air. It remained unreachable by normal human efforts. But she'd heard, over the years, of people who'd tried—thrill-seeking hikers or stupid teenagers who'd attempted to conquer her cliffs.

Arael knew Clarion watched out for them as best she could, but Clarion wasn't here now.

The sound reached her again, so faint that even she, with her celestial hearing, barely heard it. But she knew without a doubt what it was—a human cry for help. She looked back at Michael, still standing in his spot in the valley, close enough to see her but far enough for her to feel alone.

She scanned the mountainside, looking for the tell-tale aura of a human, but saw nothing. Then again, if the person were scared enough, his aura would be dark. In the night, she might not see it if he were far enough away.

The sound came again, this time more pronounced. She was sure now. Some careless hiker had gotten stuck somewhere down there.

Or...this could be a trap, she thought. But her conscience insisted that she check it out.

She contemplated asking Michael for help, but stubbornly, maybe stupidly, that was the last thing she wanted to do. She raised a hand to Michael, indicating she would only be a moment before she took off to investigate the sound. He shook his head at her, but she was already moving.

THIRTY-NINE

Somewhere in the Atlantic Ocean
Present Day

*H*mmm... A soft humming broke through the wall of Camryn's unconsciousness. It lasted a few seconds before it disappeared.

A few minutes later—or it could have been hours—it came again, this time a little louder.

The next time she heard it, the humming had turned into muffled words, coming to her through cotton balls stuffed in her ears.

"Camryn. I need you to wake up." The voice was clearer now, pulling her up through the murky haze. She recognized her name, but not the voice who spoke it. Her skin tingled with the same prickly warmth that she remembered from spring days lying in the sun.

Reluctantly, Camryn pried her eyes open and sat up, squinting into the bright light of midday. She looked up, confused, through a canopy of trees in full bloom. She was outside, surrounded by a sea of green grass and beautiful flowers.

Camryn snapped her head around to the left and right. *I know this place.* She'd woken in the woods behind her house. But how had she gotten there? And how was it so green and beautiful? She hadn't seen it this vibrant in months.

Camryn sniffed the air as a strange scent drifted past. She'd never been to the ocean but recognized it as the salty aroma of the sea.

The voice called again, urgent this time. "Camryn!"

She whipped her head toward the sound. A man sat smiling beside her with dark hair and warm, inviting eyes. He had the casual appearance of an ordinary man except for the ancient Roman battle armor that adorned his body.

He definitely had *not* been there a few moments ago.

Camryn scrambled backward away from him, but just like in a paralyzing nightmare, her body wasn't moving from its spot.

The man held his palms out toward her. "Don't be afraid," he said, and immediately, Camryn wasn't. Her fear vanished, mysteriously under the control of this man. Her heart slowed, and her thoughts cleared, but she still didn't know how she'd gotten there. The last thing she remembered, she'd been on a helicopter heading to Virginia and her town—this place—had been underwater.

"Who are you? How did I get here?"

"You can call me Sam," the man said. "And here," he gestured around and shrugged, "is a suggestive place."

Camryn narrowed her eyes. "What does that mean?"

"This is the place your mind feels safest," he explained.

Okay… "So, this is a dream?"

"Not exactly a dream, no. But I *am* speaking to you through your subconscious, and your physical body is not actually here in this meadow."

Camryn looked down at herself then back to the man. "If I'm not really here, where really am I?"

"If you're inquiring about your safety, I assure you, you are safe."

Camryn turned away from the man, clamping her eyes shut. "This isn't real. This isn't real," she repeated.

"Of course it is," Sam interrupted her. "Just not in a way you are comfortable with."

Camryn squinted. "Could you be any more vague?" She was once again grateful for her natural proclivity for sarcasm that masked her growing fear, or at least she hoped it did.

"Humans are not comfortable with things they cannot explain with logic and reasoning. Things of the spiritual and supernatural are difficult for mortals to understand. Things like telekinesis, telepathy, extrasensory perception—" he spread his hands and winked, "—divine visitations. If it doesn't fit certain rules, most humans can't accept it."

"So that's what this is then? A divine visitation? So that means you're a—like—you're an…"

"I'm an angel."

"Uh, huh." Camryn looked around, expecting someone to jump from the bushes with a camera and tell her she'd just been Prank'd.

"Just—" she held up a hand, "—give me a minute with that."

The man sat statue-like, seemingly content to give her as much time as she needed. Camryn blew out a breath, looking around. This was the strangest dream she'd ever had. Everything seemed so *real*. If this was a dream, though, at least she wasn't in any real danger.

"You don't look like an angel," Camryn said finally.

Sam laughed. "Have you ever seen an angel before? Other than pictures drawn by other humans?"

"No, I guess not."

"Then shouldn't that be an indicator to you that maybe this is real? If this were a dream, conjured up by your own imagination, I would look as you think an angel should, with wings and white robes and such."

"You haven't seen some of my dreams," Camryn said more to herself as she stood. She didn't believe the man but didn't see the harm in seeing where this would lead. No matter how terrifying a dream could get, it wouldn't have any lasting effects. She would wake up, and everything would be just as it had been when she'd gone to sleep.

"So, angels don't really have wings?" Camryn asked.

"Oh, yes, we do. But only in the spirit realm. Here, we look just like you."

"Okay, let's say you are an angel, and you're 'talking to me through my subconscious,'" she air-quoted. "Why are you here?"

"I need to show you something, and this is the safest way. Otherwise, it would be far too traumatic."

Camryn gave him a sideways look. "And it won't be traumatic here?"

"Not so much. We can proceed at a much slower pace this way. Much slower than I'd like," he added grudgingly.

The man looked to be puzzling something out in his mind for a long moment, then seemed to come to a decision. "I want to try something with you if you'll allow it."

Camryn stared back at him, taking note of all the features of his face: brown hair, blue eyes, sharp, straight nose. She thought it odd she could evoke such a person in such detail that she'd never seen before. Weren't strangers in your dreams supposed to be faceless blobs?

Camryn backed away from him. "Wh–what are you going to do?"

"I'm not going to hurt you. I would like to say I'm trying to help you, but in reality, it is I who needs your help."

Camryn's hand flew to her chest. "Me?"

"But before that can happen, there are things you need to know." The man looked uncertain. "But not things I can tell you. Things you'll have to see for yourself."

This dream was getting more and more cryptic by the moment. "Okay..."

"And I can't control how these things will come to you. I can open your mind, but when I do, I have no idea what you'll see.

It might be scary. It might be confusing or painful." He turned to look her in the eye. Camryn was surprised to see his face fraught with apprehension. He looked...apologetic? Sam reached his hands toward her, holding his thumbs and middle fingers toward her head.

At that moment, all the strange little quirks of this dream clicked together for Camryn. The sounds, the smell of ocean air that she knew she'd never smelled before, the pain in Sam's face. Only then did she realize that something was different. This was more than just a silly dream.

She knew that whatever his touch showed her would change her life forever. There might not be any waking up from this.

Sam drew his fingers closer but stopped before touching her skin. A long moment passed until Camryn, thinking he wasn't going to move his fingers any closer, closed her eyes and leaned in, bringing her forehead to rest on his thumbs.

When nothing happened, she opened one eye to look up at him, her resolve amplified by the apprehension on his face. She knew he didn't want to hurt her. "It's okay," she said with an encouraging nod, then closed her eyes again.

This time, after a moment, the trees and birds and warm grass of the clearing vanished, and she was plunged back into blackness. She heard nothing. Saw nothing. She was nowhere and everywhere all at once.

As she floated into oblivion, the nothingness that surrounded her began to press in, getting smaller and smaller around her. Camryn clutched her throat as she looked around for an escape. If she didn't find a way out, this blackness would suffocate her.

Somewhere off in the distance, she thought she could make out a door—a rectangular burst of red in the vast blackness. She tried moving toward it, but she was trudging through quicksand. The more she struggled, the farther the door drifted.

"Relax," Sam's calming voice echoed from all around her. She looked around, but he wasn't there. She tried to obey his command—closed her eyes, took a deep breath, and exhaled.

She did this again until her breathing slowed, and the crushing weight of the expanse eased a little. When she opened her eyes, she stood on the threshold of a large, red door. Not knowing what she would find on the other side, she reached out and turned the knob.

On the other side of the door, Camryn found herself standing at the end of a brightly lit hallway. The wood floor creaked under her feet, and large, wooden doors extended down each side.

Camryn had a nagging feeling in her gut, like she should be searching for something but wasn't quite sure what. *Maybe it's behind one of these doors.* Curiosity was the only thing propelling her as she trudged down the hall, her fingers trailing along the wall, skimming over each door she passed.

One door.

Two.

Camryn's mind rolled, trying to recall what she'd lost. She continued on until about halfway down the hall, a noise reached her ears. She stopped abruptly and tilted her head.

Voices seemed to be coming from behind each door, echoing ghostly whispers. No matter how hard she tried, though, even pressing her ear to the door, she couldn't make out any words. More than once, she put her hand on a knob, but something kept her from turning it. Was it fear? Or the simple knowledge that she wouldn't like what she found on the other side?

Camryn whirled around at a creaking sound behind her, but everything was as it had been. She was alone. She looked back to the doors in front of her, all the same old, red wood. Nothing to tell her which door would answer her questions.

Camryn stepped lightly, afraid of disturbing the silence around her, when her foot landed, ankle-deep, right smack in a puddle of water. She looked down to find water seeping out from under each door and inching upward.

She took a step back, her breath coming faster now. She heard the creaking again. This time from right beside her.

The door.

It gave a loud groan, levied by some unseen pressure on the other side. Actually, she realized, they all were making the same noise. All the doors bulged, threatening to burst open. Camryn looked down at the water, steadily creeping up her legs, and started to run. She turned, realizing the hall was just as long in the other direction.

Still, she ran—ran until her lungs threatened to burst from her chest. But no matter how far she traveled, just as many doors stretched out on either side of her. Water continued to rise in the hall. She'd have to start swimming soon.

Camryn put her hands on her knees, trying to catch her breath. *I've got to get out of here.* Her head snapped up then, as, with one final splintering creak, the doors burst open around her.

Camryn braced herself for the cold rush of water, but it wasn't water that swept her up. What she saw swirling around her now, were memories.

Faces.

Places.

Flashes in time.

Memories assaulted her from every direction. She closed her eyes, trying to shut them out, but they twisted around her like a cyclone.

Agonizing screams. Soft laughter.

Running. Fighting.

Soft grass. Orange dirt.

All of it was inside her, a part of her. Moments exploding from the deepest recesses of her mind. Each memory brought with it its own emotion: anger, fear, compassion, confusion.

It was too much.

Too much horror, too much regret…too much love. Too much all at once.

Her eyes jumped around, searching for an escape. Aware of every heartbeat, she felt the blood pumping through her veins, hot and cold, fire and ice.

Wake up. I have to wake up.

She clamped her hands to her temples. *You have to wake up!*

Without warning, just when she thought her heart would explode, the tornado of memories began to slow, and with it, her pulse and gasping breaths.

One of the memories swirled around her, stronger, brighter, more vibrant than the rest.

That's it.

Somehow, Camryn knew. The echo of a memory that danced just out of her reach was what she'd been looking for—the memory Sam had wanted her to see. She tried to grab onto it as it rushed by, but it escaped her grasp again and again.

She leapt for it until finally…*finally,* she caught it. And just like recalling a word that had been on the tip of her tongue, the memory came to her.

And as she feared, it changed everything.

FORTY

Somewhere in the Atlantic Ocean
Present Day

The air exploded from Camryn's lungs as her body slammed backward into the dry, orange dust of the battlefield. She tried to get up, *needed* to get up, but an immense pressure had her pinned to the ground. She raised her head and stared down, disbelieving, at the angel's sword protruding from her chest.

What the hell?

Even though Camryn wanted to make herself believe it, she knew she wasn't dreaming. This was a memory expunged from her subconscious, but from when? And more importantly, *how?*

Camryn's body felt different around her, almost as if she wasn't in a body at all. She would have marveled at the freedom she felt—like she could rise up and soar through the air, unrestricted by the laws of physics—if not for the shaft of cold metal protruding from the center of her body.

Just then, Camryn's back arched off the ground as an overwhelming, all-consuming fire erupted inside her. Some lavalike substance was flowing from the weapon in her chest and spreading throughout her body. Camryn was overcome by a strong sense of *déjà vu* as if she'd been dropped into a scene of a familiar movie.

A battle raged around her—the sounds of metal against metal grated in her ears, but the agony of the fiery substance inside her chased all thoughts from her mind.

She fought her way through the pain back to the scene unfolding around her. Above the noises of battle, she heard the screams and howls of a thousand angels being slaughtered.

Angels.

Camryn couldn't even bask in the wonder of that realization. Lying helpless on the dirt of the battlefield, Camryn closed her eyes. Nothing else existed in the expanse of time or space. Everything that had happened to her before that point—the ones she'd loved, the teenager she'd been—fled from her mind.

She wasn't Camryn anymore. Her name was Arael, and she was an ancient, powerful Archangel. And she knew the angel on the other end of this sword. His name was Michael. He was her brother, and he had sworn to protect her.

No. I don't have a brother. Camryn closed her eyes. *This cannot be happening,* she thought, but the pain told her otherwise.

In the midst of the turmoil unfurling both inside her body and on the battlefield around her, someone called out to her. Her eyes jerked open as a voice intruded into her mind. A voice not her own, but just as familiar. It spoke two simple yet powerful words, louder than the battle raging around her.

I'm sorry, the voice repeated in her mind. She turned her head in the direction of the voice, and the horror almost chased the pain away.

Ethan. But it wasn't Ethan—not the way she knew him. His black hair had been replaced by snow-white locks. His dark skin was now glowing the greenest shade of blue she'd ever seen. Everything about this angel beside her was unfamiliar. Even his eyes were a strange, blue-green shade, but she knew…he was her *qanima.* Her spirit partner in that life and in every one since.

I'm the one who's sorry, she tried to respond with her mind but wasn't sure he'd heard. Her eyes scanned over his face again—his eyes, his hair, all spattered with blood. His spirit echoed inside of her, both foreign and familiar. The fullness of it was euphoric, filling every empty space inside her.

Camryn thought back to the earthquake and the flood and remembered wishing she could save Ethan by giving her own life. At the time, it had sounded crazy, but now…

Another explosion of agony ripped through her body. Ethan's face contorted into a grimace, a mirror reflection of her own. He was feeling her pain.

Or maybe she was feeling his.

It was all happening so fast. The bond that she only just now remembered having was being burned away. For something she'd only felt for the briefest of moments, she was desperate not to lose this feeling.

From her place in the blood-soaked dirt, she reached her hand out to Ethan and he to her until their fingers touched.

Camryn knew what would come next. She'd lived through it once before. A soft whimper escaped her lips as she braced herself for darkness.

The events of her past life crashed into her then, as if the memory of Michael's betrayal had been the plug in the dam of her mind. She could have tried to fight them, tried to sort through them one by one, but they would have overtaken her. She knew what she had to do. She stopped fighting. She determined to relax her mind, float to the surface, and ride it out to the end.

FORTY-ONE

C amryn woke clutching her chest where the sword had just been. She gasped for air, and her clothes clung to her clammy skin.

She still felt its crushing pressure, but the weapon was gone. She pulled out her shirt, peeked down her collar, and let out a relieved breath. Her skin was pale and unmarked. There had been no sword, no angels battling for their place in Heaven, no mysterious angel bleeding on the ground beside her.

That was a crazy dream, she thought, but knew deep down it had been much more than a dream. No way her mind could have come up with all of that on its own.

She swung her legs over the side of the bed, hoping to find her way to the flight deck for some fresh air. She stood, turned toward the door, and screamed.

Three men congregated in the doorway, staring at her. Jay stood, leaning against the door jamb. The captain sat in a tiny chair with his elbows on his knees, and another man leaned against the wall on the other side of the hall with his hands in his pockets. They all projected the same nervous energy, as if they were anticipating some bad news.

When she saw the men's faces, her breath caught in her throat. The captain stood, worry etched in his eyes. He reached out to touch her, but Camryn shrank back from him. This man—the captain of this ship—was the man who, in her dream, had plunged a sword through her heart. Not the captain of this ship…the captain of the army of Heaven.

She wanted to scream again, but this time, terror had taken her voice. Her feet rooted to the floor. She couldn't help noticing the three men had the doorway blocked. *How am I supposed to get out of this one, Dad?*

"Please, Camryn," the captain said. "Don't be afraid."

Don't be afraid. Those were the exact words Sam had said to her in her dream.

Sam.

She squinted at the man leaning against the wall across the hall. He had brown hair, blue eyes, and a sharp, straight nose—the same man from her dream.

But she hadn't seen this man before she'd been knocked out, she was sure of it. So how had he been in her mind?

"Who are you?" she managed to ask the man, though her voice was barely a whisper.

He straightened, surprise crossing his face. "Uh, Sam, um, Samael. My name is Samael," the man said.

Camryn shook her head. How could she have known that?

"And you?" she turned her face to the captain. "Who are you?"

"I'm Michael," he said. "I'm your brother."

"No."

No, no, no, no, no, no. This couldn't be happening. No way. "You drugged me. You made me see those things."

"How could I have done that?"

"I don't know!" Camryn shrieked. "You're the military. I don't know what you can do to people with your government mind control experiments."

"Camryn," Michael said as if it should be obvious. "We're not with the military." He gestured down to his uniform. "These were for your benefit—to make you more comfortable with us." He stood and nodded at Jay, who was still peeking in through the open door.

At once, their uniforms faded away like a delicate mirage, and Michael, Sam, and Jay were left wearing the same clothes Camryn had seen in her dream. Leather belt, knee-length robe, and a sword strapped over their chests. They looked like a trio of Roman gladiators.

Camryn clamped her eyes shut. "That's not helping."

"Better?" she heard Michael ask after a moment. She peeked through one squinting eye and saw the three men now wore jeans and t-shirts.

I'm losing it. I've finally gone completely nuts. Camryn stood helpless as fear crept down her back like icy dew.

"No. This isn't happening." Her knees buckled, and she slumped against the wall to keep from falling to the ground.

Michael glared at Jay. "I knew it," he said. "This is exactly what I was afraid of. She clearly wasn't ready for this."

"Camryn," a voice came from behind her.

Camryn spun to see Ethan climbing down from the top bunk. She wondered absurdly how he'd gotten up there.

He came toward her, his movements stiff, and she could only imagine that his legs were as weak as her own. He came to face her, his face wet with tears.

"What he's saying… It's true."

Camryn shook her head.

"We've known it since the first time we met," Ethan continued. "We just didn't know what *it* was. But we both felt it, didn't we?"

Camryn didn't answer. She couldn't. It was as if she were really seeing him for the first time. She stared into his eyes—those eyes that had drawn her in across the expanse of her barn before anyone had the opportunity to drug them or plant fake memories in her mind. Those dark gray eyes that had captivated her from the first moment she'd seen them. Those eyes that she'd felt she'd known all her life.

Those eyes that she'd seen turn from a bright blue to gray as the Heavenly Fire burned the righteousness out of them.

She took a step toward him and put a tentative hand on his cheek. As soon as she touched him, a familiar warmth spread through her. She remembered how he'd held her outside of Granny's and the eerie peacefulness she'd felt on the way home that night.

His pale face and sagging shoulders reflected Camryn's own pain—not a physical ache, but centuries-worth of pure, unadulterated emotion. She couldn't argue. What they'd felt for each other from the very first sight could only be explained if these men were speaking the truth.

"Uriah," she said on an exhaled sigh, more as a statement than a question. The moment she said the name, she knew…

Ethan's face tightened as if the name brought him pain. He brought his hands up to grip Camryn's face and his forehead down to meet hers. They both closed their eyes and stood, soaking in the presence of the other.

For Camryn, they were no longer standing in a bunk room on a naval ship in the middle of a group of oversized men. It was just the two of them, like their near-kiss at Kyle's party. In that moment, she and Ethan were the only two people in the whole world.

"Is this really happening?" she managed to whisper.

His head moved up and down against hers. "Yeah, it really is."

All of a sudden, all of her self-diagnosed disorders, her visions, all the strange and unexplainable things that had happened to her all her life, all of it made sense. Maybe even her ever-present fear of impending death. *Could it really be this simple?*

Camryn laughed through her tears at her own thought. Of all the explanations for her behaviors, her being an angel was far from simple.

Camryn had read once that tears were the overflow of emotion one's body couldn't contain. If that was true, she'd often wondered why she didn't cry more than she did; she was a ball of anxiety ninety percent of the time. But it now seemed that all the tears she'd never cried were spilling out, hard and fast.

Every fear, frustration, joy, and sadness escaped down her face in heavy sheets. Her insides ached, but in a good way, like all those pent-up emotions were being expelled in her tears.

She and Ethan clung to each other until their tears slowed to a manageable flow. When Ethan finally pulled his head back and wiped her cheeks with his fingers, Camryn could barely make out the shape of his face through her swollen eyes.

"I told you I would always find you," he said with a smile.

"Well it took you long enough," a new voice said from the doorway.

Their heads whipped around as a man with a strangely familiar face and hair an unnatural shade of red entered the room. She recognized him as the man who'd greeted them at the helicopter and brought them to the infirmary. At that time, he'd been wearing a name badge that said Ray, but now she recognized him for who he really was.

He came toward her and pulled her into a giant hug. To everyone's surprise—most of all Camryn's—she hugged him back.

"Raphael!"

He held her at arm's length and smiled. She turned to Jay, who was still looking timid in the doorway. "And Japhael."

Jay gave an approving nod.

"Is everyone on this boat an angel?" Ethan asked.

"Ha! Hardly," Raphael replied. "This *is* actually a warship. There are real soldiers on board doing real military work. We're just using their facilities for our own kind of work at the moment." He gave them a wink.

"The soldiers can't see us. Or y—" Raphael stopped mid-word as if someone had interrupted him. It took Camryn a second to realize, someone *had* interrupted him—but no one else could hear it. Raphael and Michael seemed to be having a mental conversation no one else was privy to.

"No mind-talk in meetings." Samael rolled his eyes. "You know the rules."

Raphael gave him a playful shove. "This isn't a meeting, Sam. Everything doesn't have to be so formal all the time."

After a moment of an apparent silent conversation between Michael and Raphael, Michael crossed his arms in the corner, and Raphael continued. "As I was saying, the soldiers can't see us. They only see what we want them to see."

"Wait," Camryn said. "Us? As in...all of us? They can't see—" she gestured between herself and Ethan, "—us?"

Michael raised his eyebrows and waved his hand at Raphael. "Please continue," he said.

"Well, that's a little hard to explain, but the short answer is, no. They can't see you."

Camryn and Ethan exchanged a worried look.

"Don't worry. You're just as real and alive as you ever were," Jay interjected. "What Raphael is trying to say is, you're here on this boat, but you aren't really here if you know what I mean."

Camryn wrinkled her brow. "I'm sorry, no. We don't know what you mean. Are we here, or aren't we? How can we be somewhere and not somewhere at the same time? How is that even possible?" Camryn's voice had risen an octave, and her hands flew around wildly.

Ethan put a hand on her shoulder. "It's okay," he said. "I'm sure they'll explain." He looked at the men with an emphasized tilt of the head. "Won't you?"

"You're sort of...in between dimensions," Samael tried to explain. "You're not exactly in the physical world, but because you are technically human, you aren't in the spirit realm either. The soldiers on this ship, their brains simply don't register your presence. If they bumped into you, their minds would tell them they'd nudged an open door or a chair. They just wouldn't notice you."

Sam looked at the others, who nodded their approval of his explanation. "Is that a little more understandable?"

Looking at it through her seventeen-year-old eyes, it was not understandable at all. But if she stopped fighting her inclination to do so, Camryn could see time and space through Arael's eyes. Looking at it from the perspective of the immortal, celestial being that she'd once been, their story made perfect sense.

"I think we understand that," Ethan said. "But what kind of work are you doing here, exactly? And what about us?" He looked at Camryn. "Why are we here?"

All the angels exchanged a glance. "Well, as you know, the Nephilim are afraid of the water. They avoid it at all costs. They won't look for you here until ordered to do so. You'll be safe here for a few days."

"No. I mean, what are we doing *here*?" He gestured at their bodies. "How did we end up like this, in these bodies?"

"Well," Michael said, worry darkening his face. "That's something we were hoping you could tell us."

FORTY-TWO

Somewhere in the Atlantic Ocean
Present Day

About an hour had passed since the motley group had moved into a small conference room on the lower deck of the ship. They'd been allowed to shower and given clean clothes, all of which somehow fit perfectly, despite not being anything either Camryn or Ethan would have picked for themselves.

"It's what the guys are wearing these days," Jay had said at Ethan's apparent distaste when he'd handed him the dark jeans and crisp, white t-shirt.

Not this guy, Ethan had thought, but he just smiled and tried to be thankful to be out of his own filthy clothes.

He looked over at Camryn, now tugging at her tiny, hot pink t-shirt. She seemed to be just as uncomfortable as him, but of course, she still looked great.

A long table surrounded by eight chairs filled the conference room, and a television monitor hung on one wall. The room was compact, just like everything else on the ship. Ethan thought this was probably intentional, everything else being as small as possible to make room for the important stuff—like missiles and torpedoes.

He and Camryn sat alone at one end of the table while the Archangels huddled together on the other end, trying to plan their next move.

The brothers had been discouraged to discover that the last thing Ethan remembered was being left in his cell by Raphael. Ethan didn't remember how he'd gotten out or anything that came after.

Camryn's last memory of portaling out of the church and into the valley of the Alborz wasn't any more helpful. Neither of them remembered the important part—the part about what the hell they were supposed to be doing there.

On their end of the table, Camryn rubbed the back of her neck, and Ethan rolled his newly procured med bottle back and forth in front of him. At the other end of the room, things weren't faring much better.

"Her brain knows how much it can handle," Raphael was saying.

"That's a pretty inconvenient place for her memories to stop, don't you think?" Michael said, clearly frustrated.

"I'm sure the next part will be very difficult for her when it does come to her," Samael interjected. "She clearly isn't ready yet."

"Yes, well, in the meantime, she only remembers me as the guy who impaled her with a sword." He slammed a clenched fist on the table. "No wonder she doesn't trust me."

"You also pretty much kidnapped them and are holding them hostage at sea," Jay added. "I probably wouldn't trust you either."

"Why is he still here?" Michael snapped.

"He has proven an integral part of this team," Samael reminded him. "He got them here safely, didn't he?"

Ethan glanced at Camryn, who sat nervously drumming her fingers on the table.

"Don't they know we can hear them?" she said under her breath.

"I don't think they care," Ethan replied, one arm hooked around the back of his chair. "It sounds like they have more important things to worry about."

Camryn heaved a sigh and leaned her chair back, balancing it on two legs. She was restless, and for good reason. To say something big had just happened would be the understatement of the year. Something momentous had happened. Something life-changing. And Ethan was willing to bet more big things were in store. You don't just find out you're a five-thousand-year-old angel then carry on with life as usual.

The only thing they could be certain of was that they'd been sent here by Elohim.

"Every conception is God-breathed," Michael had explained. "Life is given by Elohim alone."

"So basically, we couldn't have been born without God ordaining it."

"Exactly."

"So if He knows what our mission is, why can't we just ask Him?" Ethan had asked.

All the angels had looked at him with the same dumbfounded expression. "This *not knowing* might be inconvenient for us, but none of this is by mistake," Michael had explained.

"If you were sent here with no memories, there is a reason for that. We were permitted to open your minds, but what you see and when you see it will be according to His will. We just have to figure out what to do in the meantime."

And that was where the conversation had stalled. No one could agree on anything else, let alone what their next move should be. Michael wanted to stay on the safety of the boat. Raphael seemed to think they would be just as safe in Jerusalem. Camryn and Ethan were mum on the subject. They were still trying to wrap their minds around it all.

The Archangels had retreated to the other end of the table, leaving Camryn and Ethan to wallow alone in their confusion.

Ethan looked at Camryn, now chewing her lip and sighing with every other breath. He remembered wondering, the first time he'd really looked at her, standing in her barn talking about her horses, what had drawn him to her. She wasn't what he would have called "his type."

Now that he understood, he studied her, searching for a spark of the angel he'd seen in his vision, but found nothing. This girl, Camryn, had big, brown eyes and slightly pudgy cheeks like maybe she hadn't yet lost all of her baby fat. And from what he could tell, she was nervous and unsure of herself most of the time, nothing like the angel he'd fought beside in his memories.

But there had been moments—like pulling her truck out of the mud back on her farm and in those first moments after the earthquake—when she'd needed to be, she'd been in control, focused, and confident. Those moments had been few, but Ethan knew, his *qanima* was in there somewhere.

Right now, though, Camryn was totally and completely her human self. She shifted beside him, chewing her lip and fingering the sleeve of her shirt—obviously still having a hard time accepting their angel status.

Ethan hadn't had that problem, though. He'd believed it immediately. He'd been dealing with the supernatural his whole life, after all. His being an angel was actually a giant relief. It meant that he hadn't been hallucinating all these years. He didn't have all the answers yet but knew he didn't have to be in any hurry. The answers would come in time.

Camryn didn't look so hopeful.

Ethan pulled her close, offering himself as the only comfort he could. She accepted it, as he knew she would, leaning into him and wrapping her arms around his waist while the Archangels continued to argue.

Doing his best to ignore their chatter, he leaned down and buried his face in her hair. Her hand had somehow found its way under the hem of his shirt and was sending tiny jolts of electricity through him with every stroke of her thumb against his stomach.

Two kisses. They'd had two mind-blowing kisses. Knowing what he knew now about their creation and everything they'd been through, Ethan wondered if every kiss would be like that. *Damn, I hope so,* he thought and grinned into her hair.

Obviously, things were different between them now. They hadn't had time to talk about it, but there had been a tangible shift in their relationship. There was no more hesitance, no more uncertainty. They weren't just two teenagers trying to figure out a new romance while the world went to hell around them. They were two celestial beings who had been created to guide and protect one another.

He was hers, and she was his—not in a controlling or possessive way, but in a way that said, part of her had once been part of him. She had been an extension of himself and vice versa. He could still feel the memory of that bond and felt that, whatever they were supposed to be doing here, depended greatly on them getting that connection back.

"Maybe we *should* separate them again," Samael was saying. "Give them time to remember. I can portal Camryn onto the island. Raphael may be right. We may be able to get Ethan into the church in Jerusalem without being noticed."

"No way," Ethan said, jumping into their discussion, and tightening his grip on Camryn's waist. "We've been separated long enough. Not happening." Ethan looked down at Camryn, who nodded in agreement. They'd allowed so many things to separate them—pride, vengeance, even the hope of protecting one another—but no more. He couldn't imagine being separated from her even by inches, let alone by an ocean.

All the angels stopped short, turning their heads to look at Ethan.

"Ethan," Raphael said in a patient tone. "It's too dangerous." He gestured to the air around them. "I know you can't see it, but the aura you're giving off together will be a beacon to the Nephilim. You told Jay back in Kentucky you'd only been together two days before they found you the first time. Now that they know what they're looking for, next time will be a fraction of that."

Ethan narrowed his eyes. He'd already concluded that the shadow monster they saw back on the bank of the river—and that he'd been seeing his whole life—was indeed, Nephilim. He recognized the way they moved and even the feel of them from his memories of his time as an angel. But he hadn't said anything about that to Jay.

"What do you mean 'found us?' I never told Jay about that."

Samael stopped short. "Told Jay about what?"

"About them finding us—at the river."

All the angels straightened in their chairs. "You mean you've actually seen them?"

Ethan glanced down at Camryn. "Yeah, well…" They both shrugged. "Yeah."

"When?" Samael's eyes glowed with not-so-well-contained enthusiasm. "When have you seen them?"

Ethan shrugged again. "All my life."

Michael stood and clasped his hands on top of his head. His mouth hung open, his words caught in his throat.

"And you?" Samael directed his gaze toward Camryn.

"Just yesterday. That was the first time."

"So they both have the sight," Samael said to the others. "That's promising."

"Wait." Ethan waved his hands in the air. "So if you didn't know we'd seen them, how did you know they'd found us?"

"Samael," Michael warned.

"We have to tell them," Samael argued. "Like it or not, they are a part of this now. They need to know what's going on."

Michael looked to Raphael and Japhael, obviously hoping for back-up, but they both seemed to agree with Samael.

Michael sighed. "Can this not wait until later? Don't you think they've been through enough?"

"Despite how it may seem," Samael said, "they're not children. I'm sure they can handle it."

"And it may make it easier for them to remember," Jay added.

Michael seemed to consider this. He examined the two teenagers as if he were deciding if they could, indeed, handle it.

Ethan squeezed Camryn's shoulder. "We can handle it."

Michael threw up his hands in defeat. "Just be careful," he warned. "There's too much they still don't remember."

Samael nodded. "Of course." He turned back to the two kids at the other end of the table with a look that sobered them both.

"You remember the bounty Apollyon put on Arael's head after she disappeared in Syria?" he began.

Camryn hadn't been around to witness it, but Ethan nodded. "I remember."

"Her crime? She made Apollyon look like a fool. And the longer she went missing, the angrier he became. He sent Dagon after her, for Heaven's sake."

Camryn and Ethan both stared, waiting for this all to somehow make sense.

"Well...this whole situation," Samael went on, waving his hand in the air, "and what happened before the two of you were sent here. What you don't remember—it was much worse."

Camryn and Ethan exchanged a worried glance. "How much worse?"

"Bad enough that Apollyon would do *anything* to find you. And I do mean anything. Even breaking Heavenly Law."

"What Law did he break?" Camryn asked but grimaced as if she might not want to know the answer.

"Let's just say, he knows your weakness and is willing to do anything to exploit it."

Camryn glanced around the room at all of them. "Look, I'm still a little shaky here, you might have to spell this out for me."

Before anyone could say anything, though, Ethan broke in. "Her love for humanity." He turned Camryn in her chair to face him. "Think big picture here, Camryn. He was trying to send a message, 'Give yourself up, or people are going to die.'"

Ethan felt Camryn stiffen beside him. "The earthquake? That was our fault?" she asked. The sound of the tears in her voice made Ethan want to punch something. He twisted his fingers together in front of him to keep from putting his hand through a wall.

"But we didn't know anything about any of this!" Ethan said. "How could she give herself up if she didn't even remember who she was?"

"He doesn't know that, remember? He doesn't know anything more than we do. He knows less, actually. And we weren't even aware of your memory deficits." Michael glared at Japhael, who shrank back against the wall.

"And if he thought we were hiding, like before..." Ethan trailed off, trying to work it all out in his head. He thought of Camryn's words back on her porch the night of the pine cone incident. *"It's like a cosmic riddle that no one can figure out."*

Camryn slumped in the chair beside him. "All of this is our fault," she said, finishing his thought. "All of it. All over the world."

"Technically, *your* fault. You're the one who wronged him," Japhael said, pointing to Camryn, who looked up at him in horror.

Michael glowered at him with a fierceness Jay seemed to physically feel. "Not that that's—that's not important. Sorry."

"He's not going to stop, is he?" Camryn said. "He's not going to stop until he gets what he wants."

"I'm afraid not," Raphael said.

Ethan put a hand on Camryn's shoulder and ground his jaw tight. Usually, the fire inside him combusted quickly, a spontaneous, uncontrollable rage. This time, it would be a more gradual burn, a spark igniting as he looked at Camryn, twisting her hands in her lap and looking like she might throw up.

At that moment, Ethan knew two things. He knew Camryn would want to turn herself in. To her, it would be the only way. She would take whatever punishment Apollyon could dish out in order to save even one person, that's how selfless she was.

He also knew, no matter what it took, there was no way in hell he would let that happen.

FORTY-THREE

Somewhere in the Atlantic Ocean
Present Day

C amryn lay motionless, staring into the darkness, the only movement, her slow breathing in and out…in and out. Several hours had passed since she and Ethan had grown too weary to be of any real assistance to the angels and decided it would be best to get some rest.

Ethan had fallen asleep right away, his arms wrapped tightly around her, but Camryn was wide awake. When they'd stumbled into their bunk room a few hours before, there had been no question of sleeping arrangements. They'd fallen into bed, bleary-eyed, and folded into each other like they'd been sleeping that way for years.

In the still quiet of the night, Camryn felt the steady thump-thump of Ethan's heart against her back, perfectly in sync with her own. She breathed in the smell of him, a mixture of soap and sweat and fear. She was tempted to stay there with him—the way it was supposed to be. But even as she tried to convince herself to close her eyes and *just go to sleep*, she knew she wouldn't do it.

A single tear escaped down Camryn's cheek as she eased her way out of Ethan's arms, doing her best not to disturb him. She looked down at him for only a second before tip-toeing to the door and turning the knob. As she inched open the door and slipped into the hallway, she let out a small yelp of surprise.

"What are you doing out here?" she growled at Jay, who stood like a sentinel outside their door.

"I'm on watch tonight," he said, puffing out his chest. "Don't worry, someone will be guarding you at all times. We aren't going to let anything happen to you." He smiled a wide smile while Camryn inwardly groaned.

Great, she blew out her cheeks. *Just great.*

"What's wrong?" Jay asked. "Do you need something?"

"Oh, yeah," Camryn stammered. "I'm uh, I'm looking for the bathroom."

"Oh, sure." Jay pointed down the hall. "It's four doors down on the left."

"Thanks." Camryn followed his directions even though she didn't really need to use the bathroom. *Maybe I can slip in and sneak out while he isn't looking,* Camryn thought, then frowned as she realized that would never work. Even if she was as silent as a snowflake, his angel senses would detect her movements.

Crap.

When she reached the door, she looked back at Jay, hoping he'd be looking the other direction, but nope. He was still watching her with that dang goofy grin. She waggled her fingers at him before pushing open the door and going inside.

What now?

She looked around the room, and a lead weight sank in her stomach as she saw, straight across from her, another door, apparently leading to another passageway on the opposite side of the bathroom.

Only at that moment did she realize she'd been hoping for a way out, an excuse to go back to Ethan and just go to sleep. If she'd gotten stuck in this restroom, at least she could say she'd tried, right?

But no. The path lay clear in front of her. She steeled a breath and said a silent prayer of apology to Jay—he would be in so much trouble for this—before she pushed through the door to the other side.

Standing in the next passageway, Camryn peered left then right. The hall looked the same in both directions, dimly lit and narrow. She knew where she needed to go but had no idea how to get there. And even though the halls were quiet, she knew people had to be around. A military operation like this would require round-the-clock staffing. She'd have to be careful.

She looked around again, and for no particular reason, decided to go right. All these halls seemed to be connected anyway. Surely she'd find what she was looking for eventually.

Camryn was moving as fast as possible while still doing her best to stay quiet when she heard voices approaching from an adjacent hall.

She froze.

She looked back the way she'd come but saw nowhere to hide. She was way too far from the bathroom; she'd never make it back in time. She could try another door but had no idea what or who she might find on the other side—if they were even unlocked. There was no time now, anyway.

No time.

The voices were on her now, about to turn the corner five feet from where she stood. Camryn flattened herself against the wall and squeezed her eyes shut as if that would somehow make her invisible. A half-second later, two men in Navy coveralls rounded the corner, talking in hushed voices. Camryn held her breath and braced for the worst.

They wouldn't shoot her, would they? She was just a kid.

Camryn watched in amazement as the two men walked right past her. She almost laughed when she remembered—they couldn't see her. No one on this ship could. *Except the angels.*

She straightened and shook out her fists before taking off down the hall again. She still couldn't let her guard down, though. Camryn was almost convinced the other Archangels had left the ship. Otherwise, they wouldn't have left Jay on guard duty. But she couldn't be certain.

After countless turns and so many passageways that Camryn wasn't even sure what direction she was going, she finally found the room she was looking for.

She stepped through a doorway and found herself standing in a dark dining hall.

Finally. There has to be a kitchen around here somewhere.

She saw her destination at the far end of the room and made her way quickly past metal row after metal row of tables and chairs. The vast number astounded her. There had to be five hundred chairs here. *How many people are on this ship?* she wondered absently, trying to distract herself from what she was about to do.

Camryn made her way through another set of doors into another metal room—metal ovens and stoves, metal vats and fryers, and lots of metal pots and pans. That stuff wasn't what she needed, though. This job would require something a little smaller and a lot sharper.

The galley was dark this time of night, just like the rest of this part of the ship. She could sense somehow that the space was larger than it appeared, and the whole place smelled faintly of old potatoes. She reached around to her back pocket—not for the first time since arriving on this ship—looking for her cell phone, and—also not for the first time—growled in frustration when she didn't find it there.

With no light to guide her, Camryn felt her way deeper into the galley, her hands sliding over the cold metal appliances until her eyes adjusted to the dark. When she could finally make out the objects around her, she began her search.

She walked with feather-light steps so as not to be heard, but every heartbeat pounded in her ears, and every footstep seemed to echo off the hard surfaces around her. Her palms were sweating now as doubt began to creep in.

Can I actually do this?

Camryn had begun to think she would never find what she needed when her eyes landed on it, sitting innocently on a metal countertop. She almost laughed at the irony of what she was about to do. She'd spent her whole life trying to avoid painful, agonizing death. Now she was going to bring it on herself.

But there was no other way. She knew it, and hopefully, eventually, Ethan would see it, too. She just hoped he would forgive her.

Camryn knew Ethan and Michael and any of the other Archangels would be willing to die to protect her from Apollyon's wrath. And that's what she couldn't allow to happen. If any of them got hurt—if one more person died because of her—she wouldn't survive it.

She'd spent so much time agonizing over devastating headlines, feeling a deep-rooted connection to the problems of the world. Now that she understood why and knew she could do something about it, of course, she would do it.

If Apollyon wanted her, if that's what it would take to stop him, she would go to him. Simple as that.

Camryn reached out and pulled the knife from the wood block in front of her. It was the biggest one in the group, but she still wondered if it would be big enough. She cradled it in her shaking hand. Yes, it would do the job.

She knew she should take a minute to reflect on what she was about to do—it would be more poetic that way—but she had to do this quickly before she lost her nerve.

Camryn raised the knife to her chest, placing it against the soft tissue right below her diaphragm. Tears blurred her eyes, and her breath came in quick, hitching gasps.

She'd worked this part out as she'd lain awake next to Ethan in the dark. The diaphragm would be a slower death, but easier. The path of least resistance, per se. One quick jab and the job would be done.

She wouldn't cry out. Her lungs would simply refuse to fill with air, and her vision would fade before her heart finally stopped beating. It would be just like drowning, and she had done that once already. She knew it wouldn't be pleasant, but at least this way, she'd know what to expect.

Camryn floated through the motions, not thinking, not feeling, almost as if she was already gone. Instead of her heartbeat in her ears, now a high-pitched ringing stung her eardrums.

She pressed the blade into the soft flesh, trying to steady her breaths. *You have to do it now, Camryn. Now!* She took one last excruciating breath and jerked the knife toward her.

"Hey!" a voice called from behind her. "What the hell are you doing?"

Camryn whirled around to see a young girl standing in the doorway, glaring like Camryn had just spit in her food. Camryn looked down at the knife in her hand and the growing red stain on her shirt. She'd only pierced the skin, but the blood already covered the hot pink hem of the garment.

She sucked in two big gulps of air, her body desperate for oxygen. Her eyes shot back up at the girl, still blurry with tears. Camryn wiped her face with her sleeve as she heard the girl approaching.

"You have got to be kidding me," Camryn choked out when the face came into focus in front of her. It belonged to the girl from the helicopter. The darkness shadowed her eyes, but her burnt orange hair, she would recognize anywhere. "Am I going to have to reevaluate every person I've ever met in my whole life?"

"Not your whole life," Akira replied. "Just today." She jerked the knife out of Camryn's hand. "You're still just as stupid as ever, I see."

Camryn could only stare at the girl. Her hands still shook, and her legs felt like they might drop her to the floor at any moment.

"What did you think you were going to do, kill yourself and turn yourself in?"

Well, yeah, Camryn thought but didn't trust herself to speak.

"Did you forget the part about *you're human now?*" Akira slammed the knife back into the block. "You were born into this world with a human spirit. You can't just shed this body like an extra skin and go running around the spirit realm like you could before. You're not playing by the same rules anymore."

Camryn's eyelashes fluttered. She hadn't thought of that. *Why hadn't she thought of that?* She pressed her hand over her wound. With the adrenaline fading, the pain was starting to seep in. "What are you even doing here, Akira?"

"Saving your ass, what does it look like?" Akira reached out and tried to pull Camryn's hand away. "Let me—"

"Why would you want to help me?" Camryn cut her off, jerking away from her. "You've never done anything for anyone that didn't benefit yourself."

Camryn saw that her words had stung, but she didn't care. She reached for a towel and pressed it to her wound. "You work for the *demon* who wants to kill me. As a matter of fact, you're probably working for him right now, aren't you? What are you going to do, run back and tell him where we are? Is that why you're here?"

Akira's face remained impassive, and her arms hung stiff at her sides. "You know, they told me there were things you didn't remember," she said. "But you might want to be careful."

She drew nearer to Camryn until they stood face to face. "And you might want to keep your mouth shut until you have all the information. You don't want to say—" she paused to glance down at the bloody towel, "—or do something you can't take back."

Camryn wanted to say something but thought better of it. As much as she hated it, Akira was right. Camryn didn't know everything yet, and until her memory was completely restored, what she thought she knew couldn't be a reliable source of information. This little incident served as a stark reminder of that.

Even if she'd wanted to say something, though, she wouldn't have had the chance. At that exact moment, someone came slamming through the swinging door, shining a flashlight into the room like a spotlight. Jay stood behind Ethan, panting like the sprint here had actually winded him. Ethan's frantic eyes searched Camryn's body until they landed on the bloody towel still pressed to her ribs. "What happened? Are you okay?"

"She's fine," Akira said with a roll of her eyes.

Only then did Ethan seem to notice the other person in the room. He stared at her, his mouth hanging open. "Akira?"

"Yes, it's me," she said without enthusiasm. "Enough with the introductions. Tend to your girl. I know that's what you want to do anyway."

"Akira…" Ethan looked unsure of what to do. He was seeing his best friend that he'd only hours before remembered that he even had, for the first time in this lifetime, but Camryn was hurt. Not fatally, but still hurt.

"Just…" Akira waved her hand toward Camryn and turned away, offering them some privacy.

Ethan ran to Camryn, pulling the towel away. "How bad is it? Let me see."

"I fell. It's nothing. I'm fine." Camryn tried to brush him away, but he pulled her hands away with ease.

When he got a look at the long gash, his hand stilled. He looked up at her, his face hardening. "You fell?"

"Yeah."

"That's it?" he asked, anger ringing in his voice. "That's the story you're going with?" He looked at Akira, his eyes full of questions.

Akira shrugged, uninterested. "She fell."

Ethan turned to Jay. "Get Raphael."

"No!" Camryn shouted. "I don't want Michael to know about this."

"Oh–okay," Jay stammered. "I know what to do." He turned and vanished from sight.

Ethan grabbed Camryn's wrist and dragged her toward the door. "Come on, we've got to get you to the infirmary."

Akira led the way. She seemed to know the layout of the ship pretty well. As they rushed down the dim passageway in relative silence, a boy appeared in the hall in front of them, almost as if he'd materialized out of thin air. Maybe he had. Camryn wasn't sure about anything anymore.

Looking at him now, Camryn remembered the boy as Akira's companion from the helicopter and—big surprise—she now knew exactly who he was.

Despite Ethan's anger, a smile spread across his face. He released Camryn's wrist and pulled the boy into a tight hug. "Ronan! What are you doing here?"

Ronan returned the hug and slapped Ethan on the back with a wide grin. "We thought you two might need a little help."

We? Camryn remembered that he and Akira had shown up at the same time and couldn't help wondering how in the world the two of them had ended up working together.

"I think the question is," Akira said to Ronan, looking annoyed, "where have you been?"

"Some of us still have jobs to do," he joked, but his voice trailed off when his eyes landed on Camryn and the blood-soaked towel. "Dang, Akira, what did you do?"

"Screw you, Ronan. I didn't do that."

"She fell," Ethan said in a tone that said he didn't believe that for one second and neither should Ronan.

"Ah, well." Ronan nodded in understanding. "We need to get that looked at then."

When the group reached the infirmary, Ethan turned to their companions. "I can take it from here, guys."

While Camryn usually looked forward to a stolen moment alone with Ethan, she found herself hoping for them to stay.

"Um..." Ronan looked uncertain.

"I think I know how to dress a wound." Ethan's tone let them all know he wasn't budging on the matter.

"Come on." Akira pulled Ronan away with a smirk. "Let's leave the two lovebirds alone."

Camryn couldn't help but think Akira was enjoying this...just a little.

When Akira and Ronan had gone, Ethan turned and stalked past Camryn into the exam room and began rummaging through drawers and cabinets. Camryn hung back in the doorway, unsure of what to do.

"Ethan—"

"Don't," he growled.

Camryn pressed her lips together and did the only thing she knew to do. She crawled onto the exam table.

When Ethan found what he was looking for, he turned back to her, first aid kit in hand. "Take off your shirt," he said without looking at her.

"What?" Camryn's eyes grew wide.

He finally brought his eyes up to meet hers and said through his teeth. "I can't bandage it if I can't see it."

Camryn gulped. She dropped the towel on the floor and pulled her shirt over her head. She said a silent thank you to Jay for bringing her a cute bra.

As Ethan leaned down and examined the cut, Camryn took note of the hard set of his face and tried not to wince as he poked around the tender spot.

Ethan cursed.

"What?" Camryn looked down to see blood oozing from the gash that was longer than she'd originally thought.

"It won't stop bleeding. I think you're going to need stitches." He wadded up some paper towels and pressed it to the wound.

Camryn's heart ached for him as she noticed his shaking hands. From anger? Or fear? Or both?

"Please don't be mad," she said.

Ethan's nostrils flared. "How can you even say that? Of course, I'm mad!" He blew out a breath. "I'm just glad Akira was there."

Of course, he would say that. Ethan could never see Akira for what she was: a manipulative, backstabbing traitor.

"Akira is not here to help us—" Camryn began, but her words were cut off by Ethan's sudden movement.

She flinched as the first aid kit flew through the air and crashed against the wall.

"Akira saved your life!" Ethan shouted. "If she hadn't been there, your stupid plan would've worked!"

Camryn's mouth hung open. That was a low blow, but she didn't think this the best time to argue that point.

"Do you have any idea—" Ethan slammed his palms down onto the exam table, making Camryn jump again. The air escaped from his mouth in ragged bursts.

A few moments passed before he turned his haunted eyes to look at her. His voice wavered when he spoke again.

"Do you have any idea…how much I need you?"

Camryn nodded. She did know. Because she needed him just as much. "I'm sorry," she whispered over the lump in her throat. "I'm so sorry."

Ethan was in front of her then, clutching her to him like he would never let go. She buried her face in his shirt, relishing his warmth and his sweet, intoxicating scent. How did he still manage to smell so good?

Despite the pain in her wound, Camryn wrapped her arms around him, the tears finally spilling from her eyes. "I wasn't thinking," she said. "I promise I'll never do anything stupid like that again."

Ethan pulled away and looked at her with so much sadness that she wondered if he knew something she didn't. When he spoke, his voice was a low whisper. "Please, don't make promises that you can't keep."

Ethan was still applying pressure to Camryn's wound when they heard a soft knock on the door. They both turned to see the same doctor who'd healed Camryn's knee their first night here. She appeared the same except now her purple-black hair hung straight down her back, and a bright white jumpsuit replaced her Navy uniform.

Camryn saw now that she wasn't a doctor at all. Her name was Lailah, and she was the Guardian of the sea.

"Hello again!" Lailah chirped. "I heard someone could use my help in here."

Camryn looked past her to Jay standing in the doorway. "Thanks, Jay," Camryn said with a wave. Jay nodded and disappeared again.

Lailah strolled over to the bed and turned to Ethan. "Would you mind running back to your room and grabbing another shirt for her?"

A line formed between Ethan's wrinkled brows. Camryn could understand his confusion. They didn't have any extra clothes here.

"There is a shirt. On your bed. Go get it."

Ethan glanced back and forth between the two a few times before he reluctantly obeyed.

Once he was gone, Camryn offered Lailah a meek smile, knowing the angel could have snapped her fingers and made another shirt appear if she'd wanted to. Was she in trouble with Lailah, too?

"Lie back," Lailah instructed, and Camryn obeyed. "He's much more intense than he used to be," she said, offering a bemused smile.

Camryn cringed. "You heard all of that?"

"Most of it," Lailah said, laying her hand over the still bleeding wound. "He's right, you know." She didn't have to elaborate on what he was right about. Camryn nodded.

It only took a second under the angel's hand before Camryn could feel the torn tissue connecting, the skin tightening, the pain subsiding.

"Thank you," she said when the job was done.

"My pleasure." Lailah nodded. "Let's not make this a habit, though, okay?"

FORTY-FOUR

Somewhere in the Atlantic Ocean
Present Day

"**D**o we even know this is going to work?" Camryn asked as Jay helped strap her and Ethan into the helicopter the next morning. Akira and Ronan sat across from them, expertly buckling and pulling the straps to secure themselves to their seats.

"Partly," Jay answered.

"Partly?"

"Mostly." He shrugged.

"*Mostly?*" Camryn exclaimed.

"It's going to work," Michael said, approaching the aircraft. "There's an American Air Force base in Beersheba. We can get you that far undetected. The tricky part will be getting you from the base into Jerusalem, but we have a plan for that."

"And why can't we just transport from here?" Camryn asked.

"Well, it didn't go so well the last time we tried that if you recall."

"Oh, yeah." Camryn scratched her head. "How could I forget?"

Samael popped his head between the front two seats, passing headsets back to them from the cockpit. Camryn wondered absently if he'd been their pilot on the flight from Kentucky.

"How do you know how to fly this thing?" she asked. Somehow, she couldn't imagine an Archangel taking flying lessons.

Samael looked down his nose with a playful smirk. "Please," he said. "You see this?" He pointed at an orange lever with several gauges attached to it. "I invented it."

Camryn's eyes widened. She thought back to the time of the Founders and the information they'd given the humans in exchange for human wives. She realized then that so much of human technology, the tablets and USB drives, were so much like the devices the angels had used since the beginning of time and wondered if it all came at such a price.

Ethan interrupted her thoughts with a question. "And why are we going to Jerusalem?"

"It's the safest place for you right now," Michael answered.

"Then why are we anticipating so much trouble getting into it?" Camryn asked.

"The city is heavily protected, but that's because the Nephilim presence is substantial. Apollyon has eyes and ears everywhere."

"Well, that doesn't sound very safe," Camryn said, her tone laced with sarcasm. She knew the Archangels had things under control, but she couldn't seem to control her tongue. She didn't like feeling helpless, and that's exactly how she felt—like they were playing a life or death game of chance without all the rules.

"We just have to get you to the church. The building is a fortress. Once you're there, nothing can touch you."

"And then what? What's the plan after that?"

"We wait," Michael said.

"Wait for what?" Camryn exclaimed. "I can't just sit by and wait while people are dying because of me."

"We wait for your memories to return," Michael said. "Elohim entrusted me with your protection until the time He deemed fit for you to return to us, but we had no idea when or if that would ever happen." He glanced around at the others.

"So, when you two showed up a few days ago—at just the time we'd all but given up on stopping Apollyon's plans—you've given us a renewed hope."

The others nodded in agreement.

"We are certain that you two hold the key to defeating him, so we can't be hasty. We can't do anything until you remember what you were sent here to do."

As the propellers started a slow *whomp, whomp*, Camryn sat back. She thought about Michael's words. Was it possible that she and Ethan really were the key to defeating the most powerful Fallen angel in the underworld? The thought made her stomach roil. That, and the view out her window as the helicopter lifted off the flight deck, the water drifting farther and farther from them.

The last time Camryn had been in a helicopter, she'd been almost catatonic, and it had been dark. Now, fully awake and aware that they were in a small aircraft flying over very deep, shark-infested waters, all her confidence from the night before disappeared. She squeezed her eyes shut and began sucking in air through her nose.

Ethan reached over and grabbed her hand. "You okay?"

Camryn nodded without opening her eyes.

"Hey, we're in a helicopter flown by an Archangel with a literal Guardian angel watching out for us. I don't think anything's going to happen." He smiled.

Camryn relaxed beside him but didn't remove her hand from his. Of course, that was true. She felt foolish, especially when she glanced over to see Akira glaring at her.

What's her problem now?

Camryn still hadn't quite figured out what Akira and Ronan were even doing there. None of the Archangels seemed surprised by their presence. They had to be working together. But why? Her brothers, she could understand. They were always in the middle of things like this. It was their job. But how did these two fit into the picture, especially Akira?

Camryn added Akira to her mental list of "things to talk to Michael about."

After a few awkward moments, Samael's voice crackled through the headsets. "Go ahead and settle in folks, it's going to be a long ride."

Camryn took that as her cue to catch a quick nap. Either that or spend the next hour having a staring contest with Akira.

No thank you.

Camryn closed her eyes and set about the task of replaying all her new memories over in her mind, hoping to find some connection between herself and the angel in them. She'd made no progress by the time she drifted off, her head on Ethan's shoulder.

When Camryn opened her eyes again, she stood in the valley of the Alborz facing Michael under a clear night sky. Moments before, he'd sent her emotions into a tailspin by first offering her a way home, then informing her of Uriah's imprisonment. She was angry and confused as the memory of the Heavenly Fire from the church still burned her skin.

She'd just descended from the mountain after investigating what she'd thought to be a human cry for help.

Of course, it hadn't been. It had been a trap, as she'd feared—but not the kind of trap she ever would've expected.

She stood now, no longer indecisive, and looked Michael straight in the eye.

"Have you made your decision?"

She nodded and stepped forward, placing her hands on Michael's broad shoulders—the first time she'd touched him without trying to kill him since her exile.

His shoulders that had always been so solid and strong sagged at her touch. She reached up and placed a soft kiss on his cheek. When she released him, she saw the relief flood over his face. He thinks I'm coming with him, *she realized.* And he is so happy.

"Arael," *he took her hands in his and closed his eyes. When he opened them again, a different person looked back at her. His face no longer carried the weight of a thousand burdens.*

True, he still had the world to worry about, but at that moment, he looked...peaceful. She'd never imagined it would mean so much to him to have her forgive him, that he would care that much. It was his fault, after all, that she was even here in the first place.

Immediately her stomach turned to lead, and she shivered despite the heat.

When he pulled back from her, confusion crossed his face. Could he sense her regret?

No sooner had the thought formed in her mind than the whooshing sound of an opening portal hit her ears. Michael reacted, but distracted by Arael, not fast enough. A dozen Nephilim demons surrounded him, wasting no time.

Michael released her and grabbed for his sword, but a giant beast as large as a lion and with the head of a dog jumped through the portal onto his back.

Arael gaped at the creature. What had Apollyon been doing the past thirty years? Creating his own demonic pets?

Michael swung his sword and stabbed at the beast. He managed to wound the animal with a quick slice of his weapon. It howled in pain, offering only a momentary reprieve. There was nothing Michael could do. He screamed as the creature's fangs sank into his back.

She watched, horrified, as blood oozed down his neck and onto his chest. Other demons surrounded him, clawing, biting. They grew more and more frenzied with every cry of pain. The demons that couldn't latch onto him circled above like vultures, waiting for their chance to strike.

Michael managed to send some shrieking away with his sword, but he was unfocused now, the demon venom weakening him.

Dagon stepped through the portal then, slow and purposeful, as if this was something he did every day. He came to stand beside her and placed an approving hand on her shoulder.

"You made the right choice," he said.

Michael staggered. He searched through the mayhem until his eyes found her standing with Dagon outside the horde, doing nothing to save him. She stared into his eyes, unable to look away. This was her doing, after all.

And Michael knew it.

His eyes said everything there was to say. She forced herself to watch until he finally wretched forward, the last of his strength leaving him. She would never forgive herself for her weakness, but with his fall, she turned her eyes away.

Dagon stepped forward then, and with one quick thrust of his Heavenly Fire infused staff, one end sharpened to a twinkling point, stabbed Michael deep in the side.

She jumped back as Michael's blood spattered onto her, droplets of the hot liquid spraying her face. She didn't even attempt to wipe them away.

Michael collapsed to the ground, the beast still gnawing at his back, ripping flesh until his blood carved a path in the dirt, winding like a river. Dagon held up a set of handcuffs almost identical to the ones Michael had used on her, bent down, and slung them over Michael's wrists.

Michael grunted in pain.

A tremor shuddered through her body as the sizzle of metal-burnt flesh hit her ears. What is wrong with me? This is what I wanted... Isn't it?

"Well done, Arael," Dagon said. "We could never have done this without you."

Those were the last words Michael heard before the demons dragged him away.

Camryn jerked awake with the memory still pounding in her chest.

Ethan squeezed her hand.

Akira and Ronan gaped at her.

"What is it?" all three of them asked in unison.

"God, you look terrible," Akira noted.

"Did you remember something?" Ronan asked.

Camryn could only jerk her head up and down as she bit back a sob. What had she done? What kind of horrible monster was she?

"What is it? Do you know what we're supposed to do?" Ethan asked.

"No," Camryn croaked. "It wasn't anything like that."

"Well, what was it then?" Akira demanded.

Camryn shook her head. She looked at Ethan. Did he even know? He'd been in prison when this had taken place. Did Akira and Ronan know? They had to, didn't they? But that didn't mean she wanted to sit here and talk about it with them. She didn't care what they thought of her anyway. But Ethan... What would he think when he found out?

"It's nothing," she kept saying, no matter how many times they asked. Ethan put his arm around her and rubbed his hand up and down her back. She closed her eyes and pretended to go back to sleep, but she knew she wouldn't be sleeping again for a long while.

FORTY-FIVE

Beersheba, Israel
Present Day

Camryn fought the urge to throw up as she and the others hopped off the helicopter in Beersheba. Michael's screams still echoed in her ears. If she thought she'd had night terrors before, they were nothing compared to the images she saw now when she closed her eyes. Blood and demons and… Camryn shook the memory from her head. She couldn't think about that now. Not with Michael and Jay walking right toward them.

Camryn took a deep breath. *He's fine*, she told herself. *Look at him. He's here now, and he's perfectly fine.*

But how could he be fine? She'd seen him being practically eaten alive by a demon dog right in front of her eyes. She remembered the hatred and loathing she'd felt for Michael for so many years. She remembered her thirst for vengeance. And she still had no answer for his betrayal in Eden, but the seventeen-year-old human girl inside her knew no one deserved what she'd done to him.

She wanted to run to him and wrap her arms around him and tell him she was sorry. But how would she explain that to the others? To Ethan?

Instead, Camryn bit her lip and looked away. The aversion of her eyes was a welcome distraction. She gaped at the landscape around them.

They stood on a landing pad on top of a large cinder block building. To the left lay a sea of concrete and machinery, buildings and bunkers, aircraft and tanks—a whole city in the middle of the Israeli desert. To their right, nothing but sand.

A light breeze blew, creating small dust clouds in places. What looked like sand-covered mountains loomed in the distance, probably sand dunes of some sort. One road—or path, really— led to the base, but other than that, the sand lay undisturbed, rising to soft peaks in places. It reminded Camryn of the desolate, orange dirt of Eden.

It was breathtaking.

"Hello, ladies and gentlemen," Michael said, pulling her thoughts back to the landing pad. "Welcome to Israel."

Even through her discomfort, Camryn couldn't help noticing how much Michael reminded her of a proud father returning home after a long time away. He glanced over each of them, his gaze fixing on Camryn for a long moment.

Camryn's heart seized. *He knows. He knows something's wrong.* Was it plastered on her face? Could he hear her heart beating out of her chest? Could he smell the guilt? Would he call her out in front of everyone, make her tell them what she'd done?

After an agonizing moment, Michael finally broke his eyes from hers. "Everyone ready to go?"

Camryn sighed. This was going to be a long day.

Noisy activity rang out over the base, a complete contrast to the quiet solitude on the roof. People walked in and out of buildings. Whistles blew, radios crackled. Everyone wore brownish-green t-shirts and camouflage uniform pants, but none of them seemed to notice the three men in Navy uniforms and the four teenagers following them through the base.

Michael talked as they walked. "As I said before, this area is heavy with Nephilim patrols. We won't be able to keep you hidden forever. We can shield you temporarily, so this beacon you're creating won't be seen, but the trek will be much safer underground." He stepped off the edge of the runway and lifted what looked like a round, metal hatch that, moments before, had not been visible in the sand. "We won't be seen from the air this way."

"There are tunnels under the city?" Ethan asked.

Michael looked at him with a steady gaze. "There are now."

Camryn thought about the angels' absence from the ship the night before and wondered if this was what they'd been doing.

"Hold on," Camryn interrupted. "There's nothing within miles of here. How far are we walking?"

"It's about eighty miles to the church."

"*Eighty miles?*" Camryn and Ethan exclaimed in unison. "We can't walk eighty miles."

"Oh, ye of little faith." Michael almost smiled at them as he waved them in. Akira and Ronan went first. They didn't seem to have a problem with this little arrangement.

Of course they don't, Camryn thought with a roll of her eyes. *They still have their celestial powers.* She and Ethan were a different story. They looked at each other now, though, shrugged, and stepped down into the hatch. What choice did they have at this point?

Stepping down, Camryn had to duck her head to reach the bottom of the carved-out steps, but once she did, she could stand straight with plenty of room overhead. The tunnel seemed just tall and wide enough to accommodate their larger-than-average Archangel guides and was pretty well constructed.

Actually, there was no construction to it. The sand had just been pushed aside, packed in nice and tight, and rounded into a perfect passageway. There were no lights, no lanterns or torches, but somehow the tunnel was lit just bright enough for them to see by. To top that, Camryn couldn't help noticing that her shoes didn't sink into the sand under her feet. Every step was like walking on solid ground.

The group walked in relative silence at first. Michael led the way, followed by Ronan, Akira, Camryn, Ethan, then Sam and Jay pulling up the rear.

As they trudged along, Camryn reached out and tried to poke her finger into the packed sand wall of the tunnel. It didn't budge. She thought back to a story she'd heard in Sunday School about Moses parting the Red Sea and the Israelites walking across on dry ground. Could this be like that? It sure seemed like it.

It's not going to cave in. It's not going to cave in, she kept repeating to herself as the tunnel seemed to grow narrower and narrower around her.

Ethan's fingers brushed her shoulder. "You okay?"

Camryn managed a tight nod. She longed for the confidence she'd felt that first day after Lailah had healed her leg. She thought she knew why it had disappeared. She just hoped she could get it back...and soon.

No sooner had Ethan dropped his hand from her shoulder than Akira doubled back beside Camryn and grabbed her elbow. "Can I talk to you for a second?"

Camryn's first instinct was to jerk away from her, but Akira held on.

"I guess that wasn't a request then, huh?"

Akira scrutinized her with fiery eyes. The rest of the group had stopped to stare at them both. "Go on ahead, guys. Camryn and I need to chat."

Camryn looked to Ethan, silently begging him for help. He opened his mouth to speak, but Michael grabbed his arm before he had the chance.

"Come on," Michael said to the group.

Ethan turned to give her an apologetic shrug. Camryn watched them walk away in dismay. How could Michael be allowing this? She turned back to Akira, widening her eyes to say, "Okay, get on with it," and jerked her arm from Akira's grasp.

Akira waited a few beats more, maybe to give the others time to get farther ahead, probably just to annoy her.

"I don't know what game you're playing here," Akira said finally. "But this isn't you. This isn't *the real you*. You're not this weak."

Camryn hardened her already harsh glare. "What are you talking about? I am not weak."

Akira batted her eyelashes and said in a high falsetto, "Oh Ethan, I'm so scared. Hold my hand." Then, with her voice returning to normal, "It's embarrassing."

Camryn couldn't believe what she was hearing. Akira had no idea what it was like, living with the anxiety she dealt with every day.

"Do you think I enjoy this?" Camryn snapped. "Being afraid of everything all the time? Believe me, I would change it if I could."

Akira surprised her by softening her glare and placing a hand on Camryn's arm. "We're all afraid all the time, Camryn," she said in a low voice. "But you get to choose how you let that fear affect you. It can either hold you down, or it can drive you."

The usual animosity was gone from Akira's eyes now. "There is still a lot you need to remember, Camryn, but most of all, you need to remember who you are." With her last three words, Akira poked her in the chest, then turned and left Camryn staring after her.

Camryn wanted to argue. She wanted to be angry. But what could she say? She could give her fears many names—anxiety, phobias, OCD—but they were all the same demon, really.

She'd overcome it momentarily after her first encounter with Lailah, but her near-fatal decision last night had dampened her confidence. She wasn't sure what was real and what wasn't, and that did make her feel weak. How would she ever trust herself again?

"Hey," a voice came from beside her, causing Camryn to almost jump out of her skin.

"Jesus!" She slung her arm at Michael. "You have *got* to stop doing that!"

"Not Jesus, but I have been mistaken for him before."

"Was that supposed to be a joke?"

"Sorry, I'm not really good with the humor. I was just coming to see if you were okay."

Camryn crossed her arms over her chest and glared at him. "No, actually. I'm not okay." She pointed her finger toward Akira, who was barely visible down the long tunnel now. "What the hell is she doing here?"

"Same thing as Ronan," Michael said. "They're here to help us."

"Okay, but—" She held her palms up as if weighing two options. "Ronan...Akira," she moved her hands up and down. "Not the same thing."

"There are still things you don't remember."

"Yes, I'm aware of that, as everyone so frequently keeps reminding me. I understand there's a teeny bit that I don't remember." Camryn held her thumb and forefinger close together in front of her face. "But there's a whole lot that I do remember about her, and none of it is good, okay? She's a liar and a rat who works for Apollyon if I might remind you." Camryn lowered her voice even though the group was well ahead of them. "She could be spying for him right now."

"I assure you, she's not."

Michael's placid tone grated at Camryn's last nerve. "How can you be so sure about that? She plotted to kill you numerous times. How can you so blindly trust her like this?"

"If I remember correctly, she plotted *with you* to kill me. And I'm not blindly trusting her. I know her better than you think."

313

He put a hand on Camryn's shoulder. "I understand your hesitations, but believe me when I say, I would not have allowed her here if I wasn't one thousand percent sure she was on our side."

Camryn spun on her heels and stomped away from Michael. She knew she was being immature, but she didn't care. After everything that'd happened to her and everything they'd just learned, she had a right to be a little irrational, didn't she?

"Camryn," she heard Michael's voice calling after her. "Stop being so dramatic."

Camryn's face twisted as she spun back to face him. "Dramatic? Dramatic? Are you kidding me? There couldn't be any *more* drama in our situation right now, and I think I'm handling things pretty well. I'm sorry if I'm a little worried that Miss Psycho up there is eventually going to turn on us. I've been through too much with her. There's not much else I could expect."

"Is that how we decide who we can trust, Camryn? By experience? Because, if so, please tell me who among us doesn't have a history of turning on one another."

Camryn winced as the meaning of his words struck her. Michael had betrayed her. She had betrayed him. Michael thought Uriah had betrayed her. She did see the pattern.

Camryn let out a sigh, dispelling the indignation within her. She would never make Michael understand. Not after what she'd done to him. And even after all that, he was still here helping her.

She squeezed her eyes shut as the echoes of Michael's screams reverberated in her ears.

"I'm sorry," Camryn said, crossing her arms over her chest. "Not about Akira. I'm still pissed about that." She took a deep breath and looked away. "I'm sorry about what I did to you. About...Dagon."

Michael froze beside her.

314

"I'm still having a hard time with this duality of consciousness here. So, this isn't the warrior angel talking now. This is the teenager whose only existential experience includes the past seventeen years on this earth. I don't know if she ever got a chance to tell you, but *I* am sorry."

The edge of a smile finally teased Michael's lips. "I knew you remembered something." He cleared his throat. "We can't really talk about it, but thank you for the apology."

"I know it wasn't the memory you'd hoped for."

"It's a step in the right direction. Now come on, we need to catch up with the others."

Camryn and Michael began a slow walk down the tunnel. Camryn knew Michael could have taken her hand and transported them through the tunnel to the rest of the group, but she was grateful he didn't.

She had too much to think about.

After everything, she was slowly coming to terms with her angel status. Especially after hearing Michael's screams in her vision on the helicopter, recognizing them as the same screams so deeply embedded into her subconscious that they had woken her from the verge of sleep almost every night of her life. Add that to the strange connection she'd felt with Ethan since she'd first laid eyes on him, and it was all beginning to make sense.

"He didn't do it, you know?" Camryn said after a particularly long silence.

"Excuse me?"

"Ethan." Camryn waved her hand. "Uriah. One of the last things I remember is you accusing him of leading Dagon to me in New York City. I can tell you're still angry with him, and I just wanted to make sure you know—he didn't do it."

"I know you believe that, but—" Michael shook his head, "— sometimes people surprise us. If someone would have told you before the battle that I would be the one to exile you, would you have believed them?"

"This is different, Michael. Imagine if someone accused Raphael of such a thing. It would be incomprehensible to you. I know this with every cell in my body. He would never do it."

Michael still didn't look convinced. He raised one shoulder. "We shall see. He's going to have plenty of opportunities to prove himself soon, I'm afraid."

"Well, he's going to prove you wrong," Camryn insisted.

Michael smiled down at her.

Camryn contemplated her next question for a long time, wondering if she really wanted to know the answer. She finally decided, yes, if she were going to fully trust Michael again, she had to know.

"So, why did you do it?" The question was kind of vague, but she couldn't force herself to be more specific. Besides, there was only one "it" she could be referring to.

She'd expected the question to startle him, or anger him, or elicit some kind of reaction from him, but Michael kept walking as if she hadn't spoken. The silence stretched on for so long, Camryn had given up on ever getting an answer.

Michael finally cleared his throat. "You don't know how long I've waited for you to ask me that question."

He followed his statement with another long silence.

"So…are you going to answer it?"

"I'm afraid the answer is so simple that it might not be anything like you're expecting."

"I really have no expectations, I promise you."

Michael stopped and turned to face her. The two of them were alone now. The rest of the group had been swallowed by the darkness of the tunnel ahead of them.

"I tried to talk you out of it." Michael looked down at his feet. "But you insisted on being there."

Camryn remembered the heated conversation they'd had when planning the attack on Apollyon's rebel group, back when he'd still been called Lucifer and the angels knew nothing but a life of peace and love.

"Please don't try to blame this on me." Camryn's voice was a whisper. "You know why we had to be there. Apollyon would have known we were involved."

"Yes, yes, of course. And we all agreed on that. Eventually. We had an airtight plan to protect you. It's just that—" Michael fidgeted with his sword strap and gazed off down the dark tunnel. Camryn didn't think she'd ever seen him look this uncomfortable.

"Someone showed up who wasn't in on the plan."

Camryn shook her head and pursed her lips. "I don't understand."

"It was Raphael." The words crawled from his lips. "As much as it pains me to say it, Raphael wasn't supposed to be there that day. He showed up…to help me, I suppose."

The next words didn't seem to want to come out of his mouth. And after they had, Camryn wished they hadn't.

"Camryn, it was Raphael who banished Uriah."

Camryn felt like she'd been punched in the stomach. She put her hand out to steady herself and breathed his name, "Raphael?"

She pictured the battlefield in her mind's eye. She and Uriah had been near the Conclave Hall, on the fringe of the activity. Michael had recruited two of his men to engage Arael and Uriah in a fake battle of sorts. It had to at least appear that they were participating in the conflict. Michael had been standing close by; that had been part of the plan. The one contingency they hadn't planned on, though, was Raphael. It only took a second for the puzzle to fall into place.

Raphael was Michael's *qanima*.

"It was all a mistake," Camryn whispered into the air.

"Yes." Michael breathed the word as if it weighed a thousand pounds. "He knew what was happening. I told him to stay away.

He never participates in such things. That was the first time he ever went against my wishes like that."

Michael ran his hand through his hair, a nervous gesture Camryn had never seen from him before. "Uriah was startled by his appearance. He spun. Raphael perceived him as a threat to me, and…"

"I never saw who it was." Camryn stared past Michael with blank eyes. "It all happened so fast, the face was just a blur, and then it was gone." She stood, shaking her head. How could eons worth of hatred and fighting be based on such a stupid mistake?

"And when I turned with my sword to protect my *qanima* from his attacker," Camryn continued, "from…Raphael, you did exactly the same thing."

Michael nodded. "And Camryn, I swear to you, so much was happening, there was no way I could have known it was you. It was complete chaos. I knew where you were supposed to be. I'd last seen you near the steps. Then all of a sudden, someone was thrusting a sword at Raphael. I just never expected…" His voice trailed off, unable to form the rest of the thought.

"I tried to explain this to you so many times," Michael said. "But you were so angry. And as long as you were trying to kill me, there was nothing I could do."

Something about his story still didn't make sense. She believed Michael. But something told her there had to be more to this than just a tragic mistake.

She would have asked the question, but Michael held up a halting finger the split second before Samael appeared beside them.

"Everything okay back here?" Samael asked.

Camryn and Michael both nodded. Samael glanced back and forth between them. Their stiff demeanor and tight expressions must have alerted him to their lie, but he didn't press the issue.

"Well, we are nearing our destination," he said to Michael. "I thought you should be aware."

Michael straightened, resuming his warrior posture. "Thank you, Samael. I'll be right there."

Michael stole a questioning glance at Camryn, who gestured for him to go on. They could talk more later. She wasn't sure she could take any more revelations just then anyway.

FORTY-SIX

Jerusalem, Israel
Present Day

C amryn had been certain from the beginning that this whole trip would turn into a disaster. A whole day of walking with no food and no bathroom breaks? These angels really had no concept of the limitations of the human body, did they?

But somehow, Camryn was annoyed to admit, Michael had been right again. It seemed that just being in the presence of the angels had given her and Ethan the strength and endurance they'd needed to make the long trek. And Camryn was sure it hadn't taken a whole day. They couldn't have walked more than a few hours before Michael announced their arrival at their destination.

They had come to the bottom of a stairway similar to the one they'd descended to get into the tunnel. At the top of the stairway, looking as out of place as an alligator in a swimming pool, stood a door—not a hatch like the one they'd used to get down there, but an actual door.

Camryn wanted to reach out and take Ethan's hand, but Akira's words from earlier still rattled in her mind. *I'm not weak,* she reminded herself. She needed Ethan, but not for everything.

Michael went first and held the door for the rest of the group. As soon as they stepped through, Camryn's eyes were drawn upward. The high ceiling looked to be made of dark, ancient stone. The only light in the room came from small, rectangular stained-glass windows that decorated the top edge of each wall, letting her know they were in some sort of a basement or cellar.

The Church of the Holy Sepulchre—that's where Michael had said they were headed. Tall stone pillars ran down the middle of the space—probably for support, but they made the room look like something from an Indiana Jones movie. Her gaze traveled down with the intention of taking in the rest of the space, but she didn't get very far.

Camryn's eyes landed on three more people standing in the middle of the large room. Raphael was one of them, and sitting beside him on a bright yellow cot that looked completely out of place in the ancient space were two figures she thought she'd never see again. They both stood when Michael and the others entered.

"Camryn?" They both looked confused.

Camryn wanted to run to them, but her feet wouldn't budge. Luckily, she didn't have to. They came to her—came crashing into her like a gale-force wind.

"Mom! Dad!" Camryn sobbed. "Mom…Dad." Those were the only two words she could make her mouth say.

"Shh, honey. It's okay." Her mother rubbed her hair. "We're here now." Her mother glanced at the men standing behind them. "Not quite sure how, but we're here."

Camryn pulled back to look at them. Their faces were marked with small bruises and scratches, but they seemed, otherwise, fine. "You don't know how you got here?"

Her mother's eyes were deep with concern. "We don't even know where *here* is. The last thing we remember…was losing you…in the earthquake." Her mother's words came in clipped phrases. "Then two days ago…we woke up here."

Camryn turned an accusing eye to the angels. "Two days ago? Why didn't someone tell me?"

"That was before you two even woke up," Michael replied. "Then, when you did, we had more important things to worry about."

"We meant to," Jay added, trying to soften the harshness of Michael's tone.

Camryn sighed and turned back to her parents. She examined her father's calm face and would've bet money that the angels had some kind of calming spell over him. No way would the father she knew stay nicely tucked away in the basement of a church in God-knows-where for two days without knowing exactly what was going on. She gave Raphael a questioning look, and he just shrugged.

Her eyes fell on Ethan then. He offered her a small grin, but his smile didn't quite reach his eyes.

A pang of guilt hit her, and Camryn pulled her arms to her sides. How could she be so blatantly happy about seeing her parents when Ethan's mother was dead?

With her gaze still locked on Ethan, Camryn heard a door creaking open behind her but didn't bother to look. Nothing was more important to her at that moment than taking away Ethan's pain. She took a step toward him just as his eyes broke from hers and landed on something over her shoulder. The weary sadness on his face morphed into shock.

Camryn turned her head to see a small, frail, and sickly-looking woman enter the room. Her black hair and olive skin told Camryn who she was before Ethan even opened his mouth.

"Mom?" Ethan's voice cracked. The woman's eyes were wide like she'd been caught stuffing biscuits in her purse at a buffet, as the entire room stared at her. Ethan ran and threw his arms around her.

The woman squeezed her eyes shut, and tears fell down her cheeks. "Ethan. My Ethan."

"Now, this one was harder to find," Raphael informed them. "We just got here today."

Ethan looked at Raphael. "How did you—" he started to ask but turned back to his mother, apparently deciding he didn't care.

A few minutes later, sitting on the cot between her parents, Camryn tried to put the pieces together.

"Anyway, that was it," her father said. "That's all I remember until we woke up here. I was sure I had some broken ribs, but when I woke up...nothing." He patted his sides. "Just a few scrapes and bruises."

Camryn glanced at Raphael, who, along with the other angels, was trying his best to look inconspicuous. Her feelings about him were understandably confused. He had healed her parents of whatever injuries they'd sustained, probably even saved their lives. But it had been his stupid mistake that had resulted in millennia of chaos and strife, not only for the angels but for the entire human race. He had stood by and watched her try to kill Michael at every turn and never said a word.

"It was so awful," her mom continued, looking at the floor and shaking her head. "I thought I was dead. I just couldn't keep my head above water." Tears filled her mother's eyes. "I'd lost your father." Her voice broke as she covered her face with her hands.

Camryn understood her mother's pain. She remembered the primal desperation in what she'd believed to be her last few breaths on this earth. She hugged her mother and rocked back and forth while her father wrapped his strong arms around them both.

After a moment, her mother choked out a laugh. "I'm the one who's supposed to be comforting you, not the other way around."

Lindsey took Camryn's face in her hands. "I thought you were dead, but look at you." She looked Camryn over for about the tenth time. "Not a scratch on you."

Camryn smiled. Of course, she couldn't tell her mother about her injured knee or…any other part of it, really.

"Yeah," Camryn said, a hint of nervousness in her voice. "It's crazy."

James leaned in and lowered his voice. "So, do you have any idea who these guys are?" he asked, glancing around at the strange men stationed around the room. "They've pretty much been holding us hostage here for two days. They told us it wasn't safe to leave, then you showed up here with them. Did they tell you anything? What's going on out there?"

"Oh, um…" Camryn's eye automatically shot to Michael, who was fiddling with a small television he'd brought in and positioned on a table against one wall. He gave a small shake of his head that Camryn knew was intended for her. She set her mouth in a deep frown. Did he actually think she was going to tell her parents the truth? What would she say? *"Oh, yeah, these are the Archangels who've been protecting me my whole life, and oh BTW, I'm an Archangel, too?"*

Instead, she glared at Michael and opted for silence.

"Something's happening, isn't it?" her father asked.

Camryn glanced back and forth between them. "Wh–what do you mean?"

"Honey, does this have something to do with you? Are you in danger?" Lindsey placed a hand on Camryn's knee.

Camryn's eyes darted around the room. She'd come to expect such assumptions from her father. He was the conspiracy theorist of the family, always jumping to some far-fetched conclusion at every unusual incident. But her mother was usually more level-headed.

"Why would you think I'm in danger?"

Lindsey looked down at her feet for a long moment. James put a hand on his wife's back. "Honey...we know what you can do," her mother said, looking Camryn in the eye. "We've always known."

"Well, maybe not always." Her parents shared a nervous laugh. "It was a spot of contention between us at first."

"Your dad thought I was crazy." Lindsey cut her eyes to her husband. "I can't say that I didn't agree with him sometimes, but we've seen some pretty unexplainable things, honey. And when the rain started..."

Camryn tugged at a strand of hair as she glanced back and forth between her parents. Were they serious? "What about the rain? I don't know what you guys are talking about."

"I know you think you've always hidden it from us," her father cut in. "But there were times when you were too young to know any better..."

Camryn couldn't believe what she was hearing. If her parents had really seen such things, why had they never said anything? Her eyes cut to the angels standing guard at each door. They were all feigning nonchalance, but she knew they heard every word her parents were saying. Just then, Brooke's words from the party came to her. *"Did she tell you about her superpowers?"*

"So, you think I caused the flooding of the entire midwestern United States?" she accused. "What about the droughts and hurricanes? You think I caused those, too?" The question sounded ludicrous, but she had, hadn't she? Maybe not in the way her parents suspected, but it *had* been her fault.

Without giving her parents a chance to answer, Camryn stood, marched past Ethan, her mouth set in a hard line. His body was turned away from her, his attention focused on his mother, but he looked up as she stalked past.

Camryn jerked her head toward the alcove at the back of the room. She hated to interrupt his time with his mother, but this couldn't wait.

In the alcove, she spun on a bewildered Ethan. "Back on the riverbank, when we were talking about your pills, you said when you were a kid, you used to 'do things.' What did you mean?"

Ethan ran a hand through his hair. "I don't know. What does that have to do with anything?"

Camryn glanced around, unsure how to proceed. She'd only talked about this once before, and that had had disastrous consequences. Considering that they'd just discovered they were eternal, celestial beings, though, this shouldn't be a surprising question.

When they'd first met Michael, he'd asked if they could "do things." And she remembered Ethan's reaction to Brooke's accusatory question at Kyle's party. He hadn't been surprised. Looking back on it now, it was almost as if he wanted her to tell him she had some superhuman abilities. Putting her doubts aside, she decided to jump right into it.

"Remember what Brooke said at Kyle's party, about me having superpowers?"

Ethan's eyes flitted over her face, but his expression gave nothing away.

"Well, I wasn't completely truthful about that."

Ethan shifted his weight but didn't say anything.

"Believe it or not, Brooke and I used to be friends back in elementary school." Camryn glanced up at Ethan, whose eyes had narrowed slightly. "That was until one day...I decided to tell her a secret. I...showed her something, and she totally freaked out. I don't know what she thought." Camryn shrugged. "But that's when she started telling everyone I was crazy, that I thought I had superpowers." Camryn risked another glance up at Ethan, whose face remained unreadable.

"What—" Ethan coughed into his hand. "What was your secret?"

"Um, well..." Camryn knew she couldn't explain it in words. She wasn't sure she could pull off a demonstration just then, either. It had been years since she'd used her gift or even thought of it with anything other than shame.

Brooke had made sure of that.

Camryn looked around, still keenly aware of the angels and their superhuman hearing. She stepped closer to Ethan until she could feel the heat of his skin and see the flecks of blue in his gray eyes. She put a finger to her lips and grinned.

It had been a while, but bringing the tingle back to her fingers took no time at all. She felt it first in her hands, her fingers growing colder until she squeezed them into frozen fists at her sides. Ethan's eyes grew wide as the temperature around them dropped at least thirty degrees and his breath became visible in the air between them. He wrapped his arms around himself and shivered, his eyes filled with a delighted glint.

"It's basically my Tempest power, but I don't know how extensive it is. I've only ever used it to make it snow a couple times when I was a kid. And that one time with Brooke." She looked down at her feet as the temperature returned to normal around them. "I haven't done that in years."

A smile played at Ethan's lips. "I guess I wasn't completely honest with you, either," he said, looking sheepish. "When I told you I'd been in court for vandalism." He scratched the back of his neck. "It was uh… It was actually arson."

"*What?*" Camryn let out a surprised laugh before realizing that probably wasn't the appropriate response for this particular situation. She straightened and pulled her mouth into a frown. "That's terrible."

Ethan glanced over her shoulder, and her eyes followed his to the other inhabitants of the basement. The angels were still putting on a stellar performance as uninterested military guards. Akira and Ronan were huddled together on one cot, trying their best to look the part of two distraught teenagers. Ethan's mom was picking at the hem of her oversized t-shirt, and Camryn's parents were looking at the two of them curiously.

Camryn gave them a reassuring wave as Ethan grabbed her elbow and pulled her toward the small room Elizabeth Reyes had emerged from an hour before.

It turned out to be a small bathroom, all stone walls and dark lighting. The toilet had a pull cord for flushing, and rust stains lined the porcelain sink. Everything looked so ancient, Camryn was surprised the place would actually have functioning plumbing.

"It seems so stupid now," Ethan said in a rush, "knowing everything that we know, but at the time... I was just so angry all the time. It was something I did to blow off steam. In my eyes, I wasn't hurting anyone, you know."

"Ethan, why are you explaining this to me right now? I think we have more important things to worry about than you starting a few fires."

"You don't understand." Ethan grabbed the dingy hand towel from the wall. He held the towel at arm's length and focused his eyes on it.

"Ethan, what are you doing?"

Ethan held up a finger to her and squinted in deep concentration. After a minute, the towel burst into flames.

Camryn clapped her hand over her mouth to stifle a scream. She looked up at Ethan with wide eyes.

Ethan glanced cautiously down at Camryn as he placed the flaming towel in the porcelain sink. She pulled her hand away from her mouth to reveal a mischievous smile. "That...is awesome."

Ethan let out a relieved laugh before turning on the faucet, extinguishing the flame.

"Well, I guess if we're being honest with each other," Camryn said, "there is something else I should tell you."

"What is it?"

Camryn bit her lip. "I don't know if I should say. I mean, I've never told anyone this in my entire life."

Ethan's face grew serious. "Camryn, I'm not just anyone. You should know by now, you can tell me anything."

Camryn looked at the floor and swayed back on her heels. "It's just that, if we're going to be doing this mission together, I think you should know—" Camryn looked up and grinned, "—I really do like Taylor Swift."

FORTY-SEVEN

Jerusalem, Israel
Present Day

E than had never thought of his life as normal, but after everything that had happened in the past week, he found himself longing for the predictability of his old life.

Had it really only been a week? Sunday had brought the earthquake, Monday he and Camryn had landed on the ship. From what Michael had told them, they'd been asleep for about thirty-six hours during their memory restoration, so, if Ethan's estimation was correct, that meant it must be Thursday.

Thursday.

Just seven days since he'd left his house in Franklin looking for his mother. So much had happened in such a short amount of time, he couldn't help but wonder what the next week would hold. Would they still even be alive seven days from now?

It had to be approaching midnight. Ethan lay on one of the yellow cots the angels had set up for them, but even though his eyes were closed, he wasn't asleep. Too many uncertainties weighed on his mind.

His mother's cot had been pushed flush up against his, and one of her thin, frail hands rested beside him, having dropped from his arm when she'd fallen asleep. She hadn't stopped touching him since their first hug so many hours ago.

Ethan wasn't even sure how long they'd sat on her cot and talked and hugged and cried with no sign of the perpetual anger that usually plagued their relationship. Maybe learning that someone was alive after thinking them dead for so long did that for a person. Or maybe he was learning to control it.

Ethan turned his head to look at his mother. Her lips were tight, and her eyebrows slightly pinched. Even in sleep, she looked haunted. Ethan took her hand and placed it back on her cot, trying to appreciate every small moment he had with her. He wasn't sure how many more there would be.

Camryn and her parents lay a few feet away. Their deep, even breathing told Ethan they were sound asleep. He thought of the moment he and Camryn had shared in the alcove earlier in the night and smiled. He'd been right. His *qanima* was in there. She'd been there the whole time.

They'd talked briefly with Michael about their powers but had agreed to wait until tomorrow to discuss what they meant and how they could use them. They hoped to find a distraction for their parents, but so far, they'd been unable to talk them into leaving their children's side. Camryn protested heavily, making a list of all the reasons the adults did not need to be around, but the angels weren't into infringing on free will, so the parents would stay.

Tomorrow.

Feeling restless, Ethan threw back his blanket and got up. The angels leaned, each against an exit door with their eyes closed, trying to give off the illusion of sleeping guards, but Ethan knew their senses were on high alert.

Ethan marched straight up to Michael, who reclined against the door from which they'd entered. Ethan wondered if he opened it now, what would lie on the other side. Would it be the sand tunnel? Or just another room of the large basement?

"Can I help you with something?" Michael asked without opening his eyes.

"Yeah." Ethan clenched his fists at his sides. "I wanted to talk to you and haven't really had a chance to get you alone."

"Okay." Michael raised his head.

"Did you leave me here alone on purpose?"

"You're not alone."

"You know what I mean," Ethan said. "I'm glad that you've been looking out for her while I couldn't, but I don't think it's a coincidence that the Watchers never found her. I think she's had, at the very least, supervision, if not outright protection while I was left to deal with my demons all alone."

"What makes you think you've been alone?"

"Are you kidding me? Do you have any idea what I've been through?"

"What you've been through?" Michael's voice rose, and he straightened from the wall. "What? Because your mom was an addict and you've been followed by Watchers all your life? Do you have any idea how much worse your life could've been?"

"Oh, you mean because there's always someone who has it worse? That's a load of bull, and you know it. Admit it. You were angry with me, so you abandoned me."

Michael lowered his voice and moved closer to Ethan. "Whatever my feelings may or may not be toward you has nothing to do with any of this, and you know that. I receive orders. I follow them. Bottom line. And orders were the same for both of you." He leaned his head back against the door. "And the only protection Camryn has ever had, has been her location. I'm sorry you weren't afforded that same luxury, but that wasn't my call."

Her location? Ethan almost asked, but quickly realized… "The Nephilim hate the water."

Michael nodded. "The river was the only thing that kept the Watchers away. That is until you showed up and led them right to her." He raised a brow and tilted his head in accusation.

Ethan's jaw tightened. He tried to draw up his anger at Michael's insinuation, but he couldn't deny the parallel of the situations. Ethan stuck his hands in his pockets and tapped the wall with the toe of his shoe. "I guess I can't argue with that, but it did bring us to you, so maybe you should be thanking me."

Michael seemed to ignore him as he leaned back against the wall.

"You've always been protecting her, haven't you?"

"In whatever way I could." Michael shifted on the wall. "She's never needed much protecting, though. When we figured out what she was doing in New York, we watched out for her. I thought she would need us eventually, but she never did. Not until you showed up." Michael's face remained stony.

"I told you then, and it's just as true now—I wasn't the one who brought Dagon to her, not intentionally anyway." Ethan stared, challenging Michael to argue. "I don't know why that's so hard for you to believe, but you're going to have to trust me if we're going to work together." Ethan extended his hand for Michael to shake.

Michael shifted his eyes to Ethan's hand and stared at it for a long moment before gripping it in his own. "I'll trust you as much as I have to," he said. "That's the best I can offer you."

Ethan exhaled a heavy breath and stuck his hands back in his pockets. He nodded to Michael before strolling back toward his cot. That would have to do, he supposed.

He hadn't meant to do it, but he stopped beside Camryn's cot, almost by some subconscious force. He knelt and brushed a wisp of hair from her face as her eyes fluttered open.

"Oh, sorry," he said. "I didn't mean to wake you."

"Are you kidding?" Camryn smiled. "I'm not sleeping." She used the back of her hand to wipe at her eye. "I heard you talking to Michael. What did he say?"

Ethan raised one shoulder. "Nothing really. Just talking about tomorrow." He would've felt guilty about lying to her, but her knowing grin told him she saw through his lie and was letting it slide.

A wave of something unrecognizable washed over Ethan when the smile faded from her face. It was gone so fast, he couldn't put his finger on it, but he knew... He would do anything to keep that smile on her lips.

"Ethan...I'm scared."

Her chin quivered as his eyes melded with hers. Ethan knew the vulnerability it took for her to say those words.

"I'm scared, too," he said. "But hey, we have to stop looking at this through our human eyes. We have to be Arael and Uriah now." For Camryn's sake, Ethan hoped his voice carried at least a little confidence.

Camryn nodded and clasped his hand with hers. Just as quick as they'd come, her tears were gone, and her jaw was set. She looked...determined, Ethan decided.

Ethan glanced over his shoulder to the angels standing against the wall. He would never be able to express how grateful he was—to them, to Elohim, and to whatever force had brought him and Camryn back together again.

So much had happened in the past week, so much destruction and so many lives lost. Ethan knew so much more lay ahead of them, more than they were even remotely prepared for. But right then, at that moment, with their parents alive and Camryn's hand in his, he was hit with an uncharacteristic sense of optimism.

Tomorrow would bring its own challenges, but in that brief moment of time, they were all okay.

EPILOGUE

Capitol building, Turkey
Present Day

Harriet paced in front of her desk, heart thrumming in her throat. The phone call she'd received only minutes before had so distracted her that she didn't hear the creak of the door as it opened, or notice the fresh-faced young man in a tailored suit step through.

"Should I get you some tea, ma'am?" her assistant, Reggie, asked from the door. She waved him away with a flick of her hand. She didn't want him to see her like this. She didn't want anyone to see her like this. She hadn't gotten to be president of a thriving Middle Eastern country by being easily rattled by phone calls.

She'd dined with world leaders, handled nuclear threats, and, hardest of all, gained the trust and adoration of the citizens of her country. That had all been a cakewalk compared to the guest she was about to receive.

He'd been kind enough to request a visit, but everyone knew you didn't turn down a request from men like him.

Harriet glanced at her watch, did another lap in front of her desk, then looked at her watch again. He'd said he'd arrive at five. It was one-minute till, and Harriet had no doubt he would walk through the door in exactly sixty seconds.

She circled behind the desk, sat stiffly in her chair, and draped her hands over the armrest, trying to look as casual as possible.

Her pulse was just beginning to slow when the soft buzz of her phone caused it to spike again. She picked up the receiver without speaking.

"Your guest is here to see you," Reggie said from the other end of the line.

"Send him in," Harriet croaked before standing and wiping her hands down her skirt.

The door opened, and a cold chill filled the room even before her guest stepped through. She'd only spoken to him a handful of times, but each visit was burned into her memory like a brand.

Over the forty years she'd known him, his appearance had never changed. His snowy white hair framed a face that looked more suited for a magazine than a board room. His eyes, though dark, still managed to be open and inviting. Looking at him, you'd think him as harmless as a puppy, but after knowing him for so long, Harriet would swear there was hellfire behind his eyes.

"Father," she said with a nod.

"Harriet, my love. It's been too long."

Not long enough, Harriet thought before catching herself. She had to remember to marshal her thoughts around this man.

Growing up, her mother had told her little about her father. Harriet only knew that they'd met in Paris while her mother was on holiday, spent a ravaging summer together, and after she'd returned home, unknowingly pregnant with Harriet, she'd not heard from him again.

That is until Harriet was born. Her mother hadn't even had a way to contact him, let alone tell him about the pregnancy. But somehow, he'd known. He showed up at the hospital, a different person than her mother remembered. He was no longer the charming, handsome man she'd spent countless summer nights with. He was sinister and domineering.

336

He hadn't even spoken to her mother, just held Harriet with such greedy eyes that her mother had been afraid he would run out of the hospital with her.

But he had finally placed baby Harriet back in her mother's arms. "You will do great things, my love," he'd whispered into her soft newborn head before he'd turned and disappeared out of the room.

As far as her mother knew, Harriet had never seen him again. When he'd popped into her life over the years, he'd ordered her to never speak of his visits to anyone, and no matter how much she'd wanted to tell, she'd found herself unable to disobey him.

"I know it's getting late, so I'll get right to it." He glanced at his watch, though she was sure he knew exactly what time it was. "I'm afraid there is something I need you to do for me."

It took all the willpower Harriet could muster to shake her head at him. "Things didn't turn out so well the last time I tried to help you."

"On the contrary. Things turned out just as I planned."

"You planned for Russia to attack us?" The words sounded insane coming out of her mouth, but she wouldn't put it past his abilities.

Thanks to him, she'd risen quickly—especially for a woman—from parliament, through the judiciary ranks to the position she currently held. She'd had great advantages in her political campaigns, a fact that she found herself equally ashamed and proud of. She'd known problems were coming before they'd developed, and when she'd shown up with a plan of action, the Turkish people were in awe. How could one person be so prepared? So focused and proactive? Yes, she had her father to thank for her political position, but that's about all she could thank him for.

"I planned for you to come out on top, and since the rebuilding, your citizens have prospered, have they not?"

"Millions of innocent people died." Harriet's voice was flat.

"And you were their hero," he snapped, his face hardening. Harriet knew she had crossed a line.

"Of course, I am grateful for that, but what good is it for me to be President if I have no citizens to govern?"

Her father looked at her with sadness in his eyes. "Harriet, Harriet," he tsked. "Sometimes, I wonder if you are my daughter, after all."

Harriet winced. He'd never said such a thing to her before. And as much as she feared him, she still desperately wanted his approval. She closed her eyes and sighed. "What do you need, Father?"

His face brightened, but he didn't say anything right away. Was he hesitating?

"I wish I had more time to prepare you for this, but certain new developments have sped up my timeline a bit." He seemed to be speaking more to himself than to her.

Harriet took a step back from him. "Prepare me? For what?"

Instead of answering her question, he sat in the plush orange chair in front of her desk and sighed. "Please sit down, Harriet." He gestured to the chair beside him as if this were his office and she was the guest.

Harriet sat.

"You've always known I wasn't like other fathers, haven't you?"

Harriet swallowed.

"You've never asked where I worked or where I lived or if you could come to visit."

This was all true. As a child, Harriet had concocted all sorts of elaborate scenarios that had her father traveling the globe as some sort of government spy. As she'd gotten older and her understanding of the world had grown, she always managed to reign her thoughts back to herself when they wandered to her father. She just couldn't accept the truth staring her in the face.

Her father was pure evil.

"Why are you here?" She forced the words from her mouth. She really didn't want to discuss the semantics of their relationship just then.

A pained expression crossed his face as he looked up at her. "I guess there is no harm in telling you since you won't remember this anyway."

Her father had always been cryptic in his responses, but this was getting out of hand. Harriet tried to stand but found herself paralyzed in her chair. She tried to speak again, but this time, no words came out. Of all the strange things that happened in her father's presence, this was a new phenomenon.

"Harriet, dear, the world is about to end."

Harriet was so focused on trying to wiggle her toes that she almost didn't feel him take her hand. When his words finally hit her, she wanted to laugh. He had to be joking, right? She wasn't sure if it was the paralysis or his grave expression that forced her laughter back down her throat.

"I'm sure this comes as a shock to you. Most humans stupidly believe that this meager ball floating through the galaxy is going to last forever. But I have news for you all." His voice hardened, and his grip tightened on her hand. "You are wrong."

Harriet cleared her throat and was miraculously able to force out six feeble words. "I think you need to leave," she said with as much authority as she could muster.

"I'm afraid I can't, my dear. You see, you are an integral part of my plan. As abundant as my powers are, I cannot be in two places at once. That is why I created you."

So many things were wrong with that statement. *His* plan? *Created* her?

"You...created me?"

"Oh, yes," he said wistfully. "We'd tried it before, but we were so stupid and new to the world. Most of us were running amok like toddlers with no supervision."

We... Us? Harriet wasn't sure who else he was talking about, but she didn't care to find out.

"But you—" he said, looking down at her hand in his. "Look at you. Just perfect. No one else would dare to face the wrath, but I did this," he said, caressing her hand as if it were a priceless treasure, "because I needed you."

Harriet tried to pull her hand away. She hadn't really expected him to say *because I loved you*. He'd never said those words to her before, but the comment still felt like an insult.

He stood then and reached his hands down to her. "Come," he said, and Harriet placed both hands in his, her body moving against her will.

She stood facing him.

"The hard part will come later. This part," he said with a shrug, "should be easy." He pulled two photos from his breast pocket and held them in front of her. The pictures had been taken from a distance, the two subjects unaware they were being watched. One was a young girl with sandy-blonde hair pulled into a ponytail and a worried look on her face. The other was of a boy with shaggy black hair and baggy clothes. His skin was the same tan shade of the men around him, but they both *looked* American. Harriet hoped her confusion showed on her face.

"See these two faces? I want you to memorize them. They are the only things standing in the way of our plan."

Our *plan? When did this become* our *plan?*

"Eventually, I will have to kill them. But for now, I just need to send them a message."

If talks of the world ending hadn't been bad enough, now they were discussing murder? She could not be a party to any of this.

"No," Harriet mouthed, but no sound came out.

"Oh, don't be afraid, love. I will be here to help you every step of the way." He placed his hands on either side of her head, applying the slightest pressure at her temples.

She tried to move, to back away from him, but her feet refused to budge.

"I promise this will be painless."

From her paralysis, a small whimper escaped Harriet's throat. Her father stroked her hair. "Shh...it will be okay. I'm going to give you what everyone in the world spends their life seeking. I'm going to give you answers. Knowledge. The secrets of the universe. And once I have shared my wisdom with you, you will understand the need for their destruction."

He reached behind her head and pressed on the back of her neck. Her fight or flight instinct was still in full force, trying to get her feet to move, but they were still rooted to their spot.

Harriet gasped as a white light exploded behind her eyes then disappeared, disintegrating any thoughts, desires, and aspirations she'd ever held as her own.

"See there, all done. That wasn't so bad, now was it?"

Harriet tried to make sense of his words, but she couldn't think. Her brain had turned to mush.

The next second, Harriet blinked, alone in her office. She stood in front of her desk, her pulse even and her mind clearer than it had ever been. Hadn't she been expecting someone? She glanced at her watch. Almost six o'clock. *Too late for visitors.*

Harriet shook her head, remembering something she needed to do. She walked around her desk and picked up the phone. "Reggie, I need to schedule a press conference."

ACKNOWLEDGEMENTS

One of the most important lessons I've learned on this journey is that it takes a village to write a book. And this is where I get to thank my village.

I have to first thank my husband for his unwavering support and encouragement, even when it cost him so much. He is the only reason this book exists, so if you see us together, thank him. Not me.

I owe so much to my wonderful, insightful beta readers: Amanda Asher for asking the important questions, Teresa Westmoreland and Arika Roy for suffering through an early, crap version of this story, Ansley Spring for being the grammar guru that she is, Robert Hecksher for his joyful enthusiasm, Juliette Godot for her gentle suggestions, and Taylor Bomar, for keeping the "cheese" level low.

I can't go without thanking my editor, Gina Salamon, for her insight and guidance along the way. Also, for her willingness to answer all my questions, no matter how silly.

Many thanks to my nurse friends, Alicia Petty and Amy Johnson for lending me their knowledge of psychiatric disorders and medications. Also, to my brother, Johnathon Ellington, for his invaluable input regarding the inner workings of a naval ship. You guys are rock stars!

And I probably owe the biggest thanks to my mother for reading to me every day and making sure our home was always full of books.

I love you all!

ABOUT THE AUTHOR

AE Winstead grew up in west Tennessee where she lives with her husband, two children, three cats, and one dog. You can find her online at aewinstead.com.

CPSIA information can be obtained
at www.ICGtesting.com
Printed in the USA
BVHW081442230920
589455BV00003B/254/J

9 781735 270920